MALLORY'S ORACLE

MALLORY'S ORACLE

Carol O'Connell

BEELER LARGE PRINT

Hampton Falls, New Hampshire • 1995

Library of Congress Cataloging in Publication Data

O'Connell, Carol, 1947-
    Mallory's oracle / Carol O'Connell.
    p. (large print) cm.
    ISBN 1-57490-024-2 (hardcover : alk. paper)
    1. Policewomen--New York (N.Y.)--Fiction. 2. New
York (N.Y.)--Fiction. 3. Large type books. I. Title.
    [PS3565.C497M347 1995]
    813'.54--dc20   95-21030
                                         CIP

Published in Large Print by arrangement with
G.P. Putnam's Sons

BEELER LARGE PRINT
is published by
Thomas T. Beeler, Publisher
Post Office Box 659
Hampton Falls, New Hampshire 03844

Typeset in 16 point Monotype Times New Roman type,
printed on acid-free paper and bound
in the United States of America

For Paul Sidey, with thanks

PROLOGUE

The dog came when she called. He came slowly, shivering in his pelt as he walked, picking his way lightly and gracefully on slender Doberman feet. By her voice, he was pulled along through the rooms of the apartment and past the open door to the outer hallway. He entered the kitchen with the light clatter of nails on linoleum and met his mistress there. All the muscles of his body tightened in the dog's version of attention.

The animal's eyes were soft brown wounds in a sleek black face, and there were more literal scars on the skin beneath the dark fur. He owed his life, many times over, to youth and quick recovery, but he was no longer a puppy.

The woman was seated in her chair, and the dog knew it would be a while before she moved again. It was something in the smell of her when she was in this state, even before the woman's eyes would go all wide and staring.

A small misery of crying began deep in the dog's throat. He paced back and forth before the chair, sensing the woman's temporary blindness to her surroundings, her deafness to the dog's fear.

Time. How much time before the woman came round again? The eyes were rolling back in a trance. Soon now. The dog barked. Nothing, no blink, no reflex of any kind in the woman. The dog circled the chair, fear rising up to a human crying. He moved her hand with his nose. Nothing. The hand fell limply to her lap.

The dog wailed.

Soon.

The dog's mind was breaking. Regimentation

1

instilled by pain was failing apart. He was departing from ritual, backing out of the room, terrified eyes fixed on the woman till he was clear of the kitchen. Now he turned and flung himself into the next room, racing across the carpet, passing through the open door and down the long hallway, paws touching lightly to ground in the perfect poetry of a beautiful animal in motion, muscles elongating and contracting, eyes shining with purpose. Now springing, rising, flying, crashing through the glass of the fifth-floor window.

The dog's heart was killed by the fright and strain of flight without wings. He was dead before his bones were broken on the pavement.

Chapter One

The boy's stringy brown hair fell over one eye. The other eye was fever bright. His T-shirt was grime gray and yellow in the rings of stale sweat beneath the arms. Bony knees pushed through the strained and faded threads of his jeans as he crossed the room to the pawnbroker's cage.

Safely locked behind wire and glass, the old man in the cage only feared the pain in his mind might bleed from his eyes, and so he kept them cast down as he examined again what the boy had brought him.

The police station was only minutes away. How much time had passed? he wondered. Where was Kathy? Had he been right to call her? The old man's hand trembled as he wiped his face. What would the boy make of tremors and tears?

"What's taking so long, old man?" asked the boy. "Gold is gold."

Well, no, it was not.

The pocket watch bore the name of Louis Markowitz's grandfather. And the engraved initials inside the heavy gold ring told him this was the wedding band that Helen had given to Louis. The old man had attended that wedding. And twenty years later, when Helen died, he had been at the grave with Louis and Kathy. The watch and ring were more than gold to Louis, and he would not have given them up while he lived.

The boy hovered close to the cage and then flitted across the room. He spun around, levitating off the floor. He was so thin, made all of wire, coursing with manic energy, sweat pouring off what little flesh he had, heat rising off his cooking brain, only wanting money to fill his veins with magic and fly away.

There was a light tap at the pawnbroker's window. Kathy Mallory had come. He buzzed her through the lock, and she walked in slow, stalking on long legs in dungarees. A black blazer over her T-shirt hid the gun. All the old man's compliments to her were made of hard but precious substance: her eyes were cold green jewels set in ivory and framed in an aureole of gold.

She moved on the boy in the shutter blink of the old man's eyes. It looked to him as though she had disappeared from the shaft of light by the window and then reappeared behind the boy on the other side of the room. Her lips parted, and just the tip of her tongue showed between her teeth. It must be his old eyes or his imagination—she seemed to be tasting the moment. Her hands were rising, curling.

The boy was quickly turning, and he had not faced her yet when she grabbed him by one arm and pulled it up high behind his back. The boy screamed with pain as she slammed him into the wall. And there was fear in that scream, too. He seemed younger now, a wild-eyed child caught in the claws of his nursery closet monster. This could not be happening, said the boy's eyes.

Where did you get the watch? she was asking him with another slam into the wall. Where? she asked, and never raised her voice, but tufts of the boy's hair came away in her hand when she had to ask him again.

Jack Coffey's mind was breaking with the exhaustion of nights without sleep. The question was endlessly looping back on itself: why had Markowitz gone in there alone? Why?

4

It made no damn sense at all, not for a smart cop with thirty years on the force. Raw recruits, still damp at the bib with mother's milk, were not so dumb and loved their skins more.

Lieut. Jack Coffey held his suit jacket slung over one arm. The wet stains on his pin-striped shirt were darkest at the shoulder holster. His lean and sun-brown face was slack at the jaw, and his eyes were closing to slits.

Oh, talk about rookie cops. Maybe if he'd had a decent night's sleep he might not have behaved like one himself, stumbling out to the sidewalk to lose his last meal on the pavement. And now his knees were failing him. He covered himself by leaning casually against one of the black-and-white units.

The street was crawling with black-and-whites and a few of the department's less conspicuous tan cars. The meat wagon was waiting patiently, doors hanging open. The two men from the medical examiner's office stubbed out their cigarettes and walked back inside. Nothing would get Jack Coffey back in there, nothing but the possibility of losing face in front of Kathy Mallory.

A siren cut the thick, humid air, screaming like a woman. Some fool had called an ambulance, and it was rushing toward them as though there was still time for Louis Markowitz, as though the man had not been dead for two days.

And what a place to die. The windows of the six-story building were all cracked glass and black holes. Chunks of concrete lay on the sidewalk, having fallen from the once elaborate facade. In the past few weeks, this abandoned East Village tenement had done some service as a crack house. The addicts had left a trail of works winding from the sidewalk to the door.

5

The car dipped as another, heavier man joined him on the car's fender.

"Hello, Coffey," said Chief of Detectives Harry Blakely, who was all gone to gray hair and not so lean as the younger man by forty pounds, nor so beautiful by twenty years of drink which put veins in his eyes and sallowed his flesh.

"Chief," Coffey nodded. "Riker filled you in?"

"Much as he could. It's the same freak? You're positive?"

"It's the same pattern with the wounds."

"Oh, God," said Blakely, as if God could find him in this section of lower Manhattan. Not likely, yet he wiped his face with a handkerchief and squinted up to where heaven would be if not for the crumbling brick of the tenement building. "You got a preliminary yet?"

"Yeah, but it's half-assed. Slope hasn't shown up yet. The techs figure they died maybe forty to fifty hours ago. There's plastic in the woman's wounds."

"You got an ID on her?"

"Miss Pearl Whitman, age seventy-five. She's from Gramercy Park, same as the first two."

"No shit. You know who that is? Pearl Whitman of Whitman Chemicals. You got any idea how much she's worth?"

It was like the Chief to give a credit line to a corpse. He was a good political animal.

"Look who's here." Blakely was nodding in the direction of a van with a TV news logo on the side. He gestured thumb down to a uniformed officer who moved quickly to direct the van and its cargo of reporters and cameramen onto the cross street and away from the crime scene. "Speaking of freaks. Those bastards can smell blood before jackals can."

Jack Coffey closed his eyes, but it did him no

6

good. He could see the Post's headlines on the inside of his eyelids: 'Invisible Man's Third Kill.' A rival newspaper had favored the name Gray-Lady Killer, but the public had taken more of a fancy to the supernatural aspect of the first murder.

That first old woman had been a daylight kill in the park at the center of Gramercy's square. Anne Cathery had died in full view of every window that looked out onto that square, and every bench sitter, every passerby. Yet no one had witnessed it. Her corpse had lain in anonymity among the shrubs, ignored by blasé, uncurious New Yorkers. In the early-morning hours of the following day, flies had attracted the curiosity of a resident.

The second victim had also been found in the square. But now Pearl Whitman had broken the pattern by dying at an unfashionable Manhattan address, twenty blocks south by geographic standards and miles further down by economics. Another deviation from the pattern was the death of a cop, the head of Special Crimes Section no less.

Harry Blakely lit up a cheap cigar, and Coffey bit down on his lower lip to offset a new wave of nausea and stop the onset of dry heaves. He was only hoping to keep some of his dignity, for he had nothing left of his lunch to give to the sidewalk.

"How do you suppose the perp got the old lady down here, Coffey? Any ideas?"

"Had to have a car," said Coffey, his mind working on automatic pilot now, only really concentrating on his innards. "Probably snatched her off the street in Gramercy. No rich old broad is gonna be out for a stroll in this neighborhood."

"Well now." Blakely smiled. "He has a private car. That's more than we had yesterday. So Markowitz wasn't a total loss."

7

What would they do to him, Coffey wondered, for punching out the chief of detectives? Well, he would have free beers for the rest of his natural life, but no pension.

"You're the senior man in the section, Coffey. You do right, you'll make captain before the year is out. It's your baby now."

Yeah, right. And who was going to explain that to Mallory?

Coffey was facing the long black limousine slowly pulling to the curb, but he was not really seeing it, not registering that this must be Police Commissioner Beale's limo.

"Aw, Markowitz," Blakely was saying, as much to himself as to Coffey. "This was a real bonehead mistake. He should've pulled the pin years ago."

Coffey's hand clenched wrinkles into the wilted material of his suit jacket. So all the times Lou Markowitz made the department shine had counted for nothing. He would be remembered for this last mistake. Maybe the perp was just smarter than Markowitz. Coffey had never met anyone that smart. And if and when he did? Would Blakely be sitting with someone else and remembering Lieut. Jack Coffey for *his* last mistake?

"Has anyone told Mallory?" asked Blakely.

"She's in there now with forensics."

"Oh Jesus—"

"She was the first officer on the scene. You were figuring to keep her out of it?"

"She's in there with Markowitz's body?"

"Yeah, and she's pissed off."

He was only vaguely aware of another man standing close by his shoulder and putting one bloodless, bony hand on the fender of the car. Coffey winced as the man leaned close to his ear

8

and yelled, "Are you telling me Sergeant Mallory is in there!"

Where had Beale come from on his little ferret's feet?

Still a bit slow and slightly stupid with shock, Jack Coffey turned to look down at the little man's watery gray eyes. He thought the commissioner had a very big voice for a little jerk.

Dr. Edward Slope had come straight from a poolside barbecue at his suburban Westchester home. Actually, he had escaped from his in-laws and neighbors, running from their screaming children, ducking the flying Frisbees, keeping a blind eye to the smoking hamburgers and franks on the grill, not stopping to change his clothes but only grabbing up his bag. His apologies, on the fly, had been profuse, but when he last saw his wife, she had been holding a long, sharp skewer and miming the words 'I'll get you for this' as he backed his car down the driveway and left her to the whirlwind.

In his practice as medical examiner for the city of New York, Dr. Slope usually came to his patients in a more somber suit of clothes, and not the garish splashes of Hawaiian color which competed with the blood of the crime scene. In a further, unintended rudeness, the exotic flowers of his shirt muted the dead woman's more fashionable blue dress, and drabbed the dead man's brown suit.

And he usually tended to strangers and not to a man he had known for half his life. He had walked quickly from the car to the door marked by a guard of uniformed officers. No one had caught up with him to tell him it was Louis in there. He had walked into this room and met his old friend as a corpse. Now, as he sagged against the bare brick wall, the

9

bright floodlights deepened his wrinkles and made him seventy instead of sixty.

He had to ask himself, what was wrong with this picture? Oh, just everything. Louis should be issuing orders to forensics and the photographer, and pumping him for early details and best guesses. In no scenario could Louis be one of the bodies.

And why was Kathy Mallory here? She should be sitting at a computer console back at the station, and not on her knees in the dirt and the dried blood, flies lighting on the curls of her hair and crawling over her hands and face.

The photographer and the forensic crew were standing by the door, waiting on a go-ahead from Mallory. She was kneeling on the floor, pushing a gold wedding band up the pudgy third finger on the left hand of the corpse which had been her father.

Dr. Slope turned his attention to the boy in the handcuffs. It seemed unnecessary to have such a large policeman restraining the kid. In that weakened condition he could not have outrun one of the dead bodies. The boy's head was bleeding, and half his face was swollen. Slope thought of practicing on a living patient for distraction, but then he figured he would see this one in his regular practice soon enough. The skeletal junkie was a day away from dying. Were the wounds Mallory's work? It was obvious the boy was Mallory's creature. He was tied to her by his eyes.

Mallory looked up at the boy. "You moved the body, didn't you?"

Apparently, she had trained the boy rather well in the short time they had known one another, perhaps a half hour by the recent blooding. The boy responded quick as a starving lab rat.

"Yes, ma'am. I rolled him over on his back."

10

"Tell me when I've got it right," she said, rolling the heavy body of Louis Markowitz over on his face.

Slope wondered if she had ever been on a homicide crime site before. He thought not. From her earliest days on the force, she had always been more at home with the NYPD computers than people, living or dead. A bizarre linkage of memory called up a fine spring day in Kathy's childhood when Louis had taught her the rudiments of baseball.

In a somewhat different spirit, Dr. Slope strode over to Louis's body and hunkered down beside her. He pointed to the darkened splotches on the face. "Line up the places where the blood's pooled under the skin. Line 'em up flat with the floor."

She nodded and leaned down, nose to nose with the white face of the corpse, her hands working at the dead flesh, which was deceptively warm in the August heat. When she was done, she looked up to the boy, who nodded.

Slope was checking Mallory's pretty face for signs of traumatic shock, and he was disconcerted at not finding any. She was all business, lining up the dark blood pools on the white left hand now, and looking back to the boy again. The boy nodded once more. Satisfied, she stood up and crossed the room to stand over the corpse of the old woman.

The woman's throat bore a wound resembling a second mouth. The front of the blood-crusted dress had been cut away, and the brassiere as well. One breast hung deflated against the rib cage. The other had been laid open by the knife and was covered with flies. The buzzing was nearly a roar, and the medical examiner regarded the black cluster of insects as a single feeding organism. The corpse's ancient face was a study in horror as the flies

11

crawled in and out of the open mouths of her face and throat.

Mallory stared at the old woman with as much compassion as she would give to furniture. She looked back to the boy.

"And now this one," she said.

"No," said the boy. "She was that way when I got here."

"Anything else? Did you touch anything, move anything?"

"No. I went through the dead guy's pockets and ran. I threw the wallet back there." He pointed to a loose pile of bricks and garbage in one corner of the room. The wallet lay on a torn green garbage bag.

Slope caught the eye of a forensic technician. He nodded at the bag and then made a few jots in his notebook.

"You!" said Mallory, calling the man over. "You got the kid's prints?"

The technician held up the card with the splotches of ink in neat squares which identified each printed digit.

She turned to Martin, the uniformed officer who held the handcuffed boy by one bone-thin arm.

"I don't need him anymore. Kick him loose."

Slope stopped his medical examination and watched Martin's young face and saw the patrolman's mistake in the making.

"Mallory, he robbed a corpse," said Martin. "Markowitz's corpse, for Christ's sake. You're gonna let him walk?"

"A deal is a deal. Now kick him loose," said Mallory in a voice, low and even, that said with restrained, under-the-surface violence, 'Don't you push your luck with me, not ever.' As she walked toward Martin, she seemed to grow in size and power. It was an unsettling illusion, and Slope wondered if she was even aware of it. He thought she might be.

Martin was quick to fish out the cuff key. His reddening face was turned down to the work of unlocking the irons. A moment later, the junkie was gone.

Very practical, Kathy. Why waste time on a trial?

He guessed she hadn't wasted much time on the boy's constitutional right to a lawyer, and he knew she had wasted no time at all in discouraging his right to remain silent.

Now she turned on the photographer. "Okay, it's in prime condition. Shoot."

The peripheral brightness of repeating flashes made spots in Slope's vision as he moved to the second body. He slipped plastic bags over the hands of the woman's corpse and then looked up to Mallory. "I'll get to work on it as soon as you release them."

"The old woman's the same pattern as the other two?"

"The same."

"Do Markowitz first," she said. "I'm not gonna learn anything new from her."

"You got it."

"What can you give me now? How long have they been dead?"

Like father, like daughter. He knew there was no tie of blood between them, but there was much of Louis in her.

"Two days, give or take. With the heat and the decomposition, I won't be able to pin it to within five or six hours. But I can fix a few hours of daylight on either side. Same pattern there."

"How long did Markowitz live?"

13

"Maybe thirty minutes to an hour. I'm guessing by the blood loss. I'd say the wound was enough to kill him without medical attention, but he died of a massive coronary." Markowitz had had some practice surviving mild attacks. This one must have had the force and effect of a slow train wreck.

"So he knew he was dying."

"Yes." And that hurt her, he knew. He discerned it in the slow deadening of her eyes. So Louis Markowitz had spent his last hour in pain and fear.

Wasn't life crappy that way, Kathy?

"The killer didn't take much time with him," he said. "He was more interested in the woman. Markowitz has defensive wounds on his arms. By the position of the first blood splatter, he put himself between her and the killer." And now he detected the first signs of mild shock with the slight loss of focus in her eyes. "Can I do anything for you, Kathy?"

His first error was using her Christian name on the job, and his second gross presumption was kindness. He was rewarded with universal contempt throughout the crowded tenement room. He should've known better, said the frozen silence of the uniforms, the technicians and the photographer.

"You're done with the body?" she asked, focused again, all cold to him now, all business.

He nodded.

"Okay," she said, turning to the medical examiner's men. "Bag him and take him out." Now she looked to the far corner where the old woman's body was. "And that one? How long?"

"She only lived a few minutes."

"Bag her."

Her next order cleared out all the unnecessary personnel, and that included old friends of the

14

family. Dr. Slope left in advance of his team. The way out of the building and into the light was much longer than the way in had been.

Sergeant Kathleen Mallory sat on the only chair in the room while the forensic team crawled on hands and knees, looking for fibers and hairs, the minutiae of evidence. She traced the pattern of blood. He fell there, near the door.

How could you be dead?

And he had gotten up and dragged himself along that blood-smeared wall to the window.

Did you scream for help in this neighborhood of 'I didn't see nothin', I didn't hear nothin'.'

And there by the window, where the blood had spread around his body in a wide stain in the dust, he had collapsed and died. But it had taken some time. He'd had time to think.

What did you do with the time? What did you leave behind? ... Nothing?

She looked up as they were carrying him out in a black plastic body bag.

A small notebook lay open on her lap. She drew a quick slash through the notes on Markowitz's car. It must have been stolen. Nothing had turned up on the impound lots in the two days she'd been hunting for him. It was probably in Jersey by now and painted a different color.

Why did you go in alone?

'Defensive wounds' she wrote on a clean page. So he had tailed the perp to the crime scene and gone in without backup. Why? 'Because the woman was about to die,' she wrote in a clear, neat hand. She could assume he was on foot—no car radio, or he would have called for backup. That was something. So the perp was also on foot.

15

Her pen scratched across the paper again. 'No drive-by snatch.' She was certain of that much. The killer had arranged to meet the old woman well away from Gramercy Park—a break in the pattern of the other two murders. There had to be a record on some cabby's log. A rich old woman doesn't ride the subway or the bus. And she wouldn't have come here alone to meet a stranger. 'She knew her killer.'

So she could also assume that Markowitz had figured out how the park murder was done. Smart old bastard. But if he was so smart, why did he keep it to himself? And since when did a cop with Markowitz's rank do surveillance detail?

One of the forensic techs looked her way and then nervously looked everywhere else.

Was he checking for tears, she wondered, for signs of disassembling? No way. No compassionate leave for Mallory. But Commissioner Beale was such a twit, he might order it. Then what?

The worst of the stench from the old woman's corpse still lingered. Pearl Whitman had not been such a neat kill as Markowitz. The butcher had punctured the intestine. In the absence of food, the cloud of flies was dwindling to a few annoying strafers. There were no windows that were not broken, no barriers to contain them. They whined past her ear, buzzing and black, fat with blood. Gone. All quiet now, only the sound of the brush in the hand of the man at her feet who was looking for omens in the dust and the dried blood.

"I shouldn't have called you so late."

"No, Mr. Lugar, you did the right thing."

The sleepy rabbi and the night watchman were both in their late fifties, and both were balding, but there they parted in likeness. The watchman was

16

furtive in all his movements and shaped like a beer keg on toothpick legs. The rabbi was a tall man and comfortable in his slender body. His face was catlike and tranquil in the half-closed lids of lost sleep.

The watchman jerked his head up to look at the taller man. "Wait till you see her. She looks like a little kid, just sitting there in the cold. We have to keep it cold, you understand."

"I understand."

"It's so peculiar. I worked here maybe two years now, and nobody ever wanted to sit up all night with the body. It's so peculiar. I didn't know who to call: Well then, I seen your name on the manifest for the funeral arrangements. So I gotta figure you know the family, you know?"

"I know."

He led him to the door and pointed to the square window.

"Don't she look just like a little kid?" The watchman moved his head slowly and sadly from side to side as he unlocked the door and stepped back. "I gotta go on my rounds now, Rabbi."

"Thank you for all your trouble, Mr. Lugar. It was very kind of you."

The smaller man smiled and ducked his head under the rare burden of a compliment. He turned and walked down the dimly lit hall, stiff and disjointed as though he had borrowed this body for the night and had not quite gotten the hang of walking around in it.

The rabbi pushed through the swinging doors and into a bright, cold room painted antiseptic green. She was sitting on a metal folding chair by the wall of lockers, each one home to a body, and one of those bodies was very important to Kathy Mallory.

17

Her blazer collar was pulled up against the cold, and her hands were tucked into the fold of her arms. She was hugging herself, it seemed, for lack of anyone to hold her.

She was twenty-five years old, he knew, but she was also the child who stared defiantly from the old photograph in Louis's wallet. She was not much changed since that day, fourteen years ago, when he first saw her walk into the front room of the Markowitz house, following along in Helen's wake, never going very far from Helen's side. Of course, she was taller now.

"Kathy, why are you here? Mr. Lugar was concerned about you."

"Someone's supposed to sit with the body. A relative."

"No, Kathy. That's not necessary. Louis was not so orthodox a Jew. He was only religious about our Thursday night poker games. And he missed last Thursday's game."

He bent his knees, and his body folded down in the neat illusion of shrinking until he was sitting on the backs of his shoes. It was his custom to speak to children at eye level.

"Louis was so unorthodox I caught him buying a Christmas tree one night. That would have been the first year you lived with Louis and Helen. Louis tried to fob it off as a Hanukkah bush."

"Did you ream him out?"

"Of course I did. As we were carrying it home. I was merciless."

"It was a twelve-footer. I remember that tree. It went up to the ceiling."

"So can you picture an orthodox Jew putting up Christmas trees and raising a little Gentile? You don't have to sit up with him."

"Helen would've liked it."

"You got me there." He shrugged and smiled. "She would've liked it. Louis would've liked it too."

Mallory looked down at her hands.

"It's all right to cry, Kathy."

"Don't get your hopes up, Rabbi."

Rabbi David Kaplan seemed to be growing taller instead of merely standing up. He walked over to the rear wall, where three more folding chairs rested near the door. He carried one back to the wall of lockers and dragged out the mechanics of unfolding it and settling himself into it.

"I think I'll stay too," he said.

"What for?"

"Helen would have liked it."

"I'm okay."

"Me too, Kathy. I'm okay. How long have I known you now? Since you were a little girl."

"I was never a little girl. Markowitz said so."

"Since you were a short person. I've known you that long. If you need me, I'm here."

"I'm not Jewish."

"You're telling me? But there's so much of Helen invested in you. I got to protect her investment, keep it alive, you know?" He looked up to the fluorescent lights. "It's Thursday. When I knew I would never play poker with Louis again, I cried."

"Not me."

"I believe you. Louis used to tell me—when you were very short that you had principle. 'Tears were for suckers, by her lights,' he said. I'm a sucker, Kathy. You can take from me what you want, you can tap me for lunch every now and then, for advice. Are you very angry with Louis?"

Well, that got her attention. And yes, she was very angry.

19

"He was a good cop," she said. "When a cop gets killed, it's because he got careless. How could he do that?"

"How could he do that *to you?* Louis used to worry about you working in Special Crimes.... Ah, you didn't know that? Well, you spent more time with computers than criminals. He was so proud of you. She's so smart, he would say. But these people he dealt with were so dangerous. He always knew the risks. I believe he knew it would end this way."

"I'm going after the dirtbag that did this to him."

"Your expertise is in the computer, Kathy, not fieldwork. Leave it to the others. He only wanted you to be safe. Give him that much. He wouldn't want you involved in this. Promise me you'll let go of it now. Make this promise a last gift to Louis."

She sat well back in the chair and folded her arms across her chest in the attitude of 'now it begins.' "So Markowitz spilled all of this to you. That's interesting."

"We talked. So?" He found her slow widening smile disturbing.

Louis had called it the Armageddon grin. "I was more than his rabbi. I was his oldest friend."

"And you want to help me? I'm calling you on that, Rabbi. You're either all talk, or you give me what I need."

The cold air was creeping through the light threads of his jacket. Her eyes were narrowing— another sign of trouble. How incongruous was that incredible face with those gunslinger eyes.

"So, what'd the old man say about the Gramercy Park murders?"

"Louis would come back to cut out my tongue if I led you into that mess."

She leaned forward suddenly, and pure reflex

20

made him pull back with his body and his mind. She was rising from the chair, standing over him, and he forgot that he was the taller of the two.

"Fine, then I jump into it stark naked, no defenses, none of your promised help, your hot air, your—"

"Enough.... A deal is a deal, as Louis would say. But he never told me anything concrete. He was so cryptic he could have had *my* job. He said the clues were false and they were not. He said it was complicated and simple, too. Does this help you, Kathy?"

"You're holding out on me." She sat down again and leaned forward to bring her face close to his. "He knew who it was, didn't he?"

"He never told me."

"But he knew."

"He said the only way he'd get that freak, that thing, was to catch it in the act. This one was too clever, smarter than Louis himself, so he told me, and maybe even smarter than you."

"Why did Markowitz tell all this to you and not me?"

"Oh, you know how parents are. They start to get independent of their children. Then they think they know it all, never need advice, never call the kids anymore. Like it would break an arm to pick up a phone. And you kids, you give them the best years of your lives, the cute years. This is how they pay you back, they take all the horrors of life and keep them from you."

"There's more. Give, Rabbi. Why would he do the tail himself? Why not send detectives or uniforms to do the surveillance?"

"This one scared him, Kathy. This was not an ordinary human. This was a freak from the night

21

side of the mind. How could he send in one of his beautiful young boys and girls?"

"Not good enough, Rabbi."

Her reflection elongated in the bright metal of the morgue locker, twisting in ugly distortions as she moved her head. He looked away.

"Did you know Louis was a dancing fool?"

"Rabbi."

"Patience, Kathy. He loved to dance. But there were no dancing Jews in his family. Very conservative they were, very pious, but not so much fun as you might think. So Louis would sneak out with the Irish kids, and they'd go dancing. One night, when we were young—when we were two other people, almost brand new—Louis took me with him to a nightclub. As memories go, it's right up there with the night my first child was born.

"Oh, how he could dance, Kathy. The other kids made a ring around him and his partner. They clapped, they screamed. All of us who watched on, we stamped our feet and rocked our bodies like one gigantic throbbing animal, and we made the building move with our rocking, and the band went on and on and faster and faster. And when the music did stop, the animal with two hundred mouths screamed out in this terrible, beautiful agony....

"We took the subway back to Brooklyn as the sun was coming up. I wept. Louis didn't understand. He thought this night would be such fun for me."

And now she was hearing him, not shutting him out anymore, only waiting, hanging on the end of the story.

"Louis was always on the heavy side, but such grace you won't find in a woman, and so light on his feet. I remember that lightness best. Boys who were all bones made more noise with their feet than

22

Louis. He was born to dance. He was a natural. And some say he was born to be a policeman. He could sneak up behind a criminal with his good brain and—"

"Okay, I get it. A cop with less finesse would have made too much noise."

"And Louis made almost no noise at all. And still, he died. Please, Kathy, you leave it to someone else to find out who this lunatic is."

"I think I know who it is...now."

"Then give him to the department, Kathy. Let them handle it."

"Markowitz thought the perp was so smart. Well, that dirtbag made a big mistake his last time out."

"What are you going to do, Kathy?"

"I'm gonna do it by the book. Markowitz would've liked that. My gift."

Rabbi Kaplan pulled his jacket close about his body. He was colder than he had ever been.

Chapter Two

His body was well made, and his tailored, dark gray suit was faultless. But the shaggy brown hair was the length of three forgotten appointments with his barber, and his comical face was at odds with the day as he moved in slow procession across the grass with the others. Charles Butler was in pain, and the worse he felt, the more comical he looked. His protruding eyes, overlarge in the white spaces and small in the blue-colored bits, seemed slightly zany, and his nose might perch a New York City pigeon. He was a caricature of sadness when the few drops of rain found him alone among the mourners and splashed his face and made a hash of his real tears. At six feet four, he towered a full head above the rest of them. No place to hide. There he was, the clown at the funeral.

Mallory walked just ahead of him. She might have been walking alone. It seemed accidental that she was surrounded by a throng of sad people on a common mission. He didn't find it odd that there was no sheltering arm around her shoulders, no one to take her own arm and give her support.

Charles quickened his step, and when he came abreast of her, she turned her face up to his. Her eyes were not the portals poets spoke of. They were cool green and gave away nothing. He put one arm around her. Two uniformed police officers walked alongside of them, openly marveling that he would risk that and that she did not shake him off.

Kathleen she was in all their private conversations, and Mallory she was in the public areas of NYPD. What to call her at the funeral of Louis Markowitz? She was his inheritance, and Charles was wondering just how he was going to explain that. He hoped the letter in his pocket might help.

Mallory put down the coffee cup and opened her letter. It began with a list of the deceased's regrets: Louis Markowitz regretted that his wife, Helen, had died before completing the job of housebreaking Kathy. He regretted being forced to address her as Mallory when she joined the police department. He regretted not being able to teach Kathy that it was not nice to raid other people's computers, and that he had made such good use of all her thievery and not set a better example for her.

And now the list of what he did not regret: There

24

were no regrets about arresting her at the age of ten, eleven, or twelve (they could never be sure about her age). He didn't regret handing the wild child over to gentle Helen Markowitz, who startled young Kathy speechless and kickless with a hug and an outpouring of undeserved and unconditional love. He did not regret that Kathy grew up to be a beauty with an intelligence that sometimes frightened him.

She had made Helen's last years an unreasonable joy without boundaries. And so, he could live and die with the fact that she still had the soul of a thief. And he was glad that she had made a friend in Charles Butler, who was as decent a man as God ever made, and would she please not take shameful advantage of him, but go to him if she was in trouble, if she needed help, or in the unlikely event that she needed a little human warmth. And in his postscript, he mentioned that he had loved her.

She folded her letter and looked up at the man with the sad foolish smile. Charles Butler sat on the other side of the room, quietly staring into his coffee cup.

She supposed he was waiting for her to cry.

He would wait forever.

Commissioner Beale sat down on the couch. He noted that it was a masculine thing, all dark leather and blending well with the other furnishings, massive and solid. The only feminine touch he could find in Sergeant Mallory's front room was the perfect order that men found so difficult to create, and he could find no personal effects at all. He might well be sitting in a showroom display for an upscale furniture store—entirely too upscale in his opinion. And the apartment was too large for her salary. It always worried him to see an officer living

25

beyond means, better dressed than himself, or driving a better car. The police commissioner scratched a mental note on his accountant's soul.

Sergeant Mallory returned with a tray which could only be silver, and on it was a good grade of sherry and fine crystal glasses. He made more notes.

She was smiling. So much for Harry Blakely's comment that he would have to dynamite her office before she would take compassionate leave. She had taken it rather well.

"I think we might make this an indefinite leave, Sergeant."

He did respect Blakely's advice on keeping her out of it until the case was broken, and the Chief was promising results within a few weeks. Mallory was not replaceable, Blakely had counseled. 'So don't antagonize her. Tell her it's policy.' And policy it was. Doctors did not practice on members of their families; this was no different. She had seen the wisdom of policy. She had deferred to him in everything. He liked that. He liked it a lot.

'And get her badge and her gun,' Blakely had warned him. 'You don't want her out there armed and working solo.'

Commissioner Beale had mentioned the badge and gun, but she apparently had not heard him. Her eyes had gone all soft and distant. He reminded himself that she had buried her foster father only a few hours ago. She was so pretty, so vulnerable. He didn't bring up the business of badge and gun a second time. Everything was going so well. Why spoil it? This after all was one of his most trusted officers.

Wasn't she?

"Is this a rent-controlled apartment, Sergeant? Do you mind my asking the rent?"

26

"No rent. I own it. Markowitz made the down payment for me when I moved out of Brooklyn. He wanted me to live in a doorman building with good security."

And Markowitz had probably helped with the mortgage payments and the maintenance fees. The man had certainly been on the force long enough to accumulate a nice little savings account. No, no reason to get the badge and the gun. Markowitz was as clean a cop as NYPD ever had, and this young woman had been raised by him in the best tradition of New York's Finest. Well, good enough.

Later in the day, when he would explain to Chief of Detectives Harry Blakely that he had left Mallory armed and dangerous, Blakely would roll his eyes but say nothing.

Lieut. Jack Coffey closed the door behind him and slowly sank down in the overstuffed chair in Markowitz's office. A small bald spot on the back of his head was reflected in the window behind him. The glass ran the length of the upper portion of one wall with only the interruption of the door. The window looked out on the bustle of officers and clerks in the Special Crimes Section.

The two adjacent walls were pure Markowitz, camouflaged to blend with the mess of paperwork on his desk. Floor-to-ceiling cork panels held notes on matchbook covers, duty rosters on computer printouts, surveillance and arrest reports, memos— the paperwork collage of a command position in a growing department. The decor of clutter was very like Markowitz. The entire room had been an inside-out, flattened-out model of the man's mind. He had been a lover of detail, a collector of images, a squirreler of bits and jots of data.

27

However, it was the back wall that held Coffey's attention. It was stark naked. Before the funeral, it had been covered with cork and papered over with photos, handwritten notes, news clippings, copies of statements and everything else pertaining to the Gramercy Park murders that would take a pin, the thousand details of the priority case.

He could pull most of the same information off a computer disk, and all the physical evidence was under lock, available at a call, but it would not be quite the same. The back wall had been the last available repository of Markowitz's brain. It was weird to see even one clear foot of space in the paper storm of this office, and now he was looking at a whole damn wall. He'd been raped.

He turned to his sergeant, who was looking down at his own scruffy shoes.

"How did she get it out, Riker?"

"So you think it was Mallory?"

"Cut the crap."

Riker said he never saw her take down the cork, and he hadn't. But he never mentioned that he had walked behind her through the department, past twelve occupied desks at the top of a shift, down the corridor packed with uniforms, and past the garage security guard, as she carried a long, thick roll of cork under one arm and a desk blotter under the other, with a calendar wadded in her purse and God knows what else. It was a big purse. But she had not been able to manage all that and the Xerox machine, too. Riker had carried that out for her so she wouldn't have to make two trips.

Mallory had only stolen one wall out of three. Lieutenant Coffey should be thankful she left him the desk and chair. That was the way Riker saw it.

Mallory walked into the room that Commissioner Beale had not seen. Her den had once housed only a PC and bare furnishings of one desk, one chair, and one bookcase with computer manuals and disks of countless raids on other computers. It was Spartan and clean. Even the glass of the wide window was spotless, invisible to the human eye, which found no streak or pock to stop its depth of field before it crashed into the traffic of the street running along the course of the Hudson River.

She sat down, tailor fashion, in the center of the floor and began to unroll the remarkable mind of Louis Markowitz. It was important to leave the cork intact, as the order of pinning one thing over another had been part of the man's thinking process.

The FBI profile was among the paperwork on the first layer. It described the killer as between twenty and thirty-five years old, abandoned by his father before the age of thirteen, and raised by a woman, a mother or a grandparent. But pinned over this were inventories of the first two victims' stock portfolios. Markowitz had always favored money motives. In the pinning and covering, he had rejected the profile of a sick mind. It was only the top layer he wanted to see each day from his desk across the room. And in time, the pieces of it had come together for him. It was all here.

She had done the background checks for him after the second murder. The printout on her favorite suspect had pride of place on the cork. Jonathan Gaynor didn't strictly fit the FBI profile, but he did fit the money motive as sole beneficiary of his aunt's estate. Estelle Gaynor's heir was thirty-seven. And he must be smart—thank you, Rabbi—because he had almost as many initials after his name as Charles Butler did. Gaynor might have been smart enough to make his aunt the second kill and not the first.

Henry Cathery, the heir to the first kill, was represented on the cork with her raids on a bank computer. Markowitz had probably lost interest in this one when she told him the Cathery boy had more money than the victim.

It took her two hours to xerox each scrap of paper, cut it to size and replace the copy in its exact position on the unrolled cork. The copy camera, a recent theft from the police lab, sat on the floor behind her. She lined up each glossy print of the two crime scenes with the flat board and shot them with slide film. Three-dimensional objects also went under the copy camera: matchbooks with his scribbles, a green plastic bag that was not crime-scene evidence, and a cellophane bag of beads that were evidence from the cache of a million tiny white beads found at the site of the first murder in Gramercy Park. These were Anne Cathery's beads.

The forensic tech with the least seniority had complained bitterly when the task of accounting for every damn bead had fallen to him. It had taken six hours of picking through the grass and the dirt of the park to collect every single one. It had been a day's work to track down an identical necklace and more hours to match the number of found beads to the unbroken strand. All because Markowitz loved these little details.

The doorbell chimed.

One of the neighbors? The doorman would have announced an outsider on the house telephone. On the day she had moved into this building, Louis Markowitz had put the fear of God into the doorman, that and a hundred-dollar bill. And then he had gone home alone to Brooklyn, to a dark-windowed house where he had once been a part of the little family of three: himself, the wife, and the thief.

The bell chimed again as she was crossing the front room.

Her purse lay on the table by the door, and in it was the gun, lying over the folder of her badge. It was early yet. She hadn't had time to leave any tracks, to make any noise. But when she opened the door, she had the gun in her right hand and hidden behind her back.

It was Riker who filled out the doorframe, a shaggy bear in a bad suit. By the look of his graying muzzle, he hadn't shaved since Markowitz died. A slob's idea of tribute, she supposed. Riker was looking down toward the hand he couldn't see. He raised his wrinkles in a smile and said, "You wouldn't hurt me, would you, Kathy?"

He was testing the waters. If she let him call her Kathy, she probably wouldn't shoot him. She gave him a smile. A stranger wouldn't have guessed how little practiced she was in that expression.

She opened the door wide and waved him inside. While she stashed her gun back in the purse, Riker was already moseying to the refrigerator where she kept the beer. He flicked off the cap of a cold bottle, and the metal top went spinning across the kitchen floor. Mallory stooped to pick it up and dropped it in the garbage can. She hated anything out of place. Helen Markowitz had always kept a neat, clean house.

The day after Helen died, she had begun to clean the house in Brooklyn where they had all lived together before the surgeon had cut Helen away from her. When Mallory was done with that old house, there was not a cleaner attic nor cellar, nor all

31

points in between, in all of Brooklyn. But when she took to cleaning the fireplace and then what she could reach of the chimney, Markowitz had pulled her out of there, out of the ashes which were spreading to the carpet beyond the drop cloth, and she was horrified to see the carpet smudged after half a day of scrubbing with a wire brush. She had flown into a rage as Markowitz held her tight. She had screamed and beat her fists on his chest. He let her, pretended not to notice, and held her tighter. And then she had cried. The crying had gone on for days. Then the tears were over with, and she had never cried again. It was as if Helen had taken all her tears, all at once.

Riker made himself to home on the couch.

"Coffey sent me to pick up all the stuff you pinched. But not the Xerox machine. He hasn't missed that yet." He started to drape one leg over the arm of the couch but checked himself, remembering where he was and who he was dealing with.

"You can have the Xerox, too," she said. "I'm done with it."

"Naw. I'm the sentimental type. It was Markowitz's Xerox. You hold on to it." He took a cigarette out of his shirt pocket and held it up with a question.

She nodded and pushed the ashtray across the low table.

Before he set the silver cigarette lighter back on the table, it was marred with his paw prints. "So, are you hanging in there, kid? We didn't get much chance to talk during the great precinct robbery. Jeez, the way Coffey carried on. I thought the poor bastard was gonna cry...So, how are you, Kathy?"

"Just fine."

"Anything I can do for you?"

"Yes."

One hour later, the cork roll was flattened out on the back wall of the den. It only took up half of the wall; the other half was newly covered with fresh cork. She walked up to the dividing line to approve the joining of the old and new surfaces with a carpenter's plumb line and pronounced it perfect. Riker struck in the last nail. She stepped back to the door and took in the entire room and its new character. There were snips of cut-away Xerox paper all over the floor, and empty film boxes. Two empty beer bottles had rolled to the far corner, and Riker was in the act of spilling much of the third bottle on her polished hardwood floor.

The collage of paper on the wall was a disorganized layer of trash to anyone who hadn't known Markowitz. The room was no longer a reflection of neat perfectionist Kathy Mallory. It was more like Markowitz now, as though he had recently inhabited it.

She was holding the copy of Markowitz's pocket calendar when Riker walked over to spill beer at her feet.

"You got any ideas on the Tuesday night appointments?" he asked, reading over her shoulder. "It's driving Coffey nuts."

Scrawled in black ink on each entry for Tuesday were the initials BDA, and the time, 9:00 p.m. According to older calendars, this habit of Markowitz's Tuesday nights had begun a year ago, after she had moved out of the old house in Brooklyn.

"I asked the guys in his poker game and the neighbors. They don't know where he went on Tuesday nights. Can you get me a list of the cross-offs?"

"Sure thing, kid. Just cross off every business in the phone book with those initials. And we don't have any prior arrests with those initials either."

When Riker was gone with his bag of looted paperwork and the copy camera, she went back to the den to admire the new corking stretched over the wall alongside of Markowitz's collection. This half of the wall was pristine in its emptiness, a painter's canvas in the moment before the first stroke. She stepped up to the wall and added the reports and photos from the double kill in the East Village. For this murder, she had her own glossy prints of the crime site.

There was more than an absence of paper dividing the wall between Markowitz and Mallory. Markowitz's thumbtack style was haphazard. Out of the hundreds of bits of paper, in positions she had duplicated exactly, only one was straight, and this was by accident and law of averages. On her own side of the wall, each sheet of paper and glossy print was machine-precision straight. The spaces between the statements and reports, the prints on the corpse robber, the photographs of Markowitz and the woman, each page of the preliminary medical examiner's report—all these spaces were exactly the same.

She looked at the most recent crime-site photos. There were ten. She walked down the length of the wall and studied Markowitz and Pearl Whitman killed ten times over. Below these photos, she tacked up a new printout on the Whitman Chemical Corporation, courtesy of the raided computer in the U.S. Attorney's Manhattan office. One party listed in the Securities and Exchange Commission investigation was Edith Candle, described by the

34

SEC investigator as a psychic financial adviser. She resided in Charles Butler's SoHo apartment building.

This slender case connection to Charles wouldn't have startled Markowitz. He had told her more than once that they were all only a few people removed from everyone else on the planet. The core of good police work was ferreting out those connections. 'There are no dead ends, kid. Everybody knows somebody who knows something.'

'Don't call me kid,' she had said to him then.

She had only one sheet of scant information on Edith Candle. She used the last tack and centered it at the top so the paper would hang perfectly straight. As she walked away from the cork wall, the page on Edith Candle defied the laws of perfect paper balance and dipped to hang at an odd angle, as though a hand had done it. And it was odd, too, that she did not notice this as she took one last look at the wall and closed the door behind her, car keys jingling in her jeans pocket.

In the last hours before dusk, she made a left turn on Twentieth Street, and her compact brown car left the noise of horns and sirens, street confrontations and the loud static of heavy traffic to roll quietly into another century.

Gramercy Park had lost its cobblestones and gaslights, but little else had changed in the past hundred years. The square was all sedate mansions of red brick and brownstone, marble and granite, mahogany and brass. And there was an island quality to its tranquillity. Though New York traffic drove through the square and walked through it, the formidable buildings, giant overlords with watching windows, managed to subdue what little hustle entered there on foot and to intimidate those feet to

35

a respectful march.

The grand design of the place made it clear that one who did not belong could not tarry here. The park at the heart of the square was enclosed in spiked wrought iron. Each of the residents had their own key, and all the other New Yorkers did not. For the outsiders, there was no place to pause, to rest. Each street of the square led the interloper straight out, and quickly. Only walkers of dogs might occasionally come to a halt. All others marched through and away and left no imprint in passing.

There was only an hour of good daylight left when she pulled close to the curb, well behind the cab that had carried the suspect from his last class at Columbia University. The streets were quiet around the park's iron bars, which caged only Gramercy's own. Inside the bars, women in summer dresses and winter-white hair sat on the wooden benches, talking with their hands, and a young mother walked the gravel paths with a small child. An old man sat alone but for the company of pigeons. The perfume of flowers drifted through the open window of her car.

While the suspect paid his driver, she opened her glove compartment and pulled out the folder containing the printout of his class schedule— an unwitting contribution of the university's computer—and the playbill of a student production which bore Gaynor's name on the cast listing. The murders always occurred in the daylight hours. There were gaps between his classes and the student counseling appointments. With a fast car, and some luck with the traffic lights, there was time enough for a hundred-block dash to the square and a little murder. It was only a question of when.

It didn't actually bother her that Professor

36

Jonathan Gaynor had an alibi for the time of his aunt's death. Anyone smart enough to pull off these murders was smart enough to convince a pack of students that they had seen him when they had not. That was the core of a magic act, wasn't it— convincing the audience they had seen what they had not. The daylight killing had the aspect of magic, but she was an unbeliever. It was a trick, and she would work it out.

She looked past the bars of the fence and the well-tended shrubbery and flowers, across the green grass to the murder site of the first victim. The Cathery woman had been found by one of the small brown sheds constructed as toy houses at one end of the park.

It was a maddening puzzle: so simple in its brutality, so convoluted in its accomplishment. Twenty-eight of the square's residents had admitted to being in the park at various hours of that day. Not one of them remembered any stranger entering the park, luring an old woman to the shed, cutting her up, and scattering her beads and her blood with surprisingly little cover. Well, there wouldn't have been any noise to speak of, no screaming. In Slope's opinion, the first thrust of the knife to the victim's throat had prevented that. Maybe a gurgle had come up with the blood, nothing more.

She knew she was missing something here, but damned if she could see it. There had to be a logical explanation. Smart the freak might be, but not invisible, not supernatural.

The playbill from the university theater slipped from the folder and wafted to the floor of the car. She stared down at the boldface type. *Radio Days* was the name of the production by students from Barnard College. The only segment that interested

37

her was the title of an old program from the Shadow series. She knew all the scripts by heart. In the basement of the house in Brooklyn was a space for Markowitz's old records. He had collected the gamut of popular music from Artie Shaw to Elvis, but his best-loved albums were the recordings of "The Shadow." There were others he had liked well enough—"The Lone Ranger" and "Johnny Dollar"—but he dearly loved "The Shadow." She had sat beside him on countless Saturdays, listening to recordings of the old broadcasts from the forties and fifties.

Most of the fathers in the neighborhood had workshops in the basement where they built furniture which their wives would not allow on the upper levels. In Markowitz's workshop, he was building an imagination for a child who had lived too real a life, eating out of garbage cans and holing up for the night in doorways and discarded cartons.

The hero of the old radio series had the ability to cloud men's minds and render himself invisible.

No, she was not buying it, she had told Markowitz then. 'No way could anyone pull that off,' said the child she had been.

'Make believe he can, Kathy,' Markowitz had said to her, looking down at her in the days when she was much shorter than he was.

'No. Only suckers believe in crap like that.'

'Don't say crap, dear,' said Helen, who had suddenly appeared at the foot of the basement stairs to wrap a sweater around the child who was sitting within four feet of the furnace. 'She can't possibly be cold,' Markowitz had protested. So Kathy had shivered to please Helen, and Markowitz said, 'Now you've got it, kid.'

Mallory had parked her car near the doorway of

38

the Players' Club. She shrank down in the seat when she spotted Jack Coffey chatting up the doorman. Now he was going in. This was the building the stakeout team had selected for the department's watchers on the square. This was also the spot where the second victim, Jonathan Gaynor's aunt, had been found inside a private car with tinted windows. The second murder had been daring, but not quite the stunning trick of a kill in full view of every living thing in the square.

Estelle Gaynor had also been a brutal daylight kill. Impossible, but it had happened in this place of Social Register old money and new-wealth rock stars. Pearl Whitman, the third victim, had broken the pattern by dying in low-rent environs. Why? And what had the old man seen that she was missing? Pearl Whitman was a tantalizing snag because she had left no heirs. The old SEC connection to Edith Candle, the woman who lived in Charles's building, was also nagging at her. Perhaps it was the scarcity of information on Candle that made her suspicious. This woman knew how to keep her private business underground.

Another cab pulled up to the curb on the adjacent street. The rear windows of the car were blocked by shopping bags and cloth of bright colors and, here and there, a white face and a brown one. The rear doors on both sides of the cab opened, and an endless stream of goods spilled out onto the sidewalk with the cabdriver, a small boy and a Doberman puppy. The shopping bags were every color of the rainbow, and bulged to rips at the paper seams. A flimsy circular table with folded legs leaned against the car. Boxes were being stacked precariously by the driver while the boy grappled with an antique gramophone with a large horn.

What now piled up on the sidewalk was greater than the interior volume of the cab. The magic show went on. The front passenger door opened, and an immense woman stepped out. She was at least six feet tall and simply too wide in the girth to have come out of that cab.

Now the cabby launched into a screaming match with this woman who had crossed his palm with too few dollars. He was an Arab, not too long in the country by the barely comprehensible English and the inability to deal with American women without going ballistic. He was making fisted hand gestures to go with the inarticulate screams. All Mallory could understand of the bad hollered English was, "You don't rob me, you bitch!"

He looked up at her from his height of one foot smaller. Looming over the driver, the woman seemed less the fat lady and more a regal presence. She leaned down, put her face in his face, and spoke in tones that did not carry.

The cabby nearly ripped the door off the hinges in his haste to open it. He jumped into the cab and laid a squealing strip of burning rubber all the way out of the square.

Mallory nodded in rare approval of the giantess.

Chapter Three

Charles Butler tapped his toes and willed the elevator to move faster. He would be ten minutes late if he was lucky, if the elevator made no more stops. He looked down at his shorter fellow passengers, who had conspired to slow his descent by stopping the elevator on every other floor.

40

Of course, Mallory would be on time for their appointment sixty blocks south and as many flights down. She would be knocking on the door of his empty office on the hour, not a second before or after. She was as compulsive about time as she was about neatness.

And now he remembered he had two things to be anxious about. His new office, a recently vacated apartment across the hall from his residence, would be best described as an Escher maze of tall stacks of paperwork and books, an unholy gathering of spiders and dust.

The elevator stopped again, and he glared at the boarding passenger. He was taking every stop quite personally now. These people had had all morning to ride the elevator up and down as much as they liked. However, on the upside of slowing down, Mallory might decide not to wait around. There might be a reprieve long enough to give the office a proper cleaning.

This morning, he had made a stab at straightening up, but correspondence still littered every surface. Quarterly tax forms, state and federal, bulged out of desk drawers and cardboard boxes, all waiting on a day when he was in the filing mode. And then there was all the added paperwork that went along with owning an apartment building. The hundred-odd books and a few years' worth of journals were only in proximity to the new bookshelves.

How would she react to the mess? She might assume he'd been vandalized. He could walk in behind her and feign shock.

Mrs. Ortega, his cleaning woman, had arrived while he was scrambling around on the floor, trying desperately to clear a few square feet of the carpet. Putting his head out the office door as she was

41

turning her key in the lock of his apartment, he had smiled at her, his eyes filled with hope. Her own eyes had turned hard. 'Fat chance I'm going in there,' said the back of her as she had disappeared into his residence, which was her territory and all that she might be held accountable for.

He knew Mrs. Ortega believed him to be a visitor from somewhere else—perhaps some point straight up, miles out, but nowhere on the surface of her own earth, which was square, shaped by the streets of a Latino neighborhood in Brooklyn.

And he supposed he was a bit out of the mainstream. He had grown up in the sheltered community of academia and then transferred to the closer-knit community of a research institute without stopping off in real life until very recently. A year ago, when he had given Mrs. Ortega the new address, she never asked why he would leave the luxurious boulevards of the Upper East Side for the narrower, dirty streets of SoHo. She had always known the ways of outworlders were not the ways of Brooklynites.

In the last few minutes before he'd had to leave off the cleaning up and straightening up to keep his uptown appointment sixty stories in the sky, he had considered reaming the office out with a blowtorch.

Now his stomach was rising, independent of the rest of him, as the elevator stopped again. A woman and a child got on. As the doors were closing, the child reached out and pushed ten buttons.

Mrs. Ortega's mother was Irish and had the same green eyes and red-gold hair as this stranger at the door. But Ma had not been a cop. Mrs. Ortega smelled cop when the woman ordered her to open the door of Mr. Butler's office across the hall. There was never a question of cop, or not a cop.

She turned the key in the lock and opened the door on a room in hell for cleaning women who had been sinners while they lived. She didn't like having the key to the office. Mr. Butler might get the idea that she would one day clean here, too. No way, not Shannon Ortega. She knew her rights. He couldn't make her clean it, not this mess.

She had been happy enough when he took this apartment over for his office, sweeping the whole nasty mess of papers and books across the hall. And it gave him another place to be, not underfoot while she was vacuuming and scrubbing. But no way was she going to deal with this pit, this mother of all dust collectors. All that she approved of were the freshly painted walls. The windows were at least a bucket of ammonia's worth of grime on each pane, and in the spaces between the tall stacks of paper, spiders were spinning elaborate webs with a confident sense of permanence. She had never ventured into the other rooms to see what he had done with them. She had a bum heart.

Oh, kiss a dead rat if the cop wasn't smiling. And it was not a friendly smile or a happy smile. A cat's smile it was, a cat with a live mouse in its teeth.

In the black of the stopped elevator, suspended fifteen floors above the ground, the passengers were speculating on what to do when the elevator fell. One passenger had read somewhere that it was a good idea to jump up and down. That way, the man explained to his captive audience, you had a fifty-fifty chance of being in the air when the elevator crashed.

"And breaking your legs," added Charles. "You're still failing at the same rate of speed as the

43

elevator."

Oddly enough, the eleven-year-old boy was the only one to grasp the principle of free-fall and gravity. The other passengers were now jumping up and down in the dark.

On the other side of the jammed doors, a fire marshal was urging them to remain calm via a loudspeaker. "Knock that crap off, you idiots!"

Mrs. Ortega was backing up to the wall. The cop had neatly cut off her escape route to the door.

"No English," she said, when, in fact, she did not speak any Spanish. She was fourth-generation American born and spoke only Newyorkese.

After much repetition of street names, Charles and the non-English-speaking cabdriver were finally in agreement. Once under way, the driver was disappointingly law-abiding, and not at all competitive with his fellow drivers, never changing lanes once in forty-three blocks, actually slowing down for yellow lights, and carefully looking to the left and right before proceeding across the intersection on a green light.

This was outrageous.

Charles tightly clasped his hands in his lap, lest they act as independent culprits. There was really no need to kill the driver, not on his very first day as a cabby. The next passenger would certainly do that.

Charles met Mrs. Ortega in the hall. She passed him by with her head lowered, not seeing anything but the carpet, determined that nothing would halt her steady progress down the corridor to the elevator, to freedom, muttering "Damn cops" in return for his cheerful "Goodbye. See you next week."

The office door was open. He walked through the foyer and into a perfect world of order. The windows glistened, the carpet was clear of the paper avalanche that had buried it on the very day it was put down, and the naked desk was dark wood, just as he remembered it from the Sotheby's auction of five weeks ago. Neat file holders with price tags on them were stacked on top of the antique mahogany filing cabinet. Other file holders, sans tags, were being put in their proper drawers by hands with long red nails. Twelve years of trade journals and a small library of books now filled the shelves of one wall.

Mallory strained to close the door of the filing cabinet and then turned on him. "You have to go to computers, Charles. This is just too much."

"Hello, Kathleen." He kissed her cheek and found a comfortable chair he had forgotten buying. "Sorry, I'm not usually half a day late. Oh, this is amazing." He was admiring the room, its antique furniture, its Tiffany lamps. He was not visualizing a computer or any other mechanical device in it, not even a typewriter or a pencil sharpener. "Simply amazing," he said, altogether skirting the issue of computers.

Over the two years he had known her, they'd had this conversation many times. She could never understand his resistance to the technology when he was so adept at computers and had even published an important paper on computer-mode giftedness. She had been the inspiration for that paper. Via the keyboard, she could dip her fingers into the stuffing of any software made and make it into a new animal that could sit up and bark at the moon if she wished.

"We could outfit this place with a state-of-the-art computer system," she said.

"I'd rather do it the old-fashioned way." He silently noted her use of the word *we* and wondered what to make of it.

The door buzzer went off. Charles walked across the room and out of the concept of high technology. That was it. No computers. They did not go well with his beloved antiques and the Persian carpet which fit the room so well. The carpet's weaver, a hundred years dead by now, must have envisioned this space with a mystic inner eye.

The buzzer was nagging. Most people only tapped it once. The short burst of noise was sufficiently loud and annoying. This continuation of noise, this leaning on the button, was the buzzer style of Herbert Mandrel, the tenant in 4A.

He opened the door to a small, wiry man with a fugitive face, eyes darting everywhere at once, suspecting every object of ill intentions. Nervous energy rose off the man in waves of contagion.

"You got a minute?" he asked, slipping uninvited through the narrow space between Charles and the doorframe. Herbert came up short in front of Mallory, who barred the foyer and showed no signs of standing aside.

The little man cocked his head to one side and fixed her with the intense, unwavering glare of one eye, and he did this with all the zeal of turning a cross on a vampire. Mallory, taller by six inches, looked down on Herbert with the same distaste she might show for a messy roadkill.

"Actually, I don't have a minute, Herbert," said Charles, forgetting that it had not been a question but Herbert's version of hello.

Herbert was saying, "It's getting dangerous. Everyone has guns."

"Everyone?"

"Henrietta on the third floor. She has a gun."

"Well, she's had it for quite a while, hasn't she?

Seven years, she says."

"I didn't know that. If I'd known that, I would've acted sooner." Though Herbert's feet were planted on the carpet, the rest of him was in constant motion, eyebrows colliding with each other, head jerking from side to side, one pointy finger stabbing the air as he spoke. "Do you know that a bullet can travel through four floors and kill an innocent person? You get rid of that gun or I take immediate action."

"And what sort of action might that be?" Foolish question. Herbert had only one solution to every problem from a leaking faucet to a burnt-out bulb in the hall.

"I'm calling a rent strike. All the tenants will back me on this. I want that gun out of this building. Now!" His finger was nearly touching Charles's face.

Mallory advanced a step, and Charles warned her off with a wave. He pulled the door open wider, as though that might help, as though Herbert picked up on cues less subtle than 'GET OUT!' He didn't.

"Henrietta belongs to a gun club. The gun is properly licensed and registered. There's nothing you or I can do about it."

"Yeah? You think so? Suppose I get my own gun?"

"Let's see if I'm following your logic. In the event that Henrietta accidentally discharges her gun, you plan to deflect the bullet by firing on it as it rips up through the floorboards. Have I got it right?"

"I'm gonna get a gun."

Mallory reached out and tapped him on the shoulder, smiling as she made him jump. She put one hand on her hip, drawing the side of her jacket open and exposing the .357 Smith & Wesson in her

47

shoulder holster. It was a very big gun, and Herbert's eyes were very wide.

"Not a good idea, pal." As her voice was silking along, she walked toward him, and step for step, he backed up to the door. "If I see you with a gun, if I hear a rumor that you've got a gun, it better have all the legal paperwork. You got that?" For emphasis, she reached out and touched his chest with one long red fingernail.

Charles watched in awe as the little man paled and turned smartly on one heel. Remarkably, Herbert was leaving of his own accord, and so quickly, too, not even shutting the door behind him.

Charles stared at the blessedly empty spot on the carpet where Herbert had been standing. "It's my recurring nightmare—him with a gun."

"He'll never get clearance to buy one. I'll tag his name with a psycho profile."

"You'll what?"

"I left a coded back door in the department computer. I can go in whenever I like. Nothing to it."

"Kathleen, I wish you wouldn't tell me things like that."

"You're beginning to sound like Markowitz." She turned her back on him and walked over to the century-old desk. She ran one hand across the polished surface and then sat down in the chair behind the desk as though trying it on for size.

"I stacked up the tenant paperwork in the next room, along with all the research material and the reports. You've got close to six square feet of paper in there. I can put all of that on disks with a scanner. When I'm done, it'll take up five square inches of space."

Oh, back to that again. "I prefer the idea of papers

48

I can hold in my hand. Seems more real somehow."

"You can't do that anymore, Charles. You're being buried alive by paper."

"My accountant comes by once a month and takes a bag of it off my hands."

She was not amused. "So, next month, you can send him a disk over the modem—save him a trip and a hernia."

"Ah, now you see, Kathleen, that's the problem with computers. One day there won't be any human transactions left. We'll all socialize by computer networks."

And her eyes said, 'Nice try.'

She was right; he knew that. He lacked Louis Markowitz's gift for creating order that passed for chaos. The more clutter Louis had added to his surroundings, the more details and data, the more efficiently his brain had worked. Charles's own clutter was mere confusion. He looked over the office and the perfect order she had created for him and wondered how many days would pass before he slipped beneath the snow line of the paperwork once more.

She was already reading the I-give-up signs in his face. She smiled slow and wide. "You need me. I'll start tomorrow. I can use one of the back rooms for my office."

"What? Work here? Kathleen, why would you want to work for me?"

"*With* you. I'm talking partnership." Purse and car keys in hand, she stood up and crossed the room to set a check on the cherrywood table by his chair.

The check bore the name of a major life insurance company. The claim on Markowitz's death should have taken two months, not two weeks. He wondered if she had facilitated the speed of the

49

check with her computer-hacking skills or her gun.

"That'll buy a lot of computer equipment," she said. "So, do we have a deal?"

It was hard to picture her even in temporary tandem with another human being, let alone a partnership. She hardly acknowledged that there might be one or two other officers on the same police force.

She was always such a loner, said Louis Markowitz's letter, which Charles had opened on the day the body was found. *She never hung out in cop bars, never saw the sad, mean side of burnout. She keeps company with machines.*

When Louis had given him the letter to hold against that day, Charles had felt honored, but curious, too. Why him, why not Rabbi Kaplan or someone else he had known longer?

Louis had said then, 'Kathy's a special case. You deal with special cases all the time.'

Indeed. Kaplan or any other man of the cloth would be a poor match for what Louis had described in his letter as an amoral savage:

When my Helen died a few years back, Kathy wanted to kill the whole world. It was all I could do to convince her it wouldn't be civil to gut the surgeon who failed Helen. When I'm dead, Commissioner Beale will bump her out of Special Crimes Section and put her on compassionate leave. Make her understand this is department policy, and Beale is not to be found in an alley strung up by his balls.

As he recalled, she had been very civilized about the forced leave. She had taken his advice on that matter with no argument, no protest at all. Why hadn't that made him suspicious? Well, obviously because he was an idiot.

50

He could only wonder what else had gone by him. He supposed there wasn't much point in asking her a direct question. He believed she really did like him well enough to count him as a friend, to confide in him at times, but there were limits. He would have to settle for damage control.

He looked around this perfectly ordered room. It was obvious to both of them that he needed her, even if she didn't need him—not him or any other creature on this planet. But her proposal of a partnership would cost him sleep. The things she did with other people's computers, and without their knowledge or consent.

She had a gift that would have gone begging in an era without computer technology. He marveled over the farsighted genetic blueprint. Each encounter with a human born to a specific talent, applied or not, gave him a window on the future of all mankind. But his limited window on Kathleen Mallory was frightening. The partnership was an insane idea to be considered with the same careful thought he might give to walking through a mine field or jumping out of a perfectly good airplane. And Louis would have been the first to tell him so.

In a far corner of his compartmentalized brain, he could see the specter of Louis Markowitz rolling his eyes and saying sardonically, 'Ah, Charles?' and shaking his head from side to side with the sentiment of 'No. Not a good idea. Not a good idea at all.'

"All right, Kathleen, a partnership." He extended his hand and she shook it with a firm grip.

"Call me Mallory, now that it's business."

"And you'll call me Butler, I suppose? No, I don't think so. I know you too well for that. It would seem unnatural."

51

"All right. I'll call you *Charles*. When the stuff shows up, just sign for it. Here," she said, handing him a business card. "Just a sample. You like it?"

Business cards? Hardly samples, they were printed on good stock in two colors, maroon and gray. She had to have ordered them at least two weeks ago, perhaps on the very day of the funeral.

"Kathleen—"

"Mallory."

"Sorry. I'm just a little curious about the wording. *Discreet investigations?* As in private investigations?"

"What's the problem, Charles?"

"We're a consulting firm."

"What does a consultant do, Charles?"

"Well, someone comes to me with a problem, and I look into it and come up with a solution for them."

She kissed the top of his head and walked to the door as if his own answer were answer enough. And it probably would be if his field was not finding practical applications for new modes of intelligence and odd gifts. And she was not even going to deal with the little matter that her own name preceded his in *Mallory and Butler, Ltd.*

"Wait," he called to her as she was pulling the door closed behind her. "Wouldn't I need a special license for this kind of thing?"

"You have one," she said.

"How—?" He aborted this stupid question. Of course, she had simply arranged it with a midnight computer requisition. Willing or no, he was in the computer system as a properly licensed private investigator...while she remained a police officer on compassionate leave, and with certain restrictions on her behavior.

Their partnership was minutes old, and already

52

he'd been had. This could not possibly be legal. There were rules and regulations and—

She smiled. The door closed.

He was feeling a sense of loss when she had been gone only a few seconds. She always had that effect on him. When she left a room, she left a vacuum, a hole in the air which smelled faintly of Chanel.

Only in daydreams had he considered that they might ever be more than friends. She was a beauty, while he was…a man with a prominent nose, a beak actually. And when he smiled, he had the aspect of a happy lunatic. And there were other standout qualities that some called freakish.

His eidetic memory called up the last page of Markowitz's letter. He projected it onto a clear space of the wall. The mental image was perfect to the details of the folds in the paper and the black ink blots of the fountain pen Louis favored over the ballpoint:

She never worked the field beyond her rookie days, and I don't want her working it now, dogging my last tracks. It makes me a little crazy that I won't always be there to keep her safe.

She spent most of her childhood on the streets, stealing breakfast, lunch, and dinner, and her shoes. She's fearless. She thinks there isn't a human born she can't outsmart or outshoot. The pity is that she's so freaking smart and a great shot, beautifully equipped to do the job. Scary, isn't it, Charles?

He missed Louis sorely. The day he had been given the letter was his last memory of the man. Louis had handled his sherry glass delicately. He had been graceful in all his gestures and in the way he carried himself and his excess poundage. Yet, at rest, the first creature the inspector called to mind was a fat basset hound. Then the fleshy folds of

Louis's face would gather up into a smile, dispatching the hound and exposing the great personal charm of the man. One tended to smile back, willing or no. People in handcuffs tended to smile back.

Had Louis known who his killer would be? Was it the man who killed the elderly women? He supposed he could assume it was a man. This was not the sort of violence a woman would do. And he could assume great intelligence. If Louis thought the killer was not a fair match for Mallory, that put him in the upper two percentile.

But he was thinking out the wrong puzzle. Louis had not asked him to find his murderer, he had asked him to look after his daughter, a more convoluted problem and the greater challenge of the two.

Mallory switched off the ignition and settled back to watch Jonathan Gaynor pay off the cab and enter his apartment building. Monday through Friday his routine seldom varied. She would stay on him until dusk. The daylight timing was a constant in the killing.

A shift in the September breeze carried the pungent smell of new-cut grass. She approved of Gramercy's clean streets, well-tended park and perfect order. It was so quiet here, and while the flowers bloomed, so unlike the rest of the town in the way it soothed all her senses and brought her a kind of peace unknown in her normal workaholic existence. She stared at the small park-maintenance building where Anne Cathery had lain beneath a garbage bag on the blood-soaked ground amid her scattered beads. And there, seated on a bench only a few yards from the building, was the victim's grandson, Henry Cathery.

He looked much younger than his twenty-one years; he might have been a giant twelve-year-old. He was another one who lived a somewhat routine life. Cathery's hours in the park might vary, but he was there each day, always sitting on the same bench. He had been sitting there, only yards away from the murder site, during some part of the day his grandmother was murdered.

Cathery was working at his portable chessboard, oblivious to other life forms on the planet. More than ten weeks ago, NYPD investigators had discovered that this oblivion worked both ways. The doormen and residents of the square were so accustomed to his presence, Cathery had become invisible to them. They could no more swear to his comings and goings than they could swear the fire hydrants had not been missing for a morning and then restored to their accustomed places in the afternoon.

The deceased Pearl Whitman had been Cathery's only alibi for the time of his grandmother's murder. Mallory wondered what Markowitz would have made of that. He had been no believer in coincidence. He might have wondered if Pearl Whitman had wavered in her testimony. Or was it just Cathery's hard luck that his alibi was the last victim?

Who knows what evil lurks in the hearts of men?
The Shadow knows.

Mallory smiled at the memory of the old radio program's opening line. Markowitz had never given up his lesson plans to inculcate her with a creative vision that could see around corners and beyond normal parameters. Her latest exercise in imagining was the thought that if there were aliens among us,

Henry Cathery would be one of them. His eyebrows were permanently surprised and contradicted by his half-lidded lethargic eyes, which rolled around in their sockets in a listless fashion. The mouth was small and fixed in the permanent moue of one who had recently stepped on a dog turd. He was also strange in his reclusive habits. There was an odd little relationship with a badly dressed young woman who sometimes came to sit beside him and hold one-way conversations while he ignored her, but he had no real friends.

And neither did Mallory have any friends, not now that she and Charles were business partners.

If Markowitz had abandoned the FBI profile which Cathery fit so well, he had not abandoned Cathery but only saved him off to one side of the cork board in a class by himself. Cathery would have come into a large trust from his parents' estate whether the grandmother lived or died. He didn't fit the money motive quite so well as Gaynor.

She had fixed the blind spot for the NYPD surveillance team and parked closer to Jonathan Gaynor's building. A cab pulled to curb four cars in front of her, and she made a note that the giantess and her small entourage had arrived an hour earlier this week. The boy was first to alight from the cab. Now the Doberman puppy barked as a doorman joined the cabby in unloading the paraphernalia of bags and table, gramophone and boxes. When the giantess emerged from the back seat of the cab, Mallory matched the woman, stat for stat, against the computer-raided rap sheet of a high-tech con artist whose description listed height and weight, three arrests and no convictions, companions of boy and Doberman. But not the same Doberman. The rap sheets went back for years; this dog was not six

56

months old.

So far, the only inroad on Gramercy Park was Charles's connection to Edith Candle, the woman in the SEC investigation on Whitman Chemicals, the woman who proved out Markowitz's theory on the relatedness of every living being to one another. Now, if she could only cultivate or terrorize the giantess, it could be her entrée to the community. Perhaps with a light threat, the mere twist of an enormous arm, she could leave the car, the sidewalk, and move freely among the old women of old money.

She raised up the telescoping lens of her camera and focused on the face of the giantess. This woman was not the fair mulatto Mallory had taken her for from the distance of the last sighting. The irises were dark with the cast of blue gun metal, and sliding like oiled bearings within the Asian folds of her eyes. Her complexion was the olive tone of the Mediterranean. Her nostrils and lips were classic African. Today her hair, long and reddish brown, was hanging in a straight fall below the cap of the scarf. How many races lived under that immense skin? She was the whole earth.

The giantess lit a black cheroot and called to the little boy, who moved toward her, walking as though his feet weighed twenty pounds, each one. The boy's hands hung at his sides, and his head lolled on his chest. What was wrong with him?

The giantess headed for the door to the apartment building. Beneath the long bright print of the dress, her impossibly tiny feet moved quickly along the sidewalk. The woman spoke Spanish to the cabby, French to the boy, and then chattered with the doorman in English. The babble ceased abruptly behind the glass door.

The warm sun on Mallory's face was suddenly blocked by shadow.

"Officer, I want you to arrest that person!"

What? Oh Christ, where had this woman come from?

Mallory looked up through the open car window at a pinch-faced matron in her middle fifties. The woman's hair was dark brown and unnatural for the lack of white strands to go with the sagging jowls and the puffy, lined eyes. The linen suit was Lord & Taylor, and the pearls were real.

"I said, I want that person arrested. Now!"

The woman pointed to the door which had enveloped the small troop of woman, boy and dog.

"Go get her," said the well-dressed matron in an authoritative voice accustomed to charging vicious dogs to eat delivery boys.

"I'm not a cop, lady."

"Oh, yes you are."

"Lady, I'm—"

"I did wonder at first. Your car used to be so neat. But those are takeout containers on the back seat, aren't they?"

Mallory turned around to look at the seat behind her. Newspapers and sandwich wrappers mingled with notebooks and cardboard deli containers, straws and sugar cubes, catsup and mustard packets, empty cartridge boxes and white plastic bags with the logo of the drugstore where she bought her film. A half-eaten sandwich showed dully through a layer of wax paper. How had it happened? she wondered, as if she had lost the memory of filling her car with the trash of the typical stakeout vehicle.

Why hadn't she just painted a damn sign on the side of the car? If this ever got back to Jack Coffey, he'd laugh his ass off. And then he'd change her

58

compassionate leave status to a full suspension without pay, without badge and gun.

"I'm not a cop."

"And all those coffee cups. And your car is tan, isn't it? You're a cop, and if you don't arrest that woman, I'm going to report you. I know Commissioner Beale very well. We have the same dentist."

"I'm not a cop."

"So you haven't been on stakeout every day this week and last week, too?"

"I'm a private cop."

"Pardon?"

Mallory handed her a business card. "See? Not a real cop. The commissioner wouldn't like it if I arrested somebody."

The woman stared at the card, and then her mouth hurried over to one side of her face in the slant line of the skeptic as she read the lines of maroon print. "Discreet investigations? You call this discreet?"

Jonathan Gaynor, nephew of the late Estelle Gaynor, had just stepped out onto the sidewalk. Mallory switched on the ignition and put the car in gear. He had changed his clothes and donned a baseball cap, but from any distance, she could pick him out by the body language. He had the long-legged, no-bones gait of a scarecrow, and as he moved on down the sidewalk, he seemed blown along by the wind.

He was awkward but not unattractive. She favored full beards and dark hair, and she would have found the lean, ruddy face very appealing if not for the possibility that Gaynor had gutted her old man and left him to die alone.

Gaynor waved down a cab and Mallory rolled.

She could see the pinch-faced matron in her

rearview mirror, waving the business card like a small warning flag.

Rabbi David Kaplan struggled with the legs of the card table. They were supposed to unfold from the table top, but perversely, they would not.

"My wife usually does this. She wasn't expecting anyone to come."

"Good thing I brought the beer," said Dr. Edward Slope. "Anything in the fridge?"

It would have been Louis Markowitz's turn to bring the sandwiches tonight. The doctor's own wife, Donna, had set that policy, saying, 'Don't you expect Anna to cook for you,' knowing that Anna would never have settled for cold sandwiches. It would have been a spread worthy of the Second Coming.

"I've lived with that woman for thirty-five years," said the rabbi, "and never have I seen an empty refrigerator. That's the least of my worries." One leg of the table dropped down, but he had no way to know he had accidentally moved the latch that held it in place. When his wife did this, it took three seconds. He supposed she just willed it to unfold itself and stand up on four legs. And for all he knew, it walked to the center of the room of its own accord.

Slope wandered into the kitchen to stand at the open door of the refrigerator. Louis Markowitz's refrigerator had been much like this one, as he recalled. Not so long ago, Louis's shelves had been filled with real food, built from a woman's blueprint of shopping lists and recipes, the makings of meals past and meals to come, warm colors of fruit and cool green vegetables, condiments and mysterious unlabeled jars of liquids. When the last woman had gone from Louis's house, the refrigerator had changed its character, becoming shabby in its accumulation of deli bags and frozen dinners. Everything to the rear of the shelves had resembled small furry animals which had sickened and then crawled back there to die.

Now Slope stared at Anna Kaplan's well-stocked shelves. Food is love, said this refrigerator.

He was assessing bowls and pots and checking under the lids of Tupperware when the doorbell rang. The new arrival could only be Robin Duffy. The lawyer had a hearty voice, usually upbeat. Tonight, it sounded through the walls like a mourning bell in the low octaves. Robin had known Louis Markowitz for many years, and he would be a long time getting over the death.

Dr. Slope added mustard to the tray.

Now they were three.

Two weeks had passed since the funeral. Tonight, by some connectedness of spirit, the three of them had gathered together in this place where the fourth player, Louis Markowitz, had been loved by a close circle of men.

Slope clutched a Tupperware container to his chest and made the contorted face of a man who would rather not cry. He set the plastic container on the tray. What was missing? he wondered as he picked up the tray. When the bell rang again, announcing a fourth person, the tray fell from his hands.

He sank to the floor and slowly reached out for the heavy mustard jar, sturdy thing, unbroken. He crawled about the tiles, blindly groping for each dropped item, finding the butter and the knife with his eyes screwed shut, watertight.

When he was again in full possession of

61

everything he had lost, he carried the tray down the narrow hall and into the rabbi's den, which was lined with four walls of books and two old friends, and one very large stranger, the fourth man, who was unfolding the last leg of the card table. He was well over six feet but nonthreatening in his size, perhaps because his face was so wonderfully appealing. What a nose. And those eyes. Even with the heavy eyelids, the irises were so small they left a generous margin of white on all sides, giving him the look of wide-eyed astonishment at just everything in the world.

Slope liked this man immediately. He looked at the faces of his friends, and like himself, they were unconsciously, accidentally smiling.

"Pull up a chair, Mr. Butler."

"Charles."

"Edward."

"Let me give you the ground rules, Charles," said Robin Duffy, a small and compact bulldog of a man introduced as Louis's lawyer and neighbor of twenty years.

"Louis explained the rules to him," said Rabbi Kaplan, pulling his own chair up to the table. "Charles came with twelve pounds of nickel and dime rolls."

The strained silence was broken by Robin Duffy. "I like a man who comes prepared to lose big."

"So Louis invited you to join the game?" Slope dealt out the cards, and immediately went to work on building a pastrami sandwich.

"I inherited his chair." Charles eyed the tray of sandwich makings with the discrimination of a connoisseur, and passed over the cheddar cheese for the Swiss, so as not to overpower the more delicate slices of cold chicken. He pulled the letter out of his jacket pocket and exchanged it for the jar of mayonnaise in Slope's hand.

The doctor stared down at the handwriting that had become so familiar to him over his years with the medical examiner's office. Louis's friend was pointing to the third paragraph, which indeed spelled out a legacy. The letter was silently passed from man to man as the dealt cards lay where they landed. It seemed Louis's friend had been left more than the chair.

"Well, that fits," said Duffy when he folded the letter and handed it back across the table. "I always figured the poker game was just a front for raising Kathy." He popped the cap from a bottle of beer and picked up his cards. "Did Lou ever tell you where he found her?"

"No. No, he didn't."

"She was maybe eleven. He caught the little brat breaking into a Jag. Well, he's holding her out by the collar of her jacket, and she's swinging away, little fists pounding the crap out of air. So it was take the kid home with him, or spend what's left of the wife's birthday hassling with Juvenile Hall."

"But Helen didn't understand," said Slope, picking up his cards. "She thought Kathy was a present. She wouldn't let go of the kid for twelve years."

Charles smiled down at a clear space on the table where his photographic memory projected the pages of Hoyle which dealt with the rules of poker, a game he had never played. Nowhere in the rules did it list doomsday stud with deuces wild. "Louis must have been pleased that she turned out so well, becoming a policewoman and all."

The other three men looked up from their cards, their faces all asking the same silent question: 'Are you nuts?'

"Helen Markowitz did teach Kathy table manners." Duffy examined the card which had been laid down faceup. "I'll bet a nickel. But the kid never really changed. She likes being a cop 'cause she can steal more interesting stuff with her computer. And she gets clean away with it."

"Yeah," said Slope, lighting a cigar and pushing his own coins to the center of the table. "I'll see that nickel and raise you a dime. Whatever Louis needed, Kathy could get for him. I guess he had a few occasions to worry about his pension. After she broke into the FBI computer, I saw him make the sign of the cross—Sorry, Rabbi."

"The things she's done," said Duffy, picking at his cards and trying to give the appearance that this was not a potential world-class poker hand. His dime grudgingly pushed into the small pile of coins.

"Remember when she was a little kid," said Slope. "And Helen enrolled her in the NYU computer courses for children?"

"Yeah," said the lawyer. "Helen was so happy that day. Kathy had finally taken an interest in something legal. Do you remember the way Helen cried when the kid gave her that present? You know, the one she made at computer school?"

"That transfer from the savings and loan?" Slope pushed another nickel into the pot as the next card hit the table, faceup.

"Yeah." Robin Duffy smiled, and then his mouth wobbled as he tried to take the expression back before it tipped his hand, which was somewhat improved by the card dealt him. "Kathy just couldn't understand why Helen was crying. She figured anybody'd be thrilled to have an extra twenty thou in the checking account three weeks before Christmas."

"Then," said Rabbi Kaplan, "Kathy figured, well, Helen is Jewish. Maybe different customs."

In the next four hours, Charles discovered that the game of poker could not be learned from a book, and that Helen had worked miracles with Kathy's behavior. Within six months of foster care, the Markowitzes had been able to take the child into a store with them, and even turn their backs on her for whole minutes at a time—all because theft, petty or grand, made Helen cry. Helen had done so good a job that Kathy could now pass for a young lady in any company but this one. These men knew what she was: a born thief, a hard case with no intrinsic sense of right and wrong. Yet, of all the five billion on the planet, Louis Markowitz had loved her best.

After the fiasco with Helen's present, Louis had taken Kathy out of the computer course. The NYU instructor had been sorry to lose such a dazzling student. The bank transfer had been fixed, said the pale little man with the thick glasses. The bank didn't even know the money was ever missing. So why pull the child out? he had asked, genuinely puzzled. It seemed to be upsetting the little girl, he said. 'Look, she's going to cry.'

How could Louis have explained to that kind, soft-spoken, endlessly patient man that this was not a real kid he had by the hand. You could stick pins in Kathy all damn day long and she'd never, never cry. She had no soft spots.

Later, she would cry for Helen and not stop crying for days, but that was still years and years away. These were the early days of life with the baby felon.

Determined never to sick Kathy on civilians again, Louis brought her into work with him in the

65

after-school hours and pointed at a row of computer terminals in the Special Crimes office. 'This is crap,' he explained to the skinny kid who didn't even come up to his lapel pin in those days. 'We don't have genius programmers,' he told her then, 'no decent equipment. What we got won't work half the time. And now I've got a PC that won't work at all. You're so smart? Fix it,' he told her, 'and you can play with that one.'

One night, when she was only an inch taller, she crept into his office with a strange little smile. She dumped a load of printouts on his desk and crept silently away. Long after Helen had come to take the little angel home, Louis was still at his desk reading all the department dirt he ever imagined possible. The thief had cracked every high-echelon code in existence and raided Internal Affairs.

A present.

This had been Kathy's longest lesson.

The poker game had changed to a bastard version of five-card draw, with deuces wild if you held a queen, and jacks wild if you held a ten. And Charles discovered that Slope was not only a gifted medical examiner, but he could also blow smoke rings.

Slope put up one finger and received one card in an effort to convince the others he held four of a kind. He didn't. "It drove the kid nuts for months trying to figure out why Louis didn't use the goods to blackmail his way to chief of detectives and a slew of payoffs."

Duffy chimed in, "And I'm sure Kathy was expecting a nice little cut of the action. Two cards."

"And we still have no idea what the kid made of that," said Slope, "Louis thought maybe he lost face with the little brat for a while, that she had him pegged for a sucker, turning down all that great

66

dirt."

"I'll stick with these," said Duffy. "Lousy hand that it is."

"I'm out." The rabbi put down his cards. "When she was twenty years old, Louis almost had a heart attack when she told him she was quitting college to enter the police academy."

"A license to steal *and* a gun." Duffy clinked a dime into the kitty, and as he looked up, he made his eyebrows dance. "When you see these cards, you're gonna cry, you bastards."

Slope tossed in two dimes, and after the others had followed suit, he laid out a wild card jack and three tens, glancing at Duffy with a sly smile. "Louis called in a lot of favors to keep her in Special Crimes so he could protect the city of New York from Kathy."

Rabbi Kaplan put up his hands. "Enough, Edward. You'll make Charles think he's inherited a monster."

"He has," said Duffy, spraying his wild card and three queens on the table. His short arms barely made the reach to gather in the kitty of nickels and dimes.

"Louis and Helen took Kathy off the street while she still had core emotions left," said Slope. "But she'll never be quite socialized, never altogether civilized. It was just too late, you see."

"She loved Helen at first sight," said Rabbi Kaplan, dealing out the new hand. "But it was a long road for Louis, teaching her to trust him. It was more than a year before she stopped calling Louis 'Hey Cop.' Then she got comfortable with 'Hey Markowitz.'"

"But she did love Louis," said Slope. "Some kids are a lot worse off for their time on the street. You

67

look into their eyes and there's no one home anymore. They're numb. They're the stuff that serial killers are made of. Kathy's emotions are still very much alive, but it would be a mistake to forget she's damaged."

Charles rearranged his cards, and three men knew he had two pair. He looked up to smiles all around. "You think the Invisible Man might have been a damaged child?"

Slope held up two fingers for cards. "Louis said some people were just born mean. I have to go along with that. This killer is probably just a garden-variety sociopath, nothing fancy. There are simply too many of them to categorize them as insane."

"Louis favored money incentives for murder." Duffy waved one hand to say he was sticking with the cards dealt him. "Special Crimes was set up to deal with the really brutal, bizarre stuff and a fair share of loonies. But quite a few of the perps turned out to be people with money to gain and a need for stimulation."

"Pardon?"

"Sociopaths need more stimulation. I imagine murder can be rather stimulating," said Slope. "I'm in for a nickel. And the sociopath has all the ethics of an insect."

Three hands later, Charles was down to his last roll of dimes as the rabbi explained that Kathy was predictable in her own peculiar set of ethics. "Kathy's code of behavior was shaped by Helen's character."

Rabbi Kaplan looked at Charles over the tops of some of the worst cards he'd ever held, and he smiled like a winner.

Charles was looking down on a better hand—in fact, a great hand—and as quickly as his face showed all of this to the other players, they laid down their own cards.

"You do realize," said Rabbi Kaplan, "she's going after Louis's killer."

"Louis knew who it was, didn't he?"

"It's hard to say," said Slope. "Louis knew a lot about the murderer, but it was very general stuff. He's a clever bastard, I know that much. He uses a different knife every time. Not even a similarity of serration."

Charles laid down his winning hand to the surprise of no one. "What about the second murder, the car where the Gaynor woman was found? Did the killer have to pick the lock? Wouldn't that suggest an expertise?"

"Good try, Charles," said Duffy, sadly watching the money drift by him and toward Charles's end of the table. "You take any block in New York City, and you'll find at least one unlocked car. The old man who owned that car only drove it when he went to the hospital to visit his wife. He can't remember if he locked it. It's easy to get careless in a neighborhood like that one. There's never been a car theft in Gramercy during the daylight hours."

"Doing murder in the daylight should be a bit more difficult than car theft. You think the killer belongs to the square, just blends in with the population?"

"There's no shortage of suspects in Gramercy," said Duffy. "The women left large estates. But there's nothing to tie the heirs to the crime, nothing that wouldn't be laughed out of court. If the heirs have alibis for at least one of the murders, and they do, the other murders would plant reasonable doubt even if you could get circumstantial evidence on one of them."

"This one's so clever," said Rabbi Kaplan, "Louis said he'd have to catch the killer in the act."

"Could there be two of them?"

"It's possible, I suppose," said Slope. "It wasn't Louis's theory. He always referred to one killer. He never said *them or they*. He called the killer a thing, a freak, an *it.*"

The next hand was under way and Charles dealt the last card to the rabbi. "You were saying that Kathleen's behavior is roughly predictable?"

"If you knew more about Helen, you'd know more about Kathy."

"I'll stick with what I got," said Duffy, declining more cards. "When Kathy was little, she used to steal all kinds of presents for Helen. God, how she loved Helen. She just couldn't steal enough for that woman."

"Two cards," said Slope. "I think it was Kathy's way of paying Helen for loving her."

"Of course, the presents always made Helen cry. One card."

"Well, that confused the kid a lot," said Duffy. "I mean it was free stuff, wasn't it? So why was Helen crying? Kathy was a good kid…in her own way. She did what Helen told her to do. But she didn't always understand the reasons. Finally, she arrived at a set of rules she could understand. She would never do anything that made Helen cry, even if she didn't know why Helen cried. The kid never stole another thing."

"Cards, Rabbi?"

"Well, things. She never stole things. One card, please. Kathy's moral loopholes were Helen's blind spots. Helen knew nothing about computers. So almost anything she could do with a computer was legal by Kathy's lights."

70

"And it never occurred to Helen that Kathy could kill," said Slope. "So she never told her not to."

Chapter Four

Mallory was out the door, zipping and buttoning as she flew, and 'oh shitting' her damn luck as she pulled the straps of a student book bag over her shoulders. Of all the days to sleep through an alarm. Gaynor would be en route by now, but the subway could get her to the university campus ahead of him.

It was eight-thirty rush hour when she boarded the subway car and sat in the press of cheek and thigh with the workadays who were lucky enough to find seats. Standing passengers were crushing back to the walls, already hassled and stressed by the cattle-car ambience, not wanting any trouble, yet all dressed up in their New York attitudes, up for the battle, the inevitable confrontation that followed the shove, the stepped-on toe, the briefcase pressed into back or gut.

When she got off at 117th Street, the subway's morning ammonia smell was beginning to accumulate more legitimate odors of authentic urine as she passed by a man pissing on the wall. It had become such a common sight, she had long ago forgotten it was a crime to use the city's walls for a toilet. She climbed up the stairs into the light of morning, cool air, and a whiff of hot pretzels and coffee from a nearby sidewalk stand.

Limping toward her down the sloping sidewalk was a graduate of the New York School of Begging. He carried the requisite paper cup, and his foot was turned out in a convincing twisted handicap. As he approached Mallory, something in her eyes deterred him, and he veered off sharply on two good feet.

She passed through the familiar gates of the university campus and crossed the plaza to the cover of a doorway where she could watch the street. The cab dropped Gaynor at the same place each morning and never before nine. By Markowitz's watch, it was ten before the hour. The watch had never run when the old man carried it. Repairing it had been the topic of a decade-long conversation between the Markowitzes, a few words dropped by habit in the pie-and-coffee hour after dinner. She'd taken care of that old unfinished business for them and had the watch repaired the day it had been returned to her along with the other personal effects. When it came back from the jeweler, it had been altered in another respect. Inside the gold cover and beneath the names of Markowitz's grandfather and father and his own name, it said *Mallory.*

Her gaze wandered across the plaza to the canteen's wall of glass. Sleepy students were slugging back coffee. Other students carrying trays were lining up to pay the cashier. Over the next ten minutes, she watched a few of them leave without paying. The canteen was staffed with student workers who hated their jobs and couldn't care less if the other students walked off with the tables and chairs. It was easy theft, and not worthy of her respect.

She checked the pocket watch again. Gaynor was late this morning. She pulled her notebook out of her jacket pocket and scratched a memo. Any break in a routine was noted.

But he was not late. He was early.

She watched him stroll out the front door of the canteen and cross the plaza. He carried a covered paper cup and the brown paper bag that, according to her notes, usually contained one chocolate doughnut, one napkin and three sugar packets for his coffee, which was on the light side.

She followed him to his office and leaned against a wall down the hall from his door, pretending interest in a bulletin board and waiting out his twenty-minute breakfast ritual. Exactly twenty minutes later, he emerged and locked the door behind him, stinging a book bag over one shoulder. She followed at a discreet distance as he walked to his first class.

His legs showed a decided preference for two different directions, and elbows pointed east and west. Clearly, his four limbs were only going along with the torso under duress. It was predictable that he would trip on one paving stone and stumble on one marble step before arriving at the auditorium.

His first class was gathering as he arrived. Students straggled in by ones and twos. Gaynor arranged his notes on the podium to the sounds of young bodies hitting the seats, rustling paper, books slapping to laps, yawns and coughs, settling finally to absolute quiet as Gaynor smiled and wished them good morning.

Mallory took her regular seat at the back of the lecture hall where she was lost in a sea of a hundred young faces. Notebook and pen in hand, she played the familiar role that had ceased to be pure role-playing from the first class she had attended. He was good. No one nodded off during his lectures.

When he dropped his chalk for the third time, Mallory noticed the student in the next seat was drawing a short line alongside two other lines at the top of a page. This boy would round the scorekeeping off at five before the class ended.

Gaynor was predictable in many ways, but never boring, and she was as attentive as the rest, listening to him, trying not to smile at his wry humor, trying very hard not to like him.

After a second class, they were walking back to his office again, Gaynor and his sun-gold shadow, without more serious mishap than his dropping a book and managing to trip over it.

She sat on a bench in the hall during the hours of student appointments. One after another, the students filed in and out. For the next two hours, he was never alone.

She made quick notes on the time his last student arrived, and then pulled her mail out of the canvas book bag. She looked at the letter she should have opened yesterday, weighing it in one hand. She knew, without opening the envelope, it was another request from Robin Duffy, lawyer and longtime friend of the small family that wasn't one anymore. She would have to do something about the house in Brooklyn, Duffy would say for the third time. She jammed the unopened letter into her pocket.

Not yet.

She wasn't ready to walk through the front door of the old house and sit down with the hard fact that there was no one home and never would there be.

In some dimension, Markowitz was continuing on, but not in any afterlife. Heaven would not do; it was beyond belief. She could believe in old radio heroes for an hour or more, but there were limits. Yet Markowitz had to be somewhere.

She had never returned to the small café down the street from the station house. She avoided walking on that block in the morning hours, when he might be eating breakfast there...continuing on. How could she go back to the old house in Brooklyn and not see him there, if Markowitz was to continue on outside the dark hole in the cemetery lawn.

She also continued on in her own usual way, wondering what she could do to bug his eyes out and give him a new story for the Thursday night poker game, which would always begin: 'Let me tell you what my kid did this time.'

Samantha Siddon nodded her white head at the doorman and walked slowly up the street to the next block, brandishing a silver-handled cane. She hurried along the sidewalk with a trace of a limp and the fearful memory of a bad fall which had broken one hip. The bone had taken forever to mend, and the onset of arthritis had increased her agony. She would rather be quartered by four swift horses than suffer a second fall. She never went anywhere without the cane, which bore a lion's face and lent her a little courage.

She was soon well out of the calm of Gramercy Park and into the surrounding alien atmosphere of Manhattan, taking shallow breaths, mistrusting this air. She hailed a cab and gave the driver a midtown address. Samantha was pleased and stunned to have a traditional New York cabby, a native son with a Brooklyn dialect who took risks on every block, defying death to swerve through lane changes and beat each yellow traffic light. When she stepped out of the cab on Madison Avenue, it was well ahead of the appointed hour because she had anticipated a driver who translated addresses to the wrong side of town.

With fifteen minutes to spare, she stood on a busy street corner near a public telephone and watched the parade of surefooted children of commerce marching on the avenue with the hard slaps and clicks of flat-soled shoes and high heels, eyes fixed with terrible purpose, prepared to trample old women, toddlers, anyone who impeded them on their lunch hour. Though she knew she could buy and sell any one of them with a day's interest on her capital, they terrified her. One careless shove and she might spend the rest of her days in traction or a wheelchair. The days of the walking cane were numbered as it was.

As the minutes passed by, these ideas fell away from her. When the public telephone did ring, she was ready, more than ready.

She whispered into the receiver, though the pedestrian army of that avenue was hurrying by at a heart-attack clip not conducive to eavesdropping. Her words were lost in the noise of a passing bus followed by a police car, its siren opening with a panicky scream and then switching into the nagging mode of 'Hey, get out of my way, come on, come on, move it, move it.' And at last, she was screaming to be heard above the hustle of the throng which looked through her and moved around her, and never noticed if she had two heads or one.

Her step was quicker as she walked away from the pay phone. This small intrigue had made her young again, though the bank window threw back the crawl-paced reflection of an old woman with a hump on her back.

Mallory arrived at the campus theater just behind Gaynor. She stood on the top step and casually perused the playbill set in glass to one side of the entrance. Again, she read the words she knew by heart, and gave him three minutes through the door before she followed him.

She knew this building well from student days

when she had attended Barnard College productions in its small theater. That had been another life, and when she thought back on it, it was almost as though it had happened to someone else. Some other girl had sat alone in the crowd while the babble went on around her in another language belonging to a different species of animals with bubbling mouths and the softer eyes of prey.

She entered the shoe-box lobby as Gaynor was disappearing through the door which led into the theater. A young woman stepped between Mallory and this door. Hands on hips, the woman tossed back her long frizz of brown hair, which might pass for long waves of rusted steel wool.

"You can't go in there," said the woman, in the attitude of a combative poodle which had no idea how ridiculous it looked.

This woman might be all of twenty years old, and Mallory could not miss the fact that the frizzy brunette was smaller, lighter in the framework, and had no gun. She moved past her.

"One more step and I call campus security."

Incredulous, Mallory paused and faced the poodle down. "So? You and I both know the response time for campus security is forty minutes or never."

A snicker came from the side, and the salvo was meant for the poodle. A baby-faced boy in a denim shirt and dungarees leaned one arm on the ticket counter. He stared at Mallory as he lit a cigarette and dangled it from his lip. He tipped the wide brim of an old felt hat to her, and then lowered the brim to a rakish angle. She approved both hat and boy with the slight inclination of her head.

"We're in dress rehearsal," said the poodle, still glaring up at Mallory. "No one but cast." She sniffed the air, and catching the scent of the smoke,

77

her head whipped around, followed out of sync by her body as she turned on the boy. "Put that cigarette out immediately!" Her eyebrows smashed together. "It's against the law to smoke in this building."

"But, Boo, I don't actually mind breaking the law," said the boy. His smile was charming, a child's smile.

"Put it out this minute!"

The boy bent down to stub his cigarette out on the worn sole of his shoe, but he continued to hold on to it. The unwillingness to waste the cigarette told Mallory this was a fellow scholarship child, here on merit and not family money.

"I'm ushering tonight," said Mallory to the poodle who was called Boo.

"Why didn't you say so? Here," she snapped. "You can start folding the programs." She pulled a cardboard box from the ticket counter and thrust it into Mallory's hands. When the younger woman had made her stiff exit through the stage door, Mallory turned to the boy.

"Boo? That's a name?"

"No, we call her that to jerk her chain. Bending Boo out of shape is an art form around here. You weren't half bad yourself." He relit his cigarette and smiled. "So, since when do ushers attend dress rehearsals?"

"I'm the overzealous type."

"Or crazy for punishment. I wouldn't go through it again if I wasn't in the cast." He sat down on the wooden bench and motioned her to join him. "Is it me, or does it seem a little nuts to use radio scripts in a visual medium? Does this work for you?"

"Well, it won't work for the 'Shadow' script. You can only see the Shadow on the radio." She settled

78

the box on her lap and checked her watch. "Did I see Professor Gaynor go in there?"

"Yeah, a few minutes ago."

"What's he doing here?" She already knew. His name was on the playbill which had been posted on the cork wall in her den.

"Old Boo snagged him for the role of the radio announcer."

Mallory set the box of programs to one side and stared at the double doors on the opposite wall. This, as she remembered, was the route to the balcony. There should be a staircase beyond those doors. During the daylight hours, she had never lost track of Gaynor for more than ten minutes, and she was bordering on that now. How many exits were there?

Boo came back to the lobby. She was in a foul mood by the ugly line of her mouth. When her eyes lit on the hapless smoking boy, she was reborn.

"You put that cigarette out this minute!"

Boo turned on Mallory, who slowly picked up one program and folded it in half with great concentration.

"Here." Boo held a roll of red tickets entirely too close to Mallory's face. "You can number the comp tickets, too."

The red roll and Boo's hand hung in the air, ignored by Mallory, who showed no enthusiasm for numbering tickets. Boo opened her mouth to say something as Mallory looked up at her with narrowed eyes. Boo shut her mouth quickly, as though she had been told to do it, and sat down on the far end of the bench and began to number the tickets herself. Always better to do it yourself if there's even the remote possibility of having your authority challenged. Or possibly she had just remembered that she was only twenty and had no authority.

Mallory checked the pocket watch again. He'd been out of her sight for ten minutes, hardly time enough to kill an old lady and make it back for the dress rehearsal, but she didn't like it.

The boy took the tickets from Boo's hand. "I'll do it."

The boy was relighting his very battered cigarette as Boo was passing through the lobby door to the theater. Mallory stood up quickly and crossed the room toward the double doors on the other side of the lobby, missing the expression on the boy's face as he looked up suddenly in the belief that she had vanished by magic.

She ran up the wide staircase, long legs spanning three steps at a time. She had only gone this way once before. As she recalled, it was tricky without a flashlight. The stairs wound up and around for two flights, and then a small passage led her down five steps of total blackness and into the second-tier balcony. She settled into the covering dark while Boo was commanding the lights from center stage down below. Two young women were seated in the front row, ten feet from the stage, consulting over a clipboard. They were dressed like Boo in the Barnard uniform of jeans and cowboy boots. A very unBarnard redhead was standing stage left in a dress that hemmed midcalf above stiletto heels. A young man with slicked-back hair and a forties-period suit sat on the edge of the stage, dangling his out-of-period running shoes. Boo, legs akimbo, hands on hips, screamed for the light cues, and with each call a different part of the stage was illuminated until number twenty-two blew the fuse and the theater went black.

Samantha Siddon consulted her wristwatch. In one hand she grasped the silver lion's head of her cane. She was aware of the person behind her before she heard the footfalls. All this day, she had had the sense of something momentous looming, an invisible behemoth. Now it was approaching, the moment was almost here. It was enormous in the felt wake of its coming. It was death.

The pain of her arthritis made her slow to turn around, and she was even slower to focus through the thick lenses of her glasses. Confusion added to the obscuring clouds in her faded brown eyes.

"So it's you," she said. "How odd, how very odd." She stared at the knife. It occurred to her to scream, but it was a listless thought, and she had no real heart for it. Her cane was rising to feebly block the first strike, and she had a bit of time to realize this was only the reflex of life itself, which was stubborn even when its vessel was not so set on its continuing.

*   *   *

Boo strode onto the stage with a toss of her frizzy mane, which would not toss nicely but only lumped to one side.

"Where's the lighting tech?" she called into the dark of the theater, shading her eyes with one hand and lifting her face to the second-tier balcony above Mallory's head. "It's getting late!"

And where was Gaynor? Mallory wondered. Another two minutes had passed. She'd give him two more to come out from backstage, and then she would go hunting.

Boo strutted back and forth, ordering more light cues, one through twenty this time. The lights went on and off, up and down. She screamed, "Jonathan! Where the hell are you?"

Yes, where? Mallory wondered, going on nineteen minutes, where are you, you son of a—

Gaynor ran onto the stage. He was wearing a wide-brimmed hat. His tie was loose, and he had garters on the sleeves of his shirt. And something else was radically changed. There were no jerky thrusts to his elbows, and his feet agreed to carry him in the same direction without the usual starts and stops. He made a low bow and kissed Boo's hand, neatly pulling off that gesture without looking the fool. He suddenly had style, thought Mallory. This must be what they called acting.

With the easy grace of dance steps, Gaynor quickly climbed the platform's rickety stairs which were begging for an accident, so poor was the knocked-together construction. He sat down in a straight-back chair before a desk. At the center of the desk was an old-time microphone with radio call letters crowning the top. The platform had a built-in sag toward stage right.

Boo screamed for the next cue and the houselights went down. "Where the hell is the Shadow?"

The lobby doors flew open, banging against the walls to either side. The actors onstage turned to stare as a young man strode into the theater and stood for a moment in the semidarkness. He had wild curls of dark hair, darker eyes and full lips. Just as Mallory was deciding that this was the most beautiful boy she had ever seen, he keeled over dead drunk, making a perfect three-point landing on the back of his head, his ass and one elbow. And this, she reasoned, must be the Shadow. The look of horror on Boo's face confirmed it.

82

Gaynor descended the platform stairs, stepped lightly to the edge of the stage, and jumped down to floor level to call the unconscious boy by name, to prod his body, checking for signs of life, and finally to lug the dead weight of him through the side door by grasping the boy under the limp arms which dragged along on the floor.

Mallory was wondering what had possessed Boo to cast that striking boy, sexual even when passed out cold, as the Shadow. He was definitely a poor choice for the part of a character who had the power to cloud minds and render himself invisible. Certainly no woman had a libido so dulled that even blindfolded and three days dead she could fail to notice him in any crowd.

Gaynor returned to the stage and climbed back to his mark behind the desk. The platform was so tentative, so screwy-looking, Mallory waited for it to crumble and tumble Gaynor, desk and chair to the stage. It never did, but she continued to wait, believing that it would.

It was another hour of radio plays, an old Jack Benny routine and a sketch from "Stella Dallas," an hour of Boo terrorizing a good-natured cast and crew before Mallory heard the line she had been waiting for.

Who knows what evil lurks in the hearts of men?
The Shadow knows.

Mallory's mouth moved, silently accompanying the lines of the script. When she closed her eyes, she was back in the cellar of the old house in Brooklyn, sitting with Markowitz on a rainy Saturday afternoon, sipping cocoa in the smaller audience of two dedicated make-believers.

There was a long pause in the dialogue where a pause shouldn't be. The Shadow had missed his first cue.

She opened her eyes. The star had made his entrance. With his first lines, Mallory realized that he was stone-cold sober. No hasty cup of coffee had done that for him. So the dead-fall drunk routine had been an act to torture Boo. Now the boy moved to center stage and launched into a stunning soliloquy.

Of course, the lines belonged to another character who had escaped from an entirely different play, *A Streetcar Named Desire,* and had nothing at all to do with the "Shadow" script. But the heroine gamely responded to the riveting, animalistic screams, and she came running in from the wings and bounded across the stage to leap into the boy's arms. He carried her off the stage to wild applause from cast, crew and Mallory.

Boo's shouted obscenities were lost in the fray.

The houselights were coming up as Mallory made her way down from the balcony. Outside the building, she waited on the steps with her face in a book. The actors passed by, one by one, in street clothes. A boy strolled by, playing a flute which was impossibly long. Boo sailed by, still frothing. Finally after fifteen minutes, Gaynor exited the building in his own clothes—the jeans, open-necked shirt and sports coat.

As he walked across the campus, Mallory watched the awkward gait return to his lanky legs. His elbows pointed out in sharp angles, his feet found a raised paving stone to trip over, and he was his normal self again.

The remainder of Gaynor's schedule was less spectacular. He would be on campus into the evening hours. She cared only about his time in the light, the killing hours.

Tired, and back in the subway in the middle of day's-end rush hour, she was pressed against one wall of the car. Unable to reach back to her book bag, she was reduced to reading the advertising cards above the heads of other passengers. One sign said 'Kiss warts and bunions goodbye.' Another ad was for Right to Life proponents. If you knew an unwed mother-to-be, there was a number where you could turn her in.

A passenger turned his face up to glare at her and opened his mouth to give her a ration of grief for stepping on his foot. When he looked into her eyes, he suddenly thought better of it, and he too found something to read on the walls.

*   *   *

Charles had a few pressing questions for Mallory when she walked in the door. However, by the set of her jaw and the hardness of her eyes in wordless passing, he decided it might be worth his life to annoy her just now. He gave her a few minutes' lead time before he followed her into the back room she had taken over as her private office. This room contained none but the most disturbing clues to her personality.

The three stacked units of computer terminals and printers were in precise alignment with the mobile console housing more sophisticated equipment, all robotic ducks in a row. Charles thought the bulletin board at the rear of the room lacked Markowitz's homey style of clutter; each paper was pinned at four corners and straight to within an eighth of an inch. The equipment shelved along the side wall gathered no dust, and the manuals and reference books sat solidly in the bookcase, all bindings

85

perfectly aligned.

Though he had offered her a selection of good pieces, she had furnished the room herself with standard office issue: one ersatz metal desk, one chair that swiveled and one that did not. A large metal file cabinet stood behind her desk, and without needing to pull out a drawer, he knew each paper therein would be matching corners with each other paper. There were no family photographs, and no wall hangings that did not convey charted information, and her desk was bare of any personal items. It was the room of an obsessively well-ordered human with inhuman precision of thought and deed.

Somehow, the compulsively tidy environs would not square with the young woman who took wrong turns at every opportunity, and raided other people's computers with the gusto of a Hun.

"Kathleen, could we discuss a few practical matters?"

"Mallory," she corrected him automatically as she flipped the switches to light up the first computer.

"Fine. Mallory. About my accountant? He's very upset. Thinks I'm looking for faults in his work."

"Good." She accessed a file on the accountant's floppy disk. "He'll think long and hard before he dicks around with the books."

"Arthur? He wouldn't steal a paper clip. His whole life is dedicated to honorable accountancy." Charles stood behind her chair, wondering how much of her attention he had, and what he was likely to get. "He laminated the first tax form where his child appeared as a dependent. Some people bronze baby shoes—with Arthur it's tax forms. He's a good man, and I don't want to lose him."

"I didn't accuse him of anything."

"No? You demanded a copy of his disk so you could run your own audit. How was he supposed to take that?"

She was no longer listening. She stopped scrolling and stared at the entry for apartment 3B. "This one's way behind in the rent."

He bent down to look over her shoulder at the entry for Edith Candle. "The woman in 3B doesn't have to pay rent."

Mallory's head lifted slowly, eyes holding just the hint of incredulity and sexuality.

"Mallory, go wash your eyes out with soap. She's an elderly woman and the previous owner of the building. She has a lifetime estate in that apartment. Are we done with 3B?"

The door buzzer sounded for the third time in one hour. In the past few weeks he had come to realize that Mallory had been dead right about one thing: it had been a mistake to let the tenants know he owned the building. Though he employed a full-time superintendent, every complaint came first to his own door. His clients were less troublesome traffic, coming by appointment or conducting business by mail and telephone.

"Not so fast," said Mallory. "Which one is it?"

The quick buzz was followed up by a soft knock at the door.

"Dr. Ramsharan," said Charles. "The psychiatrist in apartment 3A. Henrietta would never buzz twice. She thinks it's rude."

Mallory followed him out to the front room and watched as he opened the door. When Henrietta Ramsharan walked in, Mallory padded off to make the coffee, payment on a standing bet that he could tell her who was at the door before he opened it. It had been weeks since he'd had to make his own coffee.

He had been resistant to the idea of a coffee machine in the office, along with all the other machines—entirely too many mechanical devices in his view. Then he realized that it was Louis's coffee machine, which she had purloined from the old NYPD office. Oddly enough, he took the stolen coffeemaker as a sign of progress in her social development. It had been a theft of sentiment.

Whenever he entered the office kitchen, he avoided looking directly at that machine. If it were possible for the spirit of Louis Markowitz to inhabit an object, it would be the coffeemaker. Each time Charles glanced at it, it reproached him for not figuring out how Mallory spent her days. He had not bought the story that she preferred to work nights. He was not a complete idiot, though he felt like one.

"I'm sorry to disturb you," the polite Henrietta Ramsharan was saying as he waved her over to the couch. There were touches of gray at her temples, which only glimmered as highlights in the loose fall of jetblack hair recently escaped from the pins that held it in a tight bun from nine till five. She was wearing her after-work blue jeans, which were faded and broken in for comfort, but she had not been spending her free time in any comfortably relaxing pursuit. He noted the agitation about her eyes and mouth. The first person who leapt into his mind was the tenant who agitated everyone, even the placid Henrietta.

"Herbert, right?"

"Yes," said Henrietta. "How did you know?"

"Oh, I'm getting to know Herbert rather well."

But Henrietta knew everyone in the building. She had lived here for more than ten years, but that alone did not explain why all the tenants knew one another's history and business. At his former residence on the Upper East Side, he had gone four years without saying as many words to the people who shared one common wall with him. He had previously taken that experience as a reflection on his lack of social skills. Mallory had been the one to point out that cool-to-chilly neighbor relations were the norm, and that this building's close network of tenants was the oddity. They had no tenants' association, no focal point, no common gathering place. The small mystery nagged at him now and then. He suspected Edith Candle could explain it, but would not.

"So you think Herbert has a gun," he said.

"How did you know that?"

"You know Martin Teller, lives across the hall from Herbert."

She nodded. "Of course."

"When I passed Martin in the hall this morning," said Charles, "it was hard to ignore the bulletproof vest, particularly on a warm day. Mallory has one, but she doesn't wear it to go grocery shopping. Ergo—Herbert."

"Martin's terrified of Herbert, I know that. But were you aware of the lipstick on Edith Candle's wall?"

"No. Was her apartment—"

"No vandalism, nothing like that. You knew about the fugues? She told me she'd known you all your life."

"Fugues?"

"The automatic writing?"

No, he hadn't known. Edith had never used automatic writing in the magic act with Cousin Max. She had done a mind-reading act, he remembered that much. Something disturbing in a childhood memory began to emerge, some overheard conversation, but it was not the stuff that eidetic memory would help him with.

"Sometimes it's called trance writing," Henrietta was saying. "Edith was trying to wash the words off the wall when Martin came down to pick up his leftovers."

"His leftovers."

"He doesn't make much money from his art, not since the recession started. Edith gives him meals three times a week. She's been doing that for a few years now. So Martin just walked in on her when she was scrubbing the wall."

"Martin has a key to Edith's apartment?"

"Her door is never locked. You didn't know? You might talk to her about that. I've spent years trying to convince her it's dangerous. Strange people can always find a way into an apartment building, even one with good security."

"So it could have been vandalism."

"The writing? Oh, no. Edith does the writing, but she never has any memory of doing it."

"It's happened before?"

"Yes, but that was a long time ago."

And by her downcast eyes and shift of position, it was not open to discussion. Curious.

"What was written on the wall this time?"

"I don't know, and Martin won't tell me. You know Martin. It's a rare day if he says three words. The three he gave me were *death, here, soon*. I asked him if he was frightened of Herbert. He nodded and saved a word. That's all I know. Martin is a very fragile personality. And just the idea that Herbert might have a gun is making me a little nervous too."

Mallory was standing over them. She had just

materialized by the couch with two mugs of coffee and no warning.

"I'll fix that," she said, handing one mug to Charles and the other to Henrietta.

"No you won't. I'll handle it," said Charles. Herbert's paranoid little heart would not stand up to an interview with Mallory.

Henrietta sipped her coffee and smiled her thanks to the younger woman. "It might be a bad idea to approach Herbert directly. He's ripe for an explosion. I've seen it building up for a long time. His wife is divorcing him, and it's a pretty messy lawsuit. And then he got a layoff notice at the end of September. I don't think he can handle one more thing, not a hangnail, not anything."

Charles looked up to Mallory, who seemed skeptical. "That's clear enough?" he asked.

"Yeah. He's a squirrel," she said.

Henrietta and Charles exchanged glances, silently approving Mallory's clarity and economy of words.

The phone rang. As he was rising and reaching toward the desk, Mallory beat him to it with no apparent effort at speed. It was disconcerting the way she moved about, or rather, disappeared from one spot and reappeared in another.

She picked up the receiver of the antique telephone.

Well, it was not altogether an antique anymore, was it?

He had been dismayed to find that she had rewired it and discarded the original base for one that accommodated a plug for an answering machine. And he only discovered the job when his incoming calls were ripped out of his mouthpiece and pulled into the desk drawer.

"Mallory and Butler...Hello, Riker. Hold on a

sec." She had to open the drawer to put the phone on hold. And now they both looked down on the blinking light of four messages glowing inside the desk. If she was annoyed with him, it never showed as she walked back to her private office and pulled the door closed behind her.

He turned back to Henrietta. "Do you want me to speak to Edith?"

"No," she said, a bit too quick, too final, and in the attitude of 'absolutely not' as opposed to 'no, I don't think so.'

"Mallory, where've you been all day? I musta called a hundred times."

"Four times. Charles never looks for messages. He's pretending we don't have an answering machine."

"I got something," said Riker. "Gaynor and Cathery each have alibis for two of the murders, but together, they can't alibi all the murders."

"So? I'm not big on conspiracy theories if that's where you're going with this."

"Wait. Cathery can alibi his grandmother's murder, and Gaynor can alibi his aunt's murder—"

"Riker, I saw that movie too. It doesn't fit, not if Markowitz knew who the killer was. If the old man figured two suspects, he wouldn't have done the surveillance by himself. How could he?"

"You won't like the answer to that one, kid."

"Give."

"Coffey doesn't think Markowitz worked it out. He figures the perp suckered Markowitz. The old man got killed because he didn't know who it was, never saw it coming."

"Oh, great detective work. Coffey was the one who figured Whitman for a snatch when a half-

92

bright chimp could have told him she was meeting the perp at the scene."

"Hey, kid. This is Riker here. I'm on your side, remember?"

"Anything turn up on the BDA in Markowitz's calendar?"

"Naw," said Riker. "Coffey's off that track. I'd do it on my own, but I got no leads. I've been through the old house in Brooklyn looking through his stuff. Nothing in the credit card bills or the checkbook, but who knows. That little den of his looks just like his office. Easy to miss something in a mess like that. Maybe if you went through it? The door seals can come off anytime you want."

"Yeah, first chance I get."

When she hung up the phone, the first computer in the row of three was still screening the file on the old recluse in 3B. Charles had contributed very little information on Edith Candle in the past two weeks. He was a great respecter of privacy, and she had been unable to break him of this good quality.

Mallory looked up to the ceiling. She felt the old woman's presence before she heard the scrape of chair legs on the bare floorboards overhead. A blinking red light on the third terminal told her that Edith Candle was active again, powering up her computer and sending something out over the modem, that box which allowed the old woman to wander the electronic net from New York to the Tokyo Exchange and back again in seconds only.

Mallory picked up her test set, a black rotary dial with a handgrip. She dialed a number the telephone company used for maintenance checks as she rolled her chair over to the third terminal. Through the wires of the phone company, which led into Candle's modem, Mallory climbed up into the computer one floor above her head and watched the screen that Candle was accessing in apartment 3B. The old woman wasn't following the stock exchange figures tonight. She had patched into a small and remote commercial information network and was requesting a credit check. This J. S. Rathbone must be another wealthy spook groupie. Mallory turned back to the third screen and watched the names of stock issues scrolling by as the credit-check service fed Rathbone's stock portfolio into Candle's computer in the apartment upstairs.

So far, none of the stock activity had shown up in mergers or hostile takeovers. However, Candle had remarkable luck in selling off stocks just prior to devastating drops in value. One of these drops had been brought on by the recall of a defective and dangerous product. Candle had sold her stock just prior to the information being made public. And she also had a streak of luck in making stock purchases before sudden booms in product development—also nonpublic information. One such purchase had resulted in stock prices doubling. Scores of these instances put Candle in the realm of world-class fortune-telling or insider trading. But there was no hard evidence. No single transaction matched the huge profits on the merger of Pearl Whitman's company.

Mallory switched on the second computer and flew into cyberspace. With the tap of a key, she landed inside the Washington, D.C., data base of the Securities and Exchange Commission. No recent filings on stock activity would coincide with Candle's recent purchases, but there was a strong link to the Todd and Remmy merger of four years ago. This deal was well inside the statute of limitations, but the SEC seemed to have lost interest in Candle since the Whitman Chemicals merger in the early 1980s. Perhaps they were shy of the crystal ball defense.

Ah, gold.

Scanning the profiteer list of the Todd and Remmy merger, she found a familiar name from Gramercy Park, Estelle Gaynor, and a footnote that tied her to an old investigation. She neatly copied the block of type with five taps of the keys and shifted it onto a floppy disk. Now she patched in Candle's own credit check from the same firm that was feeding the old lady.

Apparently, Edith Candle was a longtime subscriber to this credit-check network, and when one went fishing in information networks, one also became fish food. Mallory had always avoided this by never paying for the networks she hacked into. Candle had been less prudent. The file was barebones traces of financial activity. With a quick shuffle of files, she added these new data to the old U.S. Attorney's file on the Securities and Exchange Commission action, the same document that had led her into partnership with Charles and this window on the old woman up the stairs in 3B.

Perhaps an hour had passed before she heard the door buzzer again and sounds of the door opening and closing, then the indistinct voices in conversation. She was a few minutes more putting the file on 3B in order before she closed it.

When she walked back to the reception area, Henrietta Ramsharan was gone, and the pinch-faced woman from Gramercy Park was sitting in front of Charles's desk.

"She's the one," said the woman in a shrill voice, waving the business card in Mallory's direction. "Now don't tell me you don't do this sort of thing,

95

like I've asked you to do something filthy, like a divorce case or something. One can carry discretion too far."

Charles had a trapped look about him as he slouched low in the chair behind the desk.

Mallory sat down in a Queen Anne chair to one side of the desk. "My partner handles a different kind of clientele. He deals with more unusual problems."

Charles looked at her in an openly suspicious way. His face couldn't hide a thought.

To Mrs. Pickering he said, "My usual clients are research institutes, universities, the occasional government commission. I explore unusual gifts, talents, different modes of intelligence. I also develop ways of applying these gifts to occupations or research projects. It's my partner here who does the investigative work." He swiveled his chair to face Mallory. "Mrs. Pickering was wondering what business you had in Gramercy Park."

He was smiling but hardly meaning it.

"Client confidentiality," said Mallory to Mrs. Pickering, smiling and meaning it not at all.

"Oh, back to discretion again. Why won't you take my case?"

"Did I say I wouldn't?"

"He did."

Charles leaned back in his chair and waved one hand with the attitude of 'oh, please.' "Mrs. Pickering wants us to expose her mother's pet medium as a fraud."

Mallory smiled with meaning this time. "Why not? Consider her a woman with fraudulent gifts. That puts it right in your field, Charles. Just something new and different, that's all."

"Hardly new," said Charles. "It wouldn't be the

96

first time I had a medium for a test subject. But I look on them as empathics. Some of them really are gifted."

Mrs. Pickering was rising off her chair, launching toward the ceiling. "This woman is a money-grubbing fraud!" Unspoken were the words 'you fool.' She settled back to earth and chair again, as though the exertion of accusation was simply too much for her. "You're trying to tell me this fraud can contact my dead father?"

"I'm not so sure a gifted medium gets on all that well with the dead," said Charles. "But she may be quite good at reading the living. These people have more access to their intuition than most. They take in all the details of a human being. They analyze these details and spit them out in reorganized information which the subject can't believe a stranger could possess. It's nearly magic."

But Mrs. Pickering was a typical, unmagical New Yorker. Her expression was dubious, bordering on 'you imbecile,' and this was not lost on Charles. Mallory had noticed that very little got by him, if anything at all.

"Take you, for example," said Charles. "You're recently divorced, educated at good schools. You don't sleep well, though you take prescribed medication, and sometimes you feel depression without apparent cause."

The woman was nodding, unconscious of the gesture, eyes locking on Charles in rapt attention. Mallory noted the faint white line where the wedding ring had been. The education was in the woman's voice, and fit well with the background of Gramercy Park. The dark, bruised flesh under the eyes showed through her makeup, but only on close inspection. The expertise of concealment suggested

97

the habitual loss of sleep frequently accompanied by the habitual drugs of the insomniac. And with a pinched, angry face like that, she was bound to be unhappy.

Nice going, Charles.

"You have your hair done every two weeks," said Charles.

That one was easy, thought Mallory. The roots would have to be gray; there were none showing.

"And you studied ballet in your childhood and teenage years."

Where was he getting that? Maybe she had walked in on her toes.

"You favor auctions at Christie's over Sothebys."

You gotta be kidding.

But now she took in the plethora of rings on the woman's hands. Antique settings all. Charles's freakish memory was probably calling up auction catalogs.

"You have a dog."

How did he know that wasn't cat hair on her dress? Oh, wait. That magnificent nose of his. It was a drizzly evening, and Pickering had probably walked the dog before she came. Wet fur. Cats were not walked in the rain.

"You dressed in a hurry."

Mallory found no flaws in the woman's fashionable outfit until she reached the tag showing at the nape of the neck, and just a smudge of unblended rouge on one cheek. A vain woman who doesn't scrutinize the mirror to death before she walks out the door? That was a hurry and a half.

"There are no large events in your own life these days," said Charles. "In fact, your days have a maddening sameness to them, and you're looking ahead to an endless succession of days like these.

Your mother's duplicity annoys you, maybe angers you, but your own life saddens you and frightens you.... But all this is very crude. A gifted medium could look into your feelings, note the waver of your eyes when you insisted this was for your mother's good. A gifted medium might have taken the fact that you showed anger, not concern, and done much more with that than I could."

Than you would, Mallory corrected him silently. Charles always behaved like a gentleman. She counted on that and used it against him every chance she got. It was the only edge she had on his genius IQ. But she would have to be sharper from now on. She had never planned to drag Charles into something dangerous. Use him, sure, but harm him, no. That might be unavoidable if she telegraphed her intentions by taking this case which he had just reduced to ashes.

However, the Pickering woman was offering her access to Gramercy Park and that stratum of old money. It was a better entrée than she could have hoped for. And then there was the fascinating giantess to consider.

"We'll take the case," said Mallory, all things considered at lightning speed. "That's fifteen hundred up front, and we'll bill time and expenses against the retainer."

Mrs. Pickering sat erect in her chair, not shrinking back or shrinking down, and yet she no longer seemed to take up the same space in this room. The woman was subdued to a tired nod as she fumbled in her purse for her checkbook. So Mrs. Pickering was all facade, and not the makings of the blue-ribbon bitch Mallory had first taken her for.

"My mother's name is Fabia Penworth," she said as she signed the check with the weak stroke of a

99

gold pen and then drew a small white card from her purse. "This is her address."

Mallory accepted the check and the card. She gave the woman her hand to say that a deal was done, a gesture any stranger might have mistaken for warmth. "Thank you, Mrs. Pickering."

Mrs. Pickering smiled in near shyness, stripped now to the mere human bones of a middle-aged matron out of her depth.

"Call me Marion, dear. And you are…"

"Mallory."

Mrs. Pickering rose from her chair and walked to the door with a slow, deep grace. And now Mallory guessed the ballet background. Mrs. Pickering's toes were turned out, and her carriage came from training. Her mood should have bowed her head or slumped her shoulders, had not some fiend of a dancing master with a big staff beaten that body language out of her at an early age. A similar experiment had failed with Mallory.

Charles looked rather unhappy. As the door closed, he swiveled his chair to face her. "What are you doing in Gramercy Park every day?"

She rounded her killer-green eyes ringed with thick lashes that now dropped slowly to veil seductively, and when her eyes widened again, it was a striptease. All that protected him from her was the fact that she was twenty-five and wonderful to look at, while he was thirty-nine and could not imagine why she would have any but a platonic interest in him. He was logical to a fault.

Sensing the seduction had no effect, she looked down at her red fingernails as if they might not be perfectly aligned.

"Talk to me," he said.

"I'm working on spec. It's something related."

100

"Kathleen." In those two syllables, there was only a gentle suggestion that she might be lying through her teeth.

"Mallory," she corrected him. "There *is* a con game going on in Gramercy," she said in the tone of 'I am *not* lying'—though they both knew she was. But Charles was such a gentleman, wasn't he. "I recognized the medium from a rap sheet description."

"And it's nothing to do with Louis's murder." And the sun came up twice this morning.

"No."

"I'm worried about you. You would tell me if you were mixed up in that business, wouldn't you?" And the earth might altogether stop revolving around the sun for an hour or so when that happened.

"Oh sure. Why not?"

Why not? She was genuinely fond of him. If a lie would make him feel better, she wouldn't hesitate. She liked him that much.

"So you're only interested in the medium." 'And I, Charles Butler, am Queen of the May,' said the shrug of his shoulders.

"The medium is into computer scams. Not a genius programmer, but she knows her way around the information networks. Just like the old con artist in 3B."

"What?"

"Edith Candle, the old woman upstairs in 3B. She has the same setup. Computer services for news clippings and research, magazines from all over the planet, a credit-check service."

"So you ran a background check on Edith. Please leave the tenants alone from now on. I'd rather you didn't invade their privacy. And there's nothing suspicious about Edith's information network."

101

"Sure."

"She hasn't left this building in more than thirty years, not since the year her husband died."

"I never said she wasn't nuts. I just said it's the same setup Pickering's medium had the last time she was arrested."

"Edith is a recluse, but she hasn't left the race. She uses information networks to stay in contact with the world. She can probably tell you more about what's going on out there than people who live out of doors. And the credit-check service goes with the territory of being a landlord. It's all quite harmless."

"But she's not a landlord anymore, and her subscription is up to date. It's been what?—a year since you bought the building? And why would a multimillionaire want to hole up in a SoHo apartment?"

"Edith made a reasonable fortune but nothing in the multimillions. There wasn't even a quarter-million profit in the building. It was refinanced a few years—Sorry, I forget who I'm talking to. I assume you do know the exact amount of the mortgage?"

Of course she did.

"Charles, she's got more money than God. She's a stock market freak. Did you know she had a rap sheet with the Securities and Exchange Commission?"

"What? No, scratch that. I don't want to know."

"Insider trading. I've got all the documentation on it."

"Oh, well then, it must be true if you've seen it in black and white." He threw up his hands and stared at the ceiling for a moment. His sarcasm lacked acidity, and she sometimes had to strain to catch the false notes. He went into the inner pocket of his suit jacket and pulled out his wallet.

"Let me shake your faith in all-holy documentation." He fished out his driver's license and dropped it on the desk in front of her. "Look at that. It says I was born on the twenty-sixth. My birth certificate says the same thing. The doctor was tired after sixteen hours of a difficult delivery. He put down the wrong date. So much for documentation."

"She was served with a subpoena, the SEC filed a formal order of investigation."

"I don't want to hear any more of this."

"Why not? I pulled this stuff out of the U.S. Attorney's office. That makes it credible. You want to see the printouts?"

"No!"

She had only meant to sidetrack him and now she had gone too far. It was rare to see him angry. Once before, they'd had a conversation about his aversion to invasion of privacy. She hadn't been able to make sense of it then, either, thought him deficient and handicapped, offered to straighten him out. And she could do that, she had implied then. He had come to the right place—

"I didn't mean to yell." His voice softened. "Let's try it again, shall we? Everything you learn about people redefines your relationship with them. I've known Edith since I was a child. Her husband was my father's cousin. She's all the family I have left. I don't need to know any more about her than I do."

"So you don't want to know about the insider trading."

"No!...Sorry...Suppose someone came to you and told you something unpleasant about Louis or Helen?"

"Okay. Enough," she said.

103

No, he didn't think so. That much was in his eyes. Too pat an answer, entirely too easy. She would have to watch that in the future.

They said their strained good nights to one another in the hall. She walked to the elevator and pressed the button. The doors opened on the startled face of Herbert Mandrel. His small head jerked in the way of a bird startled by the sudden display of Mallory's perfect teeth. He looked to the ceiling and walls, evaluating the limited number of exits in an elevator, and then moved as far to the rear as he could go without leaving an indent on the back wall. As the doors closed and the elevator began its slow ascent, he was puffing out his bird's chest and standing a little straighter, as though this might buy him the inches he needed to look her in the eye.

She noted the army fatigue jacket and a familiar bulge at his side. His hand moved to cover it, but too late. She was smiling down on him as she reached out to tap the red button to stop the elevator at the third floor.

The cords in his neck were bulging. He would not meet her eyes when she brought her face very close to his and said softly, "You watch a lot of television, don't you, Herbert? Cop shows, things like that? If I told you to assume the position, would you know what I meant?"

Now he did meet her eyes, and the little bird's chest was deflating. He rallied, puffing out once more, eyebrows knitting together, preamble to a New York attitude of 'get out of my face.' "You have no authority to—"

She grabbed him by one arm, spun him around and slammed him back against the wall of the elevator. With one foot, she knocked his legs apart. When he was spread eagle and somewhere between surprise and soiling his pants, she said, "If you move, I'm going to hurt you. You got that?"

He nodded and then froze. She patted him down, and then her free hand moved around to the front of his belt and unhooked the heavy metal object.

"You can turn around now, Herbert."

He was still for a moment longer in the attitude of a specimen mounted on a collector's wall. He slowly straightened and turned to face her, looking up and clearly hating her for being tall, among her other crimes against him.

"What's this?" She dangled the speedloader by its strap. "I bought it from a guy at my gun club."

"Where's the gun?"

"I don't have one."

"That doesn't work for me, Herbert. A speedloader and no gun?"

"I don't have a gun. The city's jerking me around on the license. My lawyer's working on it. Ask Edith Candle. She knows. I asked her for the name of a lawyer. I only practice shooting with the guns at the club."

"Where's the gun club?"

"West Fourteenth Street."

"Barry Allen's place?"

"Yes. He'll tell you the same thing. Check it out. Ask Barry, ask Edith."

"I will."

She pressed the button to open the doors to the third-floor hallway. She stepped out of the elevator, turned and tossed the speedloader back to him. He reached out for it and clutched air as it fell between his outstretched hands and rolled to the back of the elevator. He was on his knees when the doors closed on him.

It made sense to her. Herbert wasn't the type to

have connections to buy stolen, unregistered guns. Barry Allen was an ex-cop with a good reputation—no worries there. But how long would it be before a buddy at the gun club sold the little jerk a gun?

She dismissed the little man and turned her thoughts back to the argument with Charles. She had understood him well enough. She would have done serious damage to anyone who had maligned Helen or Markowitz. So she would let the stock scam go by. But damned if she would let slide the mention of Pearl Whitman of Whitman Chemicals in the SEC reports. Markowitz had once told her half of police work was tracking down the linkages of persons known to those unknown. Pearl Whitman had known her killer. Perhaps Edith Candle knew him too. This was her thought as she pressed the buzzer of apartment 3B.

There were muffled interior sounds of footsteps approaching, but no metallic clicks of locks being undone. The door opened on a comfortably rounded woman with white hair and the whitest skin Mallory had ever seen on a living human. It was luminous. Edith Candle smiled as though she were facing a long-anticipated friend, and not an unannounced total stranger. Mallory found this attitude far from the basic New York religion of security, which mandated one dead bolt and two sturdy Yale locks, a Doberman, a pit bull, and a peephole in the door.

"I'm a friend of Charles Butler."

"Well, any friend of Charles is welcome in my home." She stood to one side, inviting Mallory to pass through the door. As they walked into the brighter light of the living room, Edith Candle failed all of Mallory's expectations for a stock swindler. She was small in stature. Her head was disproportionately large, and a neat bun gathered at the nape of her neck. The lace collar of her wildly out-of-date dress disappeared under three chins. Her hands were knots of arthritis, and she wore glasses with thick lenses which made her eyes into expectant blue saucers.

Mallory was being pulled into the room by the gentle touch of a warm pudgy white hand on her arm. "Sit down, dear. I'll put on the coffeepot. Or would you rather have wine?"

"Coffee is fine, thanks."

She had learned enough from Charles to know the antique furniture was not a collection of cheap knockoffs. The room also housed a clutter of pricey bric-a-brac—porcelain figurines and silver candy dishes, frilly lampshades, small clusters of photographs on each broad windowsill everything designed to catch and trap dust, yet nothing did. The air smelled of pine scent and furniture wax, all the sensory cues of Helen Markowitz, world's foremost homemaker. Another familiar aroma was emanating from the kitchen, lingering after-dinner traces of pot roast from a thousand Sunday dinners and Monday morning lunch boxes.

"Who was she?"

Mallory spun on the woman suddenly and startled Edith Candle backward a step to collide with a chair and set it to rocking. The old woman adjusted her balance and her glasses. The chair continued to rock as though inhabited.

"There are memories of a woman here, aren't there?" The old woman sat down on the couch and automatically readjusted a doily on the padded arm. "There's certainly nothing in this room to say a man lived here. Was it your mother you were thinking of?"

"I never knew my mother."

107

"You breathed deep. There are no flowers in the air, only the smell of a good cleaning. And you approved the order of things. That was in your face. Apparently, you were raised right. Someone loved you. Who was she?"

"Helen. You say *was*. How did you know she was dead?"

"You were looking at a memory."

Oh Christ. So this was where Charles got it from.

"Yes, dear," she was saying when they were seated in the spacious kitchen and sipping their coffee. Edith Candle pushed a plate of brownies across the table. "His parents used to visit quite often when Charles was a child. Did you know his mother gave birth at the outrageous age of fifty-six? The Butlers were lovely people. Max and I took care of little Charles when his parents attended university conferences out of town. I used to take him to the park and watch him make false starts with the other children. He was always so hopeful and always being crushed to death. His IQ alone was enough to set him apart, but then his appearance didn't help. He was born with that nose, you know. The only newborn I ever saw with a big nose. I also spent a lot of time with him when he was doing postdoc research. He used me as a test subject. I used to be a psychic, you know."

"I know. We're working on a case with a fake medium now."

There was a humorous glint in the woman's eye at the drop of the word *fake*.

"Oh well, you came to the right person. I probably know every scam there is. But you should be a bit more open-minded. Charles can tell you that some of them have genuine gifts, an aptitude for reading souls. What I read in yours, my dear, is pain…killer

108

pain."

Two cups of coffee later, Edith Candle was opening the door at the end of the hallway. Mallory followed the old woman onto the small platform which joined the wrought-iron staircase in the progress of its winding. The railing spiraled down and around in a pattern of stark white walls and black metal. Spindle shadows slanted against the rounding stairwell, and naked light bulbs radiated from the doors of the lower platforms leading to each level of the building.

Mallory descended the stairs in the wake of Edith Candle's foray into the world beyond her five rooms. They walked down and around the circling stairs, passing the doors marked for the second and first floors, on down to the basement level and the last door. This had to be the only door without a lock in all of New York City. She put out one hand to gently restrain the old woman. She was aware of the heavy gun in her shoulder holster as she pushed through the door and into the darkness. One hand felt along the wall left of the door, seeking and finding the light switch. It didn't work.

"There's a flashlight on top of the fuse box, dear," said the old woman behind her.

Mallory opened the door wide to admit more light from the stairwell. A fuse box was mounted on the wall to the left of the doorframe. She reached up and touched the flashlight on the top of the box. It lit up at the press of the button, and she turned it on the fuse box. All the fuses were good. She tested a fuse connection, turning the glass knob.

"It's not a fuse, dear," said Edith, blinking up at her. "That light switch hasn't worked since Max and I bought the building. It was a mystery to three generations of electricians." She took the flashlight

109

from Mallory. "If I recall, there's another light by that wall. Yes, there." She picked her way across the floor, skirting boxes and trunks, to an old standing lamp with a frilled shade. She turned the switch and it lit a small area of the cellar with a soft warm glow. "I know where there's a much brighter lamp," she said, smiling. "Follow me."

Mallory walked behind her as shadows loomed up on all sides, in a makeshift corridor of shipping trunks piled high with boxes and crates. Old furniture sat under dust covers, and at the end of the aisle, a headless tailor's dummy stood off on its own.

"All of Max's illusions are down here," said Edith. "We built this storage room—it takes up half the basement." She fitted a key into a lock and the wall began to accordion, panels shifting, opening onto a cavernous space illuminated only by the light from the wide window at the sidewalk level and above her head. The source of the light was a first-floor window on the other side of the air shaft. There was light enough to see the quick movement of a rat among the garbage cans lined up near the glass.

At the basement level, Mallory could make out the edges of crates and a tall section screen standing on three panels.

"It's been a long time since I was down here," said Edith, walking in ahead of Mallory and touching a globe, which came to light and glowed dully. Within the small radiant circle of this lamp, light invaded a clear plastic garment bag, rippling through the folds of silks and bouncing off sequins.

"Other magicians have stopped by to offer condolences and ask if they could buy the mechanical devices. But I would never sell Max's secrets. It's a point of honor. Would you like to see

110

one of his most famous illusions? Do you have a strong heart? We only performed this act one time. Too much blood, the theater owner said. Are you frightened easily?"

Mallory looked down at the old woman. "Give it your best shot."

Edith switched on a footlight at the base of the section screen, which nearly touched the high ceiling of the basement. A dragon, mouth full of fire, was illuminated on three panels of delicate rice paper.

"Wait here," said the old woman. "I'll just be a moment. I have to test the equipment. It hasn't been used in more than thirty years." She handed the flashlight to Mallory and disappeared behind the screen.

Mallory felt a prickling sensation on the backs of her hands. All her good instincts made her wary. She took inventory of the shadows on the periphery of the globe lamp. The beam of the flashlight found the eyes she had only felt at her back the moment before.

Charles?

No. She was staring into the eyes of a disembodied head. The flesh had to be wax, she knew, but something icy was leaving a slick trail down her spine as she drew closer. The thing sat on a trunk at her own eye level and stared back at her with eyes entirely too real. The irises had more normal proportions of blue to white, but the wide-eyed stare of a Christmas-morning nine-year-old was definitely genetic. This was Charles's cousin.

Hello, Max.

Mallory heard her name called. She rounded the screen and walked through a passageway of wardrobe racks, stopping ten feet short of the old

111

woman, who was kneeling at the base of a guillotine fifteen feet high. The white hair was covered by a red turban, and her neck lay between the posts and locked in place by wooden braces with three openings to accommodate head and hands. Above her neck was a wide and wickedly sharp blade hanging high and waiting.

Edith smiled up at Mallory. "Pull on that, dear." She nodded to an ornate golden lever at the side of the guillotine.

Mallory only shook her head from side to side with rare wonder. Had the old woman gone crazy? This was no waxwork dummy. Edith spoke to her and the body moved, both were real, and the blade was sharp. This was not the work of mirrors.

Mallory heard the sound of metal grinding, and her eyes flashed up. Had the mechanism slipped a gear? Her stomach flipped over. She watched the blade with dark fascination. Was the blade closer now? Was the angle changed?

The blade slipped a notch.

Edith screamed as a bright light washed out the tableau and lit the entire basement with a blazing ball of sun mounted atop the guillotine. Mallory was in motion, moving toward her, eyes blinded by the light, hands reaching out, nearly there, when the blade fell and the turbaned head with its bloody stump of a neck fell from the wooden brace and rolled across the floor awash in brilliant white light. The old woman's feet spasmodically kicked out and then went limp.

Mallory froze. She was shot through with ice and her throat was paralyzed.

The head at her feet was laughing.

No, it was not. Her eyes were adapting, and she could see the head more clearly. It was only another

112

wax mock-up, a younger version of Edith Candle's head. There was no blood. An intact Edith Candle was rising off the floor.

"Oh, your face, your face," said Edith, breasts heaving, belly shaking. "That's what made the trick so powerful." She wiped tears from her laughing eyes. "People were convinced that the gears had slipped, that they were witnessing an accident. It was an amazing effect. They screamed and screamed. Most of Max's illusions were life-and-death affairs. It was his trademark."

Mallory sat down on the floor before her knees could fall and dump her there. "Christ, I hope that was your best shot."

Edith pulled a low stool out of the clutter of props and sat down beside Mallory. "I can't tell you much about Max's illusions. The magician's code, you know. But the light is the most important element of this trick. You don't see clearly while the eye is adjusting. You see what you expect to see—an accident. I can't tell you more than that. I can't even show you the mechanism that works the light. Trade secret."

Mallory grappled with previous conceptions of elderly women and made rapid adjustments in her thinking. When she looked up at Edith perched on the stool a head above her, it was with new respect. Yes, she had come to the right place.

"What kind of tricks do mediums do?"

"Well, there's quite a difference between magic and spiritualism, but illusions are all related by the same principles—misdirection, sleight of hand. A client once told me about a medium she visited on Forty-second Street who made things float through the air. I could show you something like that."

"Wires?"

"No, it's done with black art."

"Black art?"

"Nothing to do with the occult, dear. Black art is the camouflage of black on black. You need a hand-held mirror and a very dark room. The object only has to levitate a few inches. Too much is ostentatious and smacks of fakery. A few inches of levitation in an angled mirror is more believable and frightening for some reason. Your medium would need an accomplice for that, someone free to move about the room."

"She has one, a little boy."

"Well, that widens the field a bit. With a helper she can do quite a number of illusions."

"She's the high-technology type."

"Well, don't expect anything too exotic—no holographic imaging, anything like that. The simpler the illusion, the better it works. This medium wouldn't want to take any high-tech devices to a mark's home."

"She uses her computer to research the victims."

"Say *mark*, dear. *Victim* makes it sound so sordid, as if the audience isn't having a good time. Max and I created the mind-reading act while he was recuperating from an injury. A dangerous illusion had gone wrong.... But I'm digressing. You wanted to hear about the tricks. Well, I used to guess the object in the mark's hand while wearing a blindfold."

"How? Microphones?"

"No, dear. Most tricks are very simple. If you put too much credit to complexity, you'll never work them out." She pushed her glasses up the bridge of her nose, and her eyes were looking at some middle ground of memory. "Max would cue me with first words. If he said, 'Concentrate,' it was made of

114

metal. The next word would tell me if it was a coin, a watch, whatever. If he said, 'Please,' it was paper, money or a photograph. Then, when I took off the blindfold, I would read their faces and all their secrets and worries."

"You researched the marks?"

"No, dear. Max waited in line with them. We always kept them waiting a long time. People in lines can be very chatty. The audience participation was never by random selection. I know it sounds like a cheat, but every one of those people got full value for the price of admission. It was quite a show." Her smile ended in a serious afterthought.

"Then I found my true gift. A sheriff caught up to us in another town when one of my visions came true. I had seen a body and the sheriff had found it. My name was made. We went on a new world tour, and this time out, I was the headliner instead of Max. I regretted that gift after Max died. I foresaw his death, you know. You don't believe that. I can feel it. Yet it did happen to me, this terrible gift."

"Did you foresee Pearl Whitman's death?"

"No, dear. The fugue comes on a few days before the death of someone who's been recently close to me. I haven't seen Pearl in years and years."

"You don't mind talking about her?"

"No, not at all. Oh, her death was a sad business, wasn't it? She was only sixty-five when I met her. Her father had recently died. He was in his nineties, I believe. She asked me to contact his spirit. I told her I didn't do such things. I'm a clairvoyant. Lumped into the same bag with mediums, I'm afraid, but not quite the same thing."

"So, what did you do for her?"

"I advised her on stocks and business matters. That's what she wanted to talk to her father about."

"You advised her by way of a crystal ball?"

"No, dear. May I call you Kathy?...Good. I'm quite adept at playing the market. I do it with research—I have quite a data base—but I also depend on instinct. I advised Pearl on a merger that made her twice as rich as she had been before."

"And did you invest, based on that merger?"

"Oh, yes. I'd already amassed quite a bit of money on tour. And then Max and I had made a nice profit on the sale of another property. I built that sum into a rather impressive stock portfolio. I liquidated the lot and put it into Whitman Chemicals stocks. After the merger, my fortune doubled."

"Did anyone ever suggest that might be illegal?"

"Insider trading, you mean. I did get into a bit of trouble with the government people. They called me an arbitrager because I also had a slender connection to a principal in the other company. They said I was using insider information illegally. They served me with papers and questioned me for hours. In the end, they just tore up the papers. I never heard any more on it. Perhaps the U.S. Attorney would have felt a bit foolish putting an elderly psychic on the witness stand. Then Mr. Milken and the others got all that publicity, and the government people were off on another tangent. I think they just forgot all about me. It's staggering what you can get away with when you're old."

Mallory smiled, and the old woman brightened, barely suppressing a laugh over her own good joke. Gift or no gift, Mallory decided, this woman could not read her mind, or even read her smile for what it was.

'I gotcha,' said Mallory's smile.

"So, Edith...May I call you Edith?"

"Of course, dear."

"Did Pearl Whitman give up the idea of contacting her father? Or did she try someone else?"

"I don't know, Kathy. She never came back again. There was nothing more I could do for her."

"How common is it to consult a medium or a psychic about stocks and bonds?"

"Very common. If it isn't love, it's money. And the older one is, the more likely it'll be money."

"So finance is a stock-in-trade with the psychic business."

"No, dear. It does require a bit of expertise. Most of the con artists are small-time. They eke out a living, but nothing fancy. And there are truly gifted people who take no money. They work with the police department for free. But a good stock analyst is difficult to find in this world or the next."

"And you were good. The merger paid off well. Why didn't she come back?"

"Perhaps she thought she had made enough money."

"You have quite a bit of money, don't you?"

"Between us and the walls, I'm stinking rich."

"Why do you stay here? Inside, I mean, locked up?"

"What's the need of going out? The world comes here, you see. I have my services for news and research, I have television and a video service and my book clubs. I have a good relationship with all the tenants. What's the need?"

"But there's a little more to it, right? Is it something to do with your husband's death?"

"Very good, Kathy. Yes, in a way. I foresaw the death of my husband, and I was unable to prevent it. After he died, I only wanted to retire. But people will seek me out. There isn't a day without at least

117

one caller. I'm afraid I'm a bit of a failure as a recluse. I suppose I might as well go into the world again. Lately, I have thought about it more and more."

"How much do you know about mediums? You said it wasn't really your field."

"You mean the mechanics? After all my years with Max, I guess I can figure out how a trick is pulled off. But the tricks don't always indicate fraud. More a sign of showmanship, really. They've all gone to modern conveniences like the computer for research, but the old parlor tricks are still necessary. You can't bewitch a mark with circuit boards."

"How would you like to go to a séance?"

Jack Coffey would not have believed there could be so many privately owned videocams in one square block. And it seemed odd, in this one little patch of town saved off from the twentieth century, that residents should be dangling from windows and balconies, making home movies of a homicide investigation. He would have had his own film on the murder itself, but the perp had found the one blind spot in Gramercy Park. The camera had seen nothing within ten feet on either side of this basement-level janitor's apartment.

His men were doing their best superhumanly polite crowd control, but the upscale residents were vociferous in their misunderstanding of their constitutional right to attend the dog-and-pony show of a bloody crime scene. He would not be seeing Beale's limousine tonight. Nor would Harry Blakely be stopping by to answer the inevitable reporter's question: How did this happen under your nose?

Floodlights lit up the building and made the

sidewalk bright as day. The photographer, Gerry Pepper, was working without a flash as he leaned over the railing and aimed his camera down into the submerged enclosure outside the basement-level door. Pepper walked down the short flight of stairs leading below the sidewalk, the better to shoot the old woman. She was up against the wall, which was red with one of her own bloody palm prints. He shot her again and again. She looked up at him in utter calm, unprotesting, quite beyond that now. The photographer shot her face, and then suddenly stepped back as though she had just said something unpleasant.

"Hey, Gerry!" Coffey called down to the photographer. "Get me extra shots of the palm print."

The man looked up, and Coffey saw something not quite right with Gerry Pepper. Something had unsettled this seasoned pro with fifteen years of shooting corpses, every damned thing that could be done to a human, from butchered infants to overdosed junkies. Gerry had seen far worse mutilations than this opened throat and hacked breast. Coffey waved him up the stairs and over to the wall.

"What's the problem, Gerry?"

The photographer spoke in a hoarse whisper, as though anything could be heard above the babble of one hundred independent conversations in the square tonight. "It's gonna be a suicide portrait. It's crazy, I know. But, Jack, you got no idea how many suicides I've shot." He ran one hand through his hair and looked back over his shoulder before he spoke again. "I could paper my apartment with the suicide shots. And I got ten times as many murder victims, so I damn well know the difference."

Coffey had known Gerry for a long time. He wasn't about to say anything close to 'You moron, you think she mutilated herself?' It wasn't his job to demoralize the troops, that's what God created a chief of detectives for, and Blakely was never going to hear about this.

"It's crazy," said Pepper. "But you asked."

The medical examiner's techs were moving slowly up the stairs from the basement level, carrying out the body in a bag, as Dr. Edward Slope removed his rubber gloves and nodded to Coffey. In that nod he managed to convey that it was the same pattern, and that it was an insane world they lived in.

Coffey put one hand on Slope's arm. "When did this one go down? Can you give me a best guess?"

Slope closed up his bag and looked squarely at Coffey. He nearly smiled. "Well, Jack," said Slope, "I see Markowitz raised you right. It's not too difficult with this one, given the body temperature, state of the wounds and rigidity. Unless something bizarre turns up in the autopsy, I'd put it between eleven and two this afternoon. I can narrow that down a bit tomorrow."

With no good night, Slope turned and walked away, moving slow. The man's gait and posture made him years older than the last time Coffey had seen him. They had to stop meeting like this.

Riker was flipping back through the pages of his notebook. "The doorman doesn't remember when Samantha Siddon left the building. Thought it might be in the afternoon. The cleaning lady, Mrs. Fayette, saw the old woman at noon. That's when Fayette finished up for the day. She said Siddon was wearing a housecoat and slippers. Give the old lady some time to change into street clothes and that puts

120

her in the lobby around twelve-fifteen at the earliest. She had arthritis in both hands and legs. Takes longer to do the buttons. Might make it closer to twelve-thirty."

"You talked to the janitor?"

"Yeah, he's pretty shaken up. He has another job, and wants us to be cool about that if we ever meet up with the management company that runs the building. Anyway, he gets home from the second job around eleven-fifteen and walks down the stairs to the door. And it's dark. The light bulb burned out a while ago. But there's plenty of light from the street, so he takes his time about replacing it. Anyway, he sees the pile of canvas in one corner of the stairwell while he's turning his door key. So he's all ready to get bent out of shape 'cause he figures a tenant tossed something there for him to get rid of, like his doorway is the local dump. He picks up the canvas, and at first, he doesn't know what he's looking at."

Coffey looked down on the same notebook that Riker was reading from. There were four words on the page.

"Was there anything in the apartment to give us a line on next of kin?"

"There's only one relative, a cousin. You want me to send a squad car to pick her up?"

"What's the woman's name, again?" Coffey asked.

"Margot Siddon," said young Officer Michael Ohara, last of three generations of uniformed policemen. "She's a second cousin of the victim."

"Where'd you put her?"

"She's in Markowitz's office."

"Ohara, Markowitz doesn't have an office here anymore."

121

"Right," said Ohara, but without conviction. "She's in your office, Lieutenant."

Sergeant Riker moseyed after Jack Coffey, who was doing a slow burn that showed in a red stripe between his hairline and the white strip of his shirt collar. Riker smiled at his shoes as he followed Coffey into Markowitz's office.

Riker didn't believe he would ever get used to the redecorating. The walls were hung with one normal-size bulletin board and two prints of the racehorses which were Coffey's only passion in life—outside of good-looking babes.

Margot Siddon was no babe, in Riker's estimation. She sat in a chair by the desk and sipped coffee from a paper cup. She drank as though half her face were shot with novocaine. The muscles on the left side of her mouth were frozen; she could make no expression that was not a smirk. The scar on her cheek was a faint marker for the nerves that must have been severed with the flesh.

According to Riker's notes on the law firm of Jasper and Biggs, she was about to inherit a fortune, but Horace Biggs, the executor, was on vacation in Rome. Morton Jasper, pissed off to distraction at being disturbed so late, could not or would not say with any certainty that she was the sole heir.

Margot Siddon didn't look the part of an heiress. Her hair was stringy and her shoes were scuffed imitation leather. Even with the layers of clothing— the black dress, the faded tapestry vest and the flimsy shawl—she was slender by her silhouette. Legs with well-defined calves thrust out in front of her. However small her body mass, Riker would bet it was solid muscle. He guessed that dancers worked out every day. Her real weakness was in her face: the small eyes, the chin that almost wasn't there.

122

Coffey was making introductions.

"We've met," said Riker. "Miss Siddon's a friend of Henry Cathery, grandson of the first victim. She was in Cathery's apartment when Markowitz interviewed him."

The exasperation on Coffey's face said, 'It might have been nice if you'd mentioned that earlier.'

Riker took his chair at the back of the office. He was positioned to one side, facing Coffey and a bit behind Margot Siddon. He pulled a leather notebook out of his pocket and flipped back to the interview notes made at the Cathery apartment.

"So you and Mr. Cathery are friends," said Coffey.

"We knew each other," she said, making a distinction there. "I visited Cousin Samantha once a week. The Catherys lived in the same building. After Henry's grandmother died, I used to drop in now and then. He was devastated by her murder. He depended on her for everything. He wasn't managing very well after her death."

Riker nodded to Coffey. That much was true. At the top of his interview notes for that date, he had underscored the words 'victim/ nanny.' The grandmother had obviously been Henry Cathery's caretaker. Without her ministrations, the boy's flesh and laundry had gone unwashed. He had been on his own for a full month before Markowitz interviewed him. His grandmother's homicide had become the property of Special Crimes only after the second death made it the work of a serial killer. As he recalled, the apartment the kid had once shared with Anne Cathery had the smell of a cleaning woman's recent visit, but the woman's chores had not involved cleaning the boy. Body odor had been noticeable despite the floral air freshener.

123

"I helped out with small things," Margot Siddon was saying to Coffey. "I made sure he was eating regularly, things like that."

Riker nodded again when Coffey glanced his way. The next words underlined in his notes were 'Margot Siddon—new nanny.' The day the girl had opened the door to Markowitz, she had a clean pair of jeans and a man's shirt draped over one arm. There had been no doubt about who was in charge. Henry Cathery had never answered a question from Markowitz without looking first to the girl. And when the answers were slow in coming, she had answered for him. Not only was she the dominant one, but Henry even gave the impression of being the frailer of the pair, though he was of above-average height and weight, fleshy in the face and gut.

"I'm not even sure that Henry knew where the groceries came from," Margot Siddon explained to Jack Coffey. "I suppose he wondered why the refrigerator wasn't full anymore, but he didn't know what to do about it."

Riker scanned the word *groceries*. Right, the groceries had been delivered to the apartment ten minutes into the interview. Henry Cathery had given her a wad of cash to pay the delivery boy, and then she had left them for a few minutes to put the perishables in the refrigerator. Acts of charity, Riker had supposed at the time, though he didn't take the girl for the good-mother type. But they were two lonely kids, both outside the mainstream in their quirks.

He looked at the last note he had made on the day of the Cathery interview. It was written in the car after the interview was over and they were heading back. Markowitz had mentioned that the girl never

124

gave Henry Cathery the change for the groceries. Riker had written 'parasite' and underscored it.

The lighting in the Cathery apartment had been subdued. Under these brighter fluorescent lights of NYPD, Riker noted that Margot Siddon's clothes were not fashionable grunge dressing, but merely old. The elderly and wealthy cousin had not been generous with the girl.

Done with her coffee, she set the cup on the desk and folded her hands in her lap. There was a pressure on the fingers to keep them there, behaving themselves. Her less disciplined legs crossed and recrossed at the ankles.

Coffey was extending his condolences on the death of Margot Siddon's cousin. The interview went on for another twenty minutes, and Coffey glanced Riker's way several times to let him know he hadn't missed the detail that half an hour passed before Riker thought anything had been said that was worth writing down. There were those impatient looks of 'Don't needle me' in Coffey's eyes. But Riker's pen only hovered over the page.

"No, she didn't have any enemies," said Margot, accepting the photograph from Coffey's hand and nodding. "Yes, that's Samantha. Was it a serrated knife?"

"What?" Lieutenant Coffey leaned forward as though he hadn't heard her right.

"The knife that killed her. Was it serrated?"

She set the photograph down on the desk. It was a head shot for identification purposes. A white towel covered the wound to the throat. The face was unmarred and seemed at peace, only sleeping.

"Ah, we're not sure," said Coffey. "The autopsy is in progress right now."

"I can probably tell if I see the photographs of the

wounds."

"We don't expect that of you, Miss Siddon. The identification is sufficient."

"Is there some reason why I shouldn't see them?"

"We'd like to keep some of the details out of the press for now."

Big mistake, thought Riker. The kid's eyes were gleaming.

"I insist on seeing the wounds," said Siddon.

And then it was the kid's mistake to try and smile with half her face. The result was a smirk that was obviously irritating Coffey as he pulled out the envelope with the glossy prints and handed her the shot that showed only the wound to the throat.

"A long knife," she said, holding the photo close to her eyes in the way of a nearsighted person. "And not a serrated edge."

Coffey stood up and straightened his tie. He'd had enough of this—that much was in his face and the stiffness of his stance.

"Sergeant Riker will have a few questions for you, and then he'll see that you're taken home."

The lieutenant left the room.

Riker made a few notes and then looked up. Her face was all accommodation.

"Miss Siddon, do you remember where you were between eleven this morning and two o'clock this afternoon?"

"TriBeCa, in a rehearsal loft." Anticipating his next question from a childhood based on television, she said, "There were a hundred other people there for tryouts. The director will remember me. He said I was very good."

But she and Riker both knew she'd be remembered for the left side of her face.

"They told me they'd call," she said, smiling on

126

one side as the opposite cheek crinkled the scar into a hideous waning moon.

Sure they would.

"I'll drive you home, Miss Siddon."

The East Village was filled with kids from good families who affected the look of starving-artist poverty. But this young dancer with the cheap shoes was the genuine article, legitimately hungry. He had remained in the background of their first and second meetings. Now, in the closeness of the car, he detected the smell of the thrift shop, a distinct odor of secondhand clothes. And the girl also exuded a palpable energy, waves of it.

He turned off Houston and rode north for three blocks before he pulled up in front of her apartment building. A small clutch of teenagers were gathered on the near corner, taking an interest in the unmarked car. Rats scrabbled in and out of the garbage cans. The shattered bits of a syringe sparkled amid the trash on the sidewalk.

"I'll see you upstairs," he said, removing his key from the ignition.

"No, don't," she said, too quickly. "I don't want to be any trouble."

A drunk was relieving himself on the wall across the street.

"No trouble at all."

"No, I insist," she said, half smiling and no sincerity in even half of her face. She was out of the car and leaning in the window before he could open his door.

"Good night, Sergeant Riker."

He nodded and started up the car, pulling slowly away into traffic. She stayed awhile on the sidewalk to see him off and gone. In his rearview mirror, he watched her growing smaller and smaller until she

127

disappeared in the dangerous landscape of Avenue C.

He tried Mallory's home number on the car phone. He let it ring, knowing that she took her own sweet time about answering.

Before the interview with Margot Siddon, he had pointed out to Coffey that the girl would probably inherit everything the old woman had in the bank, and Markowitz had always leaned toward money motives. Coffey had pointed out, for the second time in one night, that Markowitz was dead, as if the old rummy cop could not get that one simple thing through his head. And, said Coffey, this was not a woman's crime—for the tenth time, for Christ's sake.

At the next stoplight, he made his last note of the evening: Why not a woman?

*   *   *

Margot Siddon turned on the light in her apartment, and a roach scurried across the floor underfoot. She walked through the galley kitchen and passed a rack of knives, more knives than a professional cook could find uses for. And in the alcove that passed for a bedroom, there were other kinds of knives— Swiss Army knives, common penknives, switchblade knives.

Sometimes she forgot that the rest of the world was not so preoccupied with cutlery. She had gone too far tonight. The cops had both been looking at her as though she had just dropped in from the dark side of the moon.

She thought the younger cop, Coffey, was going to drop his teeth when she asked what kind of knife had killed Cousin Samantha.

128

Dear, dead Samantha. All that lovely money.

She would inherit more than enough money to buy back her old smile, the smile she used to go around in. Her eyes gleamed and glassed as she grinned with half her face. And she began to dance. Her arms and legs were a celebration of leaps and rippling movements as she danced through the room of her dingy walk-up, kissing every wall goodbye.

Mallory passed a walking woman on the dark SoHo street. The woman gasped, not with fear but with surprise. There had been no footfalls, no noise at all. Mallory had suddenly materialized at her side and then walked beyond her.

Without turning to look back, Mallory knew by which doorway the woman behind her had left the street, that the woman had used her own key drawn from a snap-lock purse, and by the quick steps, that the woman was suddenly afraid. Good. Civilians should be afraid. They would live longer, and longer still if they were more aware of their surroundings.

She walked north to the parking garage that held her car. A block short of Houston, she stopped. She listened. She turned to stare at the space of sidewalk behind her, eyes narrowing, the better to search the empty air for traces of a human who had recently been standing there.

Nothing. No one.

She was alone on the street, said her eyes, reporting back with the facts. But she could feel that other pair of eyes on her.

A memory came jumping with light's speed to the front of her brain, all decked with flashing red warning lights. 'Most people never look up,' Markowitz had told her in her rookie days. She pulled back and looked up as a black shape was failing toward her, rushing to meet her and send her to a better world than New York City. With the married reflexes of forked lightning and quick city rats, she jumped clear as the large block of concrete crashed into the pavement beside her and left a web of cracks in its wake.

She scanned the long line of the roof and caught the movement of a dark shape against the night sky, only a shadow moving across the edge of the roof. Her gun was clear of its holster and in her hand. But she had lost that fraction of a second between here and gone. The shadow had pulled in.

She moved to the side of the building and jumped for a handhold on the ledge of the fire escape. She was shot through with adrenaline and never felt the strain of the muscles which pulled her body straight up to the first grated landing. She took the stairs of the six-story building at a dead run, rubber soles touching to metal on every third step.

On the roof, without a moon and only the glow of city lights, she saw the fast-receding shadow was rooftops ahead of her. She jumped the barriers between one roof and another, and then she was airborne in the wider gulf where two buildings did not join. The shadow was not so quick but had the advantage of time and space. Its dark coat was flapping in the high wind like the wings of a bat, and then it was flown. Gone into air.

All her senses told her she was alone in the dark. Both feet touched to ground at one time, and her gun hand came to rest at her side. She stepped lightly across the tar surfaces of the rooftops, checking fire escapes and roof doors. One door had been left open. She stared down into the dark of the stairwell, looking for disturbance's in the air, the trail of body heat, the sound and sensation of a

130

fugitive life-form. Nothing came back to her but the stillness of those nine-to-fivers sleeping therein, and she knew the thing had not gone this way. She checked the door of the roof beyond and the metal stairs of its fire escape.

Finally, she pulled her eyes back from the street below, drew back from the edge of the roof, and stared out at the skyline of lower Manhattan, the panorama of the night owls' lighted windows, all the eyes that never saw anything when the cops came knocking at the door.

Jack Coffey sat alone in his office, which was still called Markowitz's office. Margot Siddon had gotten to him. All that talk of knives, her lips curling into a smirk. He had pegged her then as another punk kid from the Village, another cop-baiter. Screw that.

Now he looked down at the file Riker had placed on his desk. Stapled to it was the requisition slip Markowitz had signed. Markowitz, the lover of details, must have ordered it after the interview in the Cathery apartment. The two-year-old account of the assault on Margot Siddon included the knife wound to the face, the cutting of the facial nerves. And the scar had been there for all to see, and all he had seen was the smirking insolence which only the knife could be accountable for and not the girl, the victim.

Oh, all the damned victims.

What else had he missed? Christ, he was tired.

Riker's own notes had been added to Margot Siddon's old file. The sergeant had tracked down the case officer for personal comments. Coffey was looking at a school photograph of a nice-looking kid with a normal smile, taken shortly before that cruel bastard had said, 'Now watch the dancing knife, little girl.' And according to the case officer's statement, Margot had actually watched the blade cutting into her skin, watched the blood flow, in shock from the violence he had already done to her, stark naked by then, covered only with blood.

All the damned victims.

He turned off the overhead lights, ready to leave but too tired to get in motion. He flicked on the desk lamp, and the softer glow illuminated the walls repainted and denuded of Markowitz-style clutter. But Markowitz had come stealing back to reclaim the place. The floor was littered with folders tonight. Another stack of case files filled the two chairs on the other side of the desk, and on the new, unmarred blotter next to his new computer terminal sat a stack of letters and diaries to read and handle in the old-fashioned way.

It troubled him that the writings of the old women had tapered off more than a year ago. Either they had ceased to have anything of interest to write about, or they had all become so fascinated by some thing or event that the writing of letters and the keeping of journals had been displaced by another, more interesting occupation. This nagged at him. In one case, all the writing he could find had been in a storage trunk. No letters of any kind had been found in the apartment. Yet the woman had the history of a dedicated diarist, not missing a day in the ten years of leather-bound books he had recovered.

All the victims had been one-dimensional before he began reading their private thoughts. None of the heirs had been able to give him even the most routine aspects of an old woman's life. Who were their friends, what interests might the victims have in common—the relatives could tell him nothing.

And the day-hire women told him only the most mundane habits of their elderly employers. Tonight he had invaded the victims' minds in search of who they had been and also rounded out the profiles of the heirs. The victims' fears had centered on losing touch with the only relations they had, their touchstones with the world, the continuity of blood.

In a fluid, old-fashioned script, one old woman berated herself for all the irrational questions asked just to keep conversation going, to prevent the rare visit from ending all too soon. And there were sometimes tear-blind rages for the lack of understanding, the inability to communicate with a generation she had nothing in common with. The crying sags, the terrible giving in to the futility of putting up any fight. The anger at being treated as a child—as though crying robbed her of her maturity. The frustration of misunderstandings that came about because the young only half listened and never did grasp the simplest fact that arthritic hands couldn't open childproof caps. The common thread that ran through the women's lives was the need to be touched.

Samantha Siddon had that need. The page open before him was the last entry in the diary of the fourth victim, dated one year ago:

She tolerates the hugs at meetings and partings. It must seem to her, in those moments, that I am clinging to my very life, and so I am. She is all the warm flesh that I may touch and be touched by. One dies without the touch. What if she should never return?

He left the light burning when he walked out of the office and moved down the hall to the incident room where they kept all the things Riker had retrieved from Mallory and all the physical evidence. It was a chaos of bloody carnage in full-color prints and bits of paper that must somehow chain together. Too many clues, Markowitz had said. And now there were too many suspects. Two of them could be working in tandem. The Cathery boy, who fit the FBI profile, was just too perfect in every respect but motive. Jonathan Gaynor, the sociology professor, had inherited the largest fortune of all. Margot Siddon was the neediest heir.

Markowitz and his damn money motives. Ah, but the old man had something. This killer was a sick bastard, no doubt about it, but not crazy. Markowitz had tipped to something. Why hadn't the old man given him a sporting chance, just a note in the dust, any damn thing at all.

"No, nothing new on my end. Thanks for calling, Riker. Yeah, see you tomorrow."

Nothing new? Well, she was still alive. That hadn't changed.

Mallory put down the telephone and walked into the den. She pinned her last surveillance notes on Gaynor to the wall. So the fourth victim had gone down between noon and two. With the best transportation, all the right connections of subway cars or traffic lights, it would take nearly an hour to make the round trip from the edge of Harlem to Gramercy Park if she only threw in a few minutes to do murder. Except for the hours of his student interviews, he had not been out of her sight for that length of time. The hall was the only exit from his office. Could Gaynor have slipped by? As Mrs. Pickering had pointed out, surveillance was not her forte. She had wanted it to be Gaynor. It would have fit so nicely.

Once, Markowitz had caught her cutting the

134

pieces of a picture puzzle to make them fit. 'Kathy,' he said, in the early days when he was still allowed to call her that, 'you can cheat the pieces to fit, but they won't show you the real picture. This is life's way of getting even with you, kid.'

She put the Gaynor notes off to one side of the board with the long shots of Henry Cathery playing chess in the park.

She needed a new best suspect and a new angle. She stared at Markowitz's pocket calendar. Suppose he had never made it to the BDA appointment that Tuesday night? He hadn't been seen since Tuesday morning. Markowitz hadn't gone to the Thursday night poker game the previous week. What if he also missed the Tuesday appointment in that week before he died? What had he been doing with his nights?

If Markowitz had figured it out, it had to be linked to one of the first two murders. Or had he worked out a connection to the third one? What had he seen that she could not see?

She loaded the slide carousel and sat watching the shots of Markowitz killed again and again, melding into shots of the first two murders, and finally her own shots of Gaynor and Cathery and the magic show of the medium, minion and baggage emerging from the yellow cab. 'Pick up all the oddball things you can find,' Markowitz had told her in her first year in crimes analysis. 'Never throw anything away, kid.'

'Don't call me kid,' she had shot back. And it was always Mallory after that. It had cost him something to call her Mallory after all the years she had been Kathy to him, as though he'd never had a hand in raising her.

She watched the slides, lights playing on her face as the images changed quickly. What would the old man make of all this? Well, first he would say she was leaving tracks, big messy ones. Markowitz the dancing fool would never do that.

So how did be get killed?

The slide carousel looped back to the first shot of Markowitz lying in his own blood. She no longer took pride in the fact that she never cried. Dry eyes closed tightly as she switched off the projector and sat alone in the dark.

The new order she had created for him permeated his entire life these days, extending even into the office kitchen. He opened the refrigerator to gleaming metal shelves which Mallory had stocked with ample makings and condiments for every kind of sandwich known to God and Charles Butler.

It was an odd moment to realize how deep his feeling did go, as he was gathering ham and pickles, mustard and mayonnaise. Thieving, amoral liar that she was, he knew with a terrible finality that he would love Kathleen Mallory till he died. Where was the cheddar cheese? And it would always be the one-sided affair of a solitary man with a ridiculous face.

His eyes avoided the expanse of yellow wall above the stove as he lit the burner and set the teakettle over the flame.

He regretted the choice of yellow paint for the kitchen. It had been an impulse decision. Like most people, he had believed yellow to be a cheerful, happy color. Too late, he had realized his mistake and called up an item on the subject of color, mentally projecting a page from an old science journal directly onto the white refrigerator door. The article had agreed with his own feeling. Yellow made people jittery.

But even if the walls had been the calming pink of drunk-tank experiments listed in the following paragraph, it might not have had any effect on his state of mind this late evening.

He slathered mayonnaise on rye bread and wondered what went on in Gramercy Park. Who was she watching, and who might be watching her? Scenarios were growing in his brain like cancers. He laid down three slices of ham and wondered about the gun she carried every day. And then there was Herbert's gun to worry about. And what had Edith to do with this?

He added on a generous slab of yellow cheese.

The teakettle screamed.

Chapter Five

"So we're back on the same pattern with this one," said Riker, slugging down his breakfast beer and spilling a few drops on his shirt. "The Siddon woman looks different from the others, doesn't she? Real peaceful." He held the photograph out to her. She only shrugged as she took it from his hand. Right. What would Kathy Mallory know of peace?

She pinned the bloody likeness of Samantha Siddon to the wall with the other on-site photos. Riker watched her all but melding into the cork, passing through the wall of it as she became absorbed by everything he had brought her.

The exterior wall in the first photograph was splattered with blood, and only patches of Siddon's fawn-colored suit were not soaked through with red. One bloody palm print stained the rough brick a few feet above the head. Mallory put her finger on this photo.

"The victim's print?"

Riker nodded.

She walked back to the other side of the wall, where Markowitz's collection had been reprinted from the slides. She stared at the park photos of the first murder and moved on to the next set. "What about the second kill? Were there any prints on the car?"

Riker leaned back against the board and paused midgulp. "Hmm?"

"Estelle Gaynor, the one found in the limo. Were there any bloody prints?"

"You got it all there in Markowitz's report. One thumb and an index finger on the window, hers—no palm prints, not hers anyway. We tracked down all the latent prints. One set belongs to a garage mechanic. Some prints from the old man who owned the car. Nothing else."

He drained the rest of his beer with one swig and moved to the Markowitz side of the wall to stand behind her. She was staring at the detail shot of the Cathery killing in the park. It showed one bloody print of a full hand on the white trim of the shed.

"You're really reaching for connections, Mallory. If you're looking for a trademark, there weren't any bloody palm prints for the Pearl Whitman site."

"It's wrong somehow," she said, crossing back to her own side of the board to stand before the Siddon prints and the separate shot of the palm's bloodstain.

Riker was hearing echoes of Markowitz, who was always listening for the off notes. "Mallory, the woman was fighting for her life." Ah, but wait. He stared at Samantha Siddon's peaceful face. It wouldn't agree with a battle on any scale.

138

"Slope can't say for sure it's the work of one perp?"

"He's still working on it. Commissioner Beale likes that idea too. It makes him feel like we know something the newspapers don't know."

"So Beale's giving Coffey a hard time?"

"You know the drill. The press crucifies Beale, Beale waves his little fists and squeaks, and Coffey pretends to be afraid of mice."

She pinned one sheet of the report to the board. "Any deviations this time? Anything odd?"

"Yeah. That one's crooked," he said, pointing to the last paper she had pinned up.

"Get serious."

He was serious. It was odd for her to make any departure from perfectionist neatness. He looked down at the chipped fingernail on her right hand, and he began to hunt the room in earnest for anything else out of place. The television and VCR had been pulled in from another room. The slide projector was new. But no dust gathered, that was certain. He supposed even a perfectionist could have an off day.

"No deviation from the MO." He shrugged. "Same old, same old. Her purse was gone. No deviations among the local corpse robbers, either."

She smiled, and that worried him. What was the deal here? Why did she find that so interesting?

"What about the wounds?" she asked. "Consistent?"

"Slope says he can't match wounds if the bastard uses a different knife every time. But the areas and the order of the cuts are the same. He always goes for the throat first."

"What odds does he give for two of them?"

"I tried that one. Slope won't give odds, and he's

139

a betting man."

As Mallory pinned up the last photo, Riker noticed her alignment was off again. Now he stepped back from the board. Markowitz's side of the wall was the usual mess. Kathy's side was neater, but with each addition to the board, less neat. Every time he came into the room, something new had been added, and item by item, her pushpin precision was going down the tubes. The preliminary report hung on the diagonal by one tack. So, what was going on here? The rest of the apartment was immaculate as always. He wondered how much time she spent in this room.

She handed him a photograph of a woman dwarfing a cabdriver. "Her name is Redwing. She's running a scam in Gramercy Park. Ever see her before?"

"She's on the park surveillance log, but I don't know her face," said Riker. Redwing was not a new element in the square, but a once-a-week pattern over more than a year. It was the shots of Jonathan Gaynor and Henry Cathery that had his full attention.

"I'm meeting her tomorrow at a séance," said Mallory. "I want some background on her, but she's not on computer as Redwing. If you tripped over an alias with a rap sheet, you'd tell me, right?...Riker?"

Riker nodded, only half listening, preoccupied with the surveillance shots. "Kid, we gotta talk about your style, okay? You don't get shots like this unless you're so close the perp can see you, too."

She turned her back on him and tacked up Redwing's shot. "You interviewed Gaynor with Markowitz, didn't you?"

"Yeah."

"Notes?"

Riker flipped through his notebook, a dog-eared dangle of pages.

"Windmill," he said, marking the note with one finger.

"Huh?"

"It's the way he moves. He makes a lot of gestures, sprawly, all arms. So, Markowitz and me, we're walkin' through the lobby with this guy, and his arms are wavin' all over the place while he talks. We pass by this group of little old ladies and they scatter like crows."

"They were afraid of him?"

"Naw, it wasn't like that. You gotta be careful with old people. They break easy. So I guess he makes them a little skittish is all, arms waving in the breeze, never looking to see where he's going."

"Like a scarecrow."

"Yeah, I like that." He scratched out 'windmill' and wrote in 'scarecrow.'

"What did Markowitz think of Gaynor?"

"I'm not sure. Markowitz spent the whole time pumping him for free professional advice."

"Gaynor's a sociologist, not a shrink."

"Yeah, but he did an article or a book or something on the elderly. Markowitz was getting into the territory, you know? This was early days, only ten hours into the second kill."

"What did he tell Markowitz?"

"Nothin' I had notes on. Old people's role in society, that kind of crap. Markowitz thought it was real interesting. I didn't."

"What's Coffey's angle these days?"

"He's got me running background on the Siddon kid." Riker pulled a videotape from his jacket pocket. "You wanna see the latest interview? I got her on tape."

141

She took the tape from his hand, fed it into the mouth of the VCR and pushed the play button.

Margot Siddon appeared on the screen, only to be ejected ten minutes later, and before the interview concluded. Mallory tossed him the tape.

"I've seen her around the park. I don't know any more than the surveillance team would. She hangs out with Henry Cathery sometimes. Most of the time he just ignores her, won't even unlock the park gate for her. He'd rather play chess than talk to girls."

Mallory stood in the fourth-floor hallway by Martin Teller's apartment and stared down at the neat stacks of books and magazines, a vacuum cleaner, a copper teakettle, and a portable electric fan assembled outside his door. These were not castaway items to be put out with the trash; this, according to Charles, was where Martin, the minimalist artist, stored everything that was not pure white.

She glanced at the door across the hall from Martin's. She had been forbidden to terrorize Herbert of 4B. Reluctantly, she turned back to Martin's door at the sound of four locks being undone. Three of the locks were shiny new metal, in contrast with the landlord's lock, which was close to twenty years old by the make.

The door opened, and she was silently invited into the apartment by the barely perceptible inclination of Martin's hairless head. Minimal Martin had also done away with unnecessary eyebrows. His white shirt, bulking out around the bulletproof vest, the white pants and socks all blended him into the white walls. The front room had the look of a vacant apartment freshly broken into. The windows were bereft of curtains, and the walls were bare except for the small collection of stamp-size artwork mounted one on each wall. Each tiny bit of art was a faint pencil line.

She preferred minimalist art over every other school; it was neat and clean and hardly there, no garish colors, nothing to think about, less work.

The doorless closet in the front room contained the minimum amount of clothes which were also white and hence invisible in these quarters. Square white pedestals passed for chairs and were indistinguishable from the square white pedestal that was his breakfast table, laid with one white dish and a single egg, Mallory had no view into the bedroom, but she could hazard a narrow mattress on the floor, covered with one doubled-over white sheet.

A bulletproof vest seemed like such a complicated addition to these rooms and to Martin.

"Martin, I'm curious about the writing on the wall in Edith Candle's apartment."

Martin merely stared, not at her but toward her, like a blind man listening for a clue as to her position. He showed no signs of a pending response. She moved into alignment with his gaze and smiled. A worry line made inroads in his brow, which for Martin was tantamount to an emotional outburst. Perhaps Martin had a truer perception of her than most people who took her smile for a smile.

"The writing on the wall, Martin?" She rose up on the balls of her feet with anticipation, further prompting the man only with her eyes. If she pressed him too hard, he might walk off into some autistic dimension and close the door behind him. And so she waited on him.

And waited on him.

Nothing.

143

Oh, of course. She hadn't asked a solid question, had she?

"Could you tell me what the writing was?"

"Red," said Martin, after she had counted off thirty seconds.

She stopped smiling.

Over the past month, she'd had occasion to observe this artist in the streets and the halls during his infrequent contacts with the humans who also lived on his planet. Martin made people nervous for all the minutes it took to determine that he was odd but harmless.

"Yes, red lipstick, but what did the writing say?"

She smiled again to worry him into a faster response. She didn't have all damn day for this crap, did she?

"Thick lines," said Martin.

The man was a badly lip-synced foreign movie with unrelated narrative. A ghost of Helen Markowitz automatically corrected the grammar of her next thought.

You can *kill him, but you* may *not.*

There was no more forthcoming. He was only standing there, not waiting, not anticipating, only occupying space. Well, he was still a man, wasn't he?

"Could you tell me what the words were?" Mallory asked gently with a low, sultry voice that pulled his eyes into hers by invisible silk strings. Martin broke the strings abruptly and turned around to face the wall. He had spent his words, said the back of him. He had none left.

Behind her own back, her hands were balling into fists. She kept the fists out of her words. "It's an interesting building, isn't it, Martin? I mean the way the tenants tuck in their heads when they slide past each other in the halls. It's like they all know what's in each other's closet and under the bed. A little mutual embarrassment. A little creepy, wouldn't you say?"

His head dropped an inch. Considering who she was dealing with, she could read much into that inch. She sat down on one of the white pedestals and stared at his back, willing him to turn around. She was not at all surprised when he did turn to face her. His senses were that acute. She wove more silk into her voice.

"There's not much turnover in this building. That's strange. New York is such a transient town. I wonder what keeps you all here. You were here when George Farmer attempted suicide ten years ago. The next tenant to leave was the one who used to live across the hall from Charles. He just disappeared one day, packed up and left no forwarding address. He abandoned his security deposit and fifteen years of interest on it. What makes a man do a thing like that?"

Martin's eyes collided with hers and rolled away in pain.

She held up both her hands, palms up with a question. "You think he saw the writing on the wall?"

Martin turned his back on her again. His head shook from side to side, not to a negative response, but as though he were shaking the words from his head.

She'd gone too far.

She rose to her feet and moved slowly to the door. As she opened it, Martin said, "Be careful. You will not know the hour nor even the minute."

When Charles returned to the office, he was

145

surprised to see Mallory there during the daylight hours. She stood at the kitchen counter putting together a plate of sandwiches garnished with the finesse of a professional chef.

"Hello, Mallory." He never slipped and called her Kathleen anymore. She was Mallory in all his thoughts, spoken and not. She had trained him well. And she fed him well and simplified his life. Even Arthur, the accountant, had praised her for making his own life easier; no more messy shopping bags of papers with coffee and tea stains washing out the figures in the amount-due columns.

Yet something told him life was just about to get more complicated.

"I had a long talk with Edith Candle," she said, ever so offhand.

He supposed it was inevitable that she should meet Edith. Every tenant in the building was drawn to Edith's apartment at one time or another. But that was another puzzle and low on his list of priorities.

"She's like a prisoner in that apartment," said Mallory.

He looked fondly at the roast beef on rye with crisp lettuce and parsley garnish. "It does look that way, I know."

The coffeemaker, haunted by Louis Markowitz, gurgled and dripped, insinuating itself into the conversation.

Perhaps he should give the puzzle of Edith more immediate consideration. Mallory was hideously single-minded, and her all-consuming interest was Louis's murderer. What was the connection?

"Do you know why she never leaves the building?" she asked.

Mallory was not given to small talk. She couldn't ask an offhand innocent question; it just wasn't in her. Well, if he never learned anything from her responses, there might be something to be had from her questions.

"She's still in mourning for her husband." And now he noticed the pastrami with mustard and mayonnaise, and he was torn between the two sandwiches.

"Nobody mourns for thirty years, Charles." One corner of Mallory's disbelieving mouth slipped into a deep dimple of skepticism, and Louis's coffee machine sputtered. "Maybe there's a little more to it?" She set the plate of sandwiches on the checked tablecloth. "Something to do with her husband's accident?"

"She told you about that?"

"Sit," she said, pointing him to a chair by the kitchen table while she turned back to the coffeemaker where Louis abided.

He had shared many meals with her, and not one of them had been in a kitchen. As he recalled, her father had been a kitchen-sitting person-but to a purpose. In Louis's opinion, conversation was greased by a kitchen atmosphere and hampered by a more formal setting.

It occurred to him that the poker players had steered him wrong. Her behavior might be more predictable if he concentrated on what she had learned from Markowitz and not Helen.

"Thirty years," said Mallory. "It's like jail time."

"I guess it does seem like a penance." He picked up a sandwich and suddenly forgot his appetite. Penance. Why had that never occurred to him before? Memories were surfacing, but still vague yet. "She might feel responsible for the accident."

"Because…" Mallory prompted him.

"I'm not sure. I was only nine when Max died."

147

"You have a memory like a computer. Now give."

"Eidetic memory doesn't work that way. I can recite chapters from books and even tell you if I spilled any coffee on the pages, but I'm not good at recalling conversations that went over my head when I was a child."

"I don't think much has gone by you since you left the womb, Charles. These conversations you can't remember, did they happen close to the day your cousin died?"

"Probably. Max lived with us for the last three days of his life."

"Only Max? He left his wife?"

"Yes, I think so. Oh, right. They'd had a quarrel. It was something to do with the new act. Edith thought it was too dangerous. I think she wanted him to give it up. But he couldn't. You see, there was a time when he'd had top billing as Maximilian the Great. Then later, he became the husband of the great Edith Candle. All of his brilliant illusions, his own gifts had gotten lost somewhere."

"So this was his comeback? He was taking another shot at it?"

"Yes. He created a fantastic new set of illusions for this act. I remember all of us, Max and my parents, sitting around the table reading the reviews the morning after his opening." His photographic memory was calling up the newspaper column that had so impressed him as a child it had remained with him for thirty years. "The *New York Times* called him a maestro." Now he was on familiar ground as he called up the printed word from another newspaper column and read the lines as though he held the paper in his hand. "'The master is incomparable at the height of his creative powers,' they said. His star was on the rise again."

148

The following morning, after the second performance had ended in tragedy, the newspapers had been kept out of his sight.

"So Max's career was on the rise. What about Edith's act?"

"Well, she still had a certain stature in psychic circles, but in one night, Max had eclipsed her, quite literally with his hands tied. It was amazing. There were lots of reviews. New York had more newspapers in those days. They all used the words *death-defying* and *dangerous* to describe the act."

"Dangerous? It was all a sham, wasn't it?"

"Oh, no. The new tricks were very dangerous. The finale required all his skill and mental discipline. While he stayed with us, he refused to give interviews. He wouldn't take any phone calls or messages."

"Not even from Edith?"

"Especially not from Edith." Why had he said that?

"Must have been quite a fight between those two."

"Well, the illusion required great concentration, no distractions."

"Like Edith predicting his death?"

The writing on the wall. What had his mother said about that?

"Yes, I suppose that was it. A few days before the opening of the new act, he found a message scrawled on the wall of his apartment. It was red lipstick."

"What did it say?"

"No idea. I'm putting this together from what I overheard. No one ever spoke to me about it. It was odd. Trance writing had never been part of the old routine."

149

"Trance writing?"

"Yes, something written without conscious thought, while in a trance. She never denied having written it, she only said she had no memory of doing it."

"Did you believe her? Whose side did you take?"

"I don't know. I was only nine years old then. I'm sure I loved them both." No, that was not true. One was loved and one was adored. "Perhaps I was closer to Max. He spent a lot of time with me. He had other things to do, I know. It was a busy period for him. But he took time out to play with me. I loved him very much,"

He picked up an olive from his plate and closed it in the palm of his hand. When he spread his fingers again, the olive was gone. He reached up and appeared to pull it from his eye socket, handing it to her with one eye closed. She laughed. Though the trick played on the simple humor of a small child, the love of all things gross and gory, she laughed as he had done all those years ago when Max was alive and beloved.

"Max died on the second night he performed the new routine with the water tank. The next day, when my parents told me about the accident, I wouldn't believe them. I just knew it had to be a trick. Edith went into seclusion after Max died. She didn't even go to his funeral. I did. The services were held in the cathedral. Magicians came from all over the world. They came in uniform, but not magician's black. They all wore white top hats, white capes and suits. The women wore white satin dresses. All the flowers were white. And later, at the cemetery, when the casket was lowered into the ground, a thousand doves flew out from under the magicians' capes. The sky was white with doves' wings. I will never see anything like that again."

"Edith must have been in pretty bad shape to miss the funeral."

"I'm sure she was."

"You don't know?"

"My parents never took me to visit her after that. My mother told me we were respecting her seclusion. The next time I saw Edith was after my mother's funeral."

The coffeemaker spat.

Edith Candle was staring at the wall but not seeing it. Looking beyond the twining roses on the wallpaper, she was probing old memories which predated the death of a magician. Her chair rocked with unconscious effort.

One could always point to a time, a choice, an act that set the tone for a life and changed a personal destiny. Her moment had come in a desolate corner of the flat midwestern landscape. The sky had been deep purple, and she recalled stars like blazing cartwheels in the triangular flaps of the tent which had been pulled back to catch the breezes of a hot summer night. Maximilian had been at the back of the tent with the mark. By code of words, he fed her the details of the watch in his hand.

"I can't see anymore," she had cried out suddenly, "The image is being drowned out by other thoughts." The other thoughts had been gleaned by eavesdropping in the line for admission. Max had overheard a woman talking about her sister Emaline's heart problem and how it worried at her night and day.

"Tell us these thoughts," said Max, cuing her to remove the blindfold and ask if the name Emaline meant anything to anyone in the audience. She

151

removed her blindfold and looked out over the silent, tense sea of faces.

She was transfixed by the boy in the front row, far from the mark at the back of the tent. The boy stared at her. He shivered and then looked guiltily away. His soft eyes shamed down to his shoes. She stared at him until the boy's eyes met hers again. He had the look of a drowning animal. The sense that he was waterbound was strengthened as the boy began to rise from the wooden bench, moving in slow motion as though the atmosphere had killing weight and pressure. An older companion, wearing the same gas station uniform as the boy's, put a hand on his shoulder to bid the boy sit down again. The boy's terrified eyes looked back to hers. He sloughed off the old man's hand and began to make his way down the aisle with the gait of too much drink, though she knew the boy was not intoxicated.

She had called out to him, "You must tell the police what you've done." The boy spun around, his face all agony, more pain than a child could stand.

"You must tell them!" she shouted.

The boy let out a strangled scream and fled up the aisle. A uniformed police officer also stood up and followed the boy out.

That night the local sheriff dug up the body of Tammy Sue Pertwee in the yard of a shantytown shack. It made the morning paper, and it made her the headliner instead of the added attraction to Maximilian's Traveling Magic Show.

Henry Cathery was sitting in the park at dusk. The streetlamps were just coming on when the pretty woman arrived. He knew she would come back. He had waited for her all through the previous day into disappointing darkness. After all the days of seeing

152

her each morning and every evening, he had felt the loss of her yesterday. Then Mrs. Siddon had died, and the pretty woman had come back to him again.

She opened the door of the tan car and stepped out on the sidewalk. She had never done that before. He followed the graceful swing of her walk as she moved down the sidewalk and toward the building across the street. So she would not be keeping him company this time. His head remained motionless while his eyes rolled after her. Her gold hair caught the lamplight and threw it back in sparks. The electric woman had wonderfully dangerous eyes.

She entered the near building through the great oaken door, held open by a doorman who stared at her with naked hurt that his chances were better to be struck three times by lightning than even to touch her. And granted, Henry thought, the doorman was very tall, good lightning rod material in a level cow pasture, but this was New York City.

Henry Cathery left his bench and walked slowly to the gate. He pressed his face to the bars and stared at her little tan car. He opened the gate and moved slowly across the street, unmindful of the fast-braking car which was now skidding around him. He stood in the street staring into the tan car's windows. The seats were much cleaner today. No trash, no coffee cups. He leaned into the narrow opening at the top of the driver-side window and inhaled deeply. So this was what she smelled like. He reached in the window, forcing the crack to widen, pushing his flesh against it until it permitted his hand to reach far enough inside to rub his palm on the upholstery of the car seat.

When Jonathan Gaynor opened the door, Mallory was close enough to notice the light sprinkle of freckles across his nose. He was only a few years shy of forty, yet the idea of a small boy with a fake beard persisted. She held up a leather folder with her shield and photo ID. He actually read the card. Most people barely glanced at it.

"Sergeant Mallory, you're right on time." He opened the door wide and stepped back as she walked in. He looked at his Rolex. "And I mean right on time, exact quartz time."

She watched his eyes drop to inspect the cashmere blazer she wore over her jeans, probably trying to reconcile the good cloth with the badge-and-gun salary. In the manner of an insurance appraiser, she noted the recent water rings on the antique woods, and a newspaper opened on a light brocade upholstery which was probably now smudged with print. Delicate pieces of collector's crystal sat on every surface—nearly every surface. Her eye for symmetry filled in the gaps on the tables where other pieces had been until recently. She sat down in the large armchair that dominated the rest of the furniture. And it was *she* who motioned *him* to sit down in the opposite smaller chair.

"You didn't mention this appointment to anyone?"

"Of course not, Sergeant." He folded his body into the chair, and his arms jutted out at risky angles to the figurines on the near tables. "I can appreciate the fact that undercover work is dangerous. You can rely on my discretion."

"Thank you. One of your neighbors believes I'm a private detective. I'd like her to go on believing that."

"Of course. How can I help you?"

"You knew Inspector Markowitz?"

"We met once. He came by after my aunt was

154

murdered. I liked the man. I was sorry to hear about his death." One hand moved of its own accord and fell over the arm of his chair. The other hand rested on his thigh, though these two body parts seemed unacquainted. No interaction of his limbs ever implied that they had met before.

"Sergeant Riker tells me Markowitz asked for your expertise, Mr. Gaynor."

"Yes. He was interested in the social dynamics of Gramercy Park, particularly the elderly inhabitants."

"There are no notes on that meeting. It might help us to follow his line of investigation if you could remember what was said."

"Well, that was over two months ago. I only recall the gist of it. He focused on all the ways elderly women connected with one another in Gramercy. This square is an interesting little nation unto itself." The hand which had been dangling now joined the rest of him, rising to the arm of the chair, knocking into the small table on its way. Gaynor never seemed to notice the hand had injured itself, he and the hand were that far removed from one another.

"Was Markowitz interested in anything more specific?"

"Yes, but I could only give him a general picture. I'm afraid I wasn't much help on particulars. You see, I hadn't moved in yet, not until weeks after my aunt's death. So at the time, I was out of touch with the square."

"Sergeant Riker seemed to think Markowitz got a great deal of help from you. The interview lasted what—three hours? His usual style was forty minutes at the outside. I call that interesting."

Gaynor appeared to be searching the ceiling for personal notes on the subject.

"He was looking for commonalities. The only

common factor I could pin down for him was the isolation of the elderly. Now, there had only been two murders at that time. I remember asking if the other woman, Mrs. Cathery, had any social network. He said no, none that they could discover. Well, neither did Aunt Estelle, and neither of them had live-in help." One hand stumbled off the arm of the chair and landed as a dead weight on top of the other one in his lap.

"But Mrs. Cathery didn't live alone. There was a grandson living in the apartment. Henry Cathery. Do you know him?"

"This is New York City. The good-neighbor thing doesn't extend to the next apartment, let alone a building at the end of the block. My aunt knew him. She said he was a recluse. And I know he's eccentric." One foot walked under the coffee table, and the accompanying shin made a thud against the hard edge. The pain was not relayed back to Gaynor, who never even winced. "According to the newspapers, he didn't even notify the police that his grandmother never came home that night. Didn't you find that odd? I mean, from the police point of view?"

"Odd? Well, he told the investigating officer he was only grateful for the peace and quiet, so it never occurred to him to go looking for her."

That initial interview with Henry Cathery had been conducted three months ago while the first kill still belonged to Homicide and not Special Crimes. The investigating officer's notes and a follow-up interview had decided Markowitz that Cathery had been truthful in this. Markowitz had always been charmed by blatant honesty.

"Mr. Gaynor, you've never spoken to Henry Cathery?"

156

"Call me Jonathan," he said, sitting back in the chair, his elbow nudging a figurine to the edge of the table on his left. "I used to see him in the park now and then. I nodded to him a few times the first week I was here. He never nodded back—just looked right through me. He's a constant fixture in the park, but I don't spend much time there anymore."

He stood up and followed his legs to the wide picture window at the far wall. He motioned her over. "There he is," he said, pointing down to the bench behind the black bars and directly across the street from the building. Henry Cathery's head was bowed over a portable chessboard as she drew closer to the window and looked down on him. Cathery chose that moment to lift his head, and she could have sworn he was looking directly at her. A reflexive instinct pulled her one step back from the window. She continued to stare down at Cathery with equal parts of revulsion and fascination.

"Bit late for him to be out," Gaynor was saying. "He's usually there during the day. See the game board on his lap? He was some sort of chess champion as a child, I think. Burned out rather early. Forgive me, I'm probably telling you things you already know."

When they turned away from the window, it was *he* who guided *her* toward the couch. "I believe your first name is Kathleen?"

She nodded. "Did you know Pearl Whitman?"

"Never met her. May I call you Kathy?"

"No."

His face reddened. Good. "Pearl Whitman visited spiritualists on a regular basis. She might be connected to a medium who comes here every—"

"Redwing?"

"You know her?"

"Who could miss a spectacle like that? How tall is she? Six foot two? And the girth." His hands made a wide circle, knocking into a slender porcelain figurine on a long table behind the couch and setting it to rocking slightly. "I passed her in the lobby of this building one day as I was leaving. The doorman told me her name. I asked my aunt about her the next time I came by. This was a very long time ago, but I remember the conversation very well. It ended in a very loud argument."

"Did your aunt attend the séances?"

"She never said. Of course she wouldn't have after that. So you think Redwing's involved in this?"

"I'm interested in everything that goes on in the square. Redwing's been coming here every week for more than a year. When you argued with your aunt, what did you have against the medium?"

His hand suddenly left him to wave in the air, and a scatter pillow sailed to the marble floor. "Well, it's a bag of tricks, isn't it? It probably wouldn't take anything very sophisticated to fool a pack of old women who really want to believe in that nonsense. It's a nasty business, victimizing the elderly. I really detest people like that."

"Would you like to take a shot at Redwing? She's giving a séance tomorrow afternoon. You'd have to be prescreened and approved. Would you be willing to call Mrs. Penworth? She's hosting the séance. I got my invitation through her daughter. It might be better if you called Penworth directly. Maybe you could tell her you'd like to contact your dead aunt?"

"Seriously?" His elbow jerked back, and his startled leg connected with the low coffee table. A delicate crystal vase skittered to the edge of the table

158

and hung there just over the wooden lip and above the unforgiving marble floor.

"I'm very serious," said Mallory. "If it wouldn't be too hard on you, it might help with the investigation."

"But why would you want me there?"

"I'd like to know if Redwing can tell me anything about your aunt that wouldn't be common knowledge."

"So you do think she's connected to the victims." One leg intended to cross the other, but a misinformed knee made contact first with the crystal vase. The vase moved over the edge of the table on one rolling foot. Mallory's hand shot out to catch it on its way to the floor. She set it back on the table in its original position.

"No. If there was a connection, we would have turned it up by now. I'm only collecting information wherever I can get it. There'll be four or five women there in your aunt's age bracket. She might have known some of them. I need a way to get your aunt's death on the same table with Pearl Whitman."

"Looking for common denominators? Very good. So you've passed yourself off as a bereaved survivor of Miss Whitman's?"

"No. I'm planning to raise Louis Markowitz from the dead. He was my father."

The vase fell to the floor and shattered into a hundred shards, all sharp as knives.

When Mallory pulled into the driveway, the old house fell far short of her imaginings after six weeks of neglect. The windows were all dark, and yet there was a lived-in look to the house and yard. There was nothing about the place to tell anyone how ruthlessly she had abandoned it. The grass had been recently

159

cut, and the walk and porch were swept. It was that time when leaves were falling, but none had landed in this yard without being raked up and disposed of. This had to be Robin Duffy's work. She looked over to the house next door.

It wouldn't be the first time this neighbor had mowed the lawn for Markowitz, who was sometimes so preoccupied with a single human hair found at a crime site that he didn't notice the grass growing in his own front yard. She wondered if Robin Duffy was also playing a game of make-believe. Did he curse Markowitz as he was mowing? Or did he break with custom this time?

Riker must have come through the back when he was last here. The police department seal was intact around the frame of the front door. She peeled away the tape and fit her old key into the lock.

If the yard had kept her illusions for her, the inside of the house told the truth. The door opened onto the smells of long-settled dust, stale air and the terrible empty silence of no one home. She flicked the wall switch, and the overhead light came on with a soft warm glow.

She stood by the love seat where Helen had done her mending in the evenings. The sewing basket was in its usual place. She had long ago come to terms with reminders of Helen. But she would not look at the overstuffed reclining chair where Markowitz had sat reading his paper every night save Tuesdays and Thursdays.

What must it have been like for him, being alone in this place? She knew she could never live here again. It had been hard enough after Helen's death.

She slowly gravitated to the kitchen, pulled along by memories of the only woman who had ever cared if her hair was combed and her nails were clean, if she had her milk money and a proper lunch to take to school. She remembered the kitchen as bigger. Perhaps she had always seen it through the eyes of the baby felon Markowitz had bagged.

'Whaddaya think you're doin', kid?' he had asked, sitting back on his heels staring at her through the low window of the Jaguar which belonged to some sucker.

'Bug off, old man, or I'll cut you,' she had said.

He had brought her back to this house that night. Four tons of paperwork at Juvenile Hall didn't fit with his plans for a birthday party, he told her. Helen's cake had been sitting in the back of his car. It had a lemon smell, and Markowitz smelled of cherry-blend pipe tobacco.

The child in handcuffs had driven Helen wild. Poor Markowitz could not get them off fast enough to please his wife. And then young Kathy had been engulfed in the plump arms of a gentle woman who smelled of laundry soap, cleaning fluid and scouring powder. Beyond Helen were the smells of steamed vegetables and pot roast. And that night, young Kathy had smelled crisp clean sheets being pulled up around her face, and the scent of talcum powder as Helen leaned down to kiss her good night.

Helen.

The house didn't smell like Helen anymore. There was dust over everything. Helen wouldn't have liked that.

Mallory climbed the stairs, heading toward the back bedroom Markowitz had used as a den. She passed by her own room, which contained all the furniture and belongings she had left behind. He had kept it the way she left it, against the day when she might want to come home again, she supposed. The doorframe had the last notch of her growing years.

161

The first notch was much closer to the floor. What a runt she had been at ten. How smug she had been at lying two more years onto her age.

Markowitz's den was disguised as the aftermath of a messy burglary, and she found nothing out of place. Riker had been careful to leave things as he found them. The bills were in the order of due dates, although a stranger would've assumed they had simply been dropped on the floor by the desk. His correspondence with the Old-time Radio Network lay on top of less important correspondence with the Internal Revenue Service. She picked up the metal wastebasket where he filed his credit card receipts and his canceled checks. Riker would have been through it, looking for a lead on BDA.

She began with the desk drawers, and an hour later, she had sifted down to the last drawer in a battered old filing cabinet to discover all her school report cards and her class photographs. She looked at the group shot from the private Manhattan day school which must have cost the old man a fortune in tuition. In that first photo, she was a standout, the only nonchild in a sea of innocence. The old man had been right; she never was a little girl.

She was downstairs again, turning out the lights and fishing in her pockets for the car keys, when she saw the pile of envelopes lying by the door under the mail slot. She leafed through the junk mail, almost passing over the flyer for the Brooklyn Dancing Academy.

BDA.

Riker said he'd been through every business listing in every telephone directory for all five boroughs. Was he holding out on her?

She walked over to the table holding the telephone and the phone books. She cradled the

162

heavy business directory in one arm, tearing the pages as she riffled through them. There was no commercial advertising for the Brooklyn Dancing Academy. She checked the white pages—no listing. Riker was off the hook; his teeth were safe.

She walked slowly to Markowitz's chair and sank into it. Her hands ran over the worn leather of the arms, and she pressed her head deep into its back cushion. She was picking up a scent which had not been obscured by the layers of dust. A tobacco pouch lay open on the small table at her right. One hand drifted down to the pipe rack and her fingers grazed the smooth worn bowls of wood. She picked up the pipe with the carved face, his favorite because she had stolen it for his birthday in those early days when she still called him Hey Cop. She held the pipe tight, her knuckles whitening as she closed her eyes, trying to imagine Markowitz in his young days.

Young Markowitz the dancing fool.

The stem of the pipe broke between her fingers. Startled, she looked down on the ruined thing. She slowly lifted the pieces of it and tried to match the jagged shards of the stem together, as though for a moment she believed she could undo the breakage and make it whole again.

Her hands dropped to her lap and the pieces of the pipe rolled out of her grasp and fell soundlessly to the rug. She began to rock slowly from side to side in a cradle motion dredged up from a time beyond her remembering, beyond the existence of hiding and running, stealing food and dodging flying broken bottles and the baby-flesh pimps. She rocked and rocked, deaf to the sound of the doorbell, to the loud banging on the door and the sounds of Robin Duffy turning his years ago-given key in the lock.

And for a time, she was deaf to the sounds of that little bulldog of a man with the frightened eyes who was shaking her by the shoulders and yelling, "Kathy! Kathy!"

A man with a knife appeared in every shadow of leaves playing on the window shade. Margot Siddon pulled the blanket up over her head in the child's conviction that blankets were protection from monsters. She had given up on sleep. She dialed Henry Cathery's number in the dark; her fingers were that practiced in this particular order of buttons. He was not happy at being awakened.

"What!" he said loudly in lieu of hello.

"Henry, it's me. Could you loan me twenty dollars?"

"Margot, are you crazy? You're rich. You've got at least a mil after taxes."

"Not yet I don't, and the apartment was sealed up by the police. I can't even get anything to pawn."

"Go to her bank in the morning. Make them give you an advance. I didn't even have to ask for my advance. The bank just sent me a draft of the repayment agreement." There was no goodbye before she heard the impersonal click of a broken connection.

She slammed the receiver to the cradle. What a weird bastard he was, or maybe, she thought, just maybe he was onto the rings she had copped from his grandmother's jewel box. He didn't live in Disneyland all the time. He had his moments of clarity, and she found those moments creepy as hell. It was like coming upon someone who had been walking in his sleep and now was awake to the nth degree, awake to the entire universe, plugged in, turned on. And in those moments, he had wired up

164

to her brain and shocked it clean of memory for days at a time, nights in succession without bad dreams. He was the only one she knew who would talk to her about the man with the knife.

She didn't recall one personal conversation with old Cousin Samantha in all the years she'd sucked up to the woman.

At first, she'd been taken to Samantha's apartment as a child. Then later, after her mother remarried and disappeared, she had gone alone. Old Samantha had been good for fifty bucks at a touch, but at the great cost of hours of monotony.

Her mother had once talked about Samantha in the days when the old woman was young and beautiful. It was hard for Margot to imagine that old bag of bones with her hump and her trembles as a beauty. When Margot was little, the old woman had called the whole world *darling,* without regard to gender, or to animate or inanimate qualities. Margot was darling and so was the bow in her hair, and each had carried the same weight in the old woman's babbling affectations and affections. Over the years Cousin Samantha's babble had become shrill, reaching, at the last, the pitch of a scream of fear.

After the man with the knife had done his work on Margot, the old woman had come to the hospital to visit her, but only the one time. Samantha had begged Margot to cover her face, to hide the scar, it was so upsetting. Then, fear filled them both, and every night. It was their only commonality after the rape. One woke up screaming with the fear of being alone. And twenty blocks south, the other woke with visions of the knife dancing up to her eyes and then down to her cheek, severing the nerve that had previously allowed her to smile on that side of her

165

face.

She stared at the wall until it lightened with the dawn, and then she scooped clothes up from the pile on the floor which was nearest the bed. As she dressed, she missed the match of buttons on her vest and never noticed. There was no food in the house. She would go shopping at the supermarket when they gave her the advance money. She would ask for all of it in cash, small bills. She would buy the whole world and meat, red meat, and a jelly roll.

Chapter Six

The banker wished he had an office with a door he could close. The unpartitioned interior of the bank had all the privacy and the proportions of two stacked ballrooms. The expansive balcony where his desk was situated was entirely too public today. People were staring at the oddly dressed young woman seated opposite him. She had a disconcerting smirk on her face, and on one cheek was the crescent moon of a fading scar. Her clothes were dirty, and she was nodding off in her chair and catching herself awake.

"Miss Siddon," said the bank officer, "I have to wait on the executor's instructions before releasing any funds. There's no way around that. And as to the advance, you haven't been able to answer a single personal question about your cousin. If you can't even give me her middle name—"

"We didn't talk much."

"Perhaps if you spoke with her law firm."

"They keep saying they'll get back to me. But no one ever calls."

166

"Have your own attorney look into it."

"I don't have one, and you know it. Look, I need money, and I need it today. What good does a million dollars do me if I starve to death, huh? Can you answer me that?"

It had to be a scam, he knew, and not very original. He'd heard similar requests. This…person must be an avid reader of obituaries. But how embarrassing if she did turn out to be the heir to the Siddon trust. One couldn't be too careful. "Do you have some form of identification? A driver's license?"

"I don't drive."

"What sort of identification do you use when you write checks to merchants?"

"I don't write checks. I don't have a damn checking account."

Now that had to be a lie. He knew for a fact that everyone on the planet had a checking account. "I can hardly give you money if you can't properly identify yourself. You can see that."

And yes, she could see that apparently, for she was rising out of the chair, dragging her body up to a stand. The long dress hung on her bones. The floppy brocade vest could not hide the thinness of her arms and face. Did she never eat? he wondered.

She was moving slowly toward the grand staircase leading down to the main floor. It had crossed his mind to give the creature some change from his own pocket, but he had thought better of it. Such a gesture might have led to a scene.

While he watched Margot Siddon's slow progress down the wide steps, he had a few spare minutes to remember he had once played lead guitar in a sixties rock band. In his wife of twenty-five years, he could find traces of the hippy girl who had sung with the

167

band and starved with the band. But who was this unmusical man who had just given the bum's rush to a woman who was certainly hungry?

He toyed with a paper clip as Margot Siddon turned at the base of the marble steps and moved, unsteady, across the wide expanse of gilded, wasted space, heading for the door. When she slipped and fell to the marble floor, he dropped his paper clip and dropped his eyes.

*   *   *

Riker kept a good distance from the glass wall of the office. He checked the exits for a fast retreat should Commissioner Beale look his way and call him in to be shot alongside Coffey. The gray little man was waving a newspaper in Coffey's face. Riker knew the headline by heart: "Invisible Man Eludes NYPD."

When the case was eight weeks old, when Markowitz was only dead forty-eight hours, it was Chief of Detectives Blakely who had told Beale the case might break at any moment. Six weeks had gone by and now Blakely rested his flabby haunch on the desk, smoked his cigar and left Coffey to fend for himself.

Coffey was standing and looking down on Beale. Riker could have told him that Blakely's was the best position. Sitting on his ass, Blakely didn't tower over the commissioner. Coffey was entirely too tall to be a good political animal in Beale's regime. And no one had taught Coffey the ingratiating smile, the prelude to bending over and begging to be kicked. The man just stood there, rock solid, and in that moment, Riker came near to liking him.

Two uniformed officers joined Riker by the watercooler, feigning thirst and watching the show.

Maybe it was time to show support for Coffey, to take his side against the commissioner. Yeah, it was time. Riker pulled out his wallet and said to the uniformed officers, "I got five dollars says Coffey's still standing when the commissioner leaves."

Margot Siddon plucked a paper cup from a trash can and held it up to a man with a tear in his sweatshirt who clinked in a dime and a quarter. Twenty minutes later, she was pushing change through a slot and asking a clerk for a subway token. She fell asleep on the train and missed her stop.

After a fifteen-block walk from the subway to her apartment, she stood outside her door with the sick realization that she had no keys. They must have rolled out of her pocket when she slid to the floor of the bank's lobby. She banged on the door of the empty apartment, crying against the wood, sinking to the hallway tiles. Her birth certificate was in there, somewhere in that pile of rubbish, and she could not get at it. She kicked the door with all the strength she had left.

Wait. The mailbox.

Her mail would identify her by name and address. But her box key was on the same lost ring with her apartment key. She pulled a switchblade knife from her pocket and danced down the steps to the mailboxes. She pried the box open, and pulled out one piece of junk mail and a utility bill.

Mallory squinted. Strong morning light poured through the long bank of tall windows, illuminating each cigarette burn on the red velvet couch. At each end of the couch sat unacquainted women who were well past a certain age, yet both sported rouge and lipstick to do a fire engine proud. An old man stood at the receptionist's desk slowly counting out dollar bills pulled from a plastic money clip which bore a dry cleaner's logo. The receptionist nodded, rippling four chins each time a dollar was plumped down on the desk in front of her.

The courtly Mr. Esteban was bending low to insert a videotape into the VCR. Mallory stared at a gray quarter inch on each side of the part in his hair, all that was not dulled with black dye.

"We tape all the students," he was saying, "every two weeks, so they can see their improvement. Usually we erase them, but not this one. No, this one is a keeper. He was a wonderful dancer, a natural." Hunched over the machine and with his nose an inch from the screen, Mr. Esteban watched the test numbers flash by on the monitor in advance of the film. "One moment and you will see."

And she did see. There was gray-haired, overweight Markowitz and a slender young dancing partner some distance from the camera. The young woman in the red dress and dancing slippers was her own age or younger, familiar and not. As the oddly matched couple danced closer to the camera, Mallory sucked in her breath.

It was Helen Markowitz.

Helen was no longer pudgy and homey, no matron in this incarnation. She was three decades younger, an impossible teenage Helen with spiked hair and a ring in her nose.

Well, why not, thought Mallory, sinking down to a tattered red velvet chair. This had been a week for ghosts.

Rabbi Kaplan had told the truth. Markowitz was a wonderful dancer, lifting his partner high in the air

170

to the music of Chuck Berry, spinning her out and twirling her back to his side. He was rocking and rolling. Illusion created of grace and fluid motion stole the years away until it was a young Louis dancing with the teenage Helen.

"What's the girl's name?"

"Brenda Mancusi."

"Where is she?"

"She doesn't work here anymore. She never came back after we heard the news about our Mr. Markowitz."

"I need her phone number, her address and a copy of that tape."

He hadn't expected to see her again, yet here she was, holding two envelopes in her grimy fist, thrusting them into his face, screaming, "Look, look!"

He took the envelopes gingerly in two fingers, wondering if lice might be transferred in this manner, and loathing himself for wondering. He nodded as he read the name appearing on the utility bill.

"This only tells me that you and Samantha Siddon have the same last name."

"I want my—"

"I did try to contact her attorney after you left the bank. He's in Europe. There's no number where he can be reached. His partner has agreed to look into the matter and get back to me."

"Sure. That bastard probably left town with all my money."

"I can assure you the money is safe in Mrs. Siddon's accounts. But those accounts will remain frozen until the bank receives instructions from the executor. And then, we'll need a picture ID. A passport or a—"

"I need money, you son of a bitch. You know what I got in my pockets? This!"

She pulled her deep vest pockets inside out. Lint-coated pennies and nickels spilled over his desk, followed by a slow-rolling moist wad of tissue, and last, the knife came tumbling out and landed in the center of his blotter. It was a switchblade.

She hadn't threatened him. He did realize it had only fallen out with the other contents of her pockets, the tissue and the coins. But a knife. Perhaps it had simply jarred him to see a knife in a bank, a weapon of any kind. Perhaps that was why he had pressed the silent alarm. He wasn't certain.

Now they both stared down at the knife as two paunchy gray-haired security guards were charging up the stairs from the lobby, their faces going red with the unaccustomed exertion.

His eyes and hers locked together in mutual disbelief.

She grabbed up the knife in one hand and ran down the stairs, passing between the old men, who reached out simultaneously and grasped the air she had passed through. They turned to follow after her as she ran the length of the lobby. The guards were so slow she had time to stumble, to collide with a patron, to burst into angry tears and beat them to the door.

"No," said Mallory. "She's only expecting me. It would've queered the deal if Redwing ran a background check on you. I'm passing you off as a friend of the family."

"Not a good idea," said Edith Candle. "It's truth, bits and pieces of truth, that makes any scam work. An outright lie will work against you. If this

172

woman's any good at all, she'll know."

"We're doing it my way."

The door was opened by a woman in a black dress and a crisp white apron. Mallory gave her name and they were ushered into the foyer. Floating on a rich sea of mingled perfumes were the sounds of teacups clinking in saucers and a gentle Chopin étude. The maid turned and hurried into the large room which opened off this small holding pen for suspicious callers. From the foyer, Mallory could hear voices: melodious laughter and high, twittering speech. The far wall was a bank of sun-bright windows. Riding below the perfume was the unaired smell of an invalid's room.

The maid was raising a sash to the noises of the street. And by that cacophony of noise, Mallory knew this could not be a parkside window. A driver was leaning on his car horn, something which was not done in the square by tacit agreement of every living and rolling thing that passed through. And on a near street, a siren careened down the block. It must have been stopped in traffic, because now the siren switched to the bleating mode, whining to get this show on the road. And inside the apartment, the old women gathered like birds on a fence, tensely perched on the furniture while the table was being set up and chairs were brought in. Women with hennaed hair chatted with blue-haired women, and all about the room was the air of things to come.

A matron in her early seventies was walking toward the foyer, smiling, her neck choked in pearls. Her head was disproportionately small, a white-haired marble atop a thick-waisted hourglass.

"Miss Mallory? I'm Fabia Penworth, Marion's mother. I'm so glad you could come, my dear. Oh, but who is this?" She stared down at Edith Candle,

173

and then back to Mallory. "This won't do. You were supposed to come alone, dear. Redwing never sees anyone without advance notice." She leaned closer and said in a stage whisper, "I've told her all about your father and his unfortunate death. She says the easiest spirit to reach is one who dies by violence. They want to contact us, they want truth to out." She suddenly remembered the annoying detail of Edith. "But this won't do."

Mallory said, "This is an old friend—"

"How do you do," said Edith, stepping forward. "I'm Edith Candle. Perhaps Miss Whitman or Mrs. Gaynor mentioned me to you. I believe you all used the same broker at one time or another."

"Why, of course. Oh, how do you do." The woman was showing all of her expensive bridgework to Edith. "Well, I'm honored, really honored. I never expected this. I don't see any problem at all, really. I'm sure Redwing will be delighted to meet you, someone of your stature in the spiritual community."

After being led into the main room and introduced to the medium, Mallory couldn't tell if Redwing was delighted or not. The medium's large, padded armchair had taken on the aspect of a throne. Imperial Redwing was dressed in Day-Glo colors, her head wound with a scarf of Indian pattern. The jewelry must weigh ten pounds, by Mallory's rapid estimate, all bangle bracelets and golden chains. Her feet were encased in tiny gold lamé sandals with delicate straps. Her eyes squinted into slits as one plump hand rose in the air to the level of Edith Candle's lips, as though she expected it to be kissed. Redwing did not rise for the older woman.

Edith took Redwing's proffered hand in her own

174

arthritic one. Mallory detected a wince of pain. Perhaps any pressure on Edith's inflamed joints might cause that, perhaps not. And now Redwing's eyes were open wide, too sharp, too bright.

The boy standing behind the armchair must belong to Redwing. Mallory assessed the genes of all races, rejumbled in this new combination: The child's eyes were yellow, the skin was golden brown and the hair somewhat kinky. The facial features were Caucasian. Though the eyes slanted up, the Asian folds were missing in this new translation of chromosomes. The boy's expression was dulled. Had he been drugged?

When the introductions were done and Redwing turned away, ending the audience, Mallory pulled Edith Candle to the only unpopulated corner of the room.

"You never told me you knew Estelle Gaynor."

"You never asked. At my age it's not unusual to know several dead people.

"Several murdered people?"

And what about Samantha Siddon? Had the fourth victim also been on nodding acquaintance with dead people before joining their company?

The doorbell chimed with light musical notes. Jonathan Gaynor was admitted. After a brief handshake with the enthroned Redwing, he allowed his introduction to be made to Mallory as though they had never met. He winked at her as his hostess led him off to another part of the room. Another white-haired woman with a survivor's eye for dangerous moving objects stepped out of his way when the sharp angles of his jutting elbows came perilously close to her.

As long as he was sitting down and not colliding with anyone, not tripping on anything, Mallory

175

thought he fit in well with the old women who fawned over him and fed him nourishing sugar cookies. He touched the wrinkled, dry hand of an octogenarian to make some point with tactile emphasis, and the woman came all undone. Mallory reevaluated her opinion on the death of sex after forty.

Her attention turned to a tall, thin woman who had joined them on the couch. The lean body was created for designer dresses. The expensive razor cut of her short white hair framed a fine bone structure beneath the webs of wrinkles. The woman was saying to Edith, "Oh yes, we knew Samantha Siddon quite well. She never missed a séance after the second murder. She said it was life on the edge, and she hadn't been to the edge for more than fifty years, and then it was only for a moment."

Mallory accepted a delicate teacup from the maid and turned back to the woman with the mannequin frame. "Ma'am?"

"Yes, dear?"

"Aren't you afraid? Three murders so close to home. Those women—"

"Oh no, dear, not at all. Now take Pearl Whitman, she wasn't killed in the square. Oh, but it was the same lunatic, wasn't it? Of course it was. You know, what frightened Pearl most wasn't death. It was the prospect of invalidism, lying in a hospital bed for years, waiting to die or waiting for someone to visit, always being disappointed, always waiting."

"Miss Whitman attended the séances, too?"

"She was a charter member. She thought murder made the whole thing more exciting."

"And Estelle Gaynor?"

"She hosted the very first one."

"No, dear," said a voice behind Mallory's chair.

176

"Anne hosted the first one."

Mallory looked up into the bright eyes of a blue-haired woman with a perfectly round face.

"Anne?"

"Anne Cathery, the woman who died in the park," said the moonfaced woman.

"You're both aware of the connection?"

"The murders and the séances? Of course we're aware. All of us." The wave of her hand included the entire room. "What's left of us. How could you fail to notice a thing like that? I swear, you young people must think we were all born with liver spots and Alzheimer's."

The mannequin leaned toward Mallory and said, more kindly, "It's all right, dear. You're supposed to take old women for doddering fools. You're young, that's your job. I certainly don't mind. I find it gives me an edge in all my dealings with your generation."

The round-faced woman winked at the mannequin. "Like that young financier you took for a ride last year?"

"Netted me a million in profit, April dear." She looked back to Mallory. "The young man assumed my position on the board of directors was some honorary title for the widow of the majority stockholder. But you seem more interested in murder than money. That speaks well of you."

"So you're not afraid."

"Of dying? I'd have to think on that, dear. Most days I'd have to say yes. But then, there are those days, you know? No, of course you don't. You're a child. You don't know the joys of incontinence and flatulence. I don't think Samantha Siddon much cared if she lived another year. She had lived too long, she thought, surviving her own children. Now there's a crime of crimes."

"Didn't she have a cousin?"

"Margot. Strange child. I don't think she cared for Margot very much. She used to brag on the child's visits every week, but I don't know that she enjoyed them. No, Samantha probably didn't mind dying."

"But a death like that—"

"There's an excitement to a quick ending," said the mannequin. "It's a momentous thing, death. But you wouldn't know that." She rested one paper-light hand on Mallory's. "You think you're immortal, don't you, dear? Of course you do."

The moon-faced woman sat down and well back in the couch cushions. Her plump feet did not quite touch the floor. "Well, anyway, the séances certainly made Samantha's last days more exciting. It was almost like a lottery. Or perhaps you'd prefer the more clichéd analogy of a Bingo game. Ah, the Bingo parlor, God's little waiting room for the blue-hair set." The woman sighed. "And now it's another month to wait for the next one."

"The next séance?" asked Mallory.

"No, dear," said the mannequin. "The séance is once a week. She's talking murder. They're usually four weeks apart."

"Did anyone mention the séance connection to the police?"

"Oh, worst possible idea. Redwing wouldn't like it. It might cause a rupture in her karma. Artists are so fragile. You're not going to rat us out, are you dear?"

Markowitz had taught her to scout the terrain. And now she was immersed in the land of canes and cataracts, blue hair and support hose, conspiracy and murder.

A bell tinkled in the hand of the maid.

178

The illusion of bird women stayed with Mallory as, from different points about the room, they rose in a flock and settled back to earth around the table with its white cloth, with whispers in the shush of material, creaks and shuffles of chairs, settling down and settling in. Mallory sat between Jonathan Gaynor and a woman with a bobbing head. Edith sat between this woman and their hostess. Redwing grasped the hands on either side of her, and the rest of the assembly followed suit in joining hands.

A dish with a black unlit candle sat at the center of the table beside a brightly painted statuette of a Madonna and Child. Piled in front of Redwing was a collection of objects. Markowitz's pocket watch was there, gleaming among other items—the rings with bright gems, a key, a ribbon-tied lock of gold hair so fine it must have belonged to a small child.

Heavy drapes were being drawn across the sunlit windows by the maid. As the room grew dark, the candle at the center of the table came to life, of its own accord, to provide all the light there was. And with that light came the sweet odor of incense, which thickened and overpowered the perfumes of the women. A trick of the wavering candle flame made the tiny Madonna statuette move in a flickering dance.

Redwing closed her eyes, and her head rolled against the back of the wing chair. "Our Father Who art in heaven," she said, and the gathering closed their eyes, all save Mallory, and repeated the words after her, all save Mallory.

Our Father Who art in heaven,

Mallory only moved her mouth in the little heresy of the handicapped make-believer with severe limitations which stopped short of buying heaven.

Hallowed be Thy name.

179

And it was only hour by hour that she kept at bay the realization that Markowitz was in that hole in the ground and feeding the worms.

Thy kingdom come, Thy will be done

The worms crawl in, the worms crawl out.

On earth, as it is in heaven.

Dust to dust, ashes to ashes, dead was dead, and a stiff was a stiff. All alone in the cold ground. Markowitz.

Forgive us our trespasses as we forgive those who trespass against us.

Never.

The boy stole up behind Redwing's chair and stood there with less life to him than the wavering statuette. Mallory was planning his incarceration in Juvenile Hall as quickly as she confirmed all the signs of a drugged child. It had always made her a little crazy to see someone strike a child, and this was worse. It called up some gray area of earliest memory which just as quickly slid away from her like a dream lost and beyond recalling. Not that she tried, for every good instinct said, 'Let it go.'

The gramophone began to play. The music was classical, melding into twenties tunes, and then to old fifties-style rock 'n' roll. Mallory lifted her chin only slightly in recognition of an album from Markowitz's basement collection.

Redwing plunged her hand into the pile of objects at the center of the table and pulled out Markowitz's watch. The music stopped.

Redwing held the pocket watch by its chain, and her eyes closed as the watch dropped lower and lower, finally lying flat on the table. The gold chain drifted from her splayed fingers. Redwing's eyes were rolling back in the sockets. Her hands pressed flat on the tablecloth. She began to rock slowly,

180

gently at first, and then faster and faster, jerking violently now and shuddering into a spasm. She jolted the table, and her chair rocked on its four legs, beating out a staccato rhythm. Suddenly, the rocking stopped, her body became rigid, leaning far back in the chair. She pressed her head into the upholstery and lowered her face until it made three chins below her open mouth.

Her face lifted and her eyes fixed on Mallory. She gathered up the flesh of her face into Markowitz's smile. The eyes all but disappeared in the merry slits melding into laugh lines at the outer edges.

Everyone else at the table was smiling. Markowitz had that effect on people. Only Mallory did not smile.

"Hey, kid, how're you doing?" said the voice of Markowitz, in his low octaves and Brooklyn accent.

Mallory and Markowitz stared at one another across the table.

"Don't call me kid," she said.

Markowitz laughed, and would not stop laughing. The table began to move, shuddering under Mallory's hands. She felt lightly drunk with the sound of his laughter.

The boy behind the armchair stepped out to the side in plain view. She watched the child going into a trance of his own. The table rocked, though Redwing's hands were splayed flat and the boy was not touching the table. The music had started again. Buddy Holly was singing about love and the roller coaster. The music couldn't be coming from the gramophone. The turntable wasn't moving, yet it came from that direction.

Markowitz stopped laughing. His smile was wide and easy now, his eyes locked with hers. "Was there something you wanted to tell me,

Kathy?...No?...Well, maybe there was something you wanted to ask?"

"Who knows what evil lurks..." she began in a small version of her own voice, which trailed off to no voice at all.

"The Shadow knows," said Markowitz.

Beside the chair, the boy's mouth moved in silent concert with the words. His thin body rocked back and forth. Markowitz began to laugh again, and the boy laughed in silent tandem, eyes closed, swaying to the music, laughing, paunching out his belly.

Everyone at the table had their hands flat on the cloth. The table continued to rock. It skittered inches left and then right. Mallory could feel the energy coming up through her palms. Her body tensed, Markowitz laughed on as her heart beat on the wall of her chest, and the table rocked with a violence, all but upending itself, energy building like the makings of a ticking bomb, blood icing, mind racing. The laughter was louder now.

The boy was no longer miming the mirth, his eyes were full of sheer terror. He was holding up his arms, fending off unseen blows, screaming in silence as the laughter rolled on. He clutched his gut in the place where Markowitz had been stabbed. The statuette rocked back and forth until it tumbled over. The small plaster head broke off from the body and rolled across the tablecloth to Mallory's hand.

She wasn't conscious of rising from the table. Consciousness surfaced as she was crossing the thick carpet of the front room, waking from a dream, heading for the door and away. Behind her, Markowitz was screaming, screaming.

The women were a chorus of twitterings and whispers. Almost at the door now. And back there, furniture was sliding across the floor away from the

182

table. She passed through the door and into the hallway as Markowitz's wailing diminished into groans. She walked quickly down the hall, seeing only the iron grille of the elevator door before her, thinking of nothing but being away and gone.

The footsteps behind her belonged to Edith Candle, who was running to catch up with her. Silently, they both passed into the elevator. The ornate iron box carried them down and down, falling, caged behind the ironwork. For three floors of deep shadow and bright light, in and out of the dark they fell, and finally, to earth.

Henry Cathery stood by the wide window of his bedroom and watched her leave the building with the old woman. She was so pretty. He had stood at the window for a long time, waiting for her to come out again, not moving from this spot, though he ached to use the toilet.

She hadn't kept him company today, either. He had to take his opportunities where he could find them. Now he was ready for her. He lined her up in the telescopic site and shot her over and over, framing her in the camera lens, her pretty face in an unsettling pain. Another shot clicked off as she walked out of the square to the place where she had parked the little tan car that smelled of her. She and the old woman disappeared into the car and it rolled out of sight. He remained at the window, staring down on the park, the ultimate game board.

The police error had been the oversight of ungifted chess players. The idiots would continue to plod on in their routine way, unimaginative players drawing only on past experience, incapable of the leap of logic, the only move that would get them to endgame.

In the coffee shop off Gramercy Park, Edith signaled the waitress for another cup of tea, and Mallory watched the door over the rim of her coffee mug. Forty minutes had passed before Jonathan Gaynor walked in and joined them at the table. He put the pocket watch down by her plate, which held an untouched croissant. She stared at the watch and wondered where her mind had gone without her. How could she have left it behind?

"Are you okay?" His voice was all concern as he eased his lanky frame into the booth beside Edith.

Mallory forgot to cut him dead, to wither him, to explain to him, with only her eyes, that he was a fool if he thought they were going to share a warm moment. She was off her stride, and rattled enough to let the kindness slide. She felt like a fool, getting suckered by Redwing. It must be showing, because Gaynor was really pushing his luck, all sympathy and commiseration in his eyes, smiling at her with an easy grin that belonged to a shy boy in a Kansas wheat field.

She smiled back and startled herself. Her smile was almost natural, nearly spontaneous.

"You shouldn't have given her something real to work with," he said.

"Well, she had to," said Edith. "Redwing would have spotted a ringer. She is talented, you know."

"The hell with talent," said Mallory. "Redwing runs her marks through an information network. The story had to check out in the computer system, so I gave her Markowitz."

"That was risky," he said. "So she also knows you're a policewoman."

184

Mallory nodded.

"It was really Markowitz you saw in Redwing, wasn't it?" Edith asked.

"A first-rate imitation, I'll give her that."

"It would be a grave mistake to underestimate her gift," said Edith.

Gaynor smiled at Edith. "Apparently you were more impressed with the show."

"Very stylish," said Edith, "Nothing tacky or flamboyant." For the third time, she signaled to the waitress with her raised teacup and hopeful eyes. The young woman in the food-spotted white uniform hurried by, eyes seeing nothing but the clock on the wall. Edith's cup settled back to the table. Hope died.

Mallory caught the waitress's eye and arrested it. Her expression gave only the suggestion of violence. A moment later, the waitress could not get more tea into Edith's cup in a big enough hurry. The young woman left the pot on the table in her haste to be anywhere that Mallory was not.

"You two missed the best part," said Gaynor. "That card table rose straight up off the floor, maybe two feet in the air." His gesturing hand swept the sugar container off the table. "It scared the life out of me." He leaned down to retrieve the container. When he set it back on the table, the pepper shaker was sent to Edith's lap. "Sorry. I wish I knew how she did it. The little boy was in plain sight a good three feet away, and Redwing's hands were flat on the table."

"That one's easy," said Mallory. "When she put her hands on the table, I saw the rings digging into her fingers. Then I saw the two ripples in the tablecloth where her rings had hooked the pins under the material. All she had to do was lift."

185

"Oh," he said, and there was some disappointment in this syllable, as though he had only lately made the discovery of Peter Pan's wires. "But there was more. Tell me, were any of the murdered women stabbed in the breast?"

"Why do you ask?"

"When she contacted my dead aunt, the boy put his hand to the right breast. He cupped his hand, like this. No doubt there was a breast there, and then it was all bloody, stabbed or slashed open."

Mallory lifted her shoulders to say 'Who knows?' and then looked around for their waitress in time to see the white flash of the uniform disappearing through the ladies' room door, which banged against the frame to say, 'Fat chance she's coming out again anytime soon.'

On the sidewalk outside the café, Edith and Mallory parted company with Gaynor. After Mallory had driven Edith Candle home and seen her to the door of 3B, she stopped the elevator at the second floor. She had two hours to kill before her last appointment of the evening.

The door was unlocked. Was Charles picking up bad habits from Edith? In the reaction time of a good New Yorker, her gun cleared the holster with speed enough to fool the eye into thinking it had simply appeared in her right hand. Gun raised, she pushed open the door. All the light came from one of the back rooms. Silently, she made her way down the hall to the back office. A cat would have made more noise with its footfalls.

Charles was sitting in a warm pool of light which spread outward from the stained-glass lamp on his desk. He was completely absorbed in the journal on his blotter, with no idea that she was in the office or in the world. She envied him his perfect

186

concentration. It was only a little unsettling to watch him reading at the speed of light.

Her gun returned to the shoulder holster as she stole back to the front room, not wanting to disturb him. There was just a little comfort in knowing he was there. Markowitz had said to go to Charles if she needed help, not if she wanted to use him and his connections. The old man would never have wanted her to drag him into this.

She sat down on the couch. It was not the typically uncomfortable antique, but well padded and more like the furniture in the Brooklyn house. It was friendly in its response to her, plumping up around the slender outline of her body. She would have liked to stop here, to not move again. This night would not be over for a long time yet, and she was already flagging, eyes closing.

However she turned the thing over, she could not see what Markowitz had seen. Logic told her Coffey was right, and Markowitz had been caught out without a clue in hell as to who the perp was. But she continued to believe in Markowitz in the same way he had taught her to believe in the Shadow. Never mind logic. It only worked half the time, anyway. Her eyes closed.

She snapped awake when the couch rearranged its stuffing to accommodate another sitter. Charles was smiling at her. He had such a wonderfully loony smile. But now, his face was slowly changing to worry lines. What was he reading in her own face? she wondered. What had she given away to tell him something was wrong? Was there really any point in holding out on him? Could she? No, probably not.

"I gather the séance wasn't much of a success."

So Edith had told him they were going to Gramercy. And what else did he know? He could

187

extrapolate volumes from near nothing.

"No, it wasn't. But I did have a nice chat with Markowitz."

Oh, she could see he didn't like that, not at all. There was more than worry in his eyes, but she could not account for it. Was he angry with her? Why?

"How did the medium know about you and Markowitz?" he asked.

His voice was very gentle. So she was not the one who angered him. Who then? Edith?

"I told her."

"That may have been a bad mistake. Did you tell Edith you were going to use Louis?"

"Yeah. I didn't have any choice. Gaynor thought it was a mistake too." If Charles was her barometer, then Markowitz the dancing fool must be rocking and rolling in his grave. She was getting too messy, too noisy, telegraphing every damn move.

"Tell me what happened."

His hand was covering hers with the human warmth that Markowitz's last letter had promised. It had been so long since she'd been touched this way, she nearly didn't recognize the sensation. 'Go to him if you need help,' said the Markowitz who lived inside her head with Helen, abiding in a detailed replica of the house in Brooklyn in the days when it gleamed with polish and smelled of canned pine trees.

She described the séance in every detail, the compulsive detail of habit. She only left out the part where she had been suckered into believing that it was Markowitz simply because Redwing had looked and talked and acted like him, because Mallory had been one beat away from taking the chance to settle old business and say goodbye, and she had blown it.

And hadn't that been the worst of it? Her eyes were open now. She had lost all the threads to make-believing, and never would she get them back. She had seen the wires behind the works.

"Charles, how could she do him so well? She knew about the wounds. Nothing that specific was in the papers."

"That computer of yours has you blindsided. With more field experience, you might have realized that quite a bit of data can be had through human networks. How many police officers were at the crime site, how many civilians, how many have wives, brothers-in-law, sisters, mothers, and who do those people talk to? If it all hangs on Markowitz's wounds, you have nothing. As to the impersonation, we've all seen Markowitz on television. He was on for days during the Senate hearings. He signed two autographs one night when we were having dinner in Chinatown."

"And the boy imitating the slashed breast?"

"The boy was imitating a woman. He made a breast. Gaynor could hardly have seen it slashed. But that's not his fault. The more people you gather into one room, the more energy there is, and mass psychosis is more possible. You can be convinced you saw all sorts of things that never happened."

"All those old women knew about the link to the séance, and not one of them thought to call the cops. How do you figure that?"

"Well, as the woman said, it's miles more exciting than waiting to die in your sleep. You don't take anything at face value, do you?"

No, she did not. "Maybe something else frightened them more than the killer did."

"Fear of the police, for instance? You think these women are a gang of geriatric criminals?"

Well, Charles had one geriatric criminal in the family, didn't he? Edith did say you could get away with a lot when you were old. But that subject was forbidden.

"Maybe Redwing has some hold on them. She's good, Charles. You should have been there. And the Markowitz imitation was Just too damn good. It took Markowitz an hour to die. Maybe Redwing had time to get to know him then."

"An incomplete portrait would have sufficed. Your memories of Louis filled in whatever she missed. You did most of the work for her. Mediums depend on that. I've watched the best of them work. They put out half a general sentence, and the client fills in the blanks. Then the medium builds on the volunteered data. It's an art form. They're also guided by subtle nuances of facial expressions. Don't underestimate the power of an observant empathic to rip your mind inside out."

"I know she's mixed up in this."

"Perhaps, but I don't think she makes a good suspect. All the victims being tied to the séances doesn't make for a very smart set of murders. I believe Louis did say the killer was smart."

"Maybe she's so smart she'd figure it that way— like a double blind."

"No, too convoluted. She may be gifted, but there's no correlation between a gift and IQ points. Redwing intuits everything."

"What about Edith? How did she know her husband was going to die that particular night? Coincidence?"

Charles sat up straighter. His eyes wandered off to the side where he was looking at something in a memory. He turned back to her. "Edith predicted the date? Is that what she told you?" His hand withdrew

190

its covering warmth. "Well then, you probably know more about the particulars than I do."

"She didn't make it up, Charles. I researched it in the periodicals section of the library. She knew the night he was going to die. She knew it days in advance. The neighbors confirmed it."

"It could easily be a coincidence that she guessed the night. It was a very dangerous trick. Death was always possible. He didn't drop down through a trapdoor in the stage, you know. He went into a tank of water, chained with iron and tied with rope. On the first night, the trick worked as it was supposed to. I went with my parents that night. I saw him struggling with the locks underwater, then working his way out of the ropes in full view of the audience. There was a large time clock onstage, set to go off at the limit of human endurance. The clock went off with an earsplitting ring. And Max wasn't free yet. He hadn't managed to undo the last coil of rope in time, and for a while, he hung there in the water like a drowned man, and all the while the clock's alarm was screaming and the audience was screaming. Then suddenly, he burst out of the ropes and pushed off against the bottom of the tank and erupted into the air. It was an amazing stunt. It took all his concentration to slow his heart and his respiratory system while he worked the locks of the chains. One slip of the mind and there you go."

"Were you scared when you thought he'd drowned?"

"Oh, no. I'd seen Max die a hundred times. Part of the fascination with dangerous stunts is that the audience believes the performer might die. Max gave them their money's worth. He died every time. I didn't see him die the last time. My parents went without me that night."

191

"And that night, the night he really died, that was the last time Edith ever left the house?"

"What?"

"She was there. You didn't know?"

"No, I didn't. She told you that?"

"No, she never mentioned it. I found her picture in the old newspaper archives."

She noticed a disturbing distraction in his eyes, but only for a moment.

"You think it's time to let me help you now?" He smiled at her. "I do understand why you have to do this. I don't like it. I worry about you. But I do understand. You don't have to do this alone anymore."

"You think I'm making a mess of this, don't you? Maybe I'm not as smart as Markowitz—"

"I'm an expert in that area. Your intelligence isn't in question. However, you might want to give some thought to the way you use it. Your strong point is gathering and analyzing data. True, you're a great shot, but that's called marksmanship. It doesn't put you in the same club with a street cop who shoots on the run. Do what you do best. Work the data, and leave the surveillance and the undercover work to the department."

"The department? Coffey thinks Markowitz botched it. He thinks the old man was sucker punched. I can't let go of the idea that Markowitz worked the whole thing out. He had to be following the suspect."

"Louis is dead. If you try to do this his way, you'll die too. You can see the logic in that. Follow his steps and you fall in the same hole. You don't know who he was following that day. You found a link to the suspects. Maybe he found another one. Who knows?"

"The Shadow knows."

"Pardon? We're not talking about *the* Shadow? The old radio—"

"It was Markowitz's all-time favorite."

"My parents loved that program."

"All right, I'm going back to collecting data. Will you do me a favor?"

"You hardly needed to ask."

"I need you to cozy up to Henry Cathery. He plays chess in the park seven days a week. Get him into a game."

"If you like, but why?"

"Because you play chess and I don't."

"No, I meant why me? I'm hardly cut out for undercover work."

"And that's why you're so perfect. Who would suspect you? Cathery's smart. He'd see through me in a minute. You're smarter."

"How did he make it to the top of your list so suddenly? I thought he was ruled out. The papers said he had an alibi."

"Never believe what you read in the papers. He's not at the top of the list, but he's pretty damn close. He's in the park every day for hours at a time. People are so used to seeing him there, they just don't see him anymore. He's a fixture, like one of the shrubs or the benches. He was probably in the park while his grandmother was being murdered."

"Well, I'm sure my key to the park wouldn't work anymore. You want me to rattle the gates and ask if he'll invite me in? You don't think he might suspect I've come to interview him?"

"Whoa. Back up. What key?"

"I have one of the original keys. It's an antique. I'll show you."

He left the office, and a moment later, she could

hear him working his key in the door across the hall. He returned to her with a velvet jeweler's box in one hand. He opened it to display a gleaming golden key nested in black satin.

"The first keys, from the last century, were all made of gold. My cousin Max gave me this one for a birthday present when I was a child."

"How did old Cousin Max happen to have a key to Gramercy Park?"

"Oh, there was always at least one Butler in Gramercy Park for a hundred years or so. Max changed his name from Butler to Candle when he left home, or rather, when his parents threw him out. After Max became a semirespectable headliner, he was reinstated in my uncle's will and inherited the house."

"He lived in Gramercy Park?"

"He and Edith only lived there for five years or so. They got a wonderful price for the house, enough to buy this building and make a few investments. It's been thirty years since she lived in Gramercy, but I'm surprised she never mentioned it."

"She's always surprising me," said Mallory. But this neatly explained Edith's ties to two old women in Gramercy Park.

"Well, I'm sure the lock's been changed many times since this key was in use. Sorry."

"Here, you can use my key." She pulled a key from the pocket of her jacket.

"Would I want to know where you got that?"

"Charles, you get more like Markowitz every day. I picked it up in Gaynor's apartment. He'll never miss it. He never goes to the park."

"Did Gaynor notice you picking it up?"

"Charles, who's the best thief you know?"

"You're the only thief I know."

194

When Edith Candle leaned back in her chair, alone in the dim window light of a fading day, she could see the whole universe spinning out from her room, stars revolving outward in galactic swirls and spinning in again. She saw how each thing set every other thing in motion. And what was once random now flowed with the predictability of a string of notes to familiar music. She saw the perfect order.

She took stock of Redwing. 'What do you make of her?' Kathy had asked. Edith had responded with a string of words: fearless, arrogant, charming, deceptive, cool under pressure, and wholly alien. But Kathy should have known Redwing best.

She's a lot like you, Kathy.

The old woman closed her eyes and gave herself over to Morpheus, god of dreams, and to the little death that was sleep.

Hours later, she was walking unsteady down the hall to bed. She was suddenly very tired, passing by the open door to the kitchen and the crude letters on the wall above the stove, paying them no attention, eyes already closing to sleep again before she opened the door on her bedroom and left the red garish message at her back.

Margot sank down at the foot of a stone lion who guarded the entrance to the public library. So many hours had passed since she left the bank, but she could feel the soreness in the bones of her legs from the hard pounding on the sidewalk. She was out of shape. When had she last been to dancing practice? Could she be that far gone in only a few days?

That little bastard of a banker had probably called the cops and told them she had pulled a knife on him. Well, that would pick their ears up. Suppose they went to her apartment and saw all the damn knives?

No, he wouldn't call. He'd been a jerk to jump the alarm. And he wouldn't risk the possibility that she might be who she said she was. Henry would know how to fix this. He'd at least be good for a loan to tide her over. But he hadn't answered the phone in the dozen times she'd called his apartment. Damn Henry, who sometimes left his phone off the hook for days at a time. What a miserable twit he was, a bastard, her only friend, her confessor, and sometimes God to her.

She would go back to the apartment in the early-morning hours, maybe break a window. Yeah, when there was less chance of being seen. The cops avoided her neighborhood at the dangerous hours. She picked another paper cup up from the sidewalk and jingled her last pennies for the late-working stragglers until the coins swelled into a subway fare.

She rode uptown and down, wondering about the time but having lost the sense of it. She had no idea what hour it might be. She leaned over to read a passenger's watch. Twenty to ten? Could she have been riding that long? The pain in her gut said it was so. How long with no food? She stared into the faces of the other passengers until their eyes met hers and their glances crashed and then fell away from her eyes, which had gone to a sleep-starved glaze.

Days ago she had believed she would never ride the subway again.

She drifted into the light sleep of the longtime subway rider.

The train slowed to a stop. The bell sounded and another passenger got on. She jerked awake and lifted her head to look at the boarding passenger.

She came hideously awake. It was him. Of course it was. It was the same train, the same time of night.

The man was not so tall as she remembered him, nor so broad at the shoulders, but then, he had become almost mythic over the past two years, growing with each nightmare. She had forgotten how very human he was, with his acne scars and his runny, large brown eyes. Was his knife also smaller than she remembered it? The knife, the knife dancing up to her eye, then ripping down her face. Perhaps he had come back for her to cut her on the other side and make her twisted smile symmetrical.

She drew her legs up to her chest and closed into a ball. The passengers on either side of her got up and moved to the far ends of the car when she began to whimper and rock, face drawn into her chest, hidden behind her knees. Her eyes darted from side to side, watching her abandonment in the ever increasing circle of alone. 'You're on your own,' said this new seating arrangement.

The train was slowing. She might make it to the door before she was hurt too badly. And then what? Would he catch up to her and drag her by the hair again, ripping handfuls from her head? There would be no cop on the platform. There hadn't been one the first time.

The train stopped. She bolted for the door. It was still closed as he came up behind her. She banged her fists on the metal until it parted, sliding back into the walls of the car. She ran through the opening, colliding with another man on the platform who was boarding. The man of the dancing knife walked past her, glancing in her direction, looking through her and then gone.

He didn't know her.

How was that possible? He was on rape-and-cut

197

terms with her, how could he not remember her?

He was climbing the stairs. She followed after him, up and out of the subway. How could he not remember her? She followed him down the street. When he entered the office building on Seventh Avenue, she watched through the glass door as he showed his pass to the security guard. So he worked the ten-to-six shift. She moved back away from the doors and crossed the street, melding in with the darkness and the trash at the curb, hearing the rats but not fearing them, settling in to keep company with vermin.

Warm rectangles of light shone from the windows of the house. Television voices emanated from within, and Mallory could smell twice-blooming roses by the porch railing. It was a living memory of the Markowitz house when people lived there—when they lived. Before she could ring the bell, the door opened and she was staring into Helen's smiling eyes. This older woman must be Brenda's mother. She was a less exact copy of Helen, only rounding out at the hips now the way Helen had rounded into middle age.

"Sergeant Mallory?"

"Yes," she said, relieved that it was not Helen's voice. She dug into her back pocket for the shield.

Mrs. Mancusi didn't wait for the identification. "Please come in," she said, standing to one side of the wide-open door.

"I'm sorry to bother you so late in the evening." She followed Mrs. Mancusi into the wide living room. It was arranged for comfort in the grouping of massive furniture and hassocks. A folded-back newspaper lay discarded by the recliner chair. Dinner smells had not yet evaporated. The interrupted carving of a Halloween pumpkin lay on the table, knife and seeds, pulp and one triangular eye cut from the orange fruit.

"You're not bothering me at all, Sergeant. Brenda called to say she's running a bit late, but she'll be home in a few minutes. I only wish my husband was here. It's his late night at the clinic." She picked up a ball of yarn and a bit of knitting from the seat of the recliner. "Sit here, Sergeant. It's the most comfortable chair." Mrs. Mancusi sat down on the couch opposite the recliner. "You must be tired working these late hours. That chair leans back. Put your feet up if you like. I know what you need, a snack. Can I get you something? Coffee? I have half a pie in the kitchen."

"Thank you, no." This woman might not have Helen's voice, but her conversation was very Helen-like, all comfort and sympathy and a belief in the healing powers of pie.

"We'd like to help you all we can. Louis Markowitz was a lovely man. I cried when I heard the dead man was Louis."

"You knew him well?"

"For a few months. We had him to dinner every two weeks or so. Brenda's known him much longer, of course. He was the one who talked her into coming back to us. She was only sixteen when she ran away."

"When he came to dinner, I don't suppose he ever discussed his work with you? It would be natural for you to be curious about a high-profile case."

"Louis never talked about business—well, police work."

"What did he talk about?"

"His family. His wife died a few years ago, and he missed her terribly. He had a daughter, though.

She's very smart, and very beautiful. He was so proud of her, you could hear it in his voice. When I read about the funeral in the paper, I tried to call her. I called every Markowitz in the phone book. You have no idea how many there are. But I couldn't find her. That poor child must have been wild with grief."

There was that catch in Mrs. Mancusi's voice to say that grief had come to this house, too.

"Brenda should be home soon. She goes to school during the day, and what do you think she does at night? She dances at the Metropolitan Opera. Louis got her the job. Said it was nothing; he'd just called in a favor. They have operas with grand ballroom scenes, and my Brenda dances. Sort of like an extra on a movie set. During the day, she dances at school. That's different, of course. She's studying modern dance and classical ballet."

Mallory heard the front door open and close. A gust of cool air came into the room with young Helen who was called Brenda. Mrs. Mancusi made the introductions, and Brenda sank gracefully to a low hassock facing Mallory. She smiled shyly—her hands entwined under her chin, arms propped on elbows, accidental elegance in every movement.

"I really loved that old man," said Brenda with a child's soft voice. "Did you know him? Did you work with him or something?"

"We were in the same department. I'm interested in the Brooklyn Dancing Academy. He never talked about it at work."

"He came regular, like every single Tuesday night for maybe a year. He paid for lessons, but he was much better than any of the instructors. He taught me old fifties-style rock 'n' roll. After work, he walked me home to my apartment.

200

"You know, I used to hate that job. Pushing old farts around the floor, fielding gropes. I hated it. I was going to quit the night Markowitz showed up. You might think an old man like that—he was pushing sixty—you might think it would look silly, he was so heavy and all, but no. He was amazing. He was wonderful."

Markowitz, you dancing fool.

Mallory closed her eyes for a moment. Then she looked up as Mrs. Mancusi was pressing a plate of pie into her hands and lowering a coffee mug to the table by her chair. She was gone back to the kitchen before Mallory could thank her. She turned back to Brenda, who was digging a fork into her own pie.

"The nights he walked you home, did he ever talk about his work?"

"Mostly we talked about me, about going home and doing it right, going back to school, stuff like that. He got me to enroll in a dance school, even loaned me the money for my first semester. I started in September."

"That's why you quit the Brooklyn Academy?"

"Well, we'd been after her to quit," said Mrs. Mancusi, reappearing with a sugar bowl and creamer which she set down on the table by Mallory's mug. "We could well afford her tuition. But she wanted to buy a gift for Louis with her own money."

"Mom and Dad insisted on paying him back for the tuition." Brenda stood up and moved toward the doorway. "I'll show you what I got for him. Wait just a minute."

Mrs. Mancusi sat down on the couch and leaned forward to whisper to Mallory, "She's hoping you'll give it to his daughter. This is very hard on Brenda. She's not over his death yet. Neither am I, really.

201

I'm not good at death."

Brenda was back, lightly tripping into the room. She danced up to Mallory with the pent-up energy that went with the territory of being seventeen years old, and put a small box into Mallory's hands. Mallory opened the box and pulled out a gold pocket watch.

Mallory pressed on the winder to open it. On the inside cover it was inscribed with the words *I love you* inside a heart that a child might have drawn. In music box fashion, the watch played the opening notes to a golden-oldie rock tune. It must have cost the girl a fortune to customize that music.

"His old pocket watch didn't work," said Brenda. "He wore a wristwatch and carried this old broken watch around in his pocket. Funny, huh? So, do you think his daughter would take it? Would it be okay, do you think? Will you give it to Kathy?"

"I'm Kathy."

A sound that might have come from a kitten escaped from deep inside Brenda Mancusi. She folded down to the floor by Mallory's feet and sat tailor fashion and silent. Her head hung low as she was trying to make sense of the world by tracing the intricate pattern of the rug with one finger, searching the weave for clues and not finding any. Failure was in her eyes when she looked up again. "Oh, I'm sorry, I'm so sorry." Her voice was cracking. "And I'm not helping you, am I? I'm not helping you at all."

"Yes you are. The watch is beautiful. He would have loved it. I love it. Thank you. It was odd, wasn't it, the way he carried two watches. Brenda, do you remember anything else that was odd, out of the ordinary?"

"He was an out of the ordinary man. God I loved

him. At least I got to tell him that before he died."

Mallory looked down to the watch as one hand closed tightly over it.

"I think I went on too long," said Brenda. "I embarrassed him maybe. He got up and left in a hurry. That was the last time I ever saw him."

A hurry? Markowitz never did hurry. He tended to mosey everywhere he went. He was a slow ambling man, easy in his steps, strolling along with an impossible grace for one so stout. Never did he do anything in a hurry.

"Do you remember the conversation? I know it was personal, but it might help me a little. What were you talking about just, before he left?"

"I was trying to tell him what he meant to me. When I took that stupid job at the Brooklyn Dancing Academy, it was all I could get. It was that or hit the streets like my roommate. She was a prossie. But the dancing turned my life around. First I did it for the money, and then he taught me to love it, and then I couldn't live without it. I told him that. I told him it was like it was meant to happen, my meeting him, one thing leading to another. It was like that meeting put everything else in motion. And then he left. So fast. Does that help? I really want to help."

"Yes, it does."

No, it didn't. It only told her what she already knew, what she already had to work with. No, wait. It told her what Markowitz knew before he died. Maybe it was time to step to the side instead of following him into the hole he had died in.

"God, I loved that old man," said Brenda, drained, exhausted, as though she had danced a hundred miles. She brought her hand up to cover her face. She cried.

And Mallory didn't.

It was a video extravaganza. The VCR sat in the far corner of the room playing the tape of Louis dancing with young Helen. And on the clear wall she projected slides of murder scenes, old ladies cut to pieces. Washes of blood flowed across the screen and covered Mallory's face with the ricochet of colored light from the projected images of death. Click: victim number one. And Chuck Berry sang to the dancers. Click: victim number two. The hard beat of the music was moving Mallory's head, manipulating the foot that tapped in rhythm.

She rigged the VCR to loop the tape for continuous play and the partners danced on through the night without tiring ever. Mallory focused on the slides, looking for something that would not jibe, something out of whack, not belonging. She knew it was there. Markowitz had seen it. It had nagged her awake, night after night. What was she missing?

No, that was a mistake. She could see that now. She was also stuck in the loop with the dancing Markowitz and young Helen. Markowitz, had he been there, would have told her to look beyond the parameters of what he knew. She had more to work with now than he had ever had.

The sky, what Margot could see of it, was the deep violet of the hours before sunrise. She watched the man saying his goodbyes to the security guard, and then pushing his way around the revolving door and into the street.

Oh, yes. He was the one.

She crawled out of the torn and discarded mattress box, out onto the sidewalk where the rats were still dancing, still brave while the dark lingered. One rat, bolder than the rest, ran across the

204

back of her spread hand. She pulled it into her chest and then looked at it as though the rat might have left prints.

The man was walking slowly, heading back for the subway station. She stood up on two feet. And only now the rats took notice of her and left the sidewalk with slithering quickness. On feet not so fast as a rat, Margot followed after the man.

Chapter Seven

They advanced across the flat stones, quick jerking shapes of light and dark, and some were spotted with brown and gray, uniform only in their forward motion, and one of them was insane.

Feet of red and red rings around the bright mad eyes, he was otherwise coal black until he passed into a dapple of sun, and iridescent flecks of green shimmered in the light. The feathers of his head were not smoothed back and rounded. Spiky they were, and dirty, as though a great fear had put them that way, and the fear had lasted such a long time, a season or more, and the dirt of no bathing or rain had pomaded them into stick-out fright, though the bird was long past fear now and all the way crazy. No fear of the human foot. A pedestrian waded through the flock, which parted for her in a wave, all but the crazy one, and it was kicked, startling the pedestrian more than the bird.

The woman shrieked and stiff-walked down Seventh Avenue. The insane pigeon followed after her, listing to one side with some damage from the kick, until he forgot his purpose.

Margot Siddon did not know how many hours she

had gone without sleep. She followed the man down St. Lukes Place heading toward Seventh Avenue under a slow-brightening sky. Streetlamps still glowed and cast her shadow slipping down into the underground. Fluorescent lights washed her face to white as she passed through the turnstile. The station was deserted at this hour but for the two of them. To be sure of this, she walked the length of the platform, checking behind each thick post.

By all the laws that governed the universe and New York City, there should be a cop here at this moment when she least wanted to see one. Apparently, even this ancient rule had crumbled in the general breakdown of law and order. They were alone.

She walked toward him, only wanting to see his eyes one more time.

He turned when she touched his sleeve. As he shook off her dirty hand, the last sound he heard was the click. He was a good New Yorker, he knew what that sound must be, and he was given part of a second, that much time to be afraid, before she slipped eight inches of steel into his ribs. By his eyes, he was surprised to be falling, dying, with no time left to ask why.

Edith Candle woke in the ghosty gray hours before sunrise. Her bare feet touched to the carpet as she pulled a woolen robe around her shoulders and plotted out the day's schedule between her bed and the bathroom. She was drawing her bathwater and had not yet looked into the kitchen. On the far wall of that room, just above the sink, a childish scrawl spread in a thick line of lipstick: THE PALADIN WILL DIE.

He approached the park with a small anxiety. More than thirty years had passed since he had last been here. To him it would always be a place of menace. All memories fashioned at the level of a child's eye were unreliable in scale, but Gramercy Park was otherwise unchanged. And so perfect was the memory of his sixth-birthday party, Charles Butler winced.

Edith had invited all the children in the square to that party, all the children who'd had nothing to do with him on previous visits. And he made no new friends that afternoon, but had once or twice been the cause of uproarious laughter which made him want to sink into the earth, to be anywhere but there.

While Cousin Max had loomed over the children, making objects go up in flames and birds go up in flight, six-year-old Charles had shrunk as much as possible, scrunching down in his chair, aiming for invisibility. For the magic show's grand finale, Max had given Charles his fondest wish. First, he made the boy the center of attention, and then, mercifully, Max made him disappear, something Charles's large nose had hitherto made impossible in any company of children.

After the show was over, Charles had reappeared against his will. The children with smaller noses and more modest brains had surrounded him and demanded to know how the trick was done. But he was honor bound not to betray Max's secrets. In slow steps, and of one mind, the children were closing the ranks of small menacing bodies while Edith and Max were packing up the magic act and trundling boxes and bags through the gates, across the street and back into the house. He was alone in the circle of faces all filled with hate, small eyes bright with anger.

207

The first punch to his stomach put him into shock, so startling it was to be hurt for no reason he could understand. He covered his stomach to protect it from the next blow, and he was kicked from behind. An open hand shot out to slap his face, and he thwarted it with raised arms. The same hand came back to him again as a fist in the side.

And now he understood them.

He dropped his hands to his sides and smiled at them, stretching his mouth to its widest, its looniest. They stood back half a step, still of one mind, and that mind was confused. What was this? asked their eyes which were one pair. In their base understanding of anger and fear, this smiling was against the rules. The tentative shot of a fist hit the back of Charles's head, but there was no real force to it. Their energy was draining off for lack of anything to feed it. There were no more blows before Edith entered the children's circle, put one hand on his shoulder and disappeared him back into the house.

During subsequent stays with Edith and Max, he had remained on the sidewalk side of the bars, where he stood now, looking in.

He opened the gate with Mallory's key and found himself a bench in a nice broad patch of October sun.

The boy at the gate must be Henry Cathery. Kathleen had supplied a more detailed description than Charles needed. The small traveler's chess set would have been sufficient to identify the boy. She hadn't needed to add the part about the visitor from another solar system. Charles, fellow alien, had a painful idea of what this boy's life must be like among the earth people.

He brought out his own traveler's set in the

minutes while Cathery was settling into his own patch of sun. Charles's ancient wooden board was inlaid with squares of mahogany and cedar. The chess pieces were made of ivory and jade. The carving had surely driven the craftsman blind with the incredible detailing of each miniature. At the bases of the figures were the pegs to correspond with holes in the board.

From a distance of park benches, he noticed that Cathery was now sliding his own chess pieces across a metal board on magnets. Cathery's concentration made him impervious to the discomfort of being stared at. The boy was alone in his own universe, and Charles, a universe away, was not likely to catch his eye in anything approaching a natural encounter. Nothing in childhood had prepared Charles for any pleasant encounter with a stranger. He had missed that stage of socialization which other people found so natural. He was not at all given to spontaneous conversation. Ah, but then they were countrymen of sorts, this fellow Martian and he. He folded his set and walked slowly across that chasm which separates strangers and their very personal territory of park benches.

When he was standing over Cathery and blocking his sun, he said, I see you favor magnets over pegs."

Cathery nodded, never taking his eyes from the board. If Charles had spoken from a burning bush, it would not have impressed Cathery sufficiently to break his concentration. Charles unfolded his own set and held it out between the boy and the metal board. Cathery looked at it and began the slow smile of a child within grabbing distance of candy.

Well, that was better.

"I've seen one like that before," said Cathery, not looking up, eyes fixed on the board and its figurines.

209

"It's a museum piece, isn't it?"

"Yes."

"Where could I get one?"

"You couldn't. There are only three of them, and two are in museums."

"You want to sell it? I don't care what it costs."

"No, I don't think so. Care for a game?"

Cathery never answered him, but put his own set to one side and looked up with the apprehension of one unaccustomed to this little social dance, unfamiliar with the steps. In that moment, Charles understood him with an insider's knowledge. This brilliant young chess master had all the socialization skills of a very small child. Charles smiled and sat down, placing the peg board on the bench between them. He held up the white to Cathery. The boy nodded. Their conversation had begun, though more than twenty minutes would pass before any more words were exchanged.

A glance at the magnet set allowed him to predict Cathery's opening, a classic game from a championship match.

Yes, that was it. Three moves later, it was apparent that Cathery was extending the chess problem to the new game. Charles called up the playing field from a page in a chess book and moved accordingly. And accordingly, Cathery's every move was predictable. If he continued to play with all the original moves, Cathery might catch on. The boy probably had no eidetic memory—that was rare—but he would certainly have committed these particular moves to what memory storage he had.

While Cathery's eyes were fastened to the board, Charles ran through the possibilities of more obscure games to match the opening. It was dishonest in a way, he supposed—Mallory had her influences on him—but if he didn't provide a master game, he might not be able to hold Cathery for long in a conversation about the weather.

"I've never seen you here before," said the boy, tossing a bishop into harm's way in a mad rush for a new queen. "You just moved in?"

"No, I don't live here." Charles spared the bishop and plotted to take down the would-be queen. "My cousin used to live in that house." He nodded to the other side of the park. "I expect it's been divided up into apartments now. It was a wonderful old place. I used to play in this park when I was a child. It hasn't changed. Peaceful, isn't it?"

Cathery nodded. "I'll never leave here."

Charles believed him. Now that Cathery was grown and beyond the torture of children, he would find this place a perfect environment for a solitary chess player. No street people, no panhandlers to interrupt his game, to break his concentration with acts of supplication or acts of insanity. Henry Cathery would thrive on simplicity. There was nothing about his person to say he went to any trouble about his clothing or his hair. The spotty beard was an obvious growth of neglect. The boy would always opt for extreme simplicity, less distraction from the game.

"Henry!"

But just now, a distraction in the form of a thin young woman was calling to Cathery from the gate. Her hair was matted and her long, dark red dress was torn. An overlarge vest of faded brocade was her only cover against the chill morning. He found it interesting that she called Cathery by his given name.

Charles waited for Cathery to move his piece and lift his eyes. He nodded toward the girl at the gate.

211

Cathery looked at her and, never changing his expression, said, "Ignore her. She'll go away in a while. Your move."

"Isn't she a friend of yours?"

"No."

Such a friendship did seem unlikely. Henry Cathery had grown up with money in a protected environment, while this one at the gate had the look of the homeless, a young woman with nowhere to be.

"I have no friends," said Cathery.

And Charles believed that, too. Again, less distraction.

"And no family?"

"Not now."

Less distraction.

The young woman paced back and forth in front of the gate. Panic was jerking and twitching in every muscle of her body. Then, suddenly, she stopped her walking to and fro. She held tightly to the bars and pressed her face to the iron. Relaxing with a gradual sag and a slant of her body, her hands dropped away from the bars. The spasmodic agitation was gone now. She slowly moved off down the sidewalk and carried herself away from the park with a poignant grace. Charles stared after her until she was out of sight. He felt an unaccountable sadness.

Cathery looked up at him with only a shading of impatience. Charles brought down Cathery's would-be queen, and that set the boy back a bit. In the time the old master's stroke had bought him, Charles turned to stare at the little buildings at the east end of the park.

"So that's where the first murder happened. I should think that would be a more interesting problem than a chess game."

Cathery had put out one fleshy hand to castle his king. The hand hovered, concentration broken, as his eyes turned to the shed.

"I don't see the problem," he said.

"A daylight murder with all these witnesses? I call that interesting."

"Nothing to it," said Cathery. "He laid her down quick, cut her throat to shut her up, and then he cut her some more. The shrubs could hide that much. She was old. She couldn't have put up much of a fight."

"How do you know her throat was cut?"

"Everyone knows her throat was cut. Ten people must have come out to took at the body before the cops showed up."

"Did you see the body?"

"Sure."

"Did you notice anything else besides the cut throat?"

"No. She was partly covered by a garbage bag. No one touched her before the police came. They only wanted to look at a dead body."

There was no pain in the recollection of his grandmother's brutal killing. It was a sterile subject and an annoying distraction.

"But those benches face the building. Not much between the benches and the spot where she died. And no one noticed a stranger in the park that day."

"Then it wasn't a stranger." Cathery shrugged. "Easier."

"No. Think it through. You're too accustomed to dealing with the flat of a board. See the face at that window?" He pointed up to a second-floor apartment window set in red brick.

Cathery squinted up. A head of white hair was bobbing behind the window glass.

"Now, look over there," said Charles.

Another face, this one much younger, looked down on them from the other side of the street.

"The police love people like that. There's at least one professional watcher in every neighborhood. How many windows in this square? Someone had to be watching, but no one came forward. Perhaps the witnesses didn't know what they were witnessing. Is that possible? That doorman faces the murder site. Maybe he was inside when it happened. But what are the odds that no one was looking at the spot at any given minute of the day? The shrubs would cover a prone body. But how do you do a violent bloody murder like that one with no real cover? And what fool would take that risk?"

"It would be the ultimate high, wouldn't it?"

"Pardon?"

"You saw that girl at the gate. When she was in high school, she used to steal things from stores. What she stole was stuff she couldn't use half the time. She said it was a rush. It was exciting."

When their game was ended in a stalemate, Charles quit the park and closed the gate behind him. He looked back to see Cathery staring up to the watcher with the white head. The watcher withdrew from the window—quickly.

Mallory had her old man's brains—Jack Coffey would admit that much. All the damn interview notes NYPD had collected in the past three months, reams and reams of notes, and no one had made the séance connection.

He looked at her sitting quietly on the other side of his desk and wished he had her back on duty again. Until this morning, he hadn't realized how much he'd missed her in the past two months. There

214

was a time, not so long ago, when he had kept track of her off-duty hours, and felt the lack of her in the way he dragged himself to work on the days when she would not be there, driving him nuts with sarcasm and just a trace of perfume. Two months was a long time to be missing her perfume.

Coffey looked up to see Charles Butler filling the doorway of his office. Butler moved across the room and folded his long self into the chair next to Mallory. While he was apologizing for being late, the man was suddenly caught short by the changes in the office. He was staring at the denuded walls, which no one, cop or civilian, had seen in Markowitz's lifetime.

"You haven't missed much," said Mallory to Charles.

Coffey wondered what *he* was missing here. Butler shows up thirty minutes late, and Mallory, the punctuality freak, lets it go by? Where was the venom, the sarcasm, the glare of 'come hither, I want to hurt you'? He faced Charles Butler, who had recovered from the mild shock of the redecorating.

"So, Charles. Wouldn't you think one of those old women would've come forward?"

"Oh, the séance ladies? I suppose it's possible they each assumed someone else would call. That's common group behavior."

"No," said Mallory. "They were playing Russian roulette."

Coffey nodded, but he wasn't buying it. It didn't fit the image formed by the elderly women in his own life, and a little old lady was a little old lady. No, something else had frightened those women, scared them off the police, and he intended to find out what it was.

"I'm arranging police protection for all of them."

215

The better to interrogate them without lawyers intervening.

"Turning into a real horse race, isn't it?" said Charles. "How often do you get such a plethora of suspects?"

"Well," said Coffey, smiling, "we usually begin with the entire population of Manhattan and then whittle it down. Right now, I got Redwing."

"What about Henry Cathery?"

"We checked him out."

"I'm just curious. If he fit the FBI profile so well, why didn't you concentrate on him?"

"I like money motives," said Mallory.

"So do I," said Coffey. "Every single one of those old women was loaded with blue-chip stocks. But then, so is Henry Cathery. He's worth a hell of a lot more than the dead grandmother."

"But you're dealing with a serial killer. Surely there's a mental disorder to consider, a pathology to the crimes."

"Hey," said Coffey. "If FBI headquarters were in New York, they'd have an entirely different set of profiles. New York City is another country."

"Coffey's right," said Mallory. "Now take cannibals, for example. Our last cannibal wasn't really hard-core."

"Yeah," said Coffey. "He was nothing at all like the Minnesota cannibal. The death was accidental. He just didn't know what to do with the body."

"Disposing of the head is always going to be a snag," said Mallory. "When we found a half-eaten head, the FBI sent us down the garden path with their psych profile."

"They never once suggested looking for a bank teller who was once a Boy Scout," said Coffey. "And as far as we knew, his parents were never cruel to him, and he had the standard complement of chromosomes."

In the attitude of only wanting to beat the dead horse one more time, Charles tried again. "But pure profit motive? No one would profit from all four killings. You think a sane murderer would kill four women if he only wanted one of them dead? Would a jury believe it?"

"A jury of New Yorkers?" said Coffey. "Oh, sure."

Mallory nodded in agreement.

"But don't you think the four-week cycles fit nicely with the pathology of a lunatic?" He looked from Coffey to Mallory. "No? But if you only considered the element of madness, it would still be an open field. I understand that Margot Siddon's alibi for the death of her cousin is a theater full of people who can't agree on the right year, much less the hour. No alibi for the Gaynor or Cathery murders. Her alibi for Pearl Whitman's death is Cathery, and he's not too committal. He's got his own alibi problems since Miss Whitman died. The medium we don't know about yet, but that's reaching. And Gaynor—"

"Gaynor? Charles, even if Gaynor didn't have Mallory for an alibi, I'm sure he could account for his time. His students make great alibis—they live on schedules, they're always watching clocks. We've got to check out his appointments for the office hours, but I don't think we're going to find gaps in his day."

"Didn't Henry Cathery also have a witness to account for his time? Pearl Whitman? How reliable was she?"

"So? What's the connection? You're not suggesting that Mallory is unreliable?" No, he could

217

see that Charles wasn't about to suggest anything like that. Mallory was already tensing. Coffey could feel it across the desk without even looking at her.

"No, of course not," said Charles, who probably loved his life as much as the next man, "but Gaynor was saved by a time constraint. No one would have an alibi for any of the murders if the women didn't die where they were found. Then it could be any of them."

"Nice try," said Coffey with no sarcasm. He really did like Charles. "But we have a lock on the crime sites. A forensic pathologist estimates the quantity of blood loss based on the victim's height and weight and the type of wound—if it's a quick kill, there's less blood loss. Then a forensic technician accounts for the blood at the crime site. The areas where the blood pools under the flesh line up with the position of the body. The first thrust gets a major artery. There's an awful lot of blood. No particles found on any of the bodies that were foreign to the site. Not even microscopic evidence to suggest they'd fallen elsewhere. So Gaynor's out of the woods."

"I'm not ruling Gaynor out," said Mallory. "Not him, not any of them."

"You're kidding," Coffey said. "What do you know that I don't?" Even as he asked the question, he knew he was being suckered. She was playing with him.

"And what have *you* got, Coffey? Any little thing you want to share with me?" Her eyes were guns. They made him nervous, and he looked everywhere for something else to be looking at. When his eyes settled on Charles Butler, the man was smiling, and there was a hint of sympathy.

"Fair enough," he said. Though he would not

218

characterize any dealing with her as fair. She'd been born to the advantages of a quicker mind and a paralyzing beauty that had done something terrible and wonderful to him the first time they met. Only Mallory could not see what a standout she was. That was the sad way of damaged kids. They grew up with distorted mirrors.

"We might have a new angle," he said, "now that Redwing links up to the victims. You'll like this one, Mallory, it's a money scam. When we started the surveillance on the square, we matched her description up with a rap sheet. We've got her under the aliases of Cassandra, Mai Fong, and—"

"And Mary Grayling." Mallory was examining her nails. "And she's changed her base of operations. Your man has been watching an empty apartment all morning."

Coffey slumped back in his chair and stared up at the ceiling for a moment. If he killed her now, everyone would know.

He lowered his gaze to stare at her, always a mistake, and he got lost for a second in her pretty eyes. In the early days of working with Mallory, she'd given him stomach flutters each time he saw her. It took him years to realize that she was all stone—no heart and nothing but contempt for a man who could be reduced to a puddle of jelly at her feet. Not that he cared. Jelly had no self-respect.

"What else have you been holding out, Mallory? Any more bombs you'd like to drop on me?"

"Play nice," she said. "You give, I give."

"You give me everything you got, and right now, or I bust you for obstruction."

Well, that certainly made her yawn.

"Mallory, I've already got you cold for working a case off the books, violating conditions of leave, interfering with police business—"

"It's my business," she said, giving each word equal weight. There was no emotion to her when she was angry, only a narrowing of the eyes to warn the poor bastard in her sights. "He was my old man, not yours."

"This case is NYPD property. I can put you on suspension, and take the badge and the gun."

"Oh damn. I left them in my other jacket."

"You hold out on me, and I swear I'm gonna nail your bleeding hide to the wall. You can't win with me, Mallory," he lied.

When jelly met stone, the outcome could not be good for jelly. He knew it and she knew it.

"You think Coffey has a line on how the first murder was pulled off?" Mallory stood at the window facing the street—the dirty, daylight life of SoHo: the trash whipping in the wind on the sidewalk below, the ragged people who had no better clothes, and the ragged people who were making fashion statements. The sash was raised to admit the aroma of refuse from another garbage collectors' strike which piled up on the sidewalk one flight below.

"Could be." Charles poured out a glass of sherry for her and watched her down it in one healthy swig. A good grade of sipping sherry was pretty much wasted on her. He sighed. "If we have to work with the parameters given, Jack Coffey has no more idea how the thing was done than you do. If the parameters are wrong—who knows?"

"You mean if he lied, if he held out on me. Count on it. You're crushed by the unmovable crime sites, aren't you?"

"Well, no. There are other possibilities. Do you

220

know what was going on in that park every hour of the day? Might there have been a distraction?"

"The homicide detectives did interviews with all the residents who were in the park that day. Nothing stands out in the reports."

"My cousin Max could distract an entire audience with one hand. The magician's buzz word is *misdirection*, sending the eye elsewhere while you work the trick. The misdirection could have been a small thing, something common, a noise or an argument."

"I'll check it out. What else have you got?"

"Did the park murder have to be planned? Couldn't it have been a crime of opportunity? A fluke of timing? Something simple?"

"No. Too methodical. The weapon was a common kitchen knife. It was brought to the park. So what did you think of Henry Cathery? Could he have pulled off something like that?"

He forgot himself and downed his sherry. "I think he's brilliant, if that's what you're asking. I don't know that he'd go to any trouble for money."

"Neither do I. Suppose he had a reason to hate his grandmother?"

"Such as?"

She handed him a folder with a recent batch of printouts. One was a psychiatrist's recommendation for short-term commitment in a sanitarium. Henry Cathery must have been twelve years old, by the date.

He read the sheets at the speed of a normal human being. Although he could easily have devoured content and sense in a fraction of the time, he hesitated in front of Mallory. He was always trying to pass as a native of normal. Henry Cathery, however, had not tried hard enough, or not cared

221

enough, and that was his only mistake.

The case psychiatrist's name was familiar. He stared at the wall and projected the page of a psychiatric journal dealing with papers on gifted children.

This reading from blank walls was one of the traits which had unsettled and alienated his cleaning woman. Once, Mrs. Ortega had hovered in his peripheral vision, watching his eyes moving rapidly back and forth, scanning lines of a text only he could see. She had jumped up on a kitchen chair and tried to pry his mouth open, having only the best intentions of pulling his tongue clear of his air passage in the belief that he was having a fit. Humiliation had taught him to be more careful in his public behaviors. But Mallory had long ago uncovered this gift. She would understand and not try to pry his mouth open.

According to the critical article re-created on the wall, Dr. Glencome was a famous popularist. He'd written several books on the socialization stages of children, forgetting ever to mention that each child was a special case, an individual. Apparently, he had diagnosed the gifted and reclusive young Henry Cathery as socially unbalanced and had committed the child.

The records detailed each passing month of the boy's imprisonment in the private hospital. Henry had gradually become more introverted, spirit all but killed and threatening the body. He had been wasting away on forced feedings until Glencome had no choice but to let Henry go free or see him wither and die, thus killing the ungifted doctor's reputation for being so very good with children. After the incarceration, the child chess master had entered no more matches.

222

Charles closed the folder. Mallory was getting more ruthless in her computer raids. This invasion of a child's life was too intrusive. But he could not forget what he had read. So the old woman had inherited the boy when his mother died. First Henry had grief to deal with. Then this gifted child had to contend with a grandparent's perception of normal, coupled with the authoritative opinion of an ass with a Ph.D.

"This isn't a valid diagnosis. It doesn't mean Henry Cathery was mentally unbalanced, that he'd be dangerous to himself or others."

"I think I guessed that," she said. "But the old lady and the shrink couldn't leave him alone, right? Suppose he held a grudge all these years? Suppose he snapped? So first he kills his grandmother, and then he learns to like it and he can't stop."

He was trying to imagine what it had been like for the Cathery boy, to be locked away from his chessboard, forced into a different mold, thwarted like a bonsai tree.

"I thought you liked money motives," he said. "Hated mental disorders."

"I'm trying to be open-minded. Here, look at this."

He took a sheaf of papers from her hand. Telephone company records of calls between Anne Cathery and the private clinic the boy had escaped from nine years ago.

"Maybe she was going to commit him before he hit his twenty-first birthday and came into his trust fund. His birthday was two weeks after his grandmother's death. Interesting, huh?"

"You're not going to give these records to Coffey, are you? This is so brutal. I can't see him standing up to Coffey, not in the face of this, a history he had

223

every right to believe was private."

"No. I'm not turning the files over to Coffey."

"Good." He was looking at her with new hope. She might eventually become altogether civilized.

"What's Coffey ever done for me?"

The buzzer went off in a short burst, the minimum intrusion, and Charles opened his door to the ever polite Dr. Ramsharan. It must be urgent. She had not changed into the soft, worn blue jeans. She stood on his threshold dressed for the office in a crisp white shirt and a linen suit of pale blue. When he stood back to allow her to enter the room, Mallory had disappeared.

"Herbert again?"

She smiled and nodded as she walked into the front room of Charles's apartment. She sat down in the chair closest to the door.

"I'm sorry to bother you with this. I suppose I could've gone to Edith. She's known Martin and Herbert for such a long time. But she's getting up in years. I'm sure you don't want her exposed to this nonsense, and neither do I."

"Wise," said Charles. "How can I help you?"

"Herbert definitely has a gun. It makes quite a bulge under his jacket. Did I tell you he's taken to dressing in an army fatigue jacket? Scary, isn't it?"

"Did you have any better luck with Martin?"

"You know how chatty Martin is."

"Hmm. I'm not sure anymore which one of them set the other one off. Maybe Martin got the vest when he saw the writing on Edith's wall. And it could have been just the sight of Martin's vest that set Herbert off. That's all it would take."

"I haven't been able to find out who mentioned my gun to him. Some of the tenants are out of town. I've had that gun such a long time, I thought Herbert

224

knew. He makes it his business to know everything that goes on in this building. Once, I caught him going through the trash."

"That seems a bit paranoid, doesn't it?"

"No. He's just a garden-variety control freak. He's something very common in any community of humans. There's one of Herbert in every crowd. And all of us have some weak point, some fracture. Herbert's fracture is widening. I need to know why."

She sank back in the upholstery and looked up to the ceiling. With added focus, she seemed to be staring through the plaster and into Edith Candle's apartment on the third floor. Her next words were predictable. "I wish I knew what was written on the wall in Edith's apartment."

"Maybe we should talk to Edith."

"Not a good idea. She was the house mother for all the years she owned the building. Old habits die hard. She'd want to take care of it herself. I don't even want her in the same room with Herbert. I told you, he's ripe for an explosion. You can trust me to know my explosives."

Charles tilted his head to one side as he listened to what Henrietta was not saying. She was not saying it might be dangerous to bring Edith into the problem; she was tap-dancing all around it. Dance was not her forte. She was not saying that Edith was the source of the problem. She knew the relationship of family and danced wide of it, and danced badly. It spoke well of Henrietta that she was no good at subterfuge. She didn't have the face to hide a boldface lie, and neither did she have the dishonest agility to lie by omission.

He was surprised. He had always believed he knew Edith Candle so well.

"All right," he said. "I won't mention anything to
225

Edith."

The tension about her mouth relaxed into an easy smile. Henrietta was her straightforward self again, done with dancing.

When he had closed the door on Henrietta, he turned to face Mallory, who was inches away from him. He'd never heard her coming up behind him. He wished he could put a bell on her neck.

Margot covered her eyes with one hand as she smashed the window leading into her bedroom. She cut her hand on the glass and never noticed. She slipped to the floor and into a deep sleep, not minding bare wood and the cold draft from the broken window. As she rolled in her sleep, the knife with the dried blood on it slipped from her pocket and thudded on the floor. She slept on without dreams.

Riker picked up the old woman at her Gramercy Park apartment. More detectives had been sent to pick up the other three séance ladies, per Coffey's orders to keep them separated. Damn waste of time. The woman was silent on the ride in. Her round face was a mask of white powder. Her eyebrows had been drawn with a shaking hand. She had not asked to see a lawyer, but neither had she asked why he was dragging her into the police station. That was interesting enough to make a note at the next stoplight. He jotted down the word *scared.*

When they arrived at the station, he ordered a uniformed officer to round the women up from the separate corners, offices and cubbyholes of the unit and put them all in the interview room together.

"Coffey won't like that," said the uniformed officer, who had started shaving only the year before.

"Yeah, he will," said Riker. "I'll take the heat if he doesn't."

He stood behind the one-way glass and watched the women file in and settle into a more comfortable silence. Minutes dragged by before the stiffness passed off and the elderly women began to talk easily among themselves. The conversation did not break off when an officer brought in a tray of covered Styrofoam cups and a box of doughnuts from the deli across the street. Riker smiled and moseyed down the hall to Markowitz's office, where Jack Coffey was waiting for him.

"You got all the old ladies from the séance?"

"Yeah."

"Put the Penworth woman in the interview room. I'll talk with her first."

"She's in there now."

He followed Coffey to the large room at the end of the hall and counted to three as the lieutenant looked in the window of one of the doors.

"All of them together," said a very testy Coffey on the third count. "I told you I wanted to see them separately." Jack Coffey looked through the glass of the interview room at four old women seated around the long table, chatting among themselves, excited, laughing.

"They're more talkative when they're all together," said Riker. "Make it more like a gossip session and you'll get more out of them."

"Riker, when I tell you—"

"Hold it, Lieutenant. You're gonna say that was Markowitz's style, right? Okay, so it's not the old man's command anymore and you're no Markowitz. Okay. But when we picked up the old ladies, one by one, they were like clams in the car. When they met up here, it all changed. They've been chattering about murder nonstop for the past twenty

"All right, Riker. We do it Markowitz's way." He looked back to the window. "Who's who?"

Riker had been primed for a fight, and now he felt somewhat let down because Coffey wasn't really such a bastard. He read off the names to match up with the woman who nodded constantly, the moonfaced woman, the one with the little head and the gigantic chest, and the skinny one with the high cheekbones who had a smart mouth and was his favorite.

They walked into the interview room and a wash of gossip running full spigot.

"Anne's death was the most spectacular," said the nodding woman, whose slight palsy happily agreed with her sentiments in the rankings of recent bloody murders in the neighborhood.

Coffey took his place at the head of the table, and Riker took the next chair, notebook in hand. They politely waited for a lull in the conversation, and Coffey introduced himself.

A round face beamed on Coffey and one pudgy white hand rested on his arm. "You know, Lieutenant, for a while, we thought it was one of us."

"Oh, yes," said the lady of the high cheekbones. "That was rather early on, of course. Pearl hadn't died yet."

"You mean you regularly discussed this possibility?"

Riker smiled down at his notebook. Coffey was having a hard time with that.

"That's practically all we talked about between séances. You thought we were discussing needlepoint?" asked the woman described in Riker's notebook as 'small head, big jugs.'

"By the time Pearl died, we'd settled on other possibilities," said the nodding woman.

"Such as?" Coffey prompted.

"The Cathery boy."

Riker flipped back through the pages of his notebook. "Miss Whitman was Henry Cathery's alibi. She said she was with the kid in the park between one-thirty and four-thirty in the afternoon of June thirtieth. They played chess for three hours. Does that sound right?"

"Yes. Pearl was quite a player when she was young. She gave it up when she turned sixty. She had more tournaments on her résumé than Henry did."

"As I recall," said the lady of the white-powder moon face, "Henry went to some trouble to remind Pearl of the hours. Pearl had been a bit confused, but she finally decided that must have been the right time."

"Cathery had to remind her?"

"Their games were haphazard. He took his chess set to the park every day, but sometimes it was in the morning, sometimes in the afternoon. If Pearl was there at the same time, she'd give him a game."

"She told us she was positive about the time," said Coffey.

"I doubt that," said the thin woman. "You know how it is. No, you wouldn't, would you? When you start to get up there in years, every time you forget your keys—well, it must be senility. That's why it was so easy to convince Pearl that she was with Henry during those particular hours."

"Since Pearl's murder," said the nodding woman, "I see Henry in the park both morning and afternoon. Maybe he always went twice a day. I'm

229

not sure. One gets so used to seeing him there."

"Right," said the moon. "His game with Pearl could just as easily have been in the morning."

"We didn't all agree on Henry, of course," said the woman with the tiny head. "I thought the lot of them, all the heirs, hired a service to do it. Maybe they got a package rate."

"Well, of course they'd get a package rate," said the nodding woman, with more enthusiasm than palsy. "This is New York. Who pays retail?"

"And do you favor the conspiracy theory too, ma'am?" asked Riker of the thin woman with the cheekbones which made him think she had been hot when she was young. "Do you think all the heirs are in on it?"

"No, dear. The smart money is on Margot Siddon."

"Margot has been so strange these past few years," said the thoughtful moon. "Or so Samantha used to say."

"Oh please," said the woman of the tiny head, with a heave of her ample chest and a diva's sigh. "Compared to whom? You don't think of Henry as the all-American boy, do you?"

The nodding woman's head began to wobble, attempting to contradict the affirmative nod with a negative shake.

The moon beamed on Coffey again. "Henry was really very little trouble to Anne. You know she took him in when his parents died."

"She took Henry and a tidy allowance as guardian and executor," said Riker's favorite. "Henry, incidentally, is worth ten times what Anne had."

"So, does Margot Siddon have an alibi, Lieutenant?" The little round face leaned forward, eyes bright.

"I don't see it as a woman's crime, ma'am," said Coffey.

She seemed affronted by this and cocked her head toward the others, who smiled with pleasant endurance and tolerance, and the thin woman's shrug said, 'Men.'

"According to the testimony of Mrs. Whitman's doorman—"

"Oh, my dear, I hope you haven't relied too heavily on the testimony of doormen," said the tiny-headed diva. "Pearl and I had the same doorman. He's drunk four days out of five."

"I have the same doorman as Anne and Samantha," said the moon. "He does the building football pool on Wednesdays. That was the day Anne died, wasn't it?"

"Now Estelle's doorman is my doorman. He's very new and very young," said the nodding woman. "You know these young people, they think we all look alike."

Coffey shot a glance at Riker, who nodded in agreement. The doormen did not make great witness material.

"Did the four victims have anything else in common besides the séances?"

"Samantha and Anne went to school together. Vassar, I think."

"Estelle and Pearl were very close," said the thin woman. "They did stocks together."

"Pardon?"

"They made the same investments with the same brokerage house. They put me onto quite a good thing once."

Riker watched Coffey make the mistake of the patronizing smile. Coffey must think these women were discussing their pin money instead of the

231

hundred-million-dollar increments they moved around the boards at the stock exchange. But Coffey had not yet read Mallory's printout on their stock portfolios and recent transactions, which companies they held stock in and which they owned outright.

The moon leaned into the conversation. "Didn't Pearl and Estelle go into partnership on a corporation?"

"That was twenty years ago, dear, and they unloaded it the following year. Things in common," mused the nodder. "Estelle and Samantha are from New York Four Hundred families. Social Register, you know. Anne Cathery and Samantha are both DAR. That's Daughters of the American Revolution."

Riker leaned forward, tapping his pencil on the notebook. "Is there any one thing they all had in common?"

"They were old."

"Thank you," said Riker.

"Ladies," said Coffey, in the same tone Riker had heard him use to address a field trip of third-graders, "do you realize that any one of you could be the next victim?"

"Well, it was something of a crapshoot at first," said the nodding woman. "But this time, we're fairly certain that Fabia's next. Show him the letter, Fabia."

The woman turned her small head down and had to lean over a bit to see beyond her large chest and into the purse on her lap. She produced a folded paper in a dramatic flourish. She was almost gleeful as Riker and Coffey read the lines that demanded her money and threatened her life.

Charles flipped through the library microfiche,

rolling by the pages of thirty-year-old newspapers. Kathleen had been right. There it was on the cover of a major daily, a photograph of the hysterical widow clinging to her husband's body.

The reporter for the *Times* speculated that Max might have survived, but the busboy had broken the glass of the water tank when he saw Max was in trouble, remaining in the dead float well past the safety margin, one leg still bound to the weight at the bottom of the tank. The broken glass had cut him to shreds, severing every major artery. Onlookers had watched helplessly while he bled to death.

And now he noticed a new detail in the photograph. His own father's face stared out at him from the crowd of nightclub patrons in the background, a small cameo of horror and disbelief.

Charles understood those disbelieving eyes so well. In childhood, it had been hard to believe that Max could ever die.

Nine-year-old Charles had been uncertain of Max's final exit from the world when he attended the funeral in the Manhattan cathedral. Holding tightly to his parents' hands, he entered that enormous place lit by a thousand candles, filled with a throng of mourners who had come to say goodbye to the master. Cousin Max lay at peace in a white coffin, dead, so the boy had been told. But Charles had held to the hope that this too was an illusion, another exit but not the final one.

The cathedral ceiling was higher than heaven. The stained-glass windows and the candles created a brilliant spectacle of unimagined space and beauty. The candles had gone out one by one, and by no human hand. Though the windows kept their brilliance, the interior dimmed to a ghostly twilight as the first magician appeared in white top hat and tuxedo with a flowing white satin cape. Out of this cape he had pulled a glowing ball of fire. Charles had seen this done onstage. It was one of Max's best illusions. The ball of fire left the magician's hand and floated over the coffin where Max slept on. A parade of men and women in white satin had come forward to circle the casket, which disappeared a moment later when they broke ranks and returned to their seats.

The casket had reappeared at the cemetery. Max's wand was broken over the open grave.

He remembered looking up to the sky, that perfect cloudless expanse of blue, as a thousand white doves took flight and blocked out the sun. He heard the thunderous rush of wings rising, and felt their wind on his face and in his hair. When he looked down again, the coffin was gone, and a scattering of white rose petals covered the earth at the bottom of the open grave. The doves soared up and up, climbing to heaven, wings working with a fury, as though they carried a weighty burden with them, up and away. The little boy followed their flight with astonished eyes.

The advantage of a prominent nose was that it missed very little. Her perfume rose up in the elevator with him. Balancing two bags of groceries and a newspaper, he followed it down the hall. At the juncture of the two apartments, he turned away from his residence to open the office door.

Mallory sat behind the desk in the front room, facing a bearded man whose gesturing put one waving arm perilously close to a delicate lampshade of glass panels. This could only be the sociologist from Gramercy Park, heir and murder suspect. He fit

234

Mallory's scarecrow description, but only in the looseness of his limbs and the awkward way they flew around without direction. His face was attractive, small regular features and warm engaging eyes. The beard suited him and saved him from the small nose, which bordered on pug and would have made him an aging boy forever.

"Charles Butler, Jonathan Gaynor," said Mallory.

"It's a pleasure, Mr. Butler."

"Charles, please."

"I love your windows." said Gaynor. "Do you know the period?"

"Thank you. The architecture is circa 1935."

This tall triptych of windows was more aesthetic than the rectangles of his apartment across the hall. Restored woodwork gleamed from the frames which arched near the ceiling. Mallory, behind the desk, was a dark silhouette in the center panel, softly backlit by the gloaming of the dinner hour.

Charles settled his grocery bags on the desk. "This room is unique. All the other windows in the building are the same period but not quite the same style."

"It's a remarkably quiet room," said Gaynor. "Double-pane glass in the windows?"

Charles nodded. At times the room was so quiet Mallory swore she could hear pins crashing to the floor, and the *'Oh shit!'s'* of spilled angels.

"You know what these windows remind me of?" Gaynor's hand sent a pencil caddie flying to the carpet. He bent down to pick it up with a lack of self-consciousness that must come from the habit of sending things accidentally away. "This whole room could be the set for *The Maltese Falcon*. It's vintage Sam Spade."

Charles sat on the edge of the desk and looked

235

around the room with new eyes. When he had taken over this apartment for his office, he had been working on the theory that a room was a three-dimensional metaphor for a human life, and a basic element of harmony. Once he had the room, he believed his life would take on a new shape, the right shape this time around. Now it was a bit of a shock to realize that his ideal room was the stereotypical setting of murder investigations. But it was.

"I've persuaded Mallory to have dinner with me," said Gaynor. Care to join us?"

Charles gathered up his grocery bags and moved to the door, looking back over one shoulder to say, "Oh, you're both invited to dinner at my place."

And the parade of three crossed the hallway.

The kitchen in his apartment was his favorite room these days. In the past year, he had grown accustomed to people dropping by at all hours. He welcomed company after all the years he had spent isolated in his room at the think tank.

The Academy of St. Martin-in-the-Fields played a Vivaldi mandolin concerto at a background level that facilitated conversation. Jonathan Gaynor made himself useful stirring the sauce for Swedish meatballs. Mallory perched on the countertop, sipping white wine to the left of Charles's chopping block, and he was unreasonably happy.

"It's wonderful," said Gaynor, sipping from the spoon. "Did your mother teach you how to cook?"

"Oh no," said Charles, smiling as he wept over the minced onions. "She only managed to cook one unburnt piece of toast in her entire life."

"Oh, right," said Mallory.

"Really, I was there that day. I remember the moment when it hit the top of the pile on the breakfast table. It was golden brown, the first I'd ever seen that wasn't black. I reached out to grab it, but my father got it first. He handed it back to my mother and said, 'This one isn't burnt yet.' She never missed a beat. She put it back in the toaster and burned it to a husk."

"All I ever had was boarding school fare," said Gaynor, holding his empty wineglass to Mallory, who filled it. "Burnt toast would've been the highlight of the meal."

Both men looked at Mallory, who had never failed to have a well-cooked, nutritionally balanced meal in all the years she lived with Helen and Louis. Just for one flickering moment, Charles believed her competitive streak might tempt her to recall a time when she lived out of garbage cans.

She jammed the cork in the mouth of the wine bottle.

"So, Jonathan," said Charles. "You have any theories on the Invisible Man of Gramercy Park?"

"It had to be a lunatic."

"Why?" Done with onions, Charles moved on to tearing small bits of bread into smaller bits.

"I look out on that park every day," said Gaynor. "I promise you, there's no way he could have killed Anne Cathery with a hope of not being seen. Therefore, it had to be a mental incompetent without the forethought to protect himself from detection."

"Good reasoning, but how do you account for the fact that there were no witnesses?"

"A fluke. And it speaks well for my theory. There was one unguarded moment when no one was looking that way."

"And no one noticed a blood-splattered lunatic strolling out of the park," said Mallory dryly.

"He could have covered his clothes with
237

something," said Gaynor.

"Wouldn't that indicate the presence of mind to protect himself from detection?" said Charles.

Gaynor sipped his wine and looked off to that corner of the eye which Charles recognized as the place where he did his own best work.

"In that case," said Gaynor, "I only have to extend my unguarded moment long enough for him to leave the park. He could have been a derelict who followed her through the gate after she unlocked it. And once he was out of the park, who would take any notice of a street person? Who would look long enough or close enough to determine that his clothes were stained with blood?"

In that same corner of the eye, Charles was reconstructing the long red dress worn by the young woman who had hailed Henry Cathery from the park gate. Gaynor might have something there. Blood, wet or dry, was not so detectable as the Technicolor paint of motion picture blood. Had the killer worn something dark or something red? Could it be that simple?

Mallory was not so open-minded.

"I can't believe it," she said.

"Of course you can't," said Gaynor, stirring the sauce dutifully, and misunderstanding her. "No sane person wants to believe that anyone is sick enough to kill a helpless old woman." Gaynor continued with his stirring and his misunderstanding of Mallory, who was not in the least sentimental about helpless old ladies. "But there are probably a lot of people who wish the Invisible Man had come to their house."

"That's cold," said Charles, crumbling raw ground beef into a bowl.

"Yes, it is," said Gaynor. "But true," He looked

up at Mallory. "Think about relatives who can't afford nursing homes. Old people are living longer, into their nineties some of them, draining the resources of their children. I don't think that series of murders enraged the public. I think it fed their fantasies. It's no accident the Invisible Man is taking on superhero proportions in the news media."

"You make it sound like the freak's performing a public service," said Mallory.

Charles could see this line of conversation was not sitting well with her. She would have given anything to watch Louis and Helen grow old. She filled her wineglass, dismissing them both with her downcast eyes.

"I know you're a sociologist," said Charles, "but do you have any expertise in sociopaths?"

"Only to the extent that they impact on society. We need them in times of war. If we don't have enough, we manufacture an artificial pathology in their basic training. As long as they're confined to a military life or a combative sport, or even a police force, we can keep them in stock. If you put them out in the civilian population, they'll cull the weak, the stragglers and—"

'The elderly,' he would have said next, if Mallory had not cut him off.

"How does insider trading impact on society?"

Charles stared at her lovely face, her Irish eyes of Asian inscrutability.

"It's potentially devastating," said Gaynor. "In the worst possible scenario, Wall Street loses the trust of the investors. Who wants to risk their savings in a rigged game? Think of the small investors who suffer the most when they're cheated. Investments fall off across the board, from mutual funds to city bonds and blue-chip stock. Then the market collapses, and we all line up with a bowl at the local soup kitchen. That pack of thieves in the 1980s scandal shook a lot of people's faith. The soup kitchen was a near thing."

"I suppose a lot of people just don't realize how wrong it is," said Mallory, swilling her wine and speaking in uncharacteristic small-talk tones, "how illegal it is."

"Very few people with the money to invest at any level can claim they don't know that insider trading is wrong, and why it's wrong."

"Including little old ladies?" Mallory smiled, and her eyes narrowed in Charles's direction.

"Oh, particularly little old ladies," said Gaynor. "They control the lion's share of the large-to-medium-investor capital."

And Charles knew that all this was for his benefit. Mallory might genuinely like Edith Candle, but Edith had not respected the law, and Mallory was the law. Apparently her code of ethics was a little more complicated than the poker players realized. Why hadn't he seen that for himself? She could have stolen the earth with her computer skills, but she had confined her theft to whatever Markowitz might need to keep the law. Perhaps she did have the unrepentant-till-pigs-fly soul of a thief, but she drew sharp lines, Markowitz's lines. There was more of him to her than Helen.

Charles nodded to Mallory, and in that nod he promised to speak to Edith about her forays into the market and what she could expect to get away with in the future.

After Gaynor said his good nights and thank-yous and closed the door behind him, after the dishes had been cleared from the table, she made herself to home on the couch, shoes kicked off, feet curling under her. When he set the tray with the coffee and liqueurs on the table before her, he saw the box with the red wrapping paper. And this was his first clue that today was his fortieth birthday.

He sat down beside her and tore the red wrapping paper from his gift. The uncovered cardboard box bore an espresso-maker logo, but when he lifted the lid, he was staring down at an object that would never make a good cup of espresso, not in this world. Not knowing quite what to say, he resorted to the obvious. "A crystal ball?"

"My idea of homage. You're the only man who ever impressed me very much. I find the rest of them boringly predictable."

As Charles held the crystal ball up to the light, his nose elongated in a dark patch of curving reflection. He put it down on the coffee table.

She would never guess how much this pleased him. Every sign of friendship was a reaffirmation that he was not so odd, not a complete freak, not entirely alien. If he could ask for more, it would only be that she were less beautiful or that his nose did not precede him by three minutes.

"You like it?"

"Very much. Not a paperweight, I take it?"

"No, it's the real article. Straight out of the department evidence room."

She was doing the service of pouring coffee and liqueurs, holding a spoon up to ask did he want sugar? No? "So, what did you think of Gaynor?"

"I suppose I liked him well enough." And it had been obvious that Gaynor liked Mallory quite a bit. "What do you really know about him?"

Her father would have asked that. Louis had remarked that one day he would have to unplug her computer for a few minutes so she could meet and marry a young man while he was young enough to hope for grandchildren. Louis had been confident that it would only take a few minutes. He had seen what she'd done to his detectives in less time.

"I've got a printout this long," she said. "I know his parents are dead. He has a summer house on Fire Island, he dabbles in stocks, and he's just inherited a few hundred million. But he wasn't starving before the old woman died. He's worth a hundred thousand on his own, all socked away in conservative investments. No arrests, no juvenile record."

So her interest in the man was all professional.

So Gaynor dabbled in stocks.

"He didn't by any chance cash in on the Whitman Chemicals merger?"

"No. I thought so at first. The timing was right. Then I backtracked the stock purchases through the computer of a financial house. He made some modest gains that year, but there was no connection. Lucky for him," said Mallory. "Estelle Gaynor got away with it. She's only a footnote in the investigation, but the SEC would've busted her nephew in a minute on sheer proximity. The government would have taken all the profits, fined him and jailed him. But none of his own transactions are linked to anything criminal. It's not like he was ever hard up for money."

"Some people never have enough money. What about the other victims?"

"There's no connection to the Whitman merger beyond Gaynor's aunt. Pearl Whitman was a principal, but she never purchased stock in the merging company. No financial history of insider trading for Samantha Siddon or Anne Cathery, but they both play the market."

"You know, it might be a good idea not to get too

242

close to any of these people until you find out what the connecting link actually was."

"I know. The séance isn't enough. I think something brought them together before the séances began."

"Maybe, maybe not. What do old women do when they meet? They talk about their children. Did you think these women might have shared a secret or a confidence?"

"Like a little lunacy in the family?"

"I hope we're not getting off on the Cathery boy again. He's socially awkward—many gifted people are—but odd behavior doesn't signify mental illness. You can't really see him hacking up an old lady, can you?"

"Oh, sure I can. And if it turns out that Anne Cathery was trying to get the kid locked up so she could get her hands on his money, I'd have to figure she had the knife coming to her. But I'd still bust him."

"All Henry Cathery seems to crave is a little solitude. He only wants to be left alone. You're not planning to torture him, are you?" Charles stared at the pattern of the carpet.

She touched his arm to call his eyes up to hers. "You liked Henry Cathery, didn't you?"

"I understood him."

"Were the old ladies helpful? Did they give you the new location for Redwing?"

"No," said Riker. "The old ladies don't contact her. She calls them. We have to wait till the next séance and tail her. And don't get any ideas, kid. Coffey's already arranged for the tail."

Riker spent the next hour drinking Mallory's beer and bringing her up to speed on Coffey's progress

243

which, according to Riker, was zip. "Dr. Slope thinks we might have a slight variation in the murders. If it's two people, then both of them are right-handed, both used incredible violence in the slashing. But the wounds are not identical. The fourth victim is slightly off, and Slope can't say for sure it's the work of one man. Maybe the guy was just in a freaking hurry this time."

"What about a man and a woman working together?"

"Naw. I'm going along with Coffey on that one. It crossed my mind, but I just don't see a woman doing that kinda job on another woman. Don't get me wrong, kid. Women can shoot and stab with the best of 'em. And they're really thorough. If I see a corpse with a whole clip emptied into it, I gotta figure a woman did that. But I can't see a woman doing these mutilations. You see something like that, it's always a man who has a problem with women."

When Riker had gone, Mallory sat down by the light of the VCR and the slide projector. She began the nightly horror show of the slides and the dancing Markowitz.

Old man, why didn't you leave something behind, a few bread crumbs?

And in her dreams, Louis Markowitz tried to teach her how to dance.

When Margot opened her eyes to the light, she could not tell if it was the gray of evening or morning. What day was it? And she was thinking of food as her stomach gnawed at her like a separate animal with teeth to bite her from the inside. The bloody knife lay inches from her face. She didn't see it for the long minutes she thought about food. She

244

daydreamed of bakery bread. The knife was kicked to one side by blind feet on the way to the door.

Out on the avenue, she had her choice of discarded paper cups. She selected one and primed it with three pennies and jingled them for the tourists.

An old woman stopped and kept Margot standing in the cold wind as she dipped a thick-veined claw into her large purse and, with maddening slowness, groped around its interior, finally extracting a change purse. Margot shifted from one foot to the other as the woman worked the clasp with arthritic fingers, at last wincing out a single dime and chiming it into the paper cup.

Margot stared at the dime keeping company with the three pennies at the bottom of her cup. A scream of outrage exploded from her mouth with force enough to push the old woman back two steps to the brick wall littered with playbills and ads and graffiti. Margot screamed at her, yelling obscenities, shrieking "Bitch, bitch, bitch" in an angry chant. She followed after the old woman, who had turned and was hurrying away with all the speed of veined and brittle legs. The woman gathered her thin coat closer about her throat, as if it might be protection from the young lunatic who was dancing alongside her, sometimes leaping in the air and screaming vile words which had the effect of physical punches and outright terror.

The old woman tried to run, and her legs failed her, falling out from under her. She heard a snap of bone when she hit the hard cement which hates old bones and breaks them when it can. The old woman never felt the jagged edge of the broken beer bottle until she looked down and saw the blood gushing from the split in her flesh. A small noise came from

245

her dry lips, a crack in the voice, a squeal of fear, more from the sight of her own blood than the pain. The old woman was crawling now, dragging her body along the sidewalk as the lunatic with the dirty, matted hair danced around her, ranting on and on, stomping and leaping, frightening the wide-eyed pedestrians who passed her quickly by, pretending not to see, not to hear, not to feel.

The old woman ceased her inching escape. She lay still in the body and quiet. Tears streamed from her eyes as her life leaked out through the jagged red hole in her leg.

Chapter Eight

With food enough and sleep enough, Margot was focused once again. In her mind, she replayed the image of the knife disappearing into his ribs in a quick thrust of the blade, she watched again as he slid to the concrete of the subway platform, gasping like an air-drowned fish, blood bubbling up from his mouth. She had stared at his eyes for a very long time. He was the one. There could have been no other eyes like those.

She would have to do something about the knife, all the knives. She wouldn't miss them any. She didn't need them anymore. How many knives did she own? She collected all the knives from the kitchen and bundled them in a towel and carried them out the door as if they had been babies. And they had been, but no more.

Riker was comfortably settled into a chair by the bulletin board in Mallory's den. He drained another beer. An empty coffee cup and a plate with the remains of Mallory's more wholesome breakfast were on the table by her computer. It would not have surprised him if she had pulled her bed into the den so she could sleep with the board as well as eat with it.

"Has Charles ever seen the board?"

She shook her head as she attached the last printout to the cork. It dangled by a single pushpin.

He wondered what Charles would think if he could see her pinning up notes and printouts in a sloppy, unMallory way. Maybe Charles would know what to do with this aspect of Mallory, this disassembling, pushpin by pushpin.

She went to the small refrigerator, a recent addition to the den, and pulled out a bottle of beer. "Now, what have you got on Redwing?" She popped off the cap and slipped the cold bottle into his hand to replace the empty one which had disappeared without his noticing.

"Okay." He looked down at his open notebook. "She has three arrests for extortion and fraud. The charges were dropped in each case."

"I've got that already."

Of course she did. She could break into the NYPD computer system in her sleep.

"I want the personal notes of the cops who busted her. The computer file won't tell me why the charges were dropped."

"They were dropped for lack of cooperation from the complainants. You know how hard it is to prosecute this kind of fraud, even when the victims do cooperate."

"Any earlier records under another alias? Maybe a little violence on her record? Assault charges?"

"No, but she's a big lady. I'd bet even money she

247

could take you." He slugged back his beer in a long thirsty draught.

"No address yet?"

"Still working on it. It's no good backtracking any of the cabs. They all pick her up in different locations and most of them are gypsy cabs, no logs." Riker looked down at his magical, bottomless beer bottle.

"So, now that Coffey has the séance connection, he must be really hot on conspiracy theories again."

"Oh yeah, he is. He's taking a real strong interest in Redwing. It's got to tie in with one of her scams, right?"

"Does Coffey understand that none of these women are going to be cheated by a small-time con artist?"

"I don't know. I think he sees every old lady in the image of his grandmother."

"What else have you got?"

"You're gonna love this. Here." He handed her a typewritten note. It was still enclosed in an evidence bag.

"Oh Jesus. Just when you think you've seen it all, somebody comes up with a new angle for a protection racket. Where did you get it?"

"One of the old ladies gave it to us during the interview. Fabia Penworth. Course she passed it around to all her friends before we ever saw it. We had to fingerprint the whole pack of them for elimination prints."

"And she was just delighted with the letter, right?"

"Yeah. Go figure. So now Coffey's off on this theory that all the old ladies who went down got death threats like that one, and either they didn't pay their own ransoms, or they were killed right after the payoffs."

"And the old ladies back that up?"

"Nope. This is the first letter they've seen, any of them."

"Then it didn't go down that way. You tell something to one of them, and you tell it to all of them. If there were other letters, they'd all know about it. Coffey's met them. What does he use for brains?"

"Hey, Kathy, ease up. Coffey didn't grow up with the old man, but he's learning. That guy don't sleep so good at night, he wants to catch this perp so bad. It's not like he's dragging his feet."

"If he knew you were feeding me—"

"Okay, that tears it. And just what do *you* use for brains, kid? Of course he knows. He always knew. What I don't know is if he figured he couldn't cut you out, or he shouldn't. And if you don't mind a little constructive criticism—and even if you do— Coffey's not half green enough to make the mistakes you've made. Your kiddy days in the department computer room don't count for squat. You got zero time in undercover work, nothing in surveillance. You figured the team in Gramercy Park didn't spot you 'cause you parked in the right place? Gimme a break, you brat. You just figured you were smarter, and maybe you are, but they got you on film. If they got you, the perp probably spotted you too. In fact, I think we can count on that. You underestimate everybody, Kathy. That'll get you killed. And Coffey shows a damn sight more respect for the old man. He figures if the perp was smart enough to kill Markowitz, he's gonna play his troops close to the vest. He can't spare one man, but he's got two of them in that Gramercy apartment, every day, dawn to dusk—one to watch the other's back. And then

249

he's still got time to worry about you."

"And you're my baby-sitter."

Oh, kiss a dead rat. He was only confirming what she already suspected. He'd been had. That was in her face, though he had to give her points for not gloating. He threw up his hands and spilled more beer in the same motion.

She turned away from him. She'd heard what she wanted to hear. He'd run his mouth nicely at ninety miles an hour, given her information, thanks, but he could stuff the rest. He stared down at his bottle. How many beers had she slipped into his hand today?

"Maybe you overestimate Redwing," she said.

"No I don't. You're right about her being small-time, little fish. When she does go for gold, she screws it up. It's a history with her. But she's smart enough to beat the charges and mean enough to do you some damage. You don't want to get too close to her."

"So she does have an assault on her rap sheet."

So much for his idea of not disclosing information on Redwing.

"You stay the hell away from Redwing."

"I know you've got a new address on her. Give it to me."

"No way." There were limits. Kathy had done a number on him, a first-class mugging, but he couldn't give her everything. How many beers had he had? And did he just tell her that he had the address?

"Kid, you just never listen. Coffey's covering for you. You make a bad mistake and he goes down with you. You don't want to screw up the way Markowitz did. Nobody goes near her without a backup. Two of the arresting cops let me read their

250

personal notes on Redwing. The charges were dropped in one case because the complainant disappeared. Another one died of a heart attack. In the case officer's opinion, the guy was scared to death."

He stared at her mask of a face in profile as she went back into the details of the bulletin board and was lost in there. He had been wrong. She did know how to listen and how to bait. Hadn't she listened as he told her the feed worked both ways, that he'd been holding out on her and shadowing her? All he had left was Redwing's address. Markowitz's daughter had the makings of a great cop.

"I was just trying to help you out, Riker. If your team is waiting for her to come back to the hole on Hudson Street, you're in the wrong neighborhood. She only uses that place because it has an underground access to a building on the next street. That's how she loses the surveillance team."

He lifted his bottle to the light and stared at it. If he put the mouth of it to his ear like a conch shell, would he hear Markowitz laughing at him?

Edith was making the kitchen noises of preparing lunch for Charles. He stood at the center of the carpet, turning slowly, sensing that something was out of place but not knowing what it might be. The further back he had to reach into the archives of his photographic memory, the more flaws he was likely to find.

The address had changed since he was a child, but not the character of the rooms. Edith and Max had re-created the interior architecture of the old house in Gramercy Park. The windows had been redone and the walls covered with matching wood panels and wallpaper. Upon his first and final

251

childhood visit to this SoHo address, at the age of nine, he had helped them to match the lesser details of each room with the photographs of his remarkable memory. They had given him this game to play during the week he had lived with them while his parents were at the other end of the world attending a conference. He had not stopped until each piece of antique furniture, each bit of bric-a-brac, photograph, and painting was set in its accustomed place.

Ten years had passed between that visit and the next. As a boy of nineteen, he had noticed one change immediately. She had taken the portrait of Max off the wall of the front room and replaced it with a good hunting print. But for that one change, Edith had kept to the original integrity of the rooms. The same museum-worthy figurines, silver dishes and ashtrays appeared on table surfaces. The same clutter of photographs and candies sat on the mantelpiece. Doilies graced the tables, and antimacassars protected the brocade of the chairs. The telephone was circa 1910. The late twentieth century was hidden away in a back room where Edith kept her computer.

He walked down the hall and entered the room which, in smaller proportions, replicated the library of the Gramercy Park house. He had not had occasion to be in this room since he was a small boy. Later visits with Edith, in his adult years, had always been confined to tea and sandwiches in the front room. But this library was the room he had loved best. The shelves were filled with tomes on magic. Most of the volumes were collector's items, some dating back two centuries. The fireplace with the ornate mantelpiece held the memories of Max's repertoire of ghost stories told on chill nights with marshmallows to toast on the fire, making white stringy goo on long sticks while Max terrified him and then made him laugh.

Charles stared at the mantelpiece. Something did not square with the child's memory. He picked up a photograph and admired the ornate silver frame. It was a good match to the other two frames which kept it company. None of them had been here when he was a boy. And now he realized another oddity. The only picture of Cousin Max in the entire apartment was this newsprint photo which accompanied his obituary. No, on closer inspection, it was not an obituary. It was an article on Edith Candle, the famed medium who had predicted her husband's death.

This must be the same article Mallory had seen. According to the text, neighbors had confirmed the death prediction from the appearance of writing scrawled on the walls of the couple's SoHo apartment.

The next newsprint photo, encased in a similar frame, was a portrait of a destroyed child. Large eyes, desolate and bewildered, peered out of a face not quite sixteen years old. This was the account of a boy's suicide. Edith's name appeared throughout the text. In the third companion frame was the posed and professionally photographed engagement portrait of a happy young woman. According to the article below the photograph, she had died in violence on the eve of her wedding.

"Charles?"

Edith was standing in the doorway, holding on to a tray of teapot and cups, condiments, sandwiches and silverware.

He took the heavy tray from her hands. "Let's have lunch in here, shall we? You know, I haven't

253

been in this room since I was a boy. Has Kathleen ever been back here?" He set the tray down on the octagonal game table surrounded by leather armchairs.

"Yes, I believe I gave her a complete tour of the apartment."

He noted the slight distraction in her eyes and an agitation to her movements as she sat down at the table and began to pour out the tea.

"What's troubling you, Edith?"

"It's Kathy. I'm very worried about that child."

"She's no child, and she's frighteningly capable."

"I don't believe she understands what she's up against. I can feel the evil, Charles. I can put out my fingers and feel it."

He looked to the photographs on the mantel. "I expect you've had these feelings before."

"I have. And the sad thing is, I was never able to avert tragedy. Perhaps it's true that destiny is writ and cannot be undone."

He walked over to the mantel and picked up the photo of the young suicide. "A case in point?"

She looked up to see what he was holding, eyes refocusing through the thick lenses, and then she looked quickly away, back to the business of pouring, a task she took exaggerated pains with. Finally done with the ritual of one lump or two, she said, "That boy's been on my conscience for years. It was a terrible tragedy. Max and I were doing a head act then. We were on the tent-show circuit in the Midwest. Oh, that was a time. A different town every night, pitching the tent in hay fields and empty lots."

She reached out for the silver frame, and Charles put it into her hand.

"It was this boy who brought out my true gift. I

254

had the sense of him close by, I could feel him. That night I took off my blindfold and looked hard at the boy. I foresaw his death. He was unkempt, he hung his head, hiding something. 'You must tell the police what you have done,' I told him. I thought if he confessed, he might be spared. The boy ran out. Later, a missing girl was found in a shallow grave in the lot behind his shack. Later still, the boy was found hanged in his jail cell."

"Was there any warning about the boy's death? Automatic writing? Anything like that?"

"No, that came later, much later."

"And it's happened again? Recently? What did Martin see written on the walls?"

She wouldn't meet his eyes. Her gnarled hands worked in her lap as she examined a lace doily with keen interest. "I didn't want him to see it. You know how sensitive Martin is. I was trying to clean it off when he walked into the kitchen. I hadn't even heard the front door open."

He could only imagine what patience it must have taken for her to build a relationship with Martin.

"The writing, what did it say?"

"It said, 'Blood on the walls and in the halls, rivers and oceans of blood.'"

The thrift store clerk was working alone. His co-workers were having an affair on the lunch hour, and he was being a good sport. Pity they weren't here now, because John and Peter would never believe this. He hardly believed it himself. The learning-disabled shoplifter had covertly deposited a load of silverware in the box for utensils.

She was moving quickly to the door with her empty towel, and then, as though she had just remembered something, she spun around on her heel

255

and returned to the box. She picked up a knife and polished it with her towel, and then another, and another. Now she was lifting the box and setting it on the floor. She sat down beside it and spilled all the utensils out on the threadbare carpet.

A middle-aged woman with iron-gray hair and the attitude of an amateur social worker was standing over the girl, speaking to her in soft words that did not carry across the room. The girl in the dirty and torn red dress only stared at the knife in front of her eyes, blind and deaf to everything else, concentrating on her work, polishing each piece of silverware. No, he realized now, it was not each piece. The girl seemed to favor the knives. She began to hum to herself as she polished them with her dirty towel.

The iron-gray woman walked up to his counter, and together in tense but companionable silence, they watched the girl working away at each blade, polishing and polishing.

The woman turned to him with fire alarms in her eyes and in her voice. "Shouldn't you call someone?"

"No reason. She's not violent."

"Seriously, you don't think that's crazy?"

"This is New York City, lady. Crazy isn't good enough. If she wants a room in Bellevue Hospital, she's gotta kill somebody to get it."

Charles set the photograph back on the mantelpiece. In the time it took to cross the small room, he had come to a few alarming conclusions about these photographs, and now he turned his mind back to the main event.

Redwing had strong powers by Edith's estimation, and she was also dangerous, reeking of

Santeria, that mix of Catholic rites and voodoo, sympathetic magic and animal sacrifice. Now he multiplied the dangers to Mallory.

"Actually, Martin saw the second writ," Edith was saying on the periphery of his hearing. "Herbert saw the first one. Well, the first prediction in years, and I don't remember making it. The words that Herbert saw were 'Death is close by time and space.'"

"Have you spoken to Herbert recently?"

"Not for a few days, no. He was quite concerned about poor Martin."

"Poor Martin?"

"Well, Martin is a bit touched, isn't he." It was not a question. She made the spinning motion of finger to temple to indicate that Martin's mind might have stripped a few gears. And he found that odd, because Martin was not the least bit insane. Henrietta, a practicing psychiatrist, had never used that word. Sensitive, she called him, and fragile, but not insane.

Martin had designed a life to complement his art. True, he had organized his private world within extraordinary parameters. Like Henry Cathery, he had opted for simplicity, even striking the noise of color from his surroundings, keeping to the hush of white, the better to listen. Martin would be sensitive to every nuance against the pure white background of his life.

Charles suspected Henrietta kept a protective watch on Martin for a reason other than impending breakdown. Might Henrietta be watching over Martin in the way a miner kept one eye to the canary's cage suspended from the rafters at the lower levels of the earth? When the fragile canary gasped and fluttered and struck its weak wings

257

against the bars of its cage, the miner would know the air had gone foul, and Henrietta would know that Edith was active again.

Edith's gifts did not extend to following the rush of an intellect that worked in microseconds. And as he picked her brains for the critical details, she mistook it all for polite conversation. Leaving his sandwich and tea untouched, he bid her goodbye and took his hurried leave.

* * *

Mallory cut the ignition and her lights while the car was still in motion. She pulled silently to the curb. "This is the building Redwing calls home this week." Leaning across Riker, she looked out the passenger-side window. "Keep an eye on the television screen in that first-floor apartment."

Riker stared into the lighted rectangle of the tenement building and the interior poverty which made a burglar gate on the window a bad investment. An old black-and-white television set was sitting on a card table. The wall behind it was a mosaic of cracks and peeling paint. A battered-to-stuffings easy chair sat to one side of the television, and all that showed above the chair's back was a balding head and tufts of dingy white hair.

Mallory was lifting her laptop computer out of its case. "Tell me when the TV picture breaks up."

Riker noted that Mallory had added a few new toys to her car. The antenna on the front fender was not made for ordinary radio reception. And he now recognized the black phone set in her left hand as telephone company equipment. "No you don't, kid. You're not doing a phone tap without a warrant,"

"No, I'm not. I won't hear one human voice. I'm

258

going to pull an electronic scramble out of the air and reassemble it on my computer. Cite me the federal code for that one."

Riker turned back to the apartment window, the better to avoid witnessing. "So what happens when the TV picture breaks up?"

"The old man sitting in front of the set will get up and start banging on it."

Riker nudged her arm. The set's screen was gone to zigzags and lost vertical hold. The old man got up from his easy chair and began pounding on the set. There was no anger in the pounder's face, but Riker thought the old man might be crying.

The screen on Mallory's laptop came to life. "We're in. The wiring in this building is the pits. Redwing doesn't know her computer busts up the old man's reception, and the old man doesn't know what a computer is. Look at the set."

Riker turned back to the window. The television reception had returned to normal. The old man walked back to his chair.

"There," said Mallory. "Now you got me on unlicensed TV repair."

How many times had she done this trick?

"I want you to promise me you won't come back here again. You can't just go into surveillance work without training," How could he explain to Mallory that she could never do covert surveillance, even with the training, because she had glorious blond hair and a face that tended to linger in memory, for years or a lifetime. "You never put in the time wetnursing sources—pimps and junkies, thieves and dealers, prostitutes—all the eyes and ears you need on the street just to get through a day on the job. A beat cop has more to work with than you do."

"Yeah, right. What about all the SEC documents

from Markowitz's side of the bulletin board? All the background checks? He got that from me, not from any of your damn street people. And who gave you the séance connection? I didn't have to pressure a pimp or roll a sick junkie to get any of it."

True, Mallory was the best source Markowitz had ever had.

"Coffey can't use the stock market material," he said. "If he calls the SEC into this too early, we'll all be up to our tails in feds. He won't let go of Lou's murder, not to them. He wants to keep it in the family, you know?"

"I know."

"But you and I need an understanding about Redwing. You could get killed pulling a stunt like this—"

"I'm not a rookie—"

"When it comes to fieldwork, you are. He screwed up, that's a fact. And you're following him into the same hole, running a surveillance with no backup."

He was talking to the air. She was staring at the screen of her computer. "So what kind of setup does Redwing have? Is she stealing money by computer hacking?"

"She wouldn't know how. Redwing is an adequate technician. She can run a computer program, but she could never design one. The past few days I've watched her scanning message centers. She's waiting for something. I'm guessing they use different message centers every time she talks to whoever's running the scam. That gives me at least one player above Redwing's level."

He looked down at the screen of her laptop computer. "Okay, what're we looking at?"

"The same thing Redwing's looking at. It's an electronic bulletin board system. Anyone in the

260

world with a telephone can log on and leave a message. The one she's lifting off the board is in code. Kid stuff. I'll break it down in another minute."

Riker looked back to the old man's window. Whatever Redwing was into, it didn't pay well. Not that the interior of one apartment was a sure indication of a bad neighborhood. And it wasn't the rats dancing on the garbage can lid; he'd seen them uptown and down. But the condoms on the sidewalk told him it was a hooker block. The next block over might be straight middle-class working stiffs. That was New York. Turn any corner and the atmosphere changed. On the next street over, a storefront window displayed toys; on this block, it was adult books and peep shows.

"I like this," said Mallory. "I like it a lot. She's not picking up background checks on victims. She's gathering stock information on mergers and takeovers. If this is nonpublic, if it doesn't tally with SEC filings, it's insider trading."

"Mallory, can you break this into simple English? I'm not a stocks-and-bonds kinda guy. I guess you didn't know that."

"Your niece works for a law firm, right?"

"Gloria, yeah. She's a paralegal."

"Let's say Gloria is working up the contract for a merger between two companies. She has a little lead time before the paperwork on the merger is filed with the SEC. Now she knows the stock will go up in value the minute the merger is made public. Suppose Gloria gives that information to a friend before it goes public? The friend makes a fortune on stock purchases and gives your niece a cut of the profits. The original stockholders are cheated because they've sold their shares to Gloria's friend,

261

and sold them for a song. The feds really hate that."

"It's like a rigged horse race?"

"You got it. You see these numbers and letters?" She pointed to the first column of type on the screen. "These are stocks. I'm guessing they're identified by current market quotations. I'll have to check the paper when we get back. The numbers following the stock IDs are purchase orders. It doesn't fit with any séance scam. She's into something too big for any one person. A medium-size bank couldn't handle these transactions."

"Suppose we get a warrant to pick up her computer?"

"No good without a direct link to the player who feeds her the information. She has a legal loophole. This bulletin board qualifies as public access, same as printing stock information in a newspaper. Now that's smart, very smart, and not Redwing's idea. You're looking for somebody with a brain, access to trading activity and organization skills."

"Coffey's gonna love this."

"Yeah, right. Tell him it's a gift from the rookie. So, what have you got for me?"

"Kid, I gave you my wad," he said, and that was the truth. She turned away from him, not believing in him anymore.

Margot held the switchblade in her hand as she listened to the phone ringing endlessly, twenty, thirty times. She knew how to wait. He would answer. The switchblade had been cleaned for the tenth time and the blade gleamed, throwing its light on the walls. No answer. She continued to wait. It was what she did best. She had waited years for the man with the dancing knife. She looked down at the blade as it caught the light in a sliver of metal.

She had decided to keep the switchblade. The blood had been boiled away on the stove. It was safe. She would keep it. It might bring her luck. It hadn't been so lucky when it tumbled to the desk in the bank, but that was before she killed the bogeyman. Maybe she'd take it back to the bank. What was she going to do about the bank? Henry would know.

The phone continued to ring.

Maybe Henry would let her use his lawyer to get the advance money. Maybe she would just go back with the knife in her pocket. She was luckier today. A tourist had put a dollar bill in her cup and now there was enough in the cup for a slice of pizza and a subway token. It amazed her how easily money could be had when one looked as she did and smelled as she did.

Thirty minutes later, she rounded the corner to Avenue C in that section of the East Village called Alphabet City. It was also called the war zone. This was where the law was not. And so it startled her to see a cop on the sidewalk talking to another cop in the car parked in front of her building.

So the banker had turned her in. Bastard. She would get the little twit for that.

She turned around and headed back to the subway, picking a cup from a trash can as she walked along the sidewalk. Don't run, she told herself, running is a dead giveaway. She panhandled her way down the street in the security that no one, cop or civilian, looked into the face of poverty if they didn't have to.

The VCR was set to loop endlessly, and so, Markowitz danced through the night. Mallory fell asleep to the lullabies of the fifties, and he rock 'n' rolled into her dreams. The dancing detective held Mallory in his arms. She was unconscious, and he was trying desperately to wake her. The dream ended with the dip. He bowed her body down until she lay upon the floor at the base of the cork wall. He was yelling at her. What was he saying? Why couldn't she understand?

She woke, lifting her head from the desk, eyes slowly adjusting to the images on the video. Markowitz danced off with young Helen, twirling away from the camera's eye, leaving Mallory alone in the dark. Her hands slowly rose above her head, curled into fists and came back to the desk as hammers.

Why had they left her all alone?

Chapter Nine

Was it night? Was it day? Margot read the time off the passenger's watch but there was no way to know if it was eleven in the morning or eleven at night. How long had she been asleep, rolling along on the subway line, back and forth, uptown and down. The subway car door opened and a passenger got on.

She watched him, her eyes doing a slow roll as he took the seat opposite hers. She stared at his mouth. It was distinctive in its cruelty, a harsh line that dipped low and mean on either side. She was not likely to forget it, ever. That mouth, that cruel twisted mouth. She had dreams about that mouth and the dancing knife. The train stopped. The man got off, and she followed after him from a small distance. It was him. He was the one. She followed him into the tunnel leading up to the next level. The knife danced out of her pocket. The blade clicked into the light.

He was the one.

*   *   *

Charles, a well-known figure at the public library, was on a first-name basis with the reference librarian in the periodicals section. John helloed him in passing. Library regulars from bums to academics recognized his nose from a distance of ten shelves, and smiled in anticipation of the inadvertently comical return smile. This time, he was hunting Fanny Evenroe instead of a book. He might have gone to the section of *Who's Who* books, but Fanny knew his quarry personally.

He found her standing at the shelves, lost in the pages of a thick volume. He approached her slowly, giving her all the time in the world to finish her perusal, and there was time to imagine the seventy-something dowager as she had once been. The remarkable bones were splendid and her back had not been bent in the least by age.

He always thought of her in the context of the first memory she had ever shared with him—her Washington, D.C., debut as a seventeen year-old girl in long white gloves and a ball gown, waltzing in a ballroom's soft glow of gaslight globes. Like all romantics of his own generation, he had missed his place in time, arriving too late for chivalry, too late for a waltz.

Fanny's face crinkled into a smile as she returned her book to the shelf and greeted him. She had the gift of making anyone believe they might be the center of her personal universe. She held out both her hands to be grasped in his, and she kissed his face on both cheeks, having to reach only a little. She was over six feet tall, but would not be exact about her height any more than her date of birth.

"It's been ages, Charles. Who is she?"

"Pardon?"

"Something new has been added to your life, and it shows."

"Well, a new problem certainly."

"And what do you call this problem?"

"I used to call it Kathleen. Just lately, I have to call it Mallory."

He brought her up to date on his new partnership as they lined up for coffee and croissants on the stone concourse between the flights of steps leading up to the formidable doors of the reference library. By the time they were seated under the shade of the table umbrella in view of the stone lions and the street traffic of Fifth Avenue, he had just broached the subject of his investigation.

"Yes, it's the same man," she said. "I knew him well. He was very handsome when he was young, a senator's aide when I met him. I danced with him more times than I can say. He was one of the few men taller than I was. I was heartbroken when he returned to his home state to practice law."

"Did you ever see him again?"

"Oh yes, years later, and neither of us had married. There were other dances. He came back to Washington as a congressman this time. He was in the House of Representatives for two terms before he ran for senator."

"Did he win?"

"Not the first time out or even the second, but finally he did. Then after he'd returned to private practice for a time, he was appointed to the Court. It

266

was an excellent appointment. He's a remarkable man. I follow his career with great interest."

"Did he ever discuss the boy with you?"

"Yes. That child was always with him."

"The case isn't mentioned in any of his published papers. I wondered if he'd simply put it behind him."

"Would you like to speak with him?"

"It's possible?"

"You're not suggesting he might have forgotten me, are you, Charles?"

"Certainly not." For she was one woman who could not be undone by time and the faultiest memory. When her name would be mentioned to the Supreme Court justice by his law clerk this afternoon, there would be no fumbling through history for her face.

When they parted company, he handed her into a cab and returned to the library to hunt down the third photograph on Edith Candle's mantelpiece.

He guessed at the rough date. He was within a year of her coverage, turning the dials on the microfiche reader as quickly as most people flipped pancakes, missing nothing on the pages. It would have happened during the years of his sabbatical in Europe.

Ah, there she was, the bride, smiling out at him, never guessing she would soon be shot to death by her fiancé on the eve of her wedding. How the devil was he going to get the particulars? Oh, foolish question. What could Mallory not get for him in the way of information? But no, it was better to bypass her on this one.

Sergeant Riker was a decent sort. He would help and not rat him out to Mallory.

Henry Cathery had a moment of utter clarity brought on by the appearance of Redwing in the street below. Wasn't it too soon for another séance? He stood by the window and his eyes cleansed of abstraction, a moment he seldom achieved away from the chessboard.

The phone was ringing behind him and had been doing so all day. Normal people were not so persistent, even annoying salespeople and policemen. It could only be Margot wanting money. She would bleed him dry if he allowed it.

He stared down at the player on the sidewalk at the edge of the flat plain of Gramercy Park. At last he saw it all in utter clarity—past, present and future. And then it was gone and he was left with the decision of whether or not to end the ringing of the telephone. He walked over to the instrument and turned off the bell. Then he wandered out to the kitchen with a thought of food, but with no idea in hell how to get it out of the cans. His IQ was 187.

"I appreciate your getting back to me, sir," said Charles. Though he was not surprised, considering his conduit.

"Well, the message intrigued me. I had no idea anyone would ever give that boy another thought. Hard to lose a case that way, whether the state sets the rope or the boy hangs himself."

The man's voice twanged in the dialect of the heartland. And there were other taut strings to the man's mood. This was no distant memory, but one oft recalled.

"The boy was guilty, wasn't he?"

"You know what that child was guilty of? He was guilty of doing the right thing by Tammy Sue Pertwee. He married her across the state line, and

268

then that fifteen-year-old boy spent the next six months working at bad jobs, night and day, to provide for her and the baby that was coming."

"A baby?"

"She died in childbirth. No one could have saved her. But that came out much later, after the boy died. The county coroner really dragged his feet on that one, the son of a bitch. They found the baby in the grave with Tammy Sue. They were lying in a crude, knocked-together box. I saw the photographs before they were destroyed. It was a heartbreaker—a dead child holding on to a dead child."

"There's no mention of a baby in any of the newspapers."

"The girl's family had that hushed. Supposedly, the photographs were lost. The boy told me they were planning to go home again when the baby's age wasn't so noticeable. Tammy Sue had been beaten by her daddy a few times, and the boy didn't think she'd stand up to another blow. The boy's family didn't even come for the body. Didn't want to acknowledge him as one of their own. It was a real circus here, midnight torch parades with signs that said 'Kill the Monster' and 'Justice for Tammy Sue.' The local merchants sold beer and hot dogs outside the jail. The boy had a clear view of the whole sideshow from his cell window.

"He cried himself to sleep every night. He was just a kid, remember. Twelve nights went by that way, till one fine summer morning, the sheriff found him dangling from the light fixture. He'd made a rope of his bedding. And then there were three dead children."

"Did Edith Candle know the whole story?"

"I told her husband, Max Candle, the magician. I expect he mentioned it to her, or maybe not. I did

269

ask him to. I thought it might help the boy's case if she made a statement to the press. But it was too late to do any good. It was the next day the boy killed himself. Max Candle sent me money to bury him, quite a lot of money. I bought that child the biggest monument in all of Claire County and buried him on the hill with the quality, and didn't the townsfolk just love that."

Before Mallory left the house, she slipped a quarter into the watch pocket of her jeans in the unconscious habit of fifteen years of telephone change. All that varied in this ritual of the coin was that it no longer came from Helen's hand. "So you can call home if you're in trouble," Helen had said each morning, whether packing little Kathy off to school or tall Kathy off to college classes, and then later, the police academy. "You only have to call, and we'll be there. We'll come for you," Helen would say as she handed Kathy her lunch box and her telephone change.

Mallory had never minded being the only one among the sophisticated Barnard women to carry a lunch box with a cartoon mouse painted on the side. She had no friends in that set, nor had she sought any.

From the age of twelve, her companions had been the computers at NYPD where she spent her after-school hours, three days a week, when Helen had committee meetings and charity work and could not pick her up at the Manhattan day school. Even in the college years, she had spent her free time among those computers, fast becoming an asset to Markowitz. But she was still a child when she hacked her way into the requisition department, and shortly thereafter, the computers became more up-

270

to-date. Packages began to arrive, containing computer components which little Kathy, and later, tall Kathy assembled into a state-of-the-art system. Markowitz had learned to avert his eyes each time he passed her computer monitor.

She fingered the quarter in her pocket. She had been such a cared-for, watched-over child, she had never needed to use that quarter. And they could not come for her now. Telephones were not so advanced. Yet the quarter rested in the pocket, connecting her by memory if not by the telephone company.

On her way to the door, she noticed the blinking light on her answering machine. She depressed the play button. Her single message was from Riker. Redwing had moved again in the night. He had neglected to tell her where.

Chapter Ten

Edith Candle peered through her thick glass lenses with a child's magnified eyes. "Best that you stay clear of her, Kathy."

"How did you get Redwing's address?"

Edith removed her glasses and went through the time-stalling machinations of cleaning the lenses. Her naked eyes took on their real and rather ordinary proportions.

Just another illusion, thought Mallory.

"She gave me the address," said Edith, restoring her magnified eyes and pushing the glasses up the bridge of her nose. "She called this morning. We had a rather long talk."

"Did she ask you to come and see her?"

271

"Yes."

"Did she tell you not to mention it to anyone?"

"She did ask me to keep her confidence, but I don't remember the exact wording."

"Give me the address."

"Did you want to come with me? I don't think she'd like that, dear. She asked that I come alone."

"I don't want you to leave the house. Give me the address."

"No, dear, I don't think I will."

Mallory sat back in her chair and stared at a point beyond Edith's white head, wondering how much it would take to bully the old woman. Edith was a little person; it shouldn't take much effort. And if she did frighten Edith—just a little—how much flak might she expect from Charles?

It was a rare win for Charles.

"Edith, what do you know about that woman that I don't know?"

"I know the underlying violence in her. It's too risky, Kathy."

Mallory noted the Rolodex sitting by the phone. It was out of place in this room of antimacassars and ancestor portraits. A ballpoint pen lay next to the Rolodex. There might as well be a neon arrow to point the way.

"How about some coffee, Edith? Will you give me that much?"

"Of course, dear."

The moment Edith was through the door to the kitchen, Mallory found the new card under the *Rs* and plucked it out of the file.

When they were done with coffee, Mallory gathered up her keys and said, "Promise you won't keep that appointment?"

"If it worries you, of course I won't. But before

272

you go, I think there's something you ought to see."
She led Mallory back to the hallway and into the
large kitchen. Faint letters worked over with
cleaning solvent were scrawled on the wall over the
stove.

Edith, with all her gifts, could not have read
Mallory's face as she turned to the young woman
and said, "Just like Max,"

Mallory only said, "Yeah, right."

Redwing's eyes rolled back when the Doberman
puppy crept into the kitchen. He was new to this
game of hers, but pain had taught him quickly. He
was also half mad with hunger and thirst.

A small plate of raw meat sat on the floor between
the woman's feet. He inched toward it, one eye to
the woman who was punishment and delight,
cigarette burns in his flesh and sensual croons and
strokes. He nosed the red meat. The odd smell of it
was familiar to him now. Every good instinct to let
it be was overcome by hunger. He tasted it. He
wolfed it. And now the thirst was stronger and the
room began to revolve. No, it was he who turned in
slow circles, his tongue dropping out between his
teeth. Thirst, terrible thirst. His dark head sank low,
close to the floor. His tongue licked the dirt of the
tiles, and his eyes closed to crazed slits of white. He
began the low growl that would build into a
howling.

It was a bright, clear day, and still warm in the
patches of sunlight. The West Village dogs gathered
in the fenced-off triangle of Washington Square
Park for the canine social hour, when they were
allowed to slip their leashes. They chased Frisbees,
sniffed one another, rolled in the dirt and grinned
273

gloriously with slobbering saliva.

In the space of seconds only, all the dogs stopped grinning at once, noses lifting to the wind, trying to identify the danger. Their humans were slower to pick up on the change in the atmosphere. The dogs moved in concert to one corner of the triangle and away from the black Labrador who had gone strange in the eyes, which were all whites now and narrowed to slits. The dark head hung low and the dog's tongue hung out. His growl was low and constant.

Something caught the dog's eye. He turned his head in tandem with the bright gold hair of the woman striding across the small West Village park on her way to the East Side. Her hair threw off sparks of sun, and the dog followed her progress with mad eyes. His was not the dog's grin, but the barred teeth of a threat. He moved in an unsteady lope toward the edge of the triangle. His human came toward him on slow, cautious feet. "Here, boy," the slender young woman called to him, holding out his collar and leash. He ignored her and hung his head over the low fence. She came closer. He spun on her quickly and nipped her hand for the first time in the seven years they had loved one another. She looked down at the teeth marks, small wells filling with blood. She was too shocked to scream.

The dog moved back a few steps and made a run at the fence, clearing the top of it by a bare inch. He was soft-pounding over the cement of the walk, following the golden woman with her sun-sparked hair. Now his human did scream and the golden one turned around to see him bounding toward her, his tongue hanging, growling low. A child passed between them, and the flash of the child's red T-shirt turned his head. He lunged for the child and

274

closed his teeth around the tiny freckled arm. The small human was alternately crying and screaming, eyes wide with terror. The dog's teeth clamped down hard until he heard the snap of the human's puny bone breaking between his jaws. Now he tossed the child back and forth with the shake of his head.

The golden girl was running toward him, calling to him, whistling high and shrill. But he was busy with the meat in his mouth. The golden one kicked him in the head, and again in the ribs. Now she had all his attention. He dropped the boy's arm from his mouth, his black lips spreading to show all his teeth as she backed away from him. His jaws opened wide and he made the leap for the golden one, who was waving him to her. It was the leap of his life, quick and with more strength than he knew he possessed. His eyes were fixed on her white throat, he was in the air, flying to her when the world exploded.

The metal in her hand smoked and his heart burst in the same moment. Her face filled his last seconds of life as she bent over him and nudged his body with the barrel of her gun. Her face was cold, without passion for the kill. The golden one was a different kind of animal than he had ever known. And then she moved on, and the dog stared at the sun until it went black.

A woman was cradling the torn and broken four-year-old boy. Mallory took the child from her arms and laid him down on the grass, elevating the bloody arm. She clamped off the fountain of blood from the severed artery with the pressure of her hand. Her eyes perused the crowd of unfamiliar faces, searching for the one who was no stranger. Riker elbowed his way through the crowd to kneel alongside of her. She had known he could not be far behind.

"Give me your belt," she said.

He stripped it off and handed it to her. She looked up to the closest civilian. "Get the ambulance. Use the phone in the NYU building. And you," she said to a nearby woman. "There's a doctor's office in that brownstone. Go get him. Tell him it's a lawful police order if he doesn't move fast enough. Riker, put some pressure on the artery."

Riker's hand replaced her own over the wound.

"That's a major artery. Keep the pressure on till the ambulance gets here."

Hands free, she bound the broken arm with the belt and a skateboard. She commandeered Riker's jacket and two other jackets to cover the child and keep him warm, to minimize the damage of shock that was already settling into his enormous eyes. The pain would come later. Now he was only crying for his mother.

She stood up, waved goodbye to Riker and moved quickly across the park, leaving him to the first aid and the paperwork of a dog bite. She smiled as she put more distance between them. Riker was a department legend. No suspect had ever shaken him off a tail. This was a first, and he would be a long time getting over it.

"Hi, Charles. It's Riker. Is Mallory around?...You got any idea where she might be?...How did you know?...Yeah, I've been following her during the day, but the brat gave me the slip.... It's important that I find her, like now, this minute. If she wanted to lose me, and she did, she's onto something.... Yeah, I'm worried too."

Riker hung up the pay phone in front of the supermarket and turned east on Bleecker Street. It

276

was early yet, not quite dark, but the Halloween costumes were spotting the streets with purple tinsel hair and monster masks. A giant tube of toothpaste walked by, and then a leafy plant on two legs. A smallish gang of werewolves and ghouls who did not come up to his recently rebuckled belt were being escorted down the street under the protective eyes of two moms. It was rare to see a child without a bodyguard in any part of the city. The smallest of the monsters wore a trendy mask from a science fiction movie.

"Boo!" the child yelled at Riker who obliged him by putting up his hands and yelling, "Don't hurt me!" The children laughed, and the bodyguards herded them on as Riker headed south toward the precinct.

Oh, kid, he said to himself, you don't know what scary is.

"'The paladin will die!' That's Mallory, isn't it? Isn't it, Edith!"

The scrawl was faint red and overlaid with scouring powder. Charles had not been breathing as he read it, and he had to make a conscious effort to resume. Edith Candle was twisting a tissue into shreds, leaving the kitchen.

He followed her down the hall, stopping at the door to Max's library. His eye for the thing out of place drew his attention to the clutter on the octagonal table. He could see the heavy scrollwork of an ornate silver frame which lay beneath a newspaper, exposed only by one corner. His eye went to the mantelpiece where the set of three frames sat intact. This one on the table would be a match.

Edith was pulling on his sleeve. "I'm very upset

just now, Charles. I'm really not up to having any company today."

Ignoring her, he walked into the library and stood by the table. Within inches of the silver frame was a large manila envelope bearing the return address of a New York clipping service. It lay on top of hastily concealed scraps of paper. As he lifted the newspaper off the frame, he uncovered a photograph of Mallory, a close-up taken at Louis Markowitz's funeral. Her beautiful face was trapped behind the glass of the silver frame. Charles crossed the room in two strides and grasped Edith by the shoulders.

"Who is going to kill Mallory, Edith? Who?"

"I can't tell. My gift is not that strong."

"Screw the gift. You set her up. Who's going to kill her?"

"You don't know what you're saying."

He went to the mantel and picked out the portrait of the young bride-to-be. "Her fiancé lived in this building. His name was George Farmer. George Farmer killed his fiancée the night before the wedding, and then he turned the gun on himself. He's a vegetable now, isn't he? Lying in a private hospital, staring at the ceiling. I'm told he drools a bit now and then. But he wasn't the one who died, so he didn't merit a silver frame. That's how it works, isn't it?"

"My gift carries a terrible burden, Charles. I tried to avert that tragedy. But I failed."

"Hardly a failure, Edith. By your obscene standards, it was a roaring success. And Cousin Max? You killed his concentration, didn't you? You were the last person he wanted to see that night. That's why my parents stopped bringing me by for visits with you. They knew you manipulated his death. And now you've set Mallory up to die. You

278

worked the damn thing out, didn't you? Of course, the old women, the séances, who would have better insider information than you? Who's going to kill her, Edith?"

"I can't believe you're saying these things."

"Originally you were planning to orchestrate an accident with Herbert and his gun. Martin was going to be the victim this time. Just a little something to keep your hand in, right? Herbert's a rather twisty, frightened little man, isn't he? Probably wasn't much of a challenge for you."

"Charles, you're distraught. You don't—"

"But then along came Mallory with all her violence, all her hate, all that beautiful young energy waiting to be fired like a bullet. And you changed your plans. Do I have it right? Where has she gone?"

"I don't know. I only know that she's in danger."

"That much I believe."

He touched the edge of the silver-framed portrait on the desk. "Kathleen Mallory is not your trophy." He brought down his fist to break the glass and free her image. The blood streamed from the tear in his hand. He left a red palm print on the door as he quit the apartment with the wadded photograph of Mallory in the closed fist of his good hand.

Mallory took stock of the VCR, the color television, and the most expensive stereo known to audiophiles and burglars. It didn't fit with the peeling wallpaper and the threadbare carpet. The air was ripe with spaghetti sauce, and the stronger smell of garbage wafted up from the air shaft window, which had been opened against the heat from the clanking radiator.

A Doberman puppy padded into the room, eyes blind to his surroundings, dazed and favoring a foreleg as he walked. The little boy sat on the floor in front of the television.

The boy looked up at her as though from a great distance and not the few feet that separated them. His yellow eyes rolled after her as she followed Redwing into the next room.

The kitchen, which was also the bathroom, had the same proportions as the front room. A purple shower curtain hid the tub, all but its lion's-paw feet. A dirty gold drape of black orchid print concealed the toilet, but not the smell of the plumbing backup.

"Sit, sit," commanded Redwing, smiling with all her teeth.

Mallory sat down at a broad table littered with the crumbs and morsels and crusted sauce of the evening meal.

"We will have tea now," said Redwing, moving slowly to a countertop lined with glass jars of unlabeled dry leaves and powders. Redwing opened a cupboard and brought out two teacups which did not match.

"None for me, thanks," said Mallory, staring at the countertop, watching the progress of a roach climbing the toaster, which held all the fingerprints laid on it since the day it was purchased. Each thing was in its proper place, but each place was coated with whatever had been spilled there—yesterday, last month. She leaned down and flicked a roach from her shoe as though she were long accustomed to doing this.

"You must drink the tea."

"Why?"

"The customs of my craft. You cops, you have your tools. I have mine. You want information, you must let me spin my craft, yes?"

Mallory nodded. The boy was standing just inside the door. He seemed to have appeared there. She looked down to his stocking feet. So quiet he was. She had never heard him speak. His eyes fixed upon Mallory and would not let go of her. Redwing spoke to him in French. He climbed a chair to fetch a tin canister from the cupboard, moving in a sleepwalk. More words were fired at him, and now he found the honey jar for Redwing, moving with no will of his own, pulled here and there by her words.

Mallory followed the boy's every move. How much damage had Redwing done to him? He was dressed like any other kid, in good jeans and a T-shirt, but all normalcy ended there. He walked slowly to Mallory, stopping at her chair and setting the honey jar on the table with automaton deliberation.

While Redwing's back was turned on them, Mallory reached out and touched the boy's face. The gentleness of her touch startled both of them. The gauze of dullness lifted from his eyes to give her a sudden window on something quick and bright which lived in there. Mallory smiled at the boy. The boy smiled back, faltering a little. 'I'm coming back for you,' her eyes said as her hand caressed his smooth young face and released it. The boy's eyes rounded, and then a curtain dropped and they were dulled again, two filmy yellow circles, nothing more, no one home.

The clock on the wall was ticking loud. The teakettle whistled and shrieked. The radiator made all the noises of tired metal being overworked, pouring out more heat than the room could hold. Redwing closed the window, the only source of air that was not sweating and stained with odors. The boy retreated to the doorway and hovered there, a

281

tentative, small body without ballast or substance.

Redwing delicately placed the teacups on the table.

"Drink."

A black fly circled Mallory's cup. She waved it off. As she raised the up to her lips, a wisp of Helen resurrected to notice the lipstick stain on the rim, and then the specter evaporated in the heat. Mallory sipped her tea. It was good, and sweet enough without the honey Redwing was spooning into her own cup.

"So you're curious about Pearl Whitman? This was the woman your father died with, was she not?"

Mallory nodded and sipped her tea.

"I once offered my services to the police," said Redwing. "Did you know that? No? They sent me away. No thank you, they said. Then last night, Lieutenant Coffey comes to ask me for information. I told him nothing. Screw the police. But you are not police anymore. With you it is personal. You I will help."

The boy appeared behind the woman's chair. As Redwing smiled broadly, the boy's eyes rolled back and his hands curled up into angry fists.

"Drink it all, and then we look into the dregs of your cup, your life."

"Just promise me you won't tell anyone I made a house call." Henrietta smiled as she snipped the last of the sutures. "Fortunately, most people forget that a psychiatrist is also an M.D. If you rat on me to the tenants, I'll be spending all my free time listening to their aches and pains."

"Not a word," said Charles.

Either she was a wildly gifted stitcher, or he was simply beyond pain. Shock could do that, he

282

supposed.

"It's been a long time since I worked on flesh and blood." She applied the gauze and then the adhesive over the stitches in his hand.

"So, what do you think of our resident medium?"

"It all fits," she said. "Other things have happened here over the years.

"You mean the murder of Allison Warwick?"

Henrietta nodded. "I didn't know George Farmer very well. I'd just moved in. He was only a nodding acquaintance when we met in the halls. But you could see the progress of the paranoia even if you weren't looking for it. I watched him change over a period of about six weeks. By then, I'd come to know Edith very well. She told me about the automatic writing."

"Don't tell me. George walked in one day and saw a message written on the wall."

"Right. The tenants were in the habit of just walking in without knocking, a custom of the house. The writing was about Allison. Edith told me she had no memory of writing it. I'm guessing there'd been quite a bit of writing on the walls in that six weeks. Whatever he saw, it ate away at him."

"It must have been something heinous."

"Not necessarily. People in love are only one step away from psychosis, and you can quote me on that. It wouldn't have taken anything blatant, Edith had time enough to tear him down."

"That was years ago. Has she done any more recent damage?"

"I've watched other things happen on a smaller scale, one tenant pitted against another. I have my suspicions about Herbert's divorce. I didn't tell you because Edith was part of your family. I'm sorry. Poor judgment on my part. Can you tell me any

283

more about these people, these suspects? Do you have a sense that one might be more dangerous to Mallory than the rest?"

"It's a crapshoot," said Charles. "Unless you want to rule out the women. People keep telling me it's not a woman's crime."

"No, I wouldn't rule them out. Is Edith on familiar terms with any of them?"

"She's met Gaynor once, and Redwing the medium, but none of the others that I know of."

"Then I'd go with the medium. Edith would work in her own territory, the surest ground, and Gaynor's probably a more stable personality. Do you have the woman's address?"

"Well, there's nothing in the telephone book under Redwing. Somehow I didn't think there would be. I have an idea Sergeant Riker might be able to get it for me."

"Good. But let's try to suppress the white knight syndrome, okay? Better to just send the police. Think of Mallory. You want someone with a gun to get there first."

"Right, and if she's not in trouble, the worst thing that can happen is that she wipes up the floor with me for interfering."

He dialed the phone and listened to it ring at the police station. After the fourteenth ring, to discourage those who were not seriously robbed, beaten or raped, the phone was answered.

"Sergeant Riker, please."

A recording advised him that all lines were busy, and would he please hold on.

Could he? It had been a long day, and no, he didn't think he could hold on any longer.

The cup was half empty when Redwing closed her

eyes and began to sway back and forth. Mallory
swayed with her, spilling a bit of tea in the motion.
She sipped from her cup and listened to the heavy
breathing. It seemed natural that the walls should
move in and out as they breathed. She could feel the
heartbeat of the house keeping time, beat for tick,
with the clock on the wall.

Redwing crooned nonsense words. Mallory
rocked with her in the same thick sea of boiling air.

The boy ceased his own swaying. Eyes rolled
back to whites, he was going through the motions of
making invisible tea, pouring the water into each
cup, dipping each bag, unscrewing the cap of a
bottle and pouring the contents into one cup but not
the other.

Mallory ceased to sway. She slowly looked down
at the dark liquid sloshing to the sides of her cup. A
yellow residue made a ring above the rich sweet tea.

Drugged.

She smashed her cup to the floor. The linoleum
rolled under her in waves. She fell twice before she
stumble-walked through the kitchen door and into
the front room where the television was pouring out
the stink of sound and sight that seared her eyes and
hurt her ears. She fell again and moved forward on
all fours. Redwing walked placidly beside her as
Mallory crawled along the dirty carpet to the door,
dragging the carpet's store of matted hair and
crumbs snagged in her broken fingernails. Redwing
opened the door wide and smiled.

Mallory stumbled to her feet and fled into the
hallway, running now for the stairs. The hall
telescoped, elongating with every step. And then she
was falling, head hitting hard corners of the stairs,
then a shoulder, a leg, assaulted by the unforgiving
stone steps. She smelled her own blood on her

285

hands. It poured out of every wound and filled the narrow lobby, spilling into the street as she opened the door and swam through it, an ocean of blood.

Out on the street, swirling stars were flying past her, and then the stars screamed at her with horns and shrieks. She listened to louder noises of the blood rushing in her veins. She could taste the color red as it ran from her eyes and flowed in rivulets into her mouth. The flying stars pulsed with color and grew fat and exploded like bloated pimples of pyrotechnics.

Markowitz was calling her. What was he saying? She smelled baking soda and floral air freshener.

"I'm dying," she screamed at him inside her brain where he lived in a corner of her gray matter that looked much like the old house in Brooklyn. Markowitz smiled. 'Don't be a sucker, Kathy.'

'You listen to your father,' said Helen, coming in from the kitchen of Mallory's mind, wearing a pair of yellow rubber gloves, holding out a lunch box. 'Do you have your quarter, Kathy?' And then Mallory was crying and wiping blood from her eyes to feed coins into a silver slot.

"I'm dying! She's killed me! Redwing killed me with the tea!" she screamed into the phone, over the wire, to terrify a gentle man, eight city blocks away, who never bothered to hang up the telephone nor lock his door behind him.

The fluorescent hospital lights made everyone look ill, but Charles thought Jack Coffey looked much worse than Mallory. By the eyes shot with red, the condition of the man's clothes and the stubble of beard, he guessed it had been at least twenty-four hours since the policeman had last seen his bed. With Sergeant Riker, it was more difficult to tell.

286

Mallory, asleep, achieved a look of innocence she could never have managed with her green eyes open. A bandage at the back of her head covered the worst of the cuts. But for the fresh bruises flowering on her bare arms, she was a study in white on white, palest skin showing above the crisp sheets. A white bandage covered the place on the inside of one arm where a tube joined her to a bottle suspended on a T-bar and dripping fluid into her vein. A machine by her bedside kept track of her life signs with low blips of sound and light.

Riker sat in the only bedside chair, eyes trained on the blips as though he were wired into them. And perhaps he was.

"Redwing's shrewd, but not too bright," Jack Coffey was saying as he leaned back against the wall by the bed. "Just for openers, we got her on possession of drugs. She had enough stuff in that apartment to open a store. It was all lying around in the open, like she didn't think we'd come looking."

Coffey was staring down on the sleeping Mallory, and Charles detected something between tenderness and aggravation in the man's expression.

"We're gonna push for dealing, too."

"What about the little boy?" asked Charles.

She had ranted on and on about the boy, even when she believed that she was bleeding from every pore and dying. The drug had ripped her mind to shreds, and yet she had fought for words to tell him about a damaged child. Mallory, the hard case. No one had ever known her, not really, except maybe Helen Markowitz who had only suspected the best of her.

Unpolished grace, unlikely paladin, thy name is Mallory.

"The kid's in custody," Coffey was saying.

287

"There's more than enough evidence of child abuse. Redwing's going away for a long time. In my sleep, I could nail her on five counts, good for five years each. And that's without the stock scam. The U.S. Attorney can try her for that one from a prison cell."

"No murder charge," said Charles. "So, you don't believe she killed Louis Markowitz?"

"Naw. I talked the DA out of it. He only liked the idea 'cause she has the size for it. But she hasn't got the brains to sucker Markowitz. Maybe we'll get something on conspiracy with the bastard she was working for."

"Redwing gave you a name?"

"She doesn't know it. She calls the head of the operation the Director. Before the surveillance team lost her, they'd tracked her through five neighborhoods, one séance for every day of the week. We figure there's more than forty people in the network. We're gonna start rounding them up this morning."

Riker was looking down on his notebook. "Mallory told me they had more action going than a medium-size bank could handle. Between all the séance groupies, there was enough capital to run a small country."

"We can count on half of them climbing over each other in a race to turn state's evidence in exchange for immunity," said Coffey. "It was one of the craziest scams I've ever seen."

"Let me guess, it's more fun that way," said Charles. "The Director used Redwing to collect insider tips from a pool of majority stockholders. Then, instructions for sales and purchases were spread over this large client base—no single transaction large enough to merit investigation. Redwing provides all the clients with the crystal ball

288

defense should the SEC ask questions. Redwing and the Director split their cut of the profits."

"Nicely done," said Coffey. "But it wasn't a split. The Director paid Redwing a very small commission. We had an SEC investigator explain it to her, just the scope of the single transaction Mallory gave us. Redwing went crazy. She had no idea that much money was changing hands. So now she's willing to cooperate, but she can't tell us much."

"If she doesn't know the Director's name, how did the two of them come together?"

"Pearl Whitman set it up. She went out shopping for mediums. She interviewed quite a few of them, Redwing says, before she found one who was reliably dishonest."

"How did the Director receive payment?"

"No idea. We assume Miss Whitman handled that."

"But the séances continued after Whitman's death. Not likely the Director would continue funneling the stock information without payment."

"The SEC man figures we'll find a foreign account set up for deposit. We won't know until we bring in the whole cartel."

"So why the attack on Mallory? It's not too bright, is it? Calling attention to herself by trying to kill a police officer?"

"She said she thought Mallory was going to expose the whole operation."

"Did she say where she got that idea? Did someone suggest it to her?"

"Dumb as Redwing is, it would've been hard to miss Mallory's brains. And then her pretty face was in the paper on the day of Markowitz's funeral, along with a nice little bio on the cop's daughter the cop. Mallory probably scared the shit out of Redwing when she had herself invited to the séance."

Mallory stirred in the white sheets, and three tired men turned to look at her. The gray window light of morning was humanizing the fluorescent lighting.

"Hey, what did the doctor say?" asked Coffey, nudging Riker's chair with one foot.

Riker looked down to his notebook again and read from the page which was blank but for the word *okay*. "It's a new designer drug. Nasty stuff. The doctor who pumped her stomach says he got three deaths put down to this junk in the last year, all from self-inflicted wounds. Victims put their eyes out, rip their veins out. There's no permanent damage to Mallory. She's got a few bruises and cuts. That's it. She'll be okay, but her reaction time's gonna be a little slow for a few days."

"She thought she was bleeding to death when Riker and I brought her in," said Charles. "But there was no blood on her except for that cut on her head and the dried blood from the dog-bite victim."

"It's a lot like LSD," said Riker. "She probably did see the wounds. Even Mallory's got to believe what she sees with her own eyes."

Charles wondered if Mallory had seen the writing on Edith's wall and believed that, too. No, not likely. Not Mallory. She had a first-rate mind. She had probably seen Edith rather clearly then.

So, she was forewarned, and yet she walked into it.

Coffey put his hand on Riker's shoulder. "You're on baby-sitting detail again. Mallory doesn't go anywhere. You got that?"

"Yeah, Lieutenant. I can handle it."

"If you need to get some sleep, have the doctor

sedate the shit out of her first. You got that, too?"

"Yeah."

"Could I have her house keys?" asked Charles. "If she's going to be here for a few days, she'll need some things from home. The nurse gave me a list."

"No problem. And thanks for the help, Charles," Smiling, he shook Charles's hand and held on to it a fraction of a second too long. "Was that old bio on the SoHo murder any use to you?" Coffey was not smiling now.

So Riker had thought it worth mentioning to Coffey. And now Coffey was waiting on Charles to give him an explanation.

"Yes, thank you," said Charles.

The young policeman's brain was not so quick as Mallory's, but worked as well in its own time. Suppose he did give Coffey his explanation? What could Coffey do about it?

Nothing.

What Edith had done he could never prove. But one day soon, he and Coffey must talk. It had to end.

Chapter Eleven

Charles dropped the duffel bag, spilling out Mallory's toothbrush, hairbrush, robe and slippers onto the hall carpet.

He wore the slack-jaw expression of a man who had Just seen a ghost. And he had.

He walked through the open doorway into the den and met Louis Markowitz. The man inhabited this room as surely as if Charles could see him in the body. Louis was at work all over the back wall, and he was as messy as he had been in life.

Charles's memory re-created one section of the den's cork wall as it had appeared in Louis's office before he was murdered. The mental photograph agreed with half this wall. The second half of the wall was also pure Louis Markowitz in style, but the man had been two days dead when the first of these photographs had been taken.

He pulled aside an overlay of paper on the right side of the cork. Photos and papers were more neatly aligned on the next layer. On the bottom layer, every bit of paper was machine-precision straight. Layer by layer, the beautiful machine had gone awry until she had captured her father's method of order passing for chaos.

On Mallory's side of the wall, an early layer of clutter held the background check on Margot Siddon. She had rejected Margot in favor of the medium on the next layer. Henry Cathery and Jonathan Gaynor were off to one side in separate categories. He pulled the photographs of Redwing off the board, eliminating the clutter of the red herring.

"Louis, talk to me," he whispered to the other side of the wall.

The bulletin board began to speak. A handwritten note jumped out at him, and credit reports, early 1980s stock transactions, and bank records. This was all Louis had to work with when he tailed the murderer to the scene of Pearl Whitman's death in the East Village. Was it the murderer he was trailing? Why had they all assumed that?

Mallory's side of the board had more financial data on the top layer, including the U.S. Attorney's probe of Edith Candle and Mallory's probe of Edith's computer. Financial statements dominated both sides of the wall with the money motive. Father and daughter were holding to the same portrait of a killer: sane but evil.

At horrific speed, he read Mallory's neatly typed and incredibly detailed surveillance notes. The medical examiner's reports he took no time with, ripping them from both sides. He knocked loose the pin which held a plastic bag to Markowitz's section. It drifted to the floor to cover the pile of rejects. The beads from Anne Cathery's necklace were also sent to the floor.

Now, with all the extraneous clutter gone, he knew why and how, but not who. Pearl Whitman tantalized him, as she must have done to Markowitz before him. But it was Samantha Siddon who finally gave up the killer's name.

Riker was the first thing Mallory saw when she opened her eyes. In her estimation, he was not a pretty sight. She thought his eyes were redder if that was possible.

His gray, unshaven face collapsed into a smile of relief.

"Hi, kid. How're you doin'?"

"Mallory to you. I feel like I've got a hangover."

"You know, this reminds me of the time you had appendicitis. You were just a little squirt."

"Riker, what's—"

"I went down to the hospital to sweat out your operation with Lou and Helen. Lou said I'd missed the best part. When the emergency room nurse pressed down on your appendix, you kicked her in the gut, he said. I laughed till I cried."

"What's going on, Riker?"

"You remember anything about last night?"

"Redwing." She sat up quickly, too quickly. "Oh

Christ, my head hurts. You got her?"

"We got her for assault and five or ten other counts. Coffey adds on a new one every time something occurs to him. The last thing I saw on his list was 'no dog tags.' He's on a damn mission."

"Where's the boy?" She pulled off the bandage which covered the needle dripping fluid into her arm.

"He's in Juvenile Hall. Don't mess with that needle or I'll call the nurse. You won't like that. She's bigger than you and meaner."

"I have to get out of here." She pulled out the needle and rubbed the hole in her arm. "Where's my stuff?"

"Not so fast, kid. You don't go anywhere, you got that? Don't give me any grief, Kathy."

"Mallory."

"This is personal, kid, not business. But I can make it business. You stay put, or I book you."

"What charge?"

"A stolen Xerox machine."

"Okay, you win."

"Naw. That was too easy, kid. You forget who you're talking to."

"I only want to go home."

"You stay here for the duration."

"I'll stay home for the duration. I'll go nuts if I have to stay here. At least at home I've got my computer."

"And Lou's bulletin board."

"That too."

"You're too weak to go anywhere."

She threw back the covers and swung her bare feet over the edge of the high hospital bed. She landed on the floor, sitting unceremoniously on her backside with a new pain to contend with.

"I told you so," said Riker.

Three women had chimed the warning bells, but they had charitably overestimated him. Bells or no bells, the village idiot was always the last to know his house was on fire.

There had been a warning of sorts toward the end of his mother's life. 'You must never break Edith's seclusion, Charles. Remember that.' And then his mother was gone. And later, when her remains were going to the ground, he was handed a telegram at the graveside, a message of condolence and an invitation to tea. His mother had said nothing about invitations to tea.

Then Mallory had tried to warn him, and how he had thanked her for that. Henrietta had not even tried, wise woman, but tripped the alarm in trying to work around him. One day, if he was to survive this life, to pick up on all the warning bells, he must get a woman of his own, and maybe a white cane and a guide dog as well.

Raindrops pocked the windows of the cab. Forked lightning lit up the streets and lifted the gloom of overcast for an instant before menacing the earth with a clap of thunder. The cabby was driving through the rain with laudable caution and no speed at all, not realizing that the house was on fire.

"Look here," Charles said to the driver. "I'll pay you ten dollars for every red light you go through."

"Oh, you crazy Americans," said the driver, whose name was made up entirely of consonants.

Charles pushed a twenty-dollar bill through the slot in the bulletproof glass.

"I love this country," said the cabby.

She sat across the kitchen table from Riker while the

295

coffeemaker gurgled between them. Her head throbbed, and it crossed her mind that the doctors had packed her braincase with cotton batting.

"Why didn't Charles come back to the hospital with my stuff and my keys?"

"Maybe he did," said Riker. "You didn't hang around very long."

Mallory shook her head. Charles had already been here, so the doorman said, and left in a hurry. She got up from the table.

"Where are you going, kid?"

"Well, not out the front door." Even the Shadow could not pass through solid oak.

After the doorman had let them in with a master key, they had reached a mistrustful standoff when Riker locked the front door dead bolt from the inside and pocketed the spare key from the ring in the kitchen. Next, he had gone to the bedroom window's burglar guard leading out to the fire escape. He had found the key to the padlock and secured that exit, too.

Now she had drunk as much coffee as she could stand, and Riker had matched her cup for cup. Her mind had cleared only a little, and he was showing no signs of the lost night's sleep. If anything, he was jazzed with caffeine, and for the first time, capable of thinking rings around her, anticipating every ploy.

Maybe.

When he was safely lost in the sports section of the morning paper, she walked into her den and pulled the door shut behind her. She dragged a chair from its position at the computer to the center of the room and sat before the board, scanning the whole of the cork wall as one unit, one mind at work. Despite the mess of papers at the baseboard, she was slow to focus, to realize there had been an intrusion here, another mind at work on the board.

Charles.

He had torn off layers of paper and rearranged the photos and printouts. Samantha Siddon had come to prominence in a centered and solitary position. Anne Cathery, Estelle Gaynor and Pearl Whitman were grouped together and off to the side, lined up in the order of their deaths. The financial data came next in Charles's own hierarchy of paper shuffling.

She was staring at the small white beads, Anne Cathery's, torn from her neck on the day of the murder in Gramercy Park. They lay scattered all over the pile of papers and the plastic bag. The ground had been soaked in blood, strewn with beads. In the slide show inside her head, the Cathery murder scene was blending with Markowitz's. She could see herself lining up the blood pools of Markowitz's face. 'Line 'em up flat with the floor,' Dr. Slope had told her then.

She walked to the baseboard and knelt down by the pile of Charles's rejects and the plastic bag. Something was missing. What had Charles taken away with him? Her drugged brain would not move quickly enough. She turned to the faster brain of her computer and called up the files to match the missing sequence numbers. And now she could see all that Charles had seen.

There was writing on the wall, and there was writing on the wall.

Charles hammered on the door.

No response.

He tried the knob. The door was unlocked. He entered slowly. The front room was curtain-drawn dark. Down the hall, a rectangle of light reflected off one wall opposite the door to the library. When he rounded the wall and stood in the open doorway, he faced a dark shape in an armchair pulled out to the center of the room and back lit by the bright light of a table lamp.

"Oh, it's you," said Edith's voice.

His eyes were slow to sort out the details of the gun's barrel and bullet chambers as she lowered it to her lap.

Edith smiled. "I suppose you think I'm a foolish old woman to be so frightened."

"Oh, no. I don't take you for a fool. And you left your door unlocked—that doesn't argue well for fear. Herbert's gun, I presume? How did you convince him to part with it? Ah, but wait. I forget. You're the one who talked him into getting it. And you were the one who sent one of the séance ladies that threatening letter. That was for Mallory's benefit, wasn't it? To send her after Redwing. Who else have you been sending notes to?"

"What are you saying?"

"This isn't a case of second sight." The wave of his hand took in the gun, and the lamp. "It's a sure thing. You're expecting an invited guest. Did you telephone or write?"

"You believe that I would deliberately use myself as bait? I'm not so brave."

"I'd say it was more like an ambush. Oh, Mallory is alive. That must be a great disappointment to you."

"Charles, how can you—"

"You knew who the murderer was. The last thing you wanted was to have the monster caught by Mallory. You were going to do that job yourself. What a coup. You protect yourself from prison and make a career comeback in one shot."

298

"If your mother could hear the things you're say—"

"My mother knew what you were," said Charles. "You've branched out a bit, though, added on a few more enterprises. I might have worked this out sooner, but it was so out of character for you to let a mark in on the action. Now there are forty of them, all in on it. Getting a bit out of hand, isn't it? Were you craving a little excitement? All those people involved in the scam. Did you enjoy the thrill to the threat of discovery? A young chess player tried to explain that special joy to me the other day. You look frightened, Edith. I think the killer has the same fears."

"I don't know what you mean."

"Read my mind—if the prospect doesn't frighten you. The Whitman merger wasn't your first or last bit of larceny. It wasn't sufficient to account for the amounts in your stock portfolio. You see these?" He pulled a wad of computer printouts from his pocket. "Mallory knew, but I wouldn't listen to her. She backtracked the increases in your fortune and tallied them with details of insider trading. The forty partners told you everything—a new product that led to an increase in stock value, a pending merger, a sale, a takeover. They even allowed you to set the dates of their transactions, just as Pearl Whitman did when her company went into merger. Then somebody started killing off your partners. The police started investigating commonalities among the victims. Exposure was a threat."

"Stop this, Charles, before you—"

"You and the murderer had so much in common. First killing for the money, then learning to love it. You were soul mates, twins, and the two of you were bound together by the same racket."

299

"This is ludicrous. You can't hold me responsible for—"

"I see your hand in everything, Edith. You primed Redwing and baited Mallory. You set Mallory up to die. That's your forte, isn't it? First you predict the death and then you make it happen. She was bright enough to expose you. That would have meant the loss of your fortune and freedom. Hers would have been a challenging death and so functional, too. How neat. But you're not orchestrating things anymore. When the killer walks in, I'll be here. Not you. Now get out of here. Go across the hall to Henrietta's apartment."

"I assure you, I'm capable of—"

"Get out!"

Mallory closed out the file raided from the last financial house on her list and pushed her chair away from the computer. Well, Edith had told her, straight out, you can get away with a lot when you're old.

She slipped by the open kitchen door. Riker was still immersed in the sports section. She walked through her bedroom and into the bathroom to turn on the shower. She left the shower running as she opened the top dresser drawer and pulled out the old .38 Long Colt which had belonged to Markowitz and his father before him. Riker had thoughtfully confiscated her Smith & Wesson, but this would do. The holes would not be so big, but the bullets would travel as far and nearly as fast. The shower was steaming the bathroom mirror as she strapped on her shoulder holster.

Edith had no police protection. They had covered the other séance connections, but they hadn't known about Edith. Mallory thought to call Coffey, and

300

then thought better of it. The evidence was so slender, it was better to catch the perp in the act. Coffey would never let her use Candle.

If she didn't act now, she'd lose the only leverage she might ever have. The séance investors were being rounded up. It was all coming undone, and it was only one newspaper edition to common knowledge. Time, she had none to spare. SEC investigators would be working the data, running the matches. If Charles had gone to Coffey with her printouts, they'd be knocking on Edith's door within the hour.

What if Charles had gone to Edith first? What was she going to do with Charles? Maybe say, 'Excuse me, would you mind turning your back while I hang old Edith out in the breeze?'

She went to the bedroom closet for her blazer. Her hand was on the door when she thought of Helen. Helen wouldn't like it if she knew her Kathy had used a little old lady to cheese the trap. That would've made Helen cry.

Well, a lot of things made Helen cry.

The first night Helen had tucked her in, Mallory smelled clean sheets for the first time in her child's memory. And there had been clean clothes to wear that next morning. The clothes smelled of fabric softener, and so did Helen on laundry day. On other days, Helen smelled of pine-scented disinfectant, scouring powder and floor wax.

She opened the door, and Helen came out of the closet in scents of sachets and mothballs. Mallory slammed the door on Helen.

* * *

Riker knocked softly on the bedroom door. No

response.

"Hey, Kathy?"

She had been moving slow and dragging, even after all the coffee she'd put away. She could be taking a nap, but he couldn't shake the feeling that he was alone in these rooms. He wandered into the den and looked at the mess of the back wall which had undergone a change of clutter style. The square computer eye was glowing blue with white type. She had left her computer running.

While she took a nap?

In a heartbeat, he was back at the bedroom door, forcing the lock and putting his shoulder to it. He was half fallen into the empty room when he heard the sound of the shower running. He knocked on the bathroom door. "Kathy, you in there?"

The burglar guard was still padlocked. The bathroom door lock was standard apartment flimsy. He kicked the door at the midsection and it gave way. The shower stall was empty and the window was open. He put his head out into the drizzling rain. It was a fourteen-foot drop to an overhang below the window. Then she would only have to walk along that overhang to gain access to the fire escape.

Not a big believer in invisible murderers, Charles had angled the lampshade to spotlight the door. Edith's ambush preparations told him he would not have long to wait.

Markowitz had been right. The evidence was so slight, there was no other way but this to end it.

He never heard the steps approaching.

A mass of energy burst through the door, with no face, no identifiable shape to the colors and materials in the rush of flying, sprawling bulk. The

302

lamp crashed to the floor. Its naked light bulb burned like a sun in the peripheral corner of his sight. And then all was still and quiet, and his attention was focussed on the point of the knife one inch from his left eyeball. When he could look beyond the knife, he was staring into the familiar eyes of a serial killer.

The lamplight from the level of the floor made the body into a giant, casting its shadow up beyond the wall, which was too small to contain it, and across the ceiling. The shape blurred as he focussed again on the point of the knife, light dancing on the sharp tip, calling his attention to the matter at hand. Any movement would cost him an eye. By great effort of will, he dismissed the knife, refusing to see it anymore, looking back to the eyes of his assailant.

"What part are you playing now, Gaynor? Jack the Ripper?" Charles smiled.

The knife pulled back only a little, a fraction of an inch. Jonathan Gaynor's eyes did the wide-then-narrow dance of 'what's going on here?' The knife came closer, all but touching Charles's eye. "Where is Edith Candle?"

Charles blinked slowly, and his smile widened into a lunatic grin. "You didn't think I'd endanger an elderly woman, did you?"

"How did you put it together?"

"You're wondering if the police could figure it out as easily as I did? They have. It was hardly challenging."

"I think you're running a bluff." The knife wavered back and forth, mimicking, in smaller degrees, the slow shake of Gaynor's head. "You never called the police. You're on your own, aren't you? You sent the note, and signed the old lady's name, right?"

"Believe what you like."

"Tell me how you worked it out."

"No, if you're going to kill me, I don't mind annoying you by taking the list of your stupid mistakes with me."

"It doesn't matter," said Gaynor, drawing the blade back an inch, hefting the weight of the hilt in his hand. "They could only have a circumstantial case. The same evidence could argue for Margot or Henry."

"Oh, sorry. I just had a chat with the police department a few minutes ago. Margot Siddon is in jail. Henry's down there now, trying to make bail for her. Not that they'll let her out. Seems she was having a bad day. She tried to kill an off-duty NYPD detective."

"You're lying, Charles."

"For the next hour or so, they'll have a score of policemen for alibis. So what now?"

"We could while away some time till Henry gets home. Or you could die in the rather boring murder of an interrupted burglary. This is New York City—unsensational corpses get stacked up like cordwood."

Never taking his eyes from Charles, Gaynor reached out one blind hand to pick up the telephone on the table next to the chair. "Dial the numbers as I call them." When the connection was made, he took the receiver and held it to his ear, waiting out the time of six rings. He put the receiver back on its cradle.

"No answer at Henry's apartment. But then I take it you'd rather not wait on Henry?"

"I've changed my mind," said Charles as the knife came closer. "I'll tell you how I figured it out. And maybe you could clear up a few small details

304

for me. Deal?" as Mallory would say.

"Deal."

"Your choice of victims wasn't very clever. You might as well have signed Samantha Siddon's corpse."

"She wasn't even—"

"Now, Louis Markowitz's key was your aunt. Louis loved money motives. Of course, you knew your aunt was mentioned in an investigator's report on the Whitman Chemicals merger."

"How do you make the leap from a recent murder to a stock market transaction in the eighties?"

"A routine background check on your aunt footnoted an SEC investigation on the merger. All the heavy profiteers were investigated. The U.S. Attorney's office elected not to prosecute. A few old women and a séance got lost in the bigger game of the junk bonds and broker swindles."

"What's the connection to me?"

"Your aunt tipped you off to the merger, didn't she? According to Mallory's reports, you made a modest gain that year, almost too modest. I found that interesting. But then, you could count on inheriting a fortune, couldn't you?"

"I never purchased any stock in Whitman Chemicals."

"I'm guessing you exchanged the insider tip for a straight percentage of profit. Perhaps you learned that trick from your aunt. She was a rather small operator up to that point, only steering the marks to Edith and making use of the dates."

"Even if you could prove that, I couldn't be prosecuted. I'm past the seven-year statute of limitations."

"But your aunt wasn't. Mallory told me you quarreled with your aunt over the séances. I believe you did. It must have been a shock to discover her activities were ongoing and so extensive. Your aunt's fortune doubled after the merger Edith arranged. But subsequent deals with the cartel made it grow to ostentatious proportions. It was out of control, wasn't it, so many people in on the action. It was only a matter of time before the cartel was exposed. And the government people routinely take all the profits, don't they? Not to mention fines in the millions of dollars. But even the SEC can't seize a dead woman's estate once it's gone through probate. Mallory's first instincts were good. She liked money motives as much as Louis Markowitz did."

"Back to Samantha Siddon, if you don't mind. I don't see the connection to me."

"It was because Siddon followed Whitman. With a few reservations, I finally gave in to Mallory's fixation with money motives, the idea that, of the four murders, there was one main target. Pearl Whitman left no heirs, no one benefited by her death. The only motive for her murder could be the framing of Henry Cathery."

"One might take the view that Pearl had changed her mind about giving Henry a solid alibi for the time of his grandmother's death."

"I wouldn't. Four murders would be too complex for a young man who thrives on simplicity and lack of distraction. He wouldn't bother to go to all that trouble—certainly not for money. I gather you didn't know he was coming into a personal fortune of his own. You seemed surprised. That's a snag, isn't it?"

"You keep digressing. How does Samantha Siddon give me away?"

"Samantha Siddon was an interesting departure from the pattern. Everyone was so busy with patterns and common motives. And that place where Louis died with Pearl Whitman, that made another interesting departure. Then I realized it wasn't a departure at all. It was business as usual with an unexpected interruption."

"You're wandering off the path again, Charles."

"Sorry. Well, the order of the murders is important. You killed Anne Cathery first to put suspicion on Henry Cathery. He was perfect, wasn't he? A strange boy, reclusive. But even if he had been arrested, there were no witnesses, no physical evidence. All that Cathery money, what were the odds he couldn't make bail? So you didn't have to worry about his confinement while you were killing your aunt. You didn't count on Henry intimidating Pearl Whitman into an alibi after the police came around a second time. Then Miss Whitman was the third victim. That would have been predictable for Markowitz, once he sized Henry Cathery up for a frame. That would have occurred to him shortly after your aunt died. He was following the money motive."

Gaynor kicked the lamp, and the shifting light made his shadow smaller. "It couldn't have been that simple."

"Did it rattle you when he followed Pearl Whitman into the building? Yes, I suppose it did. You must have thought it was all over at that point. You left the plastic bag behind. Very sloppy. It was photographed at the site."

"Siddon," said Gaynor, bringing the knife close and then drawing it back. "Samantha Siddon."

"Right. The last one. It followed Markowitz's logic for the framing of the Cathery boy. You knew about that odd little symbiotic relationship between Henry and Margot. You'd lived in the square for several months by then. I expect you'd seen them together quite a few times. You would have been interested in every aspect of Henry's routine. You couldn't count on Henry not having an alibi for all the murders, so you implicated the only other human he had any ties to. It would destroy her credibility as an alibi and lead the police down the path of a conspiracy.

"I have an unbreakable alibi for the Siddon murder."

"Well, no you don't, not if you're counting on Mallory. I'm sure you noticed her staking out Gramercy Park and following you on campus. Her tragic flaw is beauty, or rather, the fact that she's unaware of it. She actually believes she can blend into her surroundings. So you were aware of her, and you made her your alibi."

"I was never out of her sight for more than twenty minutes."

"Nineteen minutes. She's obsessive about her notes. Do you know, she even has a note about the change in your physical characteristics during the play? You do have a distinctively awkward body language, but you can lose it when you want to. Onstage, you were even graceful."

"Nineteen minutes isn't enough time to go to Gramercy Park, kill the old woman and get back to the theater again."

"Oh, I don't believe any of them were killed in Gramercy Park. The university borders a seedy area with lots of places to do a murder unobserved."

"The police have no reason to believe she wasn't killed in the park."

"You mean because of the blood at the supposed crime sites? I liked the detail of the beads spread out all over creation. You arranged the bodies as they

308

were when you killed the women. Once the bodies stiffened, it would have been easy to leave them in the same positions at another site, even working in the dark. Originally, the police believed the plastic bag was used to prevent the blood from splattering the killer. But the bags were used to retain all the blood necessary for a convincing crime scene. Excellent idea. The bag would keep it nice and moist so it would saturate the surroundings instead of lying caked on the surface. The bloody palm prints were another nice touch."

"They'll never prove it."

"No? But you've made so many errors. Shall I tell you what I believe tipped off Edith Candle? You mentioned the slashed breast from the séance. Blood and gore are not the mainstays of a medium's routine. Edith knew you'd filled the gaps in that performance from memory. You couldn't have seen it."

The knife had dropped away from his eye by a bare inch, and then another.

"It was more than money, wasn't it? I always thought that was a flaw in the police logic. You took an unnecessary risk planting the first body in the park. You craved the excitement, didn't you? How did it start?"

The lamp on the floor created the illusion of footlights and the drama of contrast. Gaynor's grin had a ghoulish aspect.

"It started with Anne Cathery's dog. He got away from her and led her out of the park. We were looking for him by the trash bins when I saw the monkey puzzle worked out for me."

"The monkey puzzle. That sounds familiar."

"When you were a schoolboy, did you have the paradigm of the monkey, the chair, the pole and the

309

banana?"

"I think so. The banana is suspended from the ceiling by a thread?"

"Right," said Gaynor. "Just out of reach. And this very hungry monkey is given the tools to retrieve the banana—a chair and a pole. But the monkey doesn't know how to use them. So he paces back and forth until he gives up and sits in the corner, beaten. Suddenly, everything falls into line. From where he sits, he can see the pole leaning on the chair and pointing up to the banana. He grabs up the pole, leaps on the chair and swats the banana down."

"So it was spontaneous?"

"Yes. She was looking for the dog by a row of trash cans. Some building super had left half a box of large plastic bags by the cans. The garbage was bagged, just waiting to be put out on the street in the morning. There was a kitchen knife on the ground—someone had discarded it for a broken handle. The hilt of the knife was touching the box of trash bags and the blade was pointing at Anne Cathery. Beyond that silly woman, on the next street, was Henry Cathery, sitting in the park playing chess with himself. I picked up one of the bags and punctured it with the knife. That gave me cover from the blood. I used another bag to put over her as soon as I'd put the knife in her throat. They were all small women. It wasn't difficult to bag her, so to speak. With the cover of a plastic bag around the body, I had all the leisure to make it look like the work of a lunatic."

"As if it wasn't."

"A profit of hundreds of millions of dollars is not the goal of the average lunatic."

"But you did like it, didn't you?"

Gaynor ignored this.

"Later, I came back for her. She was stiff by then. You were right, it was easy to arrange the body in the park so no one would know she'd been moved. Then I broke her beads and sent them flying everywhere."

Gaynor was smiling, and it was hardly an engaging smile. The man was enjoying his exposition. Of course, the downside of the perfect murder would be the lack of an appreciative audience.

"That was risky, even in the small hours of the morning," said Charles, hoping for the ring of appreciation in his own voice.

"I admit that part was exciting. But what were the odds of anyone watching at four in the morning? No one's very alert at that hour. I wore jeans and a baseball cap to pass as a maintenance man. I threw a bow-legged gait into the role. I was only carrying a large garbage bag. Nothing too sinister in that. Maintenance drones are invisible in that neighborhood. If it hadn't worked, if anyone had come forward with a description of a maintenance man with a garbage bag, it would never have come back on me. No motive. This was Henry's grandmother, not mine."

"It never occurred to you that Henry would report his grandmother missing during the night?"

"The police won't take a missing person report until forty-eight hours go by. I was hardly worried about Henry getting a posse together to beat the bushes for her. You've met him—I saw you in the park with him. It wasn't much of a risk. The worst thing that could happen was that she'd be found somewhere else."

"Where did you kill your aunt?"

"I invited her to lunch and met her on a side street

311

near the campus. She never mentioned the appointment to anyone. I had to volunteer the information to the police so they could verify my alibi for either side of the half hour when I didn't have one. I told them she stood me up."

"I suppose that was quite understandable to them, since she was being murdered at that time. And Pearl Whitman? How did you get her into that East Village neighborhood?"

"I told her I was a broker with information to give the U.S. Attorney's office about the cartel. She offered me a bribe. I told her she'd have to meet with me to work out the details. By public telephones, I led her from block to block, sort of eased her into the neighborhood by degrees."

"So, the fear of notoriety, prison and poverty overcame her fear of a bad neighborhood."

"Exactly. Samantha Siddon was only a little different. I had the impression she was looking forward to our meeting. I used a series of public phones to bring her to the theater by three different cabs. I had her walk the last few blocks and met her at the back of the building. I killed her behind a trash bin. That only took a few minutes. It took me longer to dress for the play rehearsal."

"How did you transport the body to Gramercy?"

"I usually go everywhere by cab. That day I hired a rental car for the occasion. I had to leave early, before Mallory's usual arrival time. I didn't want her to see the car."

The knife backed away another inch. He braced his arm on the arm of the chair. "But you still haven't delivered, Charles. You didn't have anything that would stick, unless there's something else you've left out,"

"Only this." Charles pushed the knife away and

blinded Gaynor with Edith's unfurled shawl. He pulled the gun from the chair cushion and leveled it at Gaynor's head as the man ripped the shawl away from his face.

"Put down the knife. The police should be here any minute now. I expect they're on the way up in the elevator."

Gaynor smiled, and it was Charles's turn to play 'What's going on here?' A child's game flashed through his brain.

Paper covers stone, scissors cut paper, stone breaks scissors.

A gun could not be outdone by a knife. So, why was Gaynor smiling?

"The police? No, I don't think so, Charles. You couldn't have known I would come—you only hoped I would. You're bluffing."

"I can't bluff. God knows I've tried. I just don't have the face for it."

The knife fell from Gaynor's hand and thudded to the carpet. "I believe you."

Well, that was more like it. Logic reigned.

Illogically, Gaynor lunged for the gun.

They were locked together, hands grappling for control of the weapon, limbs writhing, faces contorted. They were turning now, gun pointing to the ceiling, hands sweating and sliding over one another's flesh, legs kicking out, turning, turning into the dark hallway, knocking against the narrow walls and falling into the front room. They went to the floor and rolled, man over man, across the rug. The room was too dark to see the gun clearly. It was only a vague shape and cold metal, and the barrel was changing position, pointing lower. It was still in Charles's hands when it fired.

It was an explosion to crack the world. Charles

313

reached for his side, his face all in agony. Gaynor rose to his feet, sole owner of the gun. He took a handkerchief from one pocket. A plastic bag from the same pocket fell to the floor.

"You couldn't have shot me, Charles. You're much too sane and civilized." He methodically wiped the gun's barrel and then its revolving chamber and handle. "It was predictable that you'd hesitate before you took a human life. That half second has killed you." He bent down to retrieve the plastic bag from the floor and wrapped it around the handle of the gun. "And to answer your question honestly, yes, I did love it. I do love it. I'm exhilarated."

Pain was giving way to shock as he watched Gaynor ease down on the back of his heels, well out of the stream of light from the open door which now shone on Charles's face. The better to see the fear? Was Gaynor waiting for that? Yes. No killing could be complete without it.

Charles could feel the blood on his hand. The barrel of the gun was pointing to his heart, and there was no doubt that death was coming. Fear was crowded out of his mind by the approach of death, its loud footfalls, its enormity. A moment stretched out for an eternity. He was at his mother's bedside again. She had not been frightened. She had heard it coming and succumbed to the wonder of it. She had died with an expression of amazement.

He smiled at Gaynor, and the man's face clouded up with anger. The gun barrel was pressed to Charles's heart.

Soon.

He heard the bell for the elevator. So Jack Coffey had come, but not in time. There was not the space of a second to call out. He heard the shot and felt the

314

bone-shattering assault on his chest. His muscles jerked and then he lay motionless in the dark with only the light of the hall to show the outline of his body on the carpet. The higher orders of his beautiful brain were shutting down, memory was collapsing in on itself. The most primitive portion of his mind, where passion was seated, was the last repository of consciousness. The last thing in this world that his senses could reach was the voice of Henrietta Ramsharan, followed close by the sudden rush of Mallory's perfume.

Mallory shot out of Edith Candle's apartment and ran for the exit door, which was closing on its slow hydraulic. She was murderous in the eyes and the grip of her gun. She stood on the stairwell landing.

Which way? Up or down?

The noise from below was faint. Breaking glass? She looked down through the winding metal stairs to the basement door, which stood ajar. He could only be seconds through that door. But wait, something was off. Instinct kept her still. Breaking glass? The only window in the cellar was on the other side of the accordion partition where Max Candle's illusions were stored. Was Edith in the cellar? Had she opened that partition?

Now she stood in Markowitz's shoes. No backup, no time to call for help. She was going into the dark all alone.

She moved down the stairs with the silence of tennis shoes and the inherent stealth of a born thief. At each landing, she unscrewed the bulbs. When she put out the basement door's bulb, she was standing in the dark. She opened the cellar door and closed it quickly behind her. One blind hand reached up to the top of the fuse box and felt around for the flashlight.

It was gone.

The thunder made a dull sound in the basement. The glow from a streak of lightning bent its way down the sides of buildings to light up the garbage cans in the wide high window of the far wall. The window glass was broken, but not enough to allow a body to pass through the shards. He was still here.

She made her way by memory and touch, around a packing trunk, down the aisle of boxes and crates and into the wider area where Max Candle's illusions were stored, stepping softly toward the bad light from the back window. Lightning flashed and lit the guillotine, and then the thunder came crashing after it. An anticlimactic soft rain pinged off the garbage cans beyond the broken glass, and wind shears drove stray droplets through the cracked window.

She tensed every muscle in her body, watching indistinct shadows, listening for footfalls. Her eyes hardened, blind to the flight of one raindrop. It touched the sleeve of her coat and disappeared on the rough tweed, without the substance to leave a wetness or any other sign that it had ever existed. Mallory focussed on the infinitely more subtle nuances in the shadows of black on black.

'The hell of Christianity is not eternal fire,' Rabbi Kaplan had told her when she had become confused by the Christian Sunday school. (Helen had felt compelled to give the Christians equal time in Kathy's education.) 'Hell is the absence of the beloved.' The rabbi had this on the word of a Jesuit, he told her, and so it must be true. And so it was. The people she loved were killed. She wanted to kill back.

A dull globe light came on from behind the box

she was rounding. She froze. Her eyes fixed on a single shadow sliding out from behind the Chinese screen, gliding just ahead of her and to the right. She raised her gun to the level of the head which would appear in her sights any second. She planned a head shot despite the training that taught her to shoot for the widest part of the body. She licked her lips as she waited for the shadow to emerge. The rain was drumming now, harder, louder, and the wind was in a fury, sending the rain wide and far into the room.

There was a crunch of broken glass, and the head of another shadow appeared near the feet of her own. She could hear the rush of footsteps. She turned around to see the second shadow. And now the room filled with brilliant, blinding light. The silhouette moving between her and the light was small and rounded, plump arms reaching out for her.

The wrong shadow.

And now Mallory heard the sound of the shadow behind her. She spun around, too slow in her reaction time. Yet, in the split of a second, there was time to note all the details of the man as she was still turning, as the gun was rising to point the barrel. Only a few feet away. Good shot or bad, she knew Gaynor was not likely to miss at this range.

Edith Candle watched on, dispassionately. Gaynor's finger jerked the trigger, and the blue-black muzzle flashed with the explosion. It was done in a moment. And while it was being done, the rain continued to fly through the cracked glass, but for the few drops sacrificed to the heat of the gun.

In the white light of the sun-bright room, Gaynor was a chimera in Mallory's adapting eye as the bullet tore its hole in the front of her shirt. Her gold hair was flying in the wet and chill October wind whipping through the window. She was falling, falling, eyes closing before she went to the ground. She heard the soft shuffle of running footsteps and the slower heavy footfalls following after.

She was slow to open her eyes. Shielding her face from the spotlight at the top of the guillotine, she sat up with the idea that bulletproof vests were overrated. She wished she had died. Bones had been cracked by the concussion of the bullet. The vest had saved her from penetration but not from the force of the projectile fired at how many miles per second? She felt for and found the rib that was broken. Now her breath came in tears. Had she punctured a lung?

An overturned trunk lay by her side. The disembodied head of the Max Candle waxwork was lying just behind it. The resemblance to Charles was lying on its side and staring up at her.

The gun. Gaynor had taken her gun.

The rear window was still a mass of dangerous shards. He had not gone that way. And Edith— where had she gone? She must know a hundred hiding places in this cellar.

She stared up at the blazing sun atop the guillotine. Only Edith knew where the light was tripped.

There was a sharp pain in her chest as she rose to a stand. She turned off the switch for the globe lamp and then walked to the guillotine. The flashlight lay on the floor by the wooden hand locks. Edith's hands had been in the locks when the trick was done the first time. She knelt down and felt for the light switch. A small block of wood gave way under her exploring fingers. She pressed on the button, plunging the basement into the equalizer of darkness. Flashlight in hand and wax head under her

318

arm, she went hunting.

The lightning lit the window again and she saw the silhouette of Gaynor flash into brilliant tabloid detail for an instant. The gun was wrapped in a wad of shiny plastic. It was a snub-nose revolver and not the Long Colt he was holding. How many bullets? she wondered. She had stopped in Edith's apartment long enough to count two bullets in Charles's body. And then there was the second gun, hers, with a full load of ammo. She set Max Candle's head on the top of a steamer trunk, pulled loose change from her pocket, and stepping back, she tossed the coins at the trunk. She pressed the button on the flashlight and aimed the beam at the wax face which so resembled Charles.

A shot cracked in the darkness. The flashlight clicked off. The bullet had gone wild of the head. So, Gaynor's reaction time was slow, and he was a poor shot at any distance. She dropped a coin to the floor and held the beam of the light to her own face. The light clicked off and a bullet fired into the air where she had been standing.

Her foot connected with something hard. She reached down to the floor and touched a length of pipe. She picked it up and felt the solid weight of the iron in her hand. She would have to get within swinging distance before he could switch to the second gun. Now she was living intensely in the moment, excitement rising as though she were going to meet a lover and not to beat a man senseless, to let his blood, to drag out the pain, and last to kill him. She walked on through the spray of rain.

She turned the flashlight on her face and clicked on the beam.

Gaynor leveled the gun and pulled the trigger. The gun only clicked with the sound of no bullet in the chamber. The second click was lost in the roar of a gunshot followed up by the flash of lightning. For a moment, Mallory could almost believe in magic. It seemed as though his bullet had doubled back and struck him, making a bloody hole in his body. Gaynor was turning and twisting as he fell backward with the force of the bullet in his shoulder, arms waving loose and disjointed. And the surprise on his face was the dumb look of the straw man twisting in a cornfield. The gun fell from his hand and skittered across the floor.

She turned off the flashlight and watched in silence as Edith approached Gaynor's body. The old woman was holding the Long Colt that was Mallory's own. Mallory pulled back behind the trunk which held Max's head.

Edith turned slowly, eyes searching, the gun barrel following the sights of her eyes. Mallory silently circled a stack of boxes and came up behind her, grabbing the old woman's wrist with enough force to leave prints on the flesh. She twisted the gun from Edith's hand with one swift motion.

Edith gasped, turning to face Mallory, her lined face illuminated by the poor light of the back window. The old woman smiled too quickly, too wide.

"Oh, Kathy, thank God. I thought you were dead. Oh, thank God."

"Yeah, right."

Mallory clicked on the flashlight and knelt down by Gaynor's body, wholly dissatisfied with the man's continued breathing. His head had struck the wall. He was unconscious but not dead, and the wound was not life-threatening.

And a gun was in her hand.

"Kill him," said Edith, standing over Gaynor.

Kneeling down now, coming closer, her lips near to Mallory's ear, "Finish it," she whispered softly, her magnified blue eyes growing even wider. "No one will know."

"You'd like that, wouldn't you, Edith?"

Markowitz would not have liked that at all.

Mallory stared at Gaynor. Markowitz's killer was in her hands. The rain ran into her eyes as she turned to Edith. "I don't suppose I could trust you to go upstairs and call the ambulance.... No, I suppose not." She picked up the fallen snub-nose revolver. Plastic still clung to the metal by a fusion of heat. Gaynor had not fired fast enough. There was one bullet left in the chamber. She pulled the plastic loose and handed the gun to Edith, using two fingers on the rough side-grip of the handle. The old woman looked down on the weapon in her hand, eyes glistering.

Mallory checked Gaynor's pulse and then pulled back the lid of one eye. He showed no signs of coming around. "I'm going for the ambulance. I don't think you'll need to use the gun."

She wadded up the plastic bag, which had fallen away from the gun, and slipped it under her jacket.

"I understand," said Edith, nodding slowly. "I do understand." She was smiling as Mallory turned her back and headed for the way out.

After passing through the cellar doorway, she reached up to turn the overhead light bulb in its socket. When she was standing in the light again, she thought to turn around, to go back and undo this thing. She lost this thought as she stared up the winding metal of the staircase and into the eyes of Jack Coffey standing on the level above her. Beyond Coffey, a uniformed officer was motioning Henrietta Ramsharan back into the hallway and

321

closing the door.

"Mallory?" Coffey was staring from the blackened hole in her shirt to the gun dangling from her hand. Now he looked into her eyes and one hand tightened on the railing and there it froze.

She continued to hold him, to pin him to the landing with her eyes. Only a second longer.

A gunshot exploded in the room behind her.

Jack Coffey and the uniformed officer were pounding down the staircase, guns drawn, pushing past her on the way through the cellar door.

Mallory slumped against the wall of the stairwell. Later, she would have trouble remembering how much of this she had planned.

Yeah, right.

She started up the steep stairs. First her mind stumbled and then her feet. Yet she did not pick her way more carefully as she continued up and up. She was in that moment when the guts flutter and rise, the heart pounds, the brain waffles between belief and disbelief, and she did not care if she fell, nor how far.

EPILOGUE

Mrs. Ortega scanned the hospital room with the all encompassing eye of a career cleaning woman as she settled the pink geraniums into an empty water glass on the bedside table. She pulled up a chair on the other side of the bed and as far from Mallory as she could get.

"That was thoughtful of you," said Charles. "They're lovely flowers."

"They're plastic," said Mrs. Ortega. "They live

longer."

Charles gave her his widest, looniest smile and the legs of her chair scraped away from him. He turned his smile on Mallory who seemed less unnerved by lunacy.

"So, I'm assuming it was a traffic accident," said Charles. "How many accidents around the house could lodge a piece of metal so close to the heart? Am I right?"

Mrs. Ortega shifted in her chair and rolled her eyes.

"Sounds reasonable," said Mallory.

"You're not even going to give me a hint?"

"Dr. Ramsharan said it would be better if the events came back naturally. She says you may never get it all back. A lot of trauma victims never recall the last fifteen minutes of consciousness."

"And how many trauma victims have policemen posted outside the hospital room door?"

"You're a material witness in the insider trading scam."

"A witness? All the data I had was pulled off your computer."

"Memory can come back too fast, Charles. Take it easy. The SEC investigator is coming by for a statement this afternoon. If you can't remember where you got the files, that would be okay with me."

"Understood. But will you at least tell me what's been going on in the world these past two weeks? They won't let me read the newspaper or watch television."

"We locked up the case on the insider trading racket. The evidence is so tight, most of them are plea-bargaining. There's only a few holdouts for the grand jury."

"And what about Edith? Did she—"

"She made bail," said Mrs. Ortega helpfully.

"What?"

Mrs. Ortega fell silent under the icy hex of Mallory's eyes.

"People are climbing all over themselves to turn in their friends and relatives," said Mallory. "Edith didn't jump on the wagon in time to get immunity for testimony."

Mrs. Ortega looked at the floor as the headline murder charge slid under the carpet.

"What will they do with her?"

"I'm told she has the best lawyer money can buy. You're tired, Charles. We'll be leaving now. I'll be back this evening with your journals."

Mallory stood up and glanced at Mrs. Ortega. The cleaning woman jumped up from her chair and followed Mallory out of the room and into the long white corridor. She hurried along on her shorter legs to catch up with Mallory. Not that she wanted to be this near a cop, particularly not this cop, but there was something she had to know.

"Why can't he remember getting shot? How does a person forget a thing like that? If I'd been shot, I would remember a thing like that."

"Charles has soft spots and you don't," said Mallory. "You're tougher than he is."

Mrs. Ortega's dark head raised up half an inch, and she remained half an inch taller as she kept pace with Mallory's long stride.

"It's better this way," said Mallory. "The soft people always prefer the accident. They never like the version where they can be deliberately ripped open with bullets fired at ninety miles a second."

"But what happens when he reads a newspaper and finds out who shot him?"

324

"I'm taking him away for a few months, maybe a long cruise. While we're gone, the grand jury will convene and indict, and there'll be a plea bargain to waive the trial for a lesser sentence. The whole thing will be over before we get back. Maybe I'll tell him then."

Mrs. Ortega slowed her steps and watched Mallory walk on alone. As Mallory receded in the distance of the empty corridor, she seemed to grow larger instead of smaller.

"And that one's another Martian," said Mrs. Ortega.

"Kathy, you can't leave."

"Mallory, call me Mallory."

Edith Candle stood at her back as Mallory unfurled the white sheet and watched it settle as a ghost with the outline of the couch. The room was filled with such ghosts. Dust covers lay across each piece of furniture in Charles's apartment.

"The grand jury is meeting tomorrow," said Edith. "You have to testify for me."

"I haven't been asked."

Mallory walked into the kitchen. Edith followed close behind, her face wrinkled into anxious knots. Mallory opened the refrigerator. Mrs. Ortega had cleaned it out. Good. Nothing left to spoil.

"You see, Edith, I was unable to give a coherent statement to the police or the district attorney. Whenever they tried to talk to me, I would begin to cry. After a while, they decided I was bad witness material. Your own attorney came to the same conclusion."

"But I killed him to save you. You saw the writing on the wall. You have to tell them about it."

"I don't believe the grand jury is allowed to hear
325

occult evidence. They only get the solid, worldly stuff to work with. The bullet in Gaynor's shoulder came from my gun, the same gun they pried out of my hand while I was in shock. The bullet that killed him came from the unregistered gun in your possession. And so did the bullets they took out of Charles and the bullet lodged in my vest."

"Herbert's gun. But he won't—"

"Given your gift, I'm surprised you didn't foresee that Herbert would never own up to an illegally purchased gun. And Henrietta never saw the gun, did she? Well, there's Martin. But I imagine the district attorney got rather tired of trying to get three words out of Martin."

"They're going after a first-degree murder indictment and two counts of attempted murder. You know Gaynor was the killer. You know I couldn't have shot you or Charles. Gaynor had the gun in his hand. You saw it."

"I came from darkness into blinding light, and I don't remember what happened after I was shot. I'm told traumatic shock can do that. Gaynor wasn't holding a weapon when Coffey found him. You were. His hands had no trace of residue from a gun. Yours did."

No one had noticed the detail of the plastic bag which had been carried out of the cellar before the final shot, the plastic bag bearing prints and residue. Perhaps it had fallen in the street as they were loading her into the ambulance with Charles.

"You know Gaynor was the murderer. You have to tell them I shot in fear for my life."

"That's a tough one, Edith. According to the bullet trajectories for the entry wound, you shot him in the head at close range and while he was lying on the ground."

"He was a murderer!" Edith's voice was climbing to the high notes where fear was.

"The law doesn't recognize him as a murderer," said Mallory as she opened her notebook and jotted a memo to cancel Charles's newspaper subscription. "There was no evidence against him. But they did find those computer printouts with insider-trading activity on Charles's body—everything they needed to connect you to Gaynor's aunt. And then there's the note they found in Gaynor's pocket—your invitation. It doesn't look good for you, Edith."

"Help me! Do you want to see me spend the rest of my life in prison?"

Mallory smiled, and psychic Edith did not understand the meaning of it and even began to take heart from this sign of humanity in Mallory.

"Edith, there's something I've always wanted to ask you. When your husband Max was in the water tank, who ordered the busboy to break the glass, the glass that severed every artery and bled him to death? I found that busboy in a retirement home upstate. It took me a long time to hunt him down. His memory of the night was very clear. It was the biggest event in his entire life. He said he didn't see the face of the person who called out the order, but it was a woman's voice, and a woman who put the fire axe into his hand."

Edith said nothing, and the last loose end was tied by silence. "There's no justice, Edith, but it is a balanced universe after all."

"You have to help me. You're a civilized woman."

"*I* am?"

A carton of Charles's journals stood on the sidewalk by her feet. Her hand was rising to flag a passing cab when a familiar face caught her attention by the light of a streetlamp.

She dropped coins into the newspaper dispenser, plucked out a paper and looked into the eyes of Maximilian Candle. It was an old photo of Charles's cousin in his prime. The front-page article spoke of an overdue tribute to a master. Celebrity magicians from round the world planned to re-create his old routines for a charity event. Max was a headliner once more.

She found a larger photograph on the inside page, with a description of Max's magnificent funeral of thirty years ago. In the foreground of the photo, she could pick out the little figure of a child with a large nose, the small version of Charles.

When Markowitz died, the account of his less spectacular, unmagical funeral had been buried on page 15. That small column of type had been accompanied by a photograph of herself, her face dry of any of the normal signs of grief.

Of all the tears she had recently cried for Coffey who knew her better than to believe in them, and all the tears she cried for the more easily gulled district attorney who knew her not, not one drop had been the genuine article. Conversely and perversely, on principle, she had never shed one false drop for Markowitz on that day when they laid his coffin in the ground. None of the words spoken over the grave had reached her when the rabbi cast his eyes up to the sky where the God of Sunday school was hiding out, laying low, behaving like a good New Yorker who didn't want to get involved.

She had kept the integrity of the hard case, one who believed that a stiff was a stiff and dead was dead, a dedicated unbeliever in the flight of souls.

Goodbye, Markowitz.

She closed her paper and stepped into the street, putting out her hand to wave down a cab. Near by, a car alarm went off in a shriek. A burst of pigeons took flight from the overhead branches of a tree, their wings rushing, all swirling as one, soaring up beyond the lamplight, screaming as one, night blind in their flight, rising high above the woman with the wide, astonished eyes, and then gone over the rooftops, lost in the dark.

Tables and Figures

x

Contents

To my father and my mother

Published by the Press Syndicate of the University of Cambridge
The Pitt Building, Trumpington Street, Cambridge CB2 1RP
32 East 57th Street, New York, NY 10022, USA
10 Stamford Road, Oakleigh, Melbourne 3166, Australia

First published 1987

Printed in the United States of America

Library of Congress Cataloging-in-Publication Data
Christiano, Kevin J.
Religious diversity and social change.
Bibliography: p.
1. United States—Religion—19th century.
2. United States—Religion—1901–1945.   3. Cities and
towns—United States.   4. Cities and towns—Religious
aspects.   5. Religion and sociology—United States.
6. United States—Census, 11th, 1890.   7. United States
—Census, 12th, 1900. 8. United States—Census, 13th,
1910.   I. Title.
BL2525.C48   1987   306'.6'0973   87-9329

British Library Cataloguing in Publication Data
Christiano, Kevin J.
Religious diversity and social change:
American cities, 1890–1906.
1. Social change 2. United States —
Religious life and customs
I. Title
306'.6'0973   BR525

ISBN 0 521 34145 0

Religious Diversity and Social Change

American Cities, 1890–1906

KEVIN J. CHRISTIANO
University of Notre Dame

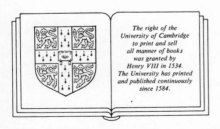

The right of the
University of Cambridge
to print and sell
all manner of books
was granted by
Henry VIII in 1534.
The University has printed
and published continuously
since 1584.

CAMBRIDGE UNIVERSITY PRESS

Cambridge

New York   New Rochelle   Melbourne   Sydney

Religious Diversity and Social Change